BOYS WITH TATTOOS

BOYS WITH TATTOOS

A NOVEL BY **EDDY PRUGH**

WEDNESDAY, JUNE 15ᵀᴴ, 2016
BEAVERTON, OREGON

Over the past eight months Danny Sheppard had sat at six different conference tables and signed six contracts. Until now the most impressive conference table had belonged to Toyota. The tables at Monster Energy and BF Goodrich had been nice, but none of them compared to the one he was sitting at now. Nike.

A sprawling slab of white marble with an imposing black swoosh in the center. Fifteen chairs on each side were positioned perfectly opposite one another. It was a fitting table for the contract he was about to sign. Three years, $6.4 million.

Danny's mind sifted through the heroes of his youth who had worn Nike. Kobe, Serena, Tiger, MJ himself—he could have gone on forever, and should have. He deserved to take a moment to appreciate the elite class he was joining. It would have been right to bask in the achievement and to congratulate himself but instead, he opted to float unbothered in the bottomless well of his thoughts.

He imagined the conference table being dropped from the St. Johns Bridge, plummeting 200 feet into the Willamette River, splashing thunderously then diving through the murky water, ribbons of bubbles streaking behind it.

Even in a moment that should have been such a celebration, the culmination of months of negotiations between Nike and Danny's representatives, he couldn't manage to take part in the joyous feeling of the room. There was a lively conversation going on just behind him but it was nothing but muddled noises as if he were hearing it through earplugs. All he wanted to do was sign the contract, shake some hands and get back to the privacy of his home.

The seven Nike executives who stood around him must have been confused by his blank stare but Danny's family was used to it. It didn't matter the occasion—during meals, watching a movie, sometimes even in the middle of interviews that he didn't particularly want to be a part of—his eyes would slowly angle off to a corner of the room and before long he would be staring into places unknown. If nobody interrupted him he could carry on for an hour or more.

This time, it was the humming click of the Nikon camera that brought him back to reality. The conference table had just crashed on the riverbed in a muddy explosion next to a sunken tire, small fish darting in every direction. He blinked a few times and glanced around, trying to adjust his senses to the mood of the room. Even though he hadn't been paying attention he sensed a shift in the tone of the conversation. It had gone from light-hearted banter to something more business-like.

As he glanced over his shoulder he saw the contract being taken out of a black folder, passed from one executive to the next then placed in front of him with almost theatrical seriousness as if the paper were made of thin glass that might shatter if not set down just right. The cream-colored paper was eggshell textured and each page was embossed with a gold swoosh.

Todd Mathers, Senior Director of Representation, reached inside his coat pocket and presented Danny with a black pen as thick as a cigar. It was real. He would be a Nike athlete. But it was far more than that. With his signature, Nike would be stepping foot into a whole new sport for the first time. Mixed Martial Arts. And Danny Sheppard was the face of it.

Nowadays his revenue seemed to come from every direction—endorsements, appearances, promotions and prize money. He didn't keep track of it with any real concern and only checked his bank account every few weeks. It wasn't about the money. It never had been. A dark, isolated bay of Danny's heart knew that the real triumph from the moment was the knowing that Lucas would have been so proud.

Since elementary school Nike always had a stronger foothold in the Sheppard house than Adidas or any other brand. As the years passed it cemented itself as the clear choice for Danny's wrestling and Lucas' football. And rightly so: they grew up in Eastmoreland, the same neighborhood as the founder of Nike, Phil Knight.

Jerry Rice, Terrell Owens, Randy Moss—all of Lucas' favorite receivers wore Nike. For the Sheppard family, back-to-school shopping had always consisted of a trip to the Nike Employee Store with passes from clients of Danny's father. In an obscure but quite meaningful way, Nike had become a part of the Sheppard family identity.

"Time for the action shot then," Danny joked as he leaned over the contract, pen at the ready. The man behind the lens of the camera smiled but didn't say anything. He hadn't spoken all day but had been orbiting close by, snapping pictures of Danny and his entourage the moment they set foot on the campus. The laughter of the Nike executives was courteously loud, a bit more than what the joke deserved. Danny's sister, Allie, passed a handkerchief to her mom after using it to dab her own eyes.

Danny's best friend, Tanner Spurling, couldn't resist a joke of his own as he started signing, "d-a-n-n-y, space, s-h-e—two p's but the second one is silent, good job." The room laughed again, more authentically this time.

Danny could feel the eyes of the Nike representatives and the ten members of his own entourage as he signed the papers…but there was more. He had the full attention of an entire audience that he couldn't see. They were back. Over the past two and a half years they had been watching him, conferring with one another in hushed voices when Danny had reached a new milestone, good or bad.

The camera fluttered again as he scrawled his name and date on the final page in a flurry. Then he carefully put the pen down and raised his head. Applause ensued. In a strong voice that had clearly been rehearsed Todd Mathers declared emphatically, "Danny Sheppard, this sport has been waiting for you. *We* have been waiting for you. The future of mixed martial arts fighting wears Nike. Welcome to the family!"

Now that the contract was signed, the "hometown advertisement", as Nike had called it, would go up downtown. He had seen a 3D image rendering on a computer in the Marketing department an hour earlier.

His face, the size of a tennis court in stencil-style grey, white, black and red would cover the entire side of an apartment building near Pioneer Square. Tanner had remarked that it sort of resembled the Obama campaign poster and he wasn't wrong.

Danny managed a watered-down smile as he shook Mr. Mathers' hand. He looked around the room at his family and coaches, then towards the employees, then towards the camera one last time. The audience of spirits or whatever they were was excited by what they were witnessing.

Danny didn't have an ounce of arrogance in his 184 lbs. but ever since he had started down this path in life he knew that a day like this had been inevitable. From the moment he decided to devote himself to the sport it was only a matter of time; he would be on top, and Todd Mathers was absolutely right; Danny Sheppard *was* the future of the sport. At only 22 years old, analysts and experts had been spot on when they described his dominance as *"unprecedented...meteoric... preposterous...simply amazing."*

Danny "The Python" Sheppard had 3.2 million followers on Twitter, 2.7 million followers on Instagram and 4.8 million fans on Facebook. Seemingly overnight—right around the time he knocked out Marcos Royer in Orlando—a new fervor started to take over the MMA world and everyone could sense the emergence of a new star. Danny could feel his fame spreading.

For the first time, a mixed martial arts fighter was attracting fans from soccer moms to politicians; beloved for his calm demeanor and soft-spoken nature in a sport where obscene arrogance was the norm; he had reached an entirely new demographic. His wrestling background and boyish good looks were able to transcend the common notion that the sport was dominated by loud-mouthed, arrogant thugs, tattooed from head to toe and sporting green mohawks.

While most 22-year-olds were applying for internships and swiping on Tinder, Danny was being credited with the huge spike in viewership of the sport and the reason ESPN had begun negotiations with The Ultimate Fighting Championship. But it wasn't just his age and incredible athletic prowess that had drawn attention. The story of Lucas was what melted people's hearts and made them turn on the TV.

The tragic passing of Danny Sheppard's All-American twin brother, Lucas, in early 2014 was the start of his fighting career. He left Oregon State University and his wrestling career behind, setting his sights, instead, on a career in mixed martial arts.

The media couldn't get enough of it, but there was far more to it. His blank stare and preference for solitude were easily attributed to Lucas' passing, but there were several missing chapters that the world would never get to read. Snapshots of those dark parts wouldn't leave his mind in peace: the pool of blood in the Safeway parking lot, the dimly lit bar, the loud metal cranking sound of the gate opening and closing, and of course Nina's beautiful, wicked smile. Every day he saw her side profile and the contour of her cheek before she turned her head to look into his eyes. It was the most potent memory, and it hadn't left him alone for almost three years.

He scanned the conference room.

This sport has been waiting for you. We have been waiting for you.

– — -

SUNDAY, JANUARY 12ᵀᴴ, 2014
PORTLAND, OREGON
5:49 A.M.

Lucas' room hadn't changed since high school. On the wall opposite his queen bed hung a wooden Wu-Tang symbol that he had sanded, polished and stained into a dark chestnut color in shop class his senior year. Above his bed was a crooked Michael Jordan poster that had been there since long before the Wu-Tang W, probably as early as elementary school years—same as the glow in the dark stars on the ceiling.

It could have been the bedroom of any average college sophomore, but it was Lucas' room, and he was anything but average. Danny was holding tangible evidence of that: the April 15th, 2013 *Sports Illustrated*.

In the week following the release of the issue the Sheppard family had been showered with copies from family friends on top of the 20 copies sent directly from *Sports Illustrated*. One had been framed and now hung in the entryway next to other family photos, Isabel had sent several to her family in Brazil, Rich had taken a few to work for the partners, and however many were left over were in a box in the basement... except for this one.

This copy was special. It was the copy that the family had actually read. In the days and weeks after its' release, it was the copy that could be found on the kitchen table one morning then stuck between the cushions of the couch the next. It had a natural tendency to curl into a baton and judging by the harsh wrinkling of water damage, it must have been left on the back porch at some point.

Each weekly issue of *Sports Illustrated* had a circulation of about three million copies. Of all the glossy issues that had raced down the print line and been boxed and shipped to newsstands all over the country...*this* copy had made it onto the dresser of the guy on the cover.

Danny remembered the day it arrived in vivid detail. Everybody had crowded around the island in the kitchen as Lucas opened the box and held up the first copy to jubilant applause and cheers of neighbors and family friends. Then he went on to read the whole article aloud. His eyes sparkled with pride as he turned the pages of the magazine.

For the past few months it had come to rest on Lucas' dresser and Danny was deeply relieved that nobody had ever bothered to throw it out. Anything that stretched into the past, confirming Lucas' existence, was priceless now; a snapshot from the 20 years that was now and forever would be referred to as... *when Lucas Sheppard was alive.*

He studied the magazine cover in the pre-dawn stillness of the bedroom. On the left was a shot of Lucas: he raised his helmet above his head as the clock ran down on UCLA. His eye black smudged onto his cheeks, his curly brown mop of hair soaked with sweat, his trademark smile beaming broadly. The backdrop was a sea of orange and black, the ecstatic student section of Reser Stadium. Lucas had three touchdown receptions in the 34-17 win for the Beavers and although Lucas had never said it out loud, Danny knew it was one of the best nights of Lucas' life.

On the right side of the cover was Danny: standing at attention on the podium while the National Anthem played. His jungle green eyes shined above his square jaw and sly grin that just bordered on a smirk.

His hair was short, almost military and a shade darker than Lucas'; the front boyishly disheveled with sweat. He had just won his first NCAA National Wrestling Championship.

"Duel Domination: Twin brothers Lucas and Danny Sheppard have lit up the gridiron and the wrestling mat for the Beavers, and they're only getting warmed up!"

Danny nearly had the entire article memorized word-for-word. It talked about the dreams of the young boys and how over time and through hard work, those dreams began to seem more and more likely to come true. Lucas wanted to play for The 49ers and Danny wanted to win Olympic Gold. Surely the leftover copies in the basement would be in high demand now.

Danny had been counting the hours as they ticked by since the announcement of Lucas' death. In just a few minutes he would be coming up on number thirty. Thirty hours of unwavering disbelief, desperately wishing to claw his way into the past. Thirty hours of begging to be told that it was all just a misunderstanding of epic proportions. It still wasn't real.

Danny had moved the mattress from the guest room into Rich and Isabel's room and it was there that everyone had curled into their grieving positions. At some point in the night, bodies began to drift back and forth between the bedroom and the living room. Danny's younger sister Allie, his younger adopted brother Rodney and Lucas' girlfriend Andrea moved as a unit for the most part.

After thirty hours, Danny needed a moment of silence away from the non-stop crying that would periodically evolve into blood-curdling shrieking. He stepped out of the bedroom, away from the mounds of crying bodies and the next thing he knew he was upstairs, standing over Lucas' bed, holding the *Sports Illustrated* from 9 months earlier.

The 30 hours that had crept by had been nothing but a barrage of unfathomable and unacceptable realizations: all the things that Lucas had yet to do and all the people he had left behind. The big ones had presented themselves almost immediately—marrying Andrea and playing in the NFL—but the small things were everywhere and at the moment, Danny stood in the midst of them.

The black and grey Dri-FIT from their Friday workout was still damp in the laundry hamper by the dresser. Lucas' bed wasn't made—it hadn't been touched since he had risen from it two days earlier... for the last time. The small things suddenly seemed sacred; the things Lucas had touched last, the things that were still affected by him. It was as if he wasn't completely gone until all the things he had last affected were changed. His bed, his dirty dishes or even the stubble left in his razor—he wasn't gone yet.

Danny was in a primitive stage of the grief, evaluating things from the ground up. First and foremost was the realization that the 20-year-old body was no more. All six feet, four inches, 205 pounds of Lucas Sheppard had stopped moving, and it would never move again. It would never catch another pass and gallop into the end zone to the thunderous cheers of 40,000 fans. It would never sprawl out on the living room couch and fall asleep with Andrea. It would never hoist Rodney up to the rim so he could dunk. It would never do *anything*... and Danny's mind wasn't registering, it didn't agree.

His body felt so foreign, as if he were missing limbs that he had had since birth but had been suddenly severed. His muscles were tingly numb and restless like an uncomfortable muscle-relaxer experience. There was a terrible pain in his chest as if a piece of his soul was trying to claw its' way out, feigning to fly away and join Lucas. Danny hadn't worked out in three days but from the tensing and shivering of the last thirty hours his muscles were sore and fatigued.

There was a stubborn part of his subconscious trying hard to convince him that it was all just an epic misunderstanding. He half expected to hear the distinct three thuds on the front porch of Lucas bounding up the stairs, hurrying home to clear things up.

He closed his eyes and basked in the silence of the room. The silence was a friend to him; between he and Lucas, he was the quiet one, notoriously. It wasn't the type of quiet that could be mistaken for shyness or insecurity but the kind of quiet that was calm and confident, easily approachable and friendly. He was most often described as sweet, gentle, reserved—*wouldn't hurt a fly*, which only intensified peoples' intrigue given that as soon as he was on the mat facing an opponent he was anything but gentle.

Lucas was the loud one. Always cracking jokes and laughing the booming laugh that was so obviously inherited from Rich. It was the most pleasant kind of loud, a joy to be around. He smiled more than Danny too. A magnificent smile: joy-filled and genuine, beaming trust and optimism like a child's smile transplanted onto a young man's face. When Lucas smiled, nobody could keep from smiling. Even though Danny didn't smile very much, his demeanor was such that people never mistook him for being unhappy or shy. Instead, he had an innocent half-mouthed grin that was adored equally as much as Lucas' smile. Both the boys emitted a calming, personable energy and in their contrasting loud and quiet ways they tended to make people feel relaxed and familiar almost instantly. At school they seemed to give no notice to their popularity, usually dressed casually in athletic clothes, talking to whomever about whatever. People always marveled at how different twin brothers could turn out and they were right to do so, it was incredible.

They were a mesmerizing duo and Allie was in no way lagging behind. All the kids had an electric sparkle of exotic beauty that could only come from parents of different races: Isabel, the Brazilian goddess and Rich, the American stallion. Eyes lingered on them a split-second longer in public places.

Judging by the way Danny's iPhone begun vibrating as he turned it on, the news had broken. Now he took it from his sweat pants' pocket to text Tanner. He hadn't been on any social media since before the accident and decided to check Twitter. He only scrolled down for a few seconds. It was all about Lucas.

"RIP #LS-80 you were the realest dude I ever met!!!!"

"can't believe you're gone...thanks for the memories #LS-80!! #beavernation"

"God always takes the best ones before there time. Prayers to his family"

The hash-tag *#LS-80* was trending nation-wide. Danny 112 messages in his inbox. He couldn't bring himself to read any of them and he knew Facebook would be even worse. He text Tanner and just as he hit send, he heard Isabel call from the top of the stairs.

"Coraçao?"

Her voice was scratchy and hoarse as it often was the day after one of Lucas' football games, but this time it was from screaming and crying. He cleared his throat as quietly as he could and forced his voice to be strong, "Sim mamãe eu estou aqui." Then, placing the magazine back on the dresser just as he had found it, he walked out of the room and closed the door firmly behind him.

– — –

Six miles southwest of the Sheppard household in a basement bedroom of a gaudy and characterless Lake Oswego mansion, Tanner Spurling's muscular, tattooed shoulders screamed for rest as they lowered his body from the chin-up bar in the doorway. He had just done his 492nd pull-up of the night since giving up on sleep at about 1:15 a.m. The high he felt from pushing his body to the limit was his favorite high. Tanner knew a thing or two about highs which, unfortunately, meant he knew just as much about lows.

Judging by his physique, nobody would be shocked to hear that he could do 500 pull-ups in a night. Not an ounce of fat could stick to the body that wrestling had given him. He wrestled at 165 lbs. and while he obviously couldn't be mentioned in the same sentence as Danny, he was still very good.

He wore a pair of basketball shorts. His sculpted upper body and dramatic tattoos drenched with stale vodka sweat. The only source of light came from a muted 14-inch flat screen on a stack of textbooks in the corner of the room. Early morning infomercials were the only tolerable form of company. The bareness of the room gave it the somewhat unmoored quality of a newly finished house that hadn't been moved into yet. The single mattress lying on the floor inspired Lucas to call the room the "Russian jail cell".

A thin line of smoke slithered towards the ceiling from the incense holder in the middle of the grey carpet, dissipating after a few feet.

A bead of sweat fell from Tanner's nose as he turned the bottle of Belvedere to the ceiling one last time, chasing it with a carton of high pulp Minute Maid. The veins on his forearms bulged, running like topographic rivers up his arms to his tattooed shoulders. The vein on the side of his forehead disappeared into his thick black hair. Inside his veins was blood, vodka and a manic rage.

His skin was clammy and uncomfortable and there was a distinctly withdrawal-like ache and soreness to his muscles. For such a young man Tanner's heart had already run quite a gauntlet. Jump-started in the third grade when his mother commit suicide, his father swiftly jogged into the abyss of vodka and opiates. Now Lucas was gone. His grief and agony was horrendous but at the same time, he was overcome by feelings of fury and desperation for vengeance. Lucas' death was no accident. Somebody was at fault. Tanner couldn't live with the notion that at that very moment, he was a free man; walking into the gas station, watching TV, talking to girls at a bar.

Trevor Ramey.

That redneck cocksucker piece of shit.

He and Danny were the only ones who knew for certain that the accident was Ramey's fault. The phone call from Lucas just before the crash had made it perfectly clear... and at the same time cast everything into complete mystery.

Tanner tumbled onto his mattress just as the shattered screen of his iPhone came to life with his 6:00 a.m. alarm. He switched it off. Lying on his back, breathing heavily, he ran his fingers over the tattoo on his rib cage. It was nothing like the dark colors and bold designs on his back and shoulders; this tattoo was hidden. Nine dots smaller than pinheads speckled a five-inch area on his upper left rib cage and onto his pectoral. It didn't appear to be anything but a few moles but a very small number of people knew that the dots were a meaningful senti-ment. It was the constellation *Vela*, in tribute to his mom, Mariel Vela. A Colombian beauty queen who had fallen in love with, and quickly married, Davy Spurling, a young American jockey from the state of Oregon. The wild stallion on Tanner's left shoulder was another tribute to both his parents, lovers of horses.

Tanner was eight when she passed. It was a cloudy but warm day in 3rd grade when he got off the school bus and walked the two blocks home to find three cop cars and an ambulance outside. It was all so confusing; the grown-ups weren't telling him something. Mariel had taken her own life, throwing up her hands and waving a white flag in her battle with depression. Several years would pass before Tanner fully understood what had happened to his mom.

Davy had struggled with prescription pills ever since the knee injury that had ended his jockey career and when Mariel died it only took him a few months to transform into a reckless, dysfunctional alcoholic while his pill habit spiraled far out of control. He loved her so much; the loss flattened him into a shadow of a man.

Tanner's aunt Judy and uncle Donnie reluctantly took custody because according to Judy, *"It's what Jesus would do."* They also assumed that Jesus would give Tanner a near-empty basement bedroom with a chin-up bar in the doorway and a bold crucifix on the center of one wall. While most kids built Legos, played video games and rode bikes, Tanner did chin-ups. Without the involvement of the Sheppard family, there's no telling what path he would have taken in life.

His aunt and uncle didn't want anything to do with him. Davy Spurling was Judy and Kim Spurling's golden-boy younger brother, soaking up all the praise with his glamorous career as a professional jockey. Tanner was the stained reminder of Davy's marriage to the South American beauty queen that neither Kim nor Judy had endorsed as anything other than a young, compulsive fling. Aunt Judy and Uncle Donnie never missed a chance to remind Tanner how blessed he was to be saved by their grace.

At recess on the very first day of 4th grade was when Tanner met the Sheppard boys. The blacktop was scorching hot under a clear blue sky when an argument over a basketball turned into a fight between Tanner and Danny, neither willing to back down. Tanner was winning when Lucas pulled him off of Danny. After fifteen minutes arguing the result of the fight in the Principal's office, Tanner reluctantly suggested that it was a tie and extended his hand in truce. Danny kept a tissue pressed to his nose with his left hand as he agreed and shook Tanner's hand with his right.

The handshake would bind the boys together like welding for the next twelve years. Evolving from playground kings to campus kings, from 4th grade at John Muir Elementary to sophomores at Oregon State University: Lucas, Danny and Tanner had shared every moment. By the time they were in high school it was only blood that kept Tanner officially out of the Sheppard family. They loved him.

His heart continued to pound as he lay on his bed, glassy eyes following the smoke from the incense. Under his mattress were a few leftover Percocet from his wrist injury but he had resisted the persuasive hiss to crush one into the vodka. For what must have been the hundredth time, he relived the moment at the hospital. A white-haired doctor of about 65 pushed through the double doors into the waiting area, a defeated slump in his shoulders. He took off his glasses and shook his head. Time was cemented still.

Isabel and Allie's legs turned to sponge as they collapsed to the floor in belligerent heaps—Tanner imagined that their shrieking was what it sounded like in hell. Lucas was older than Danny by four hours.

"My baby! Not my first baby!" screamed Isabel followed by Portuguese that Tanner knew was addressed to God because it ended in "Deus".

Allie. Beautiful, smart, kind 18-year-old Allie screamed at an ear-bleeding volume. 11-year-old Rodney buried his head between his knees, slumping against the white hospital wall before Danny knelt in their midst and scooped them together with his long arms. Rich blanketed Isabel and Allie with his massive frame. It was a tangled web of bodies locked together by clawing hugs. That's all Tanner could remember—he knew he had gone into shock almost immediately. Thinking about it sent chills up his spine and after a renewed wave of utter disbelief, he thought about Trevor Ramey. His jaw clenched shut with force.

Before the accident Tanner probably would have needed a few descriptions or stories about Ramey just to put a face to the name. He had found him on Facebook earlier in the night. Eleven mutual friends, he had gone to Sunset High, he worked for his dad's construction company and he was an only child. His most identifying characteristics were being rich, cocky and having a thunderous, cherry-red diesel truck that you could hear from three blocks away, the truck that he had been driving when he pulled out of the parking lot after Lucas. Tanner's palms sweat as his heart raced from the fantasy of pounding Trevor Ramey's skull into a crunchy pulp against the sidewalk.

He wasn't sure how the news of Lucas' death had gotten out the day before but people wanted confirmation and naturally, Tanner was the one they would ask.

Lucas Sheppard? Is it true? You're lying. No! How? Are you sure?

Beginning at around 4 p.m. Tanner's phone started to receive the distraught calls and messages, people were desperate to hear what had happened, but he hadn't responded to anybody. He was waiting for one text and one text only: Danny's.

It came at 6:07 a.m. and was as to-the-point as any of his texts.

"Come over."

"omw in 10"

Tanner's black Nissan Maxima peeled out of the driveway. His aunt and uncle had started drinking more since retiring and the fifth of Belvedere was a little more than half-full when Tanner snatched it out of their dutifully stocked liquor cabinet the night before. He knew he shouldn't be driving. The nausea had begun to creep up on him but it was impossible to tell if it was from the vodka or just the sheer grief.

The drive from Judy and Donnie's monstrosity to the Sheppard house in Eastmoreland was an agonizing 15 minutes of changing lanes and catching exits to get to the Sellwood Bridge. He crossed the bridge, hoping to feel the same soothing comfort as he had over the years when entering the lush neighborhood but he was overcome with nerves. Even after being a member of the Sheppard family for so many years, he had no idea what kind of scene he was about to encounter. After what seemed like an hour he pulled up to the forest-green two-story home in the magical neighborhood. He had grown up running amuck with the boys in the streets and parks of Eastmoreland—Allie often trailing close behind. The morning fog was thick and aided by the moisture of the golf course that was just blocks away. Streetlamps in the dim morning mist gave the street a distinct Sherlock Holmes eeriness. Tanner sat there in his car, trying to mentally prepare for what lay ahead when suddenly there was a sharp rise in his heart as if he had missed a step in the dark, goose bumps coated his arms.

There were over 3,000 songs playing on shuffle and at that very moment, the song that started playing was Lucas' favorite: *Let it Be*.

He sat in utter disbelief and listened to all 3 minutes and 55 seconds of the song, piano keys and Paul McCartney's voice drifting through his car in the dark morning. In grainy resolution like a home movie from the nineties, a highlight reel of Lucas' life played before him. It showed his defining moments. Making the entire algebra class, including Mrs. Reynolds howl with laughter. Talking football with Steve, the autistic guy who worked at Safeway, *every* time Lucas went to Safeway. Taking Andrea to prom. Catching that 30-yard touchdown pass to win the Civil War game against the University of Oregon as a true freshman.

It was too much to handle. When the song came to an end Tanner lost control punching his dashboard twice then burying his mouth in his elbow he screamed at the top of his lungs. The nausea made itself well-known then and he opened his car door and vomited onto the street.

This can't be happening. How could he be gone? He was just here.

Lucas.

Lucas Sheppard.

By far and wide the best human being Tanner had ever known had been deleted from existence. There was no way of understanding this. Lucas made everything better. He made everyone happy. When he smiled, everyone smiled. When he laughed, everyone laughed. He was the embodiment of joy and positivity, an inspiration and a guiding light to so many. He was so loved.

This isn't right.

- — -

LUCIANA CARAVELLO ARTE CONTEMPORANEA
RIO DE JANEIRO, BRAZIL

Nina hadn't moved a muscle for nearly five minutes. Her arms were folded tightly. Her weight was leaned onto her right leg and her head listed to the left in contemplation as she studied the work before her. The only light in the gallery came from what was illuminating the painting on the bone white wall.

The curator, a stringy but limber 64-year-old man with tortoise-rimmed glasses perched on the end of his nose, waited patiently for her analysis of the work. He stood several feet behind her, his fingers linked behind his back.

Nina shifted her weight and cocked her head to the other side; she moved with such a languid confidence that the curator found himself pulling his shoulders back and fixing his posture even though she was faced the opposite direction. He had heard the rumors but they seemed to be a bit of a stretch: she was too young, no older than one if his own grandchildren. Nevertheless, the curator could sense that there was something special about her.

She had started as something of a myth, brought up casually from time to time at parties by the notorious and the elite of the Rio art world. Subdued chatter about the young girl—barely in her twenties—who could look at a painting and tell you everything there was to know about it: who it was by, what time period and what was happening in the life of the painter at the time to influence the brushstrokes and colors. The final straw for the curator was the story he had heard from a close and trusted colleague, something he had seen with his own eyes a few weeks earlier at the Niterói Contemporary Art Museum.

William Santos was showing an Egyptian exhibit to invite-only guests before the display would be opened to the public. A crowd of about twenty moved as a group throughout the gallery, champagne glasses in hand, stopping at one painting after another while Mr. Santos launched into a self-indulged rant on each piece, not knowing that there was an audience member who was stockpiling the inaccuracies. After giving his analysis of the last piece of art there was a round of applause, and the room was opened for questions.

After a few mundane questions, Nina's hand became visible from the back of the crowd. "Yes, you, ma'am." Mr. Santos said, his

Portuguese bitten by the faintest Spanish accent, a wide smile spread across his face that would soon fade.

"I'm trying to understand how the work from Fathi Hassan can be described as depicting 'the learning of a new language'..."

Members of the crowd were confused at first, not sure if this young girl was arrogant or asking a quite brilliant question. William Santos' words couldn't have carried a more dismissive and patronizing tone, "Well you see, young lady, Hassan was born in Egypt but moved to Italy at the age of twenty-four, and he still lives there today. He had to learn Italian to survive and that's the primary tenant of most of his work; learning a new language. In this case, it was Egyptian—but with a Neapolitan dialect, which can be even more difficult." He said with a smug smile and a glance around the room that welcomed other guests to join him in his dismissal of the "young lady", which they hesitated to do. Nina didn't respond immediately but when she did, the rest of the room felt badly embarrassed for Mr. Santos.

"The theme of Hassan's work is not actually *learning a new language* but rather the *loss* of language through the oppression of imperialism. In reality, this theme has nothing at all to do with the fact that he moved away to Italy to study. He is referencing the Nubian language of the Nile valley, where his parents are from...geographically quite far from *Naples*."

William Santos suddenly knew exactly who this girl was, he had heard the stories, and he also knew why she was doing this to him publicly. He quickly connected dots in his head and realized that she was surely seeking retribution for how he had berated a young artist a week earlier at a downtown gallery. Nina turned to leave, but over her shoulder she added, "And he was only twenty-two when he moved to Italy."

The shocked eyes of the attendees followed her as she walked away through the open gallery, the clicking of her high heels the only sound.

Santos had organized the event himself and was left to wonder how she had managed to attend in the first place.

After hearing this story, the curator decided that it was time for him to see for himself. The only information he had to go on was that her name was Nina and that she was to be contacted through her

Instagram account: Terasina. 19K followers. There were no pictures of her, just artwork, photography, landscape and architecture.

He sent her a message introducing himself and asked if she would come to the gallery to take a look at a piece that had been puzzling him. He was made to wait a day for her response, but she agreed.

The painting in front of her would be the ultimate test of her skills. It was a trick, a riddle that even some of the most intelligent men and women in art would have difficulties with.

At last she spoke.

"The waves are Vija Celmins, I'm certain of that. But the boy... the boy is...from another brush, and not a famous one. It appears that there were two artists that worked on this separately because the water has no regard for the boy. And not only that...I believe they are from different times. The boy is far more Western."

She turned to face him so swiftly that he nearly flinched. Her gaze was bold yet subtle and the curator heard the complete confidence in her tone.

"You could have made it more difficult." She said in a voice that was part whisper and part hiss, making it hard for him to tell if she was agitated or amused. Her brilliance was confirmed. The rumors were true.

There was a long silence before a shrewd smile spread across his face. "I believe our clients would be very happy if you chose to work here."

— — -

Tanner swung his legs out of the car and onto the pavement next to the puddle of watery vomit. He continued to hyperventilate as tears welled in his eyes. He wanted to cry but the sound of the front door slamming shut made him clench his jaw and wipe his eyes. He looked towards the house. Danny's imposing frame appeared on the porch, he moved in slow motion.

Tanner turned back to the street and clenched his jaw hard, dabbing the moisture from his eyes with his sleeve one more time.

"Get it together." He ordered himself.

Danny made his way to the bottom step and sat next to the hand-prints in the smooth concrete of the driveway. Anybody who had been in the Sheppard household had seen the classic photo that had been stuck to the refrigerator for as long as Tanner could remember: 5-year-old Lucas and Danny and 3-year-old Allie proudly held up their concrete covered hands, smiling big on a summer evening in the late 90's. The photo was also folded in Danny's wallet.

In 2008 when the Sheppard's adopted Rodney they had a small square of the driveway broken up and new concrete poured right next to the handprints so he could leave one of his own. After that, the picture of Rodney holding up *his* concrete-covered hand appeared next to the original on the refrigerator.

Tanner was anxious to ask Danny about his meeting with the detective the day before. They were, after all, the only ones who knew what had actually happened to cause Lucas to crash on SW Capitol Highway. But he knew he would have to wait for Danny to start that conversation. No words seemed worth saying so he sat quietly. It felt like an hour had passed but wasn't more than a few minutes before Danny spoke, "It's gonna be on ESPN today. They called to tell us." Tanner nodded. Another 2 minutes passed before he was able to find his voice. "Who else is here?" It was almost 6:45 a.m.

Danny lay back, resting his elbows on the stair behind him, a toothpick stuck in the side of his mouth. "Nobody right now. Andrea was here until a while ago—she went home to get some stuff. Celia should be over soon. I don't know if Andrea's parents are coming over for SportsCenter." His speech was slow, his voice hollow and void of any real emotion and his demeanor matched: an unsettling, still-in-shock kind of calm. It made Tanner uneasy.

Danny was caring and empathetic to the brink of divinity. He had always put others first. At the moment, Tanner could see that he was trying to shelve his own pain and put the grief of his family ahead of his own. The one person who his heart ached for the most, was Andrea.

Lucas and Andrea would be married one day, everyone had been sure of that for a long time. Starting in elementary school, Andrea had been pulled in by the gravitational power of the Sheppard family,

Lucas in particular. Even before Lucas Sheppard had gone through puberty, he only ever looked in the direction of Andrea. The same was true for her, and they chased each other all over Eastmoreland growing up. She lived six blocks away and by the time they were in high school it was out of their hands, their hearts had decided for them.

One hot summer night in 2009 when the boys were 15, Danny and Tanner waited up until almost 4 a.m. for Lucas to get home so they could hear first-hand what it was like to have sex. When he climbed through the window their eyes were brimming with young impatient curiosity but Lucas' eyes showed something very different. He was tranquilized, a lucid trance in his stare that Danny had never seen in his brother's eyes before. Even though he didn't know what it was at the time, he could tell it was something serious, something that couldn't be easily shaken. And it hadn't been. It had never even been tested.

Danny was the opposite when it came to girls and relationships. He had never met a girl who kept his attention for longer than a few weeks. Wrestling was his first love.

Still without trying, his name was a popular one in the gossip circles of different high schools in Portland: *Have you seen those twins that go to Jesuit? One of them is a wrestler and the other plays football? From Jesuit? Oh my god—so fucking hot. I heard they are like half Brazilian or something. They go to Jesuit.*

Andrea was the type who couldn't wait to have a family of her own and she would sometimes grill Danny and Tanner about why they wouldn't settle down and have girlfriends.

"Why can't you guys just find nice girls and spend time with them and get to know them? Take them on dates. Any of my friends would jump at the chance!"

Tanner lived for set-ups like that.

"Well Andrea that sounds lovely *but*, I've already fucked every single one of your friends…some twice…a few three times." Andrea would do her best not to laugh but Tanner was just so funny and she knew it was true. All her friends adored him, as did she. She loved all three of them. It would have been impossible for her to love Lucas and not Danny and Tanner, and for that matter, Allie and Rodney too.

Danny had never lain awake and talked in a hushed voice on the phone with a girl that he had a crush on. He had never picked out a birthday present or waited at the airport for a girl. But he didn't need to do any of that to understand what Lucas meant to Andrea, and his heart was absolutely shredded for her.

The boys sat on the porch for 20 minutes without a word, the morning light trying to burn through the fog. A passerby who didn't know better would have assumed that they were brothers as people often did, they both had the faint hint of something not entirely Caucasian. Tanner's mind was so deeply immersed in memories that he was startled when Danny spoke, "What'd you do yesterday?"

Tanner thought about it for a second. "Um. I worked out for most of the day. Couldn't really sit still. Um. Went for a run. Listened to music."

More time passed before Danny rose. "Let's drive."

The Maxima pulled away from the curb and around the corner, the thickness of the fog fluctuated in different parts of the neighborhood.

Danny tilted his seat back and stared out the sunroof, watching the branches rush overhead and occasionally disappearing into the fog. They crept slowly through the neighborhood, passing manicured lawns and gardens and clean black asphalt driveways occupied by Volvos, Audis, Mercedes and Subarus.

They passed Mrs. Gibbons who was walking Charlie, her golden retriever, but that was the only sign of life on the street, it was a quiet Sunday morning. They cruised along the fog-blanketed Eastmoreland Golf Course three blocks north of the house. Both Tanner and Danny had lost their virginities on the secluded eighth hole green: Tanner first, Danny a week later. Same girl. Felicia Stenvall, a Swedish exchange student.

After fifteen minutes cruising slowly through the neighborhood they pulled back up to the house. Danny pulled his hood on halfway.

Tanner stole a quick look at him and didn't like what he saw. His eyes were strange. They were open, but there was no life in them: ghostly, unoccupied mannequin eyes, far away in a daydream—or a nightmare, more likely. It was the same look he had seen in his dad's eyes in the months after his mom passed away: slumped on the couch with a week of stubble and a plastic half-gallon of Nikolai on the coffee table amongst empty prescription bottles. A classic Scarface quote dashed through his mind.

"The eyes Chico… they never lie."

He must still be in shock, Tanner thought. Danny took the toothpick out of his mouth and used it to motion towards the broken display of the dash.

"What happened to your dash?"

Tanner didn't have the heart to tell him about *Let it Be* playing the moment he pulled up to the house. His hand still hurt.

"I smashed it. I was mad."

Danny didn't respond.

"Well when we get inside, go brush your teeth and wash your face and stuff. You know mom will freak out if she smells booze."

Tanner nodded, ashamed that he had let himself drink like he had the night before. Rich and Isabel were wary of the history of dependence in his family and they had kept a watchful eye on him over the years. Thankfully, his favorite fix came in the form of a chin-up bar.

Once inside the house, Tanner headed straight to the bathroom and after brushing his teeth and splashing water on his face he made his way through the kitchen to the living room: his real home. The mammoth brown sectional couch under the low slanted ceiling was his favorite place in the world and there was nothing he loved more than spending a rainy Sunday under blankets in the cave of a room watching movies or a football game. He sat on the couch and was sleeping in a matter of minutes.

— — -

After Allie had walked Andrea back to her house at around 5:30 that morning she returned home and was finally able to close her eyes. At about 9:30 she shivered as she woke, Rodney had stolen all the covers. She wandered into the kitchen to get some more fruit—anything more substantial than fruit or juice was impossible to chew and swallow. *SportsCenter* was in a half an hour so she decided to take her apple and grapes down to the couch and wait for everybody else, she knew they had their alarms set for the broadcast, she wouldn't need to wake them.

She didn't know that Tanner had come over while she was asleep and seeing him on the couch gave her a start. She nestled into his side like a cat, secretly hoping he would wake up, which he did. Foggily he came to consciousness and became aware of her presence. He adored Allie as if she were his own little sister. Draping an arm over her he let his cheek rest on top of her head.

Until middle school she had always gone by Alexandra. It had been Tanner who had started calling her "Allie" and now it was only strangers that called her Alexandra. Even on her University of Portland Women's Tennis bio it read,

Allie Sheppard
Class: Freshman
Hometown: Portland, OR
High school: Jesuit HS
D.O.B: 10-17-1995

Just as the boys belonged on the cover of *Sports Illustrated*, Allie may as well have stepped off the cover of *Seventeen*. At Jesuit, it was the overwhelming consensus that she was the hottest girl in the school. In truth, she was just a young Isabel. Long athletic legs, almond skin, jungle green eyes (like Danny) and deep dimples on her round face. The attention and praise she received hadn't spoiled her and she had remained kind, caring and genuine. Spending her childhood trying to keep up with her brothers had made her tough so the twins weren't very protective of her, but Tanner was.

He tried to focus on the shadows moving across the ceiling over the banister in the kitchen. Allie followed his attention, answering the question that he hadn't asked, "Celia and Dre's parents just got here."

"What time is it?" he asked, wiping his eyes and trying to rouse his senses.

"Like nine forty-five. SportsCenter is on pretty soon." Tanner tried wearily to push himself off the couch but Allie latched onto his arm and he let himself doze off again. Moments later the whole group was settling around them: Rich, Isabel, Celia, Rodney, Andrea and her parents, and Danny. The couch was big enough for everyone.

Commercials for Wendy's, StateFarm, Univeristy of Phoenix and a preview for the *Captain America* movie played before the broadcast started. Danny sat forward on the couch, his sleeves pulled up to his elbows, face pale, eyes empty.

"This. Is. *SportsCenter.*" Declared the deep voice followed by the trademark "Duh-na-na. Duh-na-na." The camera swooped through the air and landed on a composed and professional Chris Berman at a grand broadcasting table. It was immediately clear by his face: this was not a typical broadcast. Through the years Stuart Scott, Linda Cohn, Chris Berman and Dan Patrick had captivated the boys' imaginations with their electric commentating on the sports stars of the 90's and 00's.

The first time Lucas was on ESPN had been indescribable: the footage of his second touchdown reception in the early season game against Eastern Washington. With each game of his freshman season everybody got more and more accustom to seeing him on TV as his success continued to soar. Now he had an entire segment dedicated to him...for the worst possible reason.

— — –

"This morning, our hearts are heavy as we send our thoughts to Oregon State University and Beaver Nation, following a tragic loss. Reports coming out of Portland this morning are that the Beaver's twenty-year-old, All-American wide-receiver Lucas Sheppard was tragically killed in a car accident, early Saturday morning."

Wrong. The crash was before midnight so it was Friday night but Lucas wasn't pronounced dead until after midnight.

Tanner was irritated by the small inaccuracy.

Trevor Ramey.

Jaw Clench.

As Chris Berman began recalling his accomplishments Lucas' highlight reel started to play.

"In just two seasons, Sheppard established himself as one of the best wide receivers in college football. As a true freshman for the Beavers he caught fifty-two passes for seven hundred and thirty-four yards on his way to being named PAC-12 Offensive Freshman Player of the Year as well as being tabbed a Freshman All-American by every major publication in the country. This past fall in his sophomore season Sheppard picked up right where he left off, catching ninety-two passes for one thousand two hundred and fifty-one yards and being named PAC-TEN Offensive Player of the Year as well as being a consensus First Team All-American selection."

The clips of Lucas' best catches were painful to watch but when they showed a clip of him smiling on the sideline a chorus of cries broke out from several places on the couch, sending shivers through Tanner's body. Berman continued, "Joining us on the phone from Corvallis, Oregon is Beavers Head Coach, Tony Marshall."

Footage of Coach Marshall patrolling the sideline during various games of the season with his headset on was shown on the left of the screen. "Coach Marshall thank you for joining us on what must be an extremely difficult morning." It took a second for the low raspy voice to come over the phone.

"It's a terrible morning here, Chris." Coach Marshall sounded utterly flattened. "I think people are still in shock, myself included. Everybody loved this kid. You know, when you're a recognizable athlete on a big campus, it's easy to take up the label of *athlete* and nothing more, but with Lucas, people still knew him as a nice person, not just a football player. That's just what kind of character this kid had. As good as he was on the field, he will be missed just as much in the locker room and around campus."

"That sure seems to be something we've heard repeatedly with everybody we've spoken to about Lucas—and you're not lying when you say that he was good on the field. Where did Lucas Sheppard rank in terms of receivers you've coached over the years?" Berman asked.

"Lucas was... *without question*... one of the most exciting talents that I've ever coached. I mean, *massive* potential. More raw talent than most players would even know what to do with. Most importantly, he had the right attitude, the right mindset—he was a very smart kid.

His maturity as a freshman—a *true* freshman, I should clarify—was remarkable. No occasion was too big, he was a born leader—I mean the list just goes on. One of the jokes in the coaching staff last year was that the only certainties in life are death, taxes, and that number eighty is going to be open. He was an amazing player."

"We understand that students and players are still on Christmas break and won't return to class for another week but what will protocol be for players once they return to campus?" Berman asked, looking as professional and composed as always. Tanner felt a fleeting moment of gratitude that it was Chris Berman who was the one talking about his friend.

He. Could. Go. All. The. Way.

"Well, there will be counselors available for players and staff but the most important thing is that we deal with this as a team. Lucas had contact with everyone. He was everywhere. He didn't necessarily have a *specific* group of friends on the team—he was a friend to everyone— offense, defense, special teams—everyone. We're going to be there for each other and we are going to go to practice everyday with Lucas in our hearts."

Berman thanked Coach Marshall for joining the broadcast, and continued.

"Lucas Sheppard came from one of the most athletic families you are ever likely to meet. His father, Rich Sheppard, played quarterback for Portland State University in the late 80's and his mother, Isabel Silva, a native of Rio De Janeiro, Brazil, played tennis for University of Portland during the same time period. His younger sister, Allie is currently following in her mothers' footsteps and has just finished her freshman season on the tennis team at the University of Portland. Lucas' twin brother, Danny, is nothing short of a wrestling prodigy, also currently attending Oregon State. Out of high school Danny was ranked by several publications as the number one recruit in the country in the 184-pound weight class. He strolled to an undefeated national championship in his freshman season and is currently undefeated in his ongoing sophomore season with a record of twenty-two wins and zero losses. ESPN analysts believe he could be on course to become just the fifth NCAA wrestler in history to be a four-time National Champion.

Our thoughts and prayers are with the Sheppard family and the rest of Beaver Nation during this difficult time."

Tanner could recall ESPN mentioning the deaths of a few college athletes over the years, but nothing to this extent.

Guess it's different if you're a consensus All-American.

In the same box on the screen where the video of Coach Marshall on the sidelines had just been, ESPN switched to a live feed from a camera in one of the press boxes in Gill Coliseum. School wasn't even in session for another week but the bleachers and coliseum floor were filled with what had to be at least a few hundred people, milling about in orange and black, consoling one another with candles in their hands. Center court was filled with stuffed animals, flowers and lit candles. The live feed expanded to fill the whole screen, and remained there in deafening silence for ten seconds until it transitioned to Lucas' roster headshot above the sobering statistic of his life span:

Lucas Michael Sheppard
November 3rd 1993 - January 11th 2014

Allie buried her face in Tanner's shoulder. She couldn't bear to look at Lucas' shaggy brown hair and vast white smile looking back at her. Everyone had done their best to refrain from crying out loud during the broadcast but once the commercials came, nobody held back, it was an orchestra of sobbing. Danny rose from the couch and headed for the sliding door that led to the porch and back yard. He gave Tanner a commanding flick of his head for him to follow. Tanner squeezed Allie's arm and got up.

Near the fire pit by the line of trees at the back of the yard there was an old wooden picnic table that had been there since the boys were in elementary school. The years of Portland rain had badly warped all the flat surfaces and its' legs had been somewhat reclaimed by the earth. Danny stepped up onto it, Tanner stayed on the ground.

Nothing was important enough to be said out loud. There was no need for 'I can't believe he's gone' or 'It doesn't seem real', the obvious response to which would have been 'No shit'.

Danny stood on the table with his arms folded, staring vaguely toward the roof of his house as the silky spray fell. Tanner was almost certain now that he was still in some state of shock. He had been hoping that Danny would tell him something about what was said with the detective, but it didn't come.

A few silent minutes went by before Danny stepped down from the table. Watching him do that for Tanner felt as though somebody had taken a baseball bat to his chest. He was known for doing backflips off the table. With typically stunning athleticism, he would turn towards the line of spruce trees and launch himself off the table into a slow rotating backflip, landing on the ground, one leg before the other. Lucas would too. It was a trick they'd done consistently since middle school.

One of their Brazilian uncles, Paolo, was a somewhat famous practitioner in the world of capoeira and had started teaching the boys when they were five years old. Spending their summers in Rio, they would stay at the beach for hours, whipping themselves through the air at the instructions of Paolo until the sun would set. They had become incredibly good at it over the years and their choreographed routines were amazing to watch; the flips, kicks and spins that demanded such athleticism and coordination. Tanner loved to watch it and had even gotten pretty good at some of it himself, but to see Danny simply step down was powerful in the most unimaginable way. He might never do a backflip off the table ever again. As soon as the sliding door shut behind Danny, Tanner sat on the picnic table, hung his head and started to cry.

– — -

LEO GOIA PRISON
RIO DE JANEIRO, BRAZIL

The camera clicked as the flash turned the room white.

"Esquerdo." The military guard's deep voice announced. Joris knew the basics of Portuguese well enough to know that it meant 'left'. He obeyed, turning to face the other wall. Another click. Another flash.

Presídio Leo Goia would be home for the next 18 months.

At 31 years old, Joris Wijndal was stepping into incarceration for the fourth time on a third continent. The first stint had been in his home country of The Netherlands when he was 22. The sentence had been a walk in the park; four months playing chess, backgammon and learning to play the guitar while sleeping in a cell as nice as some of the hotels he'd stayed in on his travels. Next was Sweden when he was 26. The prison had been equally if not more hospitable than The Netherlands but this time, he was in for a year. The noble attempts of the civilized countries to rehabilitate him were futile. He was a criminal, a narcotics entrepreneur. He couldn't change.

This was the trajectory his life had been set on since he was 12 years old. At the age when he was just beginning to rebel against structure and authority—cut school, smoke cigarettes and drink vodka in the streets with the other misguided youths of Amsterdam. It was a Thursday afternoon, he didn't know why he remembered something so trivial, but it was the day when everything changed.

Joris was folding the €60 he had just won in a card game at a popular fountain where the street kids often loitered. He didn't notice the sleek silver Mercedes pull up or the slick-haired, handsome Turkish man with a wide jaw and piercing brown eyes who stepped out. Kerem Demirelli. A well-known and well-respected figure in the darker parts of Amsterdam—he would sometimes buy a stick of gum or a cigarette from one of the kids for €100. He was best known for fixing lower league soccer games, but he did much more than that.

"Good day for you?" He asked as Joris organized his cash.

They started to talk card games and the rest was history. Unlike all of the other kids, who admired Kerem for his luxury sedan, gold jewelry, leather jackets and clean Chuck Taylor's, Joris was far more enamored with the wisdom and stories, tales of far-away lands and dangerous adventure…that came with big rewards. It was then, at the age of 12, that he decided what he wanted from life: to experience all that he could. None of the other kids saw the world beyond the streets of Amsterdam, but Joris began to marvel at the vast possibilities.

Kerem was quick to recognize Joris' intelligence and ambition and he plucked him from the streets and began apprenticing him in different illegal trades: fixing soccer games, smuggling ecstasy into

England, passport modifications and even a little counterfeiting. It became his life: messy wads of Euros or crisp folds of pound notes, dim brothels, sticky black tar, white powders, bags of multicolored pills, bloody pavement, the angry hiss of Eastern European languages, Louis Vuitton luggage or duct-taped bundles. It suited him and by the time he was 19, he was running his own show.

The way a normal person might fear prison and the lawful powers of retribution, Joris came to fear the monotony of a modest existence. While he was locked up in Stockholm's Österåker Prison, he met Arnel, a Filipino man who laid an enticing new prospect in front of him. He would mule heroin from Thailand to Brussels.

It had led to his third prison stint and compared to The Netherlands or Sweden, it was hell on earth: two years inside Klong Prem, Thailand. The first three runs had been successful, about four kilos of heroin on each trip back to Belgium, netting him about €200,000.00 on each haul. But he would come to live out the cliché that he had heard a thousand times, every mule had: the final haul is where it always goes to shit.

Sitting shirtless on the itchy cotton sheets of the cheap hotel in Bukkhalo, he inhaled thickly on a sticky joint while waiting for Prakit to return with the bundle. The wait was longer than it had been any of the other times but he didn't worry—any number of things could be holding him up. The sound of mopeds whizzing by on the street below floated into the third-floor window of the hotel. He pondered a vacation destination after this last run—Morocco, New Zealand or somewhere in Central America maybe, Costa Rica sounded nice.

He had just dabbed out the joint in the ashtray—as if some higher power had allowed him to finish it—when everything came crashing down. Car doors slammed outside. In the exact same moment that he stuck his head out the window and looked down to see if it was Prakit getting out of a taxi, two police officers looked up, directly in his face. It was perfectly obvious to both parties: sunburnt pink face with red hair and the faded rose tattoo on his neck. There was no point in running.

The following two years were horrific. Sleeping on the half-inch thick pool chair cushion amongst a gathering of cockroaches every night in the sweltering heat was the lighter side of his worries.

When he was finally processed and set loose into the courtyard of Leo Goia he was pleasantly surprised by the conditions, although anything would have been an upgrade from Klong Prem. Ever since he was a child he had been a devout optimist and even then, upon his induction into the fourth major prison stint of his life, his mind went directly to potential silver linings.

This won't be so bad, I can learn Portuguese and maybe find a card game. Surely I can get my hands on a guitar, too.

Even after experiencing some of the darkest sides of humanity his positivity and sense of humor hadn't deserted him. He scanned the rising walls of cells that boxed him in. Seven levels. He sighed deeply as unfamiliar faces shot glances at him from every direction. "Eighteen months and counting." He said to himself.

– — -

Only ten minutes away from Joris' new home in Leo Goia was the hillside home of Isabel Silva's parents. The scene in the living room mirrored the scene in the Sheppard house 6,850 miles away; grief, like love or any powerful human emotion was the same in any culture. Isabel's four older brothers, their wives and all eleven of their children had gathered at Edson and Rosa's house after the news came over the phone. It was unbelievable. Lucas was gone.

The boys and Allie had spent their summers in Rio ever since they were born and even though they lived on separate continents, there was never any disconnect between Isabel and her family.

It had never been her intention to stay in America after she finished studying but as she learned, intentions were brittle when they stood in the path of love. When the twins came along Isabel and Rich made a promise that they wouldn't let her culture be watered down in thier children, they would be Brazilian and American, starting with the naming of the boys. Rich wasn't having any part of Márcio or

Rafael, but Lucas was a good name and he warmed to Danilo since his own father's name had been Daniel. Alexandra was easily agreed upon.

There was no pre-determination for which name they would give to which twin. They agreed that it was wrong to assign them names before having taken their first breaths but when they were born, it was somehow obvious which one was Lucas and which one was Danilo.

"This is Danilo." Rich said with certainty, holding the tiny being for the first time. Isabel smiled, exhausted but knowingly, "I know. Because this is Lucas."

Rich had held Danny first and Isabel had held Lucas first. After a few minutes, they switched, Isabel holding Danny and Rich holding Lucas. After a few more minutes, they switched again.

Isabel Silva had grown up as an urban princess in the mountainside neighborhoods of Rio. The whole Silva family was unofficial royalty; Edson and Rosa were beloved from the poverty-stricken favelas to the gated communities in the basin of the city. Isabel's brothers were all well known and well respected for their different talents and contributions to Rio De Janeiro. She could have stayed in Rio and married a doctor or Real Estate mogul, she was the subject of constant attention growing up...and she couldn't wait to escape it. Tennis was her first love and she jumped at the allure and promised adventure of an athletic scholarship to an American university.

Fate took the steering wheel and seven years later, Isabel Silva was Isabel Sheppard. Her husband was a strong, handsome American football player named Richard Thomas Sheppard. Soon after they were married she was pregnant with twin boys. They bought a small home in the quant Eastmoreland neighborhood and her life had become unrecognizable in the most magical way.

– — -

The day wore on; Danny continued to count the hours as they sluggishly ticked by. Isabel was on and off the phone with family, answering question after question through tears, "Não... esperando e esperando... Eu não sei... Ele não tinha cinto de segurança...Meu menino."

First at noon and then again at about 7:00 p.m. she had broken down as if she were hearing the news for the first time, her shrieking in Portuguese was blood-curdling. Rich had been pretty consistent throughout the day, mainly just sitting at the kitchen counter in sweats and a t-shirt, looking at photo albums, dabbing his moist eyes and crying infrequently.

Even with puffy red eyes he was still *Big Rich* or *Grizzly Rich* as Tanner called him sometimes. The definition of a man's man: wide-shouldered, barrel-chested six feet and four inches tall with huge, calloused hands. His wide stature and thick circle of facial hair around his mouth was intimidating but anybody that knew him knew that he was only intimidating in the courtroom when the wellbeing of a child was at stake. He and Isabel shared a staunch compassion for all of humanity and a deep distress for the suffering of others. The grace of the Sheppard family had shown brightest in 2008 when they adopted Rodney.

Earlier in his career Rich practiced primarily Criminal Law before transitioning to primarily Personal Injury. On a blustery day in April a handsome light-skinned black man with short dread-locks strolled into Rich's office. The first thing Rich noticed were the two tear-drop tattoos on the left side of his face. The next thing he noticed was the suit: charcoal Armani. The man studied Rich and his office without shame. He was big. Probably as tall as Rich and maybe even heavier. After a long enough pause Rich said,

"Tight-end?"

The man continued to eye him before his expression softened slightly.

"Defensive back."

Rich nodded.

"Sheppard. They say you're the man to talk to when the day comes. Well…the day is here." Rich sensed a slight Chicago accent. He then dropped a Louis Vuitton duffle bag on the table that Rich hadn't even noticed was in his hand. He unzipped it and began taking out crisp stacks of $100 bills. "Thirty five for a retainer. Who do I talk to about the intake." It wasn't a question.

The man had hired Rich to defend Rodney Jones Sr. who had just been arrested in Gresham and was being charged with Unlawful Possession of a Dangerous Drug: eight kilos of methamphetamine. Little did law enforcement know if they had arrested Rodney Sr. earlier in the day it would have been ten times as much. The Westside Interagency Narcotics team had been after Jones for three years since he dodged a lengthy sentence on a previous charge. The prosecution's case was strong and the charges were enough to send him away for more than 20 years even after he accepted a plea. Rodney Sr. wasn't a dealer that was standing on any street corner.

According to the District Attorney, he was "a shark amongst fish in the Portland drug world. The city will be a far safer place with him off the streets" which wasn't a lie. Three weeks after being hired to defend Rodney Sr., five-year-old Rodney Jr. sat in the waiting room of the firm, feet dangling off the edge of the chair.

Rich was walking to the copy room when he past the waiting area and did a double take. There was a lone little boy in their reception. He turned to the receptionist with the question obvious on his face.

"Rodney Jones' son. His mom dropped him off about ten minutes ago. Said she'd be right back."

Rich peered into the waiting room where the little boy sat on one of the big leather couches, feet dangling, stare transfixed on the waterfall in the corner of the room.

By the time 3:30 p.m. turned to 7:30 p.m., all six attorneys had left and Rich had sent their secretary, Christine, home for the night, assuring her that he would take care of the situation. They didn't know how to get ahold of this woman who had dropped him off. Rodney Sr. wasn't married and when Rich had asked Rodney Jr. if he knew his mommy's cell phone number, he shook his head confused and most likely terrified. Rich couldn't speak to Rodney Sr. on such short notice and a home phone number listed in his case file in Gresham was disconnected.

Finally at 8:15, Rich said, "I'm hungry. What do want to eat?" Rodney had Taco Bell in the car on the way home to Eastmoreland. Rich could hardly get a word out of him. Even when Isabel smiled and asked him his name he just looked up at her with big brown scared and confused eyes. Rich did his best to explain to him that he was going to spend the night with them and that they would find his mommy the next day and everything would be fine.

The next morning Isabel had a buffet of four kinds of cereal, doughnuts, eggs, bacon, waffles, and fruit on the kitchen counter. "I like those." Rodney said timidly, pointing to the Lucky Charms. "Oh good!" she squealed, her smile warming the whole room around her. When Allie joined them in the kitchen she almost got Rodney to smile once when she said, "Rodney you look like Allen Iverson with those cornrows."

Rodney Sr. was white and his girlfriend, Rodney's mother, was black. Rodney Jr. had lived most of his life in central Oregon and Rich had trouble fathoming the hellish circumstances he must have endured being the black son of a white meth dealer in rural Oregon.

For the rest of the day, Rodney Jr. experienced the phenomenal power that was Isabel, Allie… and a credit card. Meanwhile, Rich showed up to work and found a series of voicemails from Child Protective Services that explained the situation. Rodney's mom was in a holding cell in Multnomah County jail. After dropping him off at the office she had gone to offload another 200 grams at a stash house in Tigard but was busted coming out the back door and was now looking at 5-7 years. Small credit to her, she had in fact told them that her son was waiting at the attorney's office but there seemed to have been some sort of miscommunication along the line because nobody even knew that she had a child until later that night when she asked about him during interrogation.

There was nobody to take care of Rodney except for the State. Rodney Sr. no relatives or parents. When asked if he had an associate or friend who might be able to care for Rodney Jr., Rodney Sr. said, "I wouldn't trust my son to any of my *associates*."

Rich was able to arrange temporary custody so Rodney could stay at their house for the next week. He opened up a little more each day, helped by the fact that he loved sports. On what was meant to be his last night with the Sheppard family they ate Pizza Schmizza on the couch while watching the Lakers play the Nuggets. Rodney loved Kobe. At a commercial break, Lucas asked, "Rodney did you have fun this week?"

Sitting cross-legged on the carpet in his new Jordan hoodie, his cornrows freshly twisted, he was glued to the TV and didn't realize that the room had gone quiet; they wanted to hear what he would say. He loved being there. All he did was play football, basketball and soccer with Lucas and Danny, eat Isabel's delicious cooking, and sleep in a comfortable bed without the late-night commotion of drug transactions taking place in the living room.

"Yeah I like to play with you and Danny. Nobody ever wants to play with me at home." There was no self-pity in his voice; he was just stating a fact. Before anybody could say anything the game came back on and Rodney shot his fists into the air, "Come on Kobe!"

After that it would have been impossible for Rich or Isabel to simply turn him over to the State. Family meetings were held over the next two or three days before it was decided: they would adopt Rodney. One of Rich's partners practiced Family Law and it wasn't a complicated process since both Rodney Sr. and the mother agreed to it, admitting that it was by far the best option for him.

— — —

Six years had passed since the night of Pizza Schmizza and the game between the Lakers and the Nuggets. Now at 8:30 p.m. Rodney was in Rich and Isabel's room wrapped in blankets with Allie and Andrea, crying tears for his big brother who he thought was the second coolest person in the world, behind Kobe. He had come out of the room a couple times but had only ended up in Isabel or Celia's arms crying even harder.

Celia had taken on the responsibility of planning the services when it was decided that they would take place on Saturday and Sunday. Saturday would be the public service at Gill Coliseum in Corvallis and on Sunday there would be a private service at church in Portland. Somebody—most likely Celia—had ordered pizza. A stack of boxes had appeared on the island in the kitchen.

Celia Ramsey had lived in Eastmoreland since 1976, long before the Sheppard's had moved into the neighborhood.

To her, 6'4" 205 lb. Lucas Sheppard would forever be a little boy who never checked for cars before sprinting across the street to give her a hug. By the time Rich and Isabel moved into the neighborhood Celia had finished raising her three daughters and already lost her husband to cancer. She had watched Isabel's belly grow big with the boys. She had taken the family pictures every year on the first day of school. She had been ever-present at sporting events and birthday parties from the very beginning, usually with a camcorder—and eventually an iPhone—glued to her hand. She had taken the family pictures every year on the first day of school. She had dinner with the Sheppard family on a weekly basis. They ended every conversation with 'I love you'. Like Tanner and Andrea, she was family.

Danny had been the first one of the kids to start tagging along with Celia on her neighborhood walks and as a small child he found out that the wisdom of older people was both fascinating and addicting. In middle school he developed a strong interest in history and he would stockpile questions about historical events to ask her on their walks. It soon became at least a weekly routine for everyone in the family: walks with Celia. No topic was off-limits and none of the kids kept any secrets from her. Growing pains were alleviated, stories were told, advice was given, jokes were laughed at and debates were had. So many lessons were learned from her, none more important than kindness.

Needless to say, Celia was heartbroken beyond words. Somehow, she had remained the most composed out of anyone throughout the day. Like Isabel she had been on and off the phone, coordinating and organizing the services, often stepping onto the back porch with her cell phone to talk to a planner of some sort.

Danny and Tanner had remained on the couch for the most part. Danny only left to check on the girls and Rodney or to give Isabel a neck to latch onto. Danny was an observer; his quiet nature had allowed him to excel at reading people's expressions and body language. At the moment it was easy for him to see that Tanner was desperate to talk about Trevor Ramey. His sadness was clear, but there was something beneath it, something itchy and antsy, almost energetic in the way he curled his thumbs into his palms, exhaled sharply and frequently shifted his position.

He knew Tanner would be that way until they got word from the detectives. For the time being, he and Tanner were the only ones who felt the anger along with the pain. Nobody else had been there for the phone call.

"It's being investigated. There's nothing we can do right now but wait." Danny said unprompted.

It wasn't enough for Tanner. "And—*what?* They're going to call Trevor Ramey and ask him if he ran him off the road?" Tanner's voice agitated and impatient. Danny closed his eyes and bowed his head ever so slightly, meaning he didn't appreciate tanner's inability to control his emotions. Tanner promptly resumed silence. A minute passed.

"They'll look at the car, they'll talk to people—Ramey and other people. They'll take care of it. I have the detective's number and dad is in contact. They'll get him for it."

Tanner wasn't satisfied but he wasn't going to press on. His insides were on fire and what he wished Danny would say was,

"Tanner, go kill that motherfucker."

– — –

Saturday, January 18th arrived with the still impossible to grasp realization that there was a service for Lucas. Danny drove Celia's Audi SUV with Celia sitting in the front seat and Rodney and Tanner in the back. Rich drove Isabel and the girls in his car and Andrea's parents drove separately. Corvallis, a two-hour drive south on

I-5, was a lovely college town surrounded by lush Oregon forests, but there would be nothing lovely about it today.

Leaving the house had turned into an ordeal after Allie attempted to make a joke, "I didn't think I'd ever get a chance to wear these all-black Vans!" It had the opposite effect of a joke and she and Andrea spent the next half hour sobbing in each other's arms. Tanner was finally able to usher them to the car with some light encouragement, "Let's just get through today and get back to the couch alright?"

It seemed to help, and they were on the road by 9:15. The rain fell harder the closer they got to Corvallis but it hadn't seemed to prevent anybody from making it to the service. There was private parking for them in the little parking area between the Sports Performance Center and the Coliseum.

All three cars arrived within 10 minutes of each other and as soon as everybody was there, a security guard led them through a side door and down a set of stairs to a makeshift waiting area of folding chairs in the dim tunnel that led from the Coliseum floor to the basketball locker room. Danny and Tanner knew the building well.

The light crept up the tunnel but wasn't strong enough to illuminate them 30 feet from the threshold. The commotion of roughly 5,000 people settling into their seats was audible and inspired Rodney to curiously wander down the tunnel and poke his head out. The light cast his small body into a perfect silhouette—a quite picturesque scene that everybody seemed to notice in silent unison.

For the next 20 minutes, there was eye dabbing, feet shuffling and Allie mumbling her speech to herself from a wrinkled notecard. The girls had decided to give a speech together. Finally, the same security guard made his way up the tunnel, "We'll have you guys out on the stage now—if you're all ready?" As they rose to their feet there was a collective sigh as if to say, *Here we go*.

The service made one thing glaringly obvious: Lucas was loved. Danny had underestimated. There had to be at least 6,000 people in attendance. Gill Coliseum held about 10,000 and it was well over half full. The majority of the crowd wore black and orange.

The football team had all come back early from Christmas break for the service and were sitting in the front, dressed sharply in program-provided black suits. Little orange "80" pins were on almost everyone's shirts. They must have been giving them out at the entrances. Danny remembered the exact moment when Lucas found out he would get to wear number 80 as a freshman. He was so excited. Jerry Rice wore number 80 when he played for the 49ers; he was Lucas' all-time favorite.

After the first semester of their freshman year the boys had driven to Newport on the Oregon coast before heading home for Christmas break. They rolled up their pants and strolled down the beach, running from the waves. Conversation inevitably rounded back to the incredible season Lucas had just finished. Everyone knew he would do well, but not *that* well. Danny was expected to win. Of course everyone was proud of his first national championship but there was little surprise in it. The boys sat in the dunes and stared out at the Pacific Ocean. Tanner tried to wrap his head around this new not-so-impossible idea that one day, Lucas could be mentioned in the same sentence as Jerry Rice himself.

–   —   –

"Let's call it a day." Celia sighed as they climbed back into her Audi. The service had gone as well as it could have. She had opened the eulogies, introducing herself as "Lucas' stand-in grandma" explaining that she had watched the kids grow up from across the street since they were born. There wasn't a single nerve in her voice as she addressed the crowd of 6,000, speaking with eloquence and clarity that made it impossible to believe she was 84 years old.

Danny shared a heart-piercing story from their childhood about how Rich had told Danny that he needed to throw Lucas as many passes as there were blades of grass in the backyard. Then he said that by the time they were in middle school, he had probably thrown him as many passes as there were blades of grass on the golf course by their house.

Tanner's speech was nothing short of extraordinary. He was so gifted with words. Rich stood with Isabel, who of course managed to look graceful and gorgeous as she recited a prayer in Portuguese. Then in his deep gravelly voice, Rich told the crowd how proud he was of the man his first-born son had become.

Hanging boldly in the center of the Coliseum floor was a Brazil flag and the American flag either side of a huge, orange "80". It would have been wrong to have no acknowledgment of Lucas' Brazilian heritage.

Each speech was more heartbreaking than the previous but if there was a dry eye in the crowd before Andrea and Allie's speech, there certainly wasn't afterwards; rhythmically finishing each other's sentences while sharing the things they loved most about Lucas. Even the toughest 6' 5", 270 lb. linebackers were turned into blubbering babies. Tanner had helped Rodney write some touching things from the perspective of someone who looked up to Lucas and it turned out great. There were also words from Coach Marshall, Athletic Director Alec Durr, and School President John Woodward.

Danny started the car. "Let's call it a day." He echoed. In that moment, he didn't want to be sitting next to anybody in the world but Celia.

There had been so many people at the service that there was some traffic on the way to I-5. It took about two and a half hours to get home, slightly longer than normal. The rain had thinned into a mist. Tanner's encouragement from that morning had turned out to be spot-on as everyone changed from funeral attire to sweats and hoodies and went straight back to the couch. Isabel had a typically delicious smelling pot of Brazilian stew on the stove. Danny's appetite had come back a little bit and for the evening, everything was relatively calm. As they sat on the couch with the TV on, Danny peered at Andrea out of the corner of his eye.

Her curly golden hair was pulled into a ponytail but a bouncy strand fell next to her face. Danny hadn't met another quite like her; kind, considerate, intelligent, fun to be around and so beautiful—the female version of Lucas. Her eyes had a natural slant that squinted adorably when she smiled and made her look "White-Asian" or "perma-stoned" as Tanner often joked—he loved giving her a hard time about it. Sometimes she would walk into the room and Tanner would gasp, "Oh my God Dre! How high are you right now? Did you smoke the *entire* bag?" She always laughed at the joke, which only made her look even more "perma-stoned".

It was perhaps the worst realization of the whole thing: Lucas and Andrea would never be married.

Danny winced from the thought.

What are you supposed to do now? I'm so sorry Dre.

– — –

Everybody had filled and refilled their bowls until the pot was empty. The feijoada was Tanner's favorite. Nobody had eaten or slept much the previous few days but when Rodney woke from the couch at around 3:00 a.m., the lights of an infomercial were dancing across sleeping bodies all around him. He sleepily pushed the power button on the TV and headed for his bedroom, which made him sad because Lucas used to carry him to bed when he would fall asleep on the couch. Sometimes he would wake up in Lucas' arms on the way but pretend to be asleep until he got put to bed then try to scare him. Lucas would always fake a heart attack from shock.

He didn't think anybody had woken up but as he made his way through the kitchen he heard Danny quietly call after him, "Rod?" Then he heard him getting up from the couch. Even though Lucas was 2 inches taller and 25 pounds heavier, Danny somehow always seemed to be the bigger one to Rodney. As he came up the short flight of stairs from the living room, Rodney tucked his chin to his chest and held his arms up as the tears began to roll down his cheeks yet again. Danny scooped him up with the incredible ease that always amazed Rodney.

Nobody is stronger than Danny.

"Why did he crash?" Rodney wailed. "Shhhh. Shhhh." Danny whispered into his ear, cupping the back of his little brother's head, attempting to suppress the impending sobbing fit. "I don't know. I don't know." He set Rodney down and took a knee in front of him, squeezing his shoulders squarely. Rodney had a knuckle buried in his eye as he struggled for a full breath between sobs. Danny spoke clearly, "Rod listen." He held his little shoulders firmly, "Lucas loved you, Rod. A lot. What I'm going to tell you is for grown-ups, but you're a big boy now and you need to know this."

Rodney was able to nod and choke out an, "Okay."

"It's okay to feel sad, Rod. It's okay. Mom, Dad, Tanner, Celia, Dre and Allie, all our other friends, the football team—everyone's sad. It's okay. But you know he doesn't want us to be sad forever, right? He wants us to keep living and he wants us to do fun stuff. He wants you to play soccer and laugh with your friends—and work hard in school, of course," Danny paused and swallowed hard to clear away the lump in his throat, "...and do all the other stuff that makes you happy, but it's okay to be sad buddy."

It was perfectly true. Danny knew Lucas better than anybody ever would and he knew it's what he would want for his family, but it would be impossible. Nobody would be picking up life where they had left off. Everything was fucked. It was so unreasonable for him to be expected to carry on; to go back to Corvallis, walk around campus, sit in a classroom, to wrestle with the same competitive drive. It wasn't going to happen. He picked up Rodney and carried him to Lucas' room where they both fell asleep.

– — –

When Tanner woke up the next morning he just knew; *Today is the day*. The day that the phone call would come from the detectives and the whole thing would turn from an accident, to an accident that was somebody else's fault. Tanner didn't know how things would change, knowing that it was a murder and not human error. He wanted to see the public react with outrage. He wanted to see the footage of Trevor Ramey handcuffed in an orange jumpsuit, walking into a courthouse for sentencing as his attorney pushed the cameras out of his face.

The call came at around noon. Danny and Tanner were half-heartedly shooting free throws with Rodney in the driveway. Rich answered his cell phone. The conversation lasted about 4 minutes and was ended with a flimsy commitment to "stay connected should something come to our attention. Again, we're very sorry for your loss."

Rich called the boys into his office and informed them of the news. There was no evidence to support the claim that the crash was caused by an act of road rage. Trevor Ramey was, and would remain a free man. Rich passed the news to the boys far too nonchalantly for their liking. Nobody understood like they did, they hadn't heard the phone call. It was *100%* Trevor Ramey's fault, they were certain. They knew what they heard. Rich hadn't taken them seriously enough for their liking and he thought they were grasping for something that wasn't there.

It was a crushing blow, too much for Tanner to take and his

emotions got the best of him. This time Danny didn't do anything to calm him.

"He didn't just crash his car on his own! Lucas didn't even text and drive, he was a good driver. This is *bullshit* Rich. That motherfucker..." Tanner yelled as tears of anger welled in his eyes. Nobody said much for the rest of the day.

– — -

LEO GOIA PRISON
RIO DE JANEIRO, BRAZIL

It only took six days for Joris to carve a niche for himself in Leo Goia. He now had a single mattress against a wall in one of the spacious second floor cells and a shelf in a refrigerator in another second floor cell where his food was guaranteed safe. But most importantly, he had Michel, a valuable person to be friends with inside Leo Goia.

He had met Michel on the morning of his second day inside. Joris was leaned against the wall of the courtyard scanning the activities ahead of him as well as the areas of concentrated commotion on the cell levels above him. He considered how he would go about approaching someone. He was correct in his assumption that there would be a few other European inmates. In total he estimated there to be about 300 inmates and among them were a few Germans.

From his time in Klong Prem he anticipated being singled out as an outsider, but so far nobody had shown him an angry eye. In the first 48 hours inside nobody had cast him anything more hostile than a *Welcome to Leo Goia* glare. In fact, as far as he could tell, there didn't seem to be any real animosity among the inmates, cliques of friends were evident, but no gang tension. He had been aware of a steady commotion from a cell on the ground level directly opposite the courtyard. He ventured across the cracked pavement and peered inside the open doorway from a respectful distance. It was a gym. A cell devoted to exercising. Steel chin-up bars were bolted to the concrete wall. Dumbbells, benches, bars and different sized plates were organized neatly at one side. The guys working out were all big so it seemed that there was some sort of exclusion for who was allowed to workout there but there was also assorted workout equipment scattered in the yard for the rest of the population.

As he turned to head back to the far side of the courtyard he was approached by a stout man with a round face and chubby cheeks. He looked to be in his mid thirties and wore a faded yellow Ralph Lauren polo and stained jean shorts.

"Colocar uma aposta para a luta?" He asked in what sounded to Joris like a friendly enough tone. Joris flattened his hand in the air in front of him and rotated it like a ship at sea, "Meu portugues não é bom." He knew enough of the language to say that his Portuguese wasn't good. The man seemed eager to try out his English, "Make bet? For fight?"

And just like that, Joris had the *In* that he needed. They exchanged enough broken Portuguese and English for him to find out that there were fights on Friday nights that everyone bet on, and this man was one of the bookies. They spoke for almost 15 minutes. At one point when two military guards made their way behind them Joris attempted to shush Michel but when Michel followed Joris' eyes over his shoulder he laughed when he saw them, "They do not make problem! *They* make me bets!"

Joris laughed, pressing a hand over his heart in mock relief. Then in Portuguese too native and fast for Joris to understand Michel exchanged a joke with the guards as they passed. After learning that family members of inmates could bring them nearly anything from the outside Joris asked how he could get his hands on money on the inside. Michel rattled off a few options that he could pursue—sewing soccer balls together for a manufacturer, painting the aqua walls of the intake offices—but as soon as he said it, Joris clenched his fists in excitement, his knees nearly buckled with the news. There was a card game. It was played on the fourth level.

Within 15 minutes Joris had become likable enough for Michel to invite him to the poker game that evening and to lend him R$15 to use. He had turned it into R$132 and promptly paid back Michel then placed R$40 on an unknown fighter in the fight that would happen on Friday, just to maintain a connection with Michel.

Life in Leo Goia was shaping up nicely for Joris. During the days he cold play futsal or backgammon in the courtyard and he could buy marijuana and tobacco from inmates on the fourth level of cells.

The card game was profitable. He was able to win enough (and lose enough back to the important players) for food and liquor orders from Michel's wife who visited every other day. Pretty soon he would have enough money for a cheap guitar. For Joris, there was nothing in the world more relaxing than having a guitar in his arms.

— — —

SUNDAY JANUARY 19TH, 2014

Tanner couldn't stop thinking about the date. He remembered dates, and now Lucas Sheppard's funeral had one: Sunday, January 19th, 2014.

The final head count was 64. All six of Rich's partners at the firm and their families were there. Celia's oldest daughter and her family had come down from Seattle. Mark Rollins and his wife Tricia were obviously there—Mark had been Danny and Tanner's high school wrestling coach at Jesuit and he and Tricia had become good friends of the family after the four years they had spent with him. He had since opened a mixed martial arts gym in Beaverton that Tanner and Danny promised to come visit soon.

Andrea had chosen to invite four of her closest friends who were friends of Danny and Tanner and of course Lucas. Allie's group of six best friends and two of their families were there and then Tanner and Danny had the difficult task of deciding which of their and Lucas' friends to invite. It could only be the ones who had been around from the very beginning but even then there were quite a few. They finally settled on 11 but could easily have stretched that to 20.

St. Patrick's Catholic Church was located in North West Portland, close to the Pearl District. It was the church that Isabel had started going to when she was in college across the river at University of Portland. There was hardly any planning necessary for the funeral but Celia had still gone ahead with a few things. Danny had no idea where she had found it but somehow she had unearthed a stunning picture of Lucas at football practice from the season before. It was taken during

46

a water break while he was standing in his practice jersey and shorts, flanked by tight end Jordan Reynolds and quarterback Tyler Armstrong. The three of them stood in the sunshine, holding their helmets and water bottles, looking at something beyond the camera, laughing.

It was a magnificent picture, brilliantly capturing Lucas in his most pure form: smiling in the sunshine, playing football with his friends. Celia had blown it up into a poster board and it stood on a display tripod in the entryway between grand bouquets of dark red roses. Danny and Tanner had stationed themselves there to greet everyone as they came in and every single person had stopped and taken time to marvel at the picture. It was where the tears of the afternoon would begin for most. Danny had never seen the picture before and had absolutely no idea where Celia had found it. That was Celia though.

Even though Lucas would have a headstone at the graveyard on Skyline that overlooked the city with snow-capped Mount St. Helens and Mount Hood looming in the distance, it was decided that he would be cremated. It went without saying that a part of him needed to come to rest in Brazil, he would have wanted it that way.

Often times it slipped under the radar or was lost in the commotion of their achievements just how Brazilian the kids actually were. They were *half* Brazilian. Their *mother* was Brazilian. They had spent two months out of every year of their life in Brazil. They loved it there. They loved their grandparents and all their aunts and uncles and cousins. They felt the culture in their bodies and spoke Portuguese to each other on a daily basis even when they were in Portland. This was the first half of his burial. The American half of Lucas Sheppard would be laid to rest. The Brazilian half would happen soon enough.

Allie wandered into the entryway from the chapel, unnoticed by the boys. Before she got their attention she watched them. Danny and Tanner in their jet-black three-piece suits. They both looked striking enough to be an advertisement for a suit company, especially since Tanner had cut his black hair short like Danny's.

That week Tanner had told her about what happened in the hours leading up to the accident; about Trevor Ramey, about the phone call from Lucas. When she asked her dad about it Rich had told her that there was nothing to it. That they shouldn't worry about it and it was probably just something that they had made important in their minds as some sort of coping method. She hadn't asked Danny about it yet and she decided that she wouldn't until things settled down a bit.

She was worried about him. He had been unrecognizable all week, a ghost in a human body. When he spoke it was as if he were talking to himself and when he looked at someone it were as if he was looking through them.

Allie decided to give them their space and she ducked back into the chapel before they noticed her.

"We're going to start in just a few minutes everyone." It was 11:55 a.m. and the Priest, David, made his way through the huddles that had started to form near the back of the chapel. A very handsome black man in his mid-sixties, his hair was only just beginning to grey at the sides. Tanner had joked with him in the past that he should be in a "Just for Men" commercial. His teeth were straight and white above his clergy shirt and sleek black jacket. He spoke Spanish, Italian, Portuguese and some French. Isabel had always adored him for that.

She had never forced the kids go to church growing up but they knew it made her happy so they would usually go at least once a month. They enjoyed it. David was fantastic to listen to. His sermons usually began as seemingly random stories with a few well-timed moments of comic relief and then just when it seemed that the story was in fact random, it would unfold beautifully into a moral and lesson for the day. It was what church was supposed to be, sending everyone home on Sunday mornings feeling lifted and closer to the people around them.

The Sheppard family along with Andrea and her parents, Tanner and Celia settled into the front row. David began in his booming voice that Tanner had likened to James Earl Jones—"I'm telling you, this guy could narrate shit." Tanner had once whispered years earlier at a Sunday service, making everybody in his vicinity chuckle.

"I'd like to welcome everybody. Welcome to the commemoration, the funeral, the service, the celebration of life—whatever you choose to call it, for an incredible young man. We are all here because we were blessed beyond words to have known Lucas Michael Sheppard."

Another common feature of David's speeches were short pauses so people could reflect on what he had said. He let a few seconds pass before continuing.

"I attended the public service yesterday in Corvallis as I'm sure most of you did. What a magnificent event, wasn't it? Being able to hear about Lucas from the people close to him—the different perspectives—it was quite special. Now you get to hear about him from the perspective of *Priest*, and right away, I can tell you that without a shadow of doubt, Lucas was doing it *right*." He said, pressing his thumb and index finger into the 'OK' sign and holding it in front of him for three seconds of a seven-second pause.

"In fact, Lucas was so *correct* in how he lived his life, that it provided us with faith—I'll elaborate on that in just a moment. You see, people come to church for many reasons, and one of those reasons is that they gain a sense of comfort, a sense of peace or assurance. They feel closer to God, and they like the belonging and certainty that feeling gives them."

David scanned the crowd with understanding in his eyes. "People assume that because I have been to *Priest school*," he said, using finger quotes, "that I know more than you about God and his will. But I'm going to let you in on a secret. Nobody knows *more* or *less* about God than anybody else. God is as *much* or as *little* as one chooses to make him. He is as *important* or as *unimportant* as one chooses to make him. To *me*," David flattened his hand against his chest, "God... is a person like Lucas Sheppard. His kindness. His smile, and his laugh, his understanding and his sense of humor."

Another few seconds passed. "I am a man of God. I see God in many places and in many ways, in the faces of many people—*all* people in fact. However, in the faces of some, I see a *concentration* of God, if you will. When I see a handsome, intelligent, athletic young man who uses the gifts that he has been blessed with to make those around him happy, I have to believe that God is revealing a tiny bit of himself to the world. *My* faith in God is strengthened by the existence and the actions of people like Lucas Sheppard."

He continued, "So. I suppose the question that inevitably arises...

is *why?* Why, why…why?" he said quietly, clenching his fists in front of him, "I know you have all asked *Why* in that same manner. Indeed it's probably the very first question each of you had when you received that phone call last week. I don't blame you. For a moment, I *myself* had the same question. Why *would* God take a person from us who spreads so much joy? It's true that God works in mysterious and sometimes seemingly senseless ways, but *Lucas Sheppard?* Could he really be so cruel as to take *Lucas Sheppard* from us? Surely that one was a *mistake?* No?" David looked around with a wrinkled brow as if to say, *Are you serious?*

"When God takes anybody from the earth, especially when it's before his or her time, he lays a challenge for the rest of us. The challenge is this…" he raised an instructive index finger, "can we *succeed* in honoring their memory?" He slowly lowered his finger and rested his hands squarely on the podium, continuing in a voice that was just loud enough to be heard.

"Sitting in a church, sitting in a Coliseum, reminiscing about Lucas' life… this is one form of honoring. However, the type of honoring that I am speaking of, the type of honoring that needs to occur now… is less complicated, and far more important."

Five seconds passed. "A smile is all it takes. None of us can share *Lucas'* smile." David chuckled as his tone briefly changed from his formal speech voice to something far more personal, "What a smile Lucas had." Heads throughout the audience nodded as their faces gave way to the reflex grin that came when they pictured Lucas' smile.

David cleared his throat. "There's a reason why more than six *thousand* people showed up in Corvallis yesterday. And it's *not* because Lucas was one hell of a football player. It's because he smiled. Lucas was always smiling, wasn't he?"

Heads nodded again as tears flowed. "It may not be in all of our nature. But can we change? Can we allow the nature of someone, whom I think it's safe to say we all admired, change us?" Five second pause.

"We must. We must allow ourselves to be inspired by the life of an amazing young man." For a moment, it seemed like David might actually tear up, something that nobody had ever seen him do. He leaned forward on the podium, demanding attention, "The answer that

I see to the question of *Why...* is this..." after taking a deep breath he answered, "So we can spread Lucas' magnificence. It is up to us now, to make Lucas' death and more importantly, his life, touch as many people as possible. If we can live in the way we believe Lucas would have wanted us to live, the joy that Lucas spread will never cease, and Lucas will never *truly* die."

The final words seemed to strum the heartstrings of everyone and crying became audible throughout the audience. Tanner had goose bumps. He looked to his left, Danny's head was bowed, his eyes closed. It was as much emotion as Tanner had seen from him that week. Everyone else on the front bench was crying. Isabel in Rich's arms, Allie and Andrea sandwiched Rodney in a three-way hug. Celia dabbed the corners of her eyes with a silver handkerchief.

David began a closing prayer and Danny started to feel that the curtains were closing on Lucas. This was the end. Not the moment in the hospital a week earlier, but right then. He became frantic with anxiety—something was being forgotten. His heart began to speed up and his mind scrambled for something. He needed the congregation to understand that something wasn't right.

Do none of you realize what is happening?

It was as if the end of the service would bring the *true* end to Lucas' life, and it would usher in the next period of time when the intent would be to *heal*. He tried to catch Andrea's eye as if she too would certainly share the same fear. To Danny, *healing* was the same as turning his back. He didn't want to *heal*. It angered him. People would be trying to *heal* now. Before he knew it the prayer ended and he felt emptiness more profound than anything he had ever felt in his life.

Lucas is gone.

The truth hadn't hit him with such force until right then.

Nothing will ever be the same. Nothing will ever be good.

—   —   —

Everybody except Danny's spirits had been noticeably lifted from the service. Tanner had gone back to his aunt and uncle's house for the night. Celia was at her house. The girls and Rodney were back on the couch and Rich and Isabel were getting some much-needed sleep.

Danny scoured the buffet of dishes on the island in the kitchen, knowing he didn't have the appetite to eat even a bite. He had to get out of the house. He needed to drive.

"Dre. Can I take your car to Safeway?" The keys came flying over the banister. "Thanks. Anybody want to come? Anybody need anything?" Three *no thank-yous* and two *Love yous*, echoed back over the banister.

Each minute of the next few hours would become welded in his memory in perfect clarity. For years to come he would wonder… what if one of them had just said *yes* to his invitation? Surely his life would have turned out so, so different.

- — -

RIO DE JANEIRO, BRAZIL

The Basquiat exhibit had been opened two days earlier at the gallery and ever since laying eyes on the piece that was titled, *Untitled*, Nina had been seeing it in her dreams. The massive skull drawn in what first looked to be an erratic fashion but to Nina, it was anything but erratic.

When she dreamt of it there was a heavenly sound that accompanied it but she could never recreate it in her mind after she had awoken. The more she thought about it the more she felt at peace; knowing that the painting had travelled directly from his hand through time, unchanged and unaffected by the world around it. It had no political affiliation or opinions on social issues. It didn't make small talk or care about money or material things. It didn't desire power or notoriety. It didn't worry about the future. It simply wanted to exist and go through life alongside the masses of people who gathered to marvel at it.

Untitled.

Tonight she was going to get into Jean-Michel Basquiat's mind. She had swallowed the capsule a half an hour earlier and was beginning to feel the numbness snake into her limbs. She rarely did drugs, but when it was for the purpose of seeing a work of art in the state under which it had been created, it was a magical thing. She took a deep breath and exhaled slowly. The guards at the entrance and exit of the room had disappeared behind the walls.

"You are untitled." She whispered to the painting.

"It is true. How could you ever have a title?"

It needed no name. Every day that week she had spent between forty-five minutes to an hour looking at it in silence after the gallery was closed to the public. She could hear it, and when she stepped closer it grew louder like the wings of a wasp flying closer and closer. It was love.

– — –

Danny backed Dre's silver Honda Accord out of the driveway and headed toward the Sellwood Bridge that would take him to the West side of Portland. He knew where he was going. The Sellwood Bridge would put him onto Barbur Boulevard, which would take him along the river towards downtown Portland, past the penthouses at John's Landing. Then he would exit onto Naito Parkway, the four-lane street that separated the fountains and sculptures of the riverside parks from the towers of downtown. It was a roughly two-mile stretch of road that travelled under the many overpasses of the bridges that connected East and West Portland.

The homeless drifted from one underpass to the next, pushing carts and hefting garbage bags, feeding their dogs scraps of food.

Past the modern townhouses and apartment buildings of the Pearl District, past the train station, under the overpass of I-5 he waited at the last stoplight on Naito after which it would turn into endless warehouses of the Northwest Industrial area.

The industrial area was a lonely place at night, not even the homeless ventured that far out. He thought back to a time from his youth: sitting on Rich's shoulders to get a better view of the launching of a newly built ship into the Willamette. The splash had been enormous as the massive ship rocked back and forth before coming to balance in the river as the crowd cheered.

There wasn't a car in sight in either direction. He commanded the steering wheel with his right hand as he reached the St. John's Bridge that would take him back to the East side.

"Portland, Oregon." He said out loud. Even 12 miles from home, in the middle of the St. John's Bridge, gazing back at the lights of downtown, he felt as if he were just around the corner from his house. He loved his city.

Andrea's "summer '08" playlist was playing quietly as his thoughts drifted back to her. He could see her sitting on the couch at that moment, her thumb steadily stroking her iPhone screen, towing down her Twitter feed so she could read all the nice things people had to say about the love of her life. Danny winced at the thought. He headed south on MLK. Everything he passed brought up a different memory.

The playlist had the same nostalgic effect as the drive. It was the soundtrack to the carefree fall semester leading up to graduation from high school. Colleges had been chosen, commitments made, scholarships accepted, classes were easy and life was as fantastic as it had ever been.

– — –

As in most catastrophic life missteps, it was so close to being avoided entirely: a *left* when it was supposed to be a *right*, a *sure, why not?* when it so easily could have been a *no thanks*. In Danny's case, it was a split-second decision between going home and falling asleep on the couch with Andrea and Allie, or driving to Safeway. Not until he was at the exit of 99E, just four blocks from home, did he decide that he actually *did* want to go to the store; he would get doughnuts for the next morning, just like Lucas loved on Saturday mornings growing up. It would lift everyone's spirits.

The winding road led him along the golf course to Reed College then up the hill on Woodstock Boulevard. The rain began to fall. The closer he got to Safeway, the harder it fell and the more he felt like being under a blanket on the couch.

Memories of late night trips for snacks came flooding back to him as he parked in more or less the middle of the deserted parking lot. The healthy downpour continued. Danny hoped Steve wouldn't be working.

The autistic man who had worked there for years and who Lucas would always take the time to talk football with for a few minutes. Danny's empathy took over again as he felt a sharp pain for Steve. Every time he saw the Sheppard family in the store he lit up and if Lucas wasn't there, he would always send a message for them to pass on to him.

Danny reclined his seat back as far as it would go. The car was still running but the tapping of the rain on the hood drowned out the idling engine. Danny turned off the music. The unblemished silence greeted him like an old friend, but the quiet would last only a few minutes. He had been aware of a distant rumbling in the near distance and it had only grown louder over the last few seconds until the rainy parking lot roared with the sound of a grunting diesel engine. He propped himself up on his elbow just in time to catch a flash of cherry-red in his rear-view mirror. He would forever hate the noise of a diesel truck engine. Three rows of empty parking spaces behind him a cherry-red truck sat idling.

There's no way that's him. There are a hundred cherry-red F-250's in Portland.

He knew it wasn't Trevor Ramey but his heart had started racing nevertheless. The engine went silent. He stared in his rear-view mirror as the passenger side door opened. A tall, lanky guy hopped down to the ground. He was wearing a brown hoodie and a backwards baseball cap that rested so far back it looked like it was about to fall off his head. He reached into his bottom lip and flicked a fat wad of dip onto the asphalt. Then the back passenger door opened. Another tall guy—this one heavily built—climbed down from the cab looking as though he had just finished a shift on a construction site. His jeans and boots were splattered with cream-colored paint. He was wearing a baseball cap also but it was pulled low over his eyes. It certainly seemed like Trevor Ramey's crowd.

Danny tried to control his breathing as if he were worried about drawing attention to himself, his heart pounded faster. His eyes, which had grown steadily wider since the passengers had stepped out, stared crazily into the mirror and it wasn't until they started to water that he realized he needed to blink.

"There's no chance…" he said aloud.

The driver's door had opened but whoever got out was out of Danny's line of sight. The two passengers made their way to the front of the truck and huddled around a tin of chew that the driver held in the middle of them… still he couldn't see the driver. They were talking loudly but the rain on the roof of the car drowned out their voices. Seconds passed like minutes, but when they started for the entrance of Safeway, Danny's heart leapt up his throat like an animal trying to claw its' way out of a well. It was Trevor Ramey. The facial features couldn't be made out but it was definitely Ramey. The curly blonde hair was all he needed to see.

This is impossible. This is impossible. Impossible.

It was so hard to believe that for a moment Danny questioned whether or not he had taken some sort of medication in the day that had caused him to hallucinate. He couldn't breathe. It was so hot inside the car.

There must be some mistake. That's not him.

But there was no mistake. It was Ramey. The curly blonde hair had been making unwanted appearances in Danny's mind for a week, and now the real thing was right there in the parking lot, just yards away.

His ears were ringing. A light-headed, dreamy, haze took him into a nearly post-concussion state. He had never felt anything like it; he seemed to be watching himself from outside the car. Even stranger, he felt like he had the attention of many more people. He couldn't see them but he could feel their excitement all around him. High in the balconies of an invisible theater, they observed, knowing what was about to happen, an unseen audience watching the play that he was the star of.

Time was moving in frames in sync with his heartbeat. Each time he would regain cognizance, he was looking at a new frame. First was the dashboard and the sprinkled windshield, the rain falling through the yellow glow of a tall light pole. Then it was a frame of the door panel and his hand reaching for the handle. Next was black asphalt and a white parking line under a wide puddle, rain drops peppering its' surface.

He leaned out and vomited up the entire water bottle that he had downed on the drive. Then there were no more frames, just the color red. A deep, passionate burgundy red so dark and hot that it almost turned purple. He couldn't feel his legs as he moved and it wasn't until he had taken several steps that he himself became aware that he was outside the car, and moving towards them.

– — –

The power to reason and think clearly had deserted him; he was operating on nothing but instinct. There was no taking a deep breath, no counting down from ten. He wanted to get his hands on Ramey. He was *starving* for it. 30 yards away, 25 yards, 20 yards—he was closing fast. The lanky guy was the first to notice Danny and he gave Ramey a frantic nudge with his elbow. Danny saw their expressions turn from confused to a wide-eyed cocktail of confusion and fear. He had their full attention but he still screamed.

"RAMEY! YOU KILLED MY BROTHER! MEU IRMÃO GÊMEO, SEU FILHO DA PUTA!"

His bloodshot stare must have been terrifying because Ramey went ghost-white when he realized first, who it was, and second, what his intentions were. He must have been so confused. As far as he knew he was in the clear. Nobody knew what he had done a week ago on SW Capitol Highway. How could they?

The scene unfolded with a Hollywood aesthetic as if it were being directed. The invisible audience looked on with excitement: the bad guy retreating while sending his goons to kill the hero. Ramey backpedalled as the lanky guy and the big guy stepped in front of him, albeit faint-heartedly and with more peace-making intentions than fighting—they clearly didn't have a clue of the severity of their situation.

"Hold up there big guy," the lanky guy said stepping forward with a puffy bottom lip of fresh chew, holding out his hand for Danny to stop. It was almost comical how easily Danny dispatched him, brushing his arm out of the way and striking him squarely in the jaw so hard that his long arms flew up in front of him as he was propelled backwards onto the asphalt. His arms remained rigid in front of him and his head was locked in a tilted back position as a disturbing nasal grunting started. The bigger guy put his fists up but he was clearly shaken by what he had just seen, his stance was twitchy and uncertain. Through his clenched teeth Danny hissed, "Get the fuck out of my way."

There was a split-second when confusion reigned in the eyes of the big redneck. He tried to study the look on Danny's face to learn something about the situation. Whatever it was that he saw was more than enough to convince him to surrender, "I got no beef with you man." He said putting his hands above his head and turning toward the truck.

"What the *fuck* Kevin?" Ramey whined nervously taking another step back. He was hopelessly exposed now; a baby gazelle separated from its' mother on the prairie. Surfer boy blonde curls and a cut off T-shirt exposing his tanned, steroid-filled biceps: the poster child for excessive privilege, arrogance and bottomless second chances.

Trevor was scared, but he should have been terrified. Even after seeing what Danny had just done to his friend he was still too non-chalant, confident that he would still get out of it somehow. Danny headed straight at him with chilling enthusiasm, forcing Ramey into a spontaneous apology that only hurt his cause.

"Dude, I'm sorry. It was an accident—I didn't mean to hurt him." It was a feeble attempt at an apology—as casual as if he were apologizing for spilling someone's beer. He obviously had never apologized for anything in his whole life but it didn't matter. The words were drowned out by the ringing in Danny's ears. By the time Ramey realized that he should probably try to run it was far too late, still he tried.

"Oh no you don't."

He had transformed into something he had never been before. His eyes were no longer vacant; they were full of life—a primitive, animalistic kind of life. He toyed with his prey, kicking Ramey's trailing leg behind his front leg as he turned to run. Ramey yelped like a dog getting its' tail stepped on.

"You're in trouble." Danny said with calm certainty. He let Ramey scamper to his feet just so he could tackle him to the ground again. The next thing he knew, he was looking down at Trevor's completely exposed and vulnerable face, flopping to either side desperately trying to find some sort of shelter. His arms were pinned to the asphalt beneath Danny's knees.

It was the last moment, the edge of the skyscraper rooftop. The choice was still available: he could step back to safety, or he could step off the edge.

He jumped.

The first punch he savored; the loud slap of bone on bone, it was fulfilling. To have the exact human that he had been thinking about all week right there underneath him was a gift, a dream come true. The cracking and slapping of his punches grew faster and harder. He started dropping the point of his elbow straight onto Ramey's face, then back to punches, then back to elbows. Trevor's legs kicked wildly and he squirmed with all his might but it was useless, he wasn't escaping. He would have stood a better chance escaping the jaws of a crocodile.

Danny continued to watch himself from outside his body as he pounded Trevor Ramey's skull into the asphalt. Feeling a solid connection from his elbow or his fist was quenching some indescribable thirst inside of him. He couldn't get enough of it. If Kevin hadn't been there, there was no telling how long it would have lasted.

He was still throwing punches when he felt the arms around his chest. He had forgotten about Kevin and he had no idea how much time had passed. He panted as he sat on the ground, just feet from Ramey's body. He was exhausted, taking labored breaths, not totally convinced by his surroundings as if he had awoken from sleepwalking in a new place. He pushed himself to his feet and bent over, hands on his knees, trying to slow his breathing.

In through the nose... out through the mouth, in through the nose... out through the mouth.

He glanced back at a distraught Kevin who was hovering nervously a few yards away, not sure if Danny would turn his aggression towards him next. Behind Kevin was the lanky guy, still unconscious; Danny had to think for a moment... *oh that's right, I hit him first.*

He turned back to study Ramey. His head rested at an awkward slant, blood ran from his nose and mouth, mixing with the rainwater on the asphalt. His cheekbones were already enormously swollen.

"Danny?" Kevin's voice quivered. Danny stood over Ramey's motionless body. There was no response. The ringing in his ears had become more deafening, Kevin's voice sounded as if it were coming from underwater. "Oh my *fuck*." Kevin managed with a just-before-tears shiver in his voice. Danny knew exactly what he was thinking because he was wondering the same thing.

Is he dead?

He linked his fingers over his head and took a few steps in the opposite direction of Safeway. Then he squatted by a puddle and splashed water on his hands, rubbing his knuckles slowly. Wiping his hands on his sweatshirt as he walked back to the car. Out of his peripheral he noticed a skinny figure silhouetted in the entrance of Safeway. It was Steve, smiling and waving as if it were just another day. Danny waved back.

"Hey Steve!"

– — –

Just like the moments that followed the news that Lucas had passed, Danny didn't remember pulling out of the parking lot. His mind couldn't quite believe what had just happened.

What if he's dead? Mom... I have to call Tan—Celia is going to— where should I go right now? Deus no puede ser real.

He sped home.

He had to be dead. He looked dead. His head was all fucked up. I just murdered a guy...with my bare hands.

The Honda screeched to a stop in front of the house. The sadness he had felt all week was now overpowered by a new combination of fear and regret. He was frantic.

He sat in the car and forced himself to take deep breaths, he needed to gather his thoughts as best he could and decide on a course of action.

The cops have been called to Safeway. Kevin will tell them what happened, he knows who I am. It will take them five minutes to figure out where I live. They'll be here in maybe 15 minutes, tops...

He had already made one decision that would change his life forever, and now he had yet another decision of the same magnitude.

I'm not getting arrested tonight.

It was decided, and it turned into a race against time. He bounded through the front door, up to his room, grabbed his Nike duffel and started stuffing it with whatever he saw—workout clothes, a pair of sandals, his iPod and headphones. He moved swiftly across the hall to Lucas' room, snatching the *Sports Illustrated* off the dresser. The red glow of the clock from the bedside table read 12:46 a.m. He sandwiched his phone between his shoulder and ear while he darted back to his room grabbing whatever else he thought he might need.

"Yeah," Tanner answered almost immediately.

"Dude. I need you to pick me up behind Kay's as soon as you can. Leave now." Tanner could hear the urgency and didn't ask questions.

"Leaving now." He said and hung up. Kay's was a bar in Sellwood, half a mile of quaint neighborhood streets towards the river. The only problem was he would have to cross the bridge over 99E where he would be a sitting duck to any police coming from that direction. Time was ticking, but he couldn't leave without saying something to the girls and Rodney.

He left his bag in the kitchen and tiptoed down the stairs, dropping softly to his knees in front of the couch. They were so peaceful in their sleep and it seemed cruel to wake them. He beat away a fleeting rational thought to stay on the couch and wait for the cops. He gently squeezed their shoulders. Andrea rubbed her eyes with one hand and stuck out her other arm for a hug. He took full advantage. Clenching his eyes shut he plunged his face into her shoulder and cleared his throat.

"I'm so sorry Dre." He squeezed her tighter. "I'm so, so sorry. I love you." She could sense that something was awry; his angst was obvious but never in her wildest dreams could she fathom what had just happened.

"Love you more." She said softly as she started to cry. There wasn't time for anything else. He released her and moved on to his little sister who had a confused, sleepiness in her eyes but she was more than happy to be engulfed by his hug.

"Love you little sister. Você é uma princesa." He kissed the top of her head and held her in silence as she too began to cry, pressing her eyes into his sweatshirt to soak the tears. It stung him deep in the chest to let her go, but there was no time.

Rodney. Danny scooped him off the couch and spun him through the air making airplane noises before bringing him in for a hug. "Remember. Lucas doesn't want us to be sad forever okay? I love you, dude." Then he tossed him back onto the couch.

"Goodnight guys." He said as he bounded up the stairs to the kitchen, snatched his bag off the island and slung it around his neck. For a moment he stopped in front of his parent's bedroom door. They would be so ashamed when they found out. He hated himself for what he had just done, and what he was about to do. Just as he was about to push open the front door, his eyes grew wide. He had nearly made a catastrophic mistake, forgetting to pack the most important thing... his passport.

– — -

He was sweating. Puddles exploded under his feet as he sprinted down the middle of Bybee Boulevard; the arterial that weaved through East-moreland. It would be the street the cops would take to get to the house regardless if they were coming from the direction of Safeway or downtown.

The adrenaline was finally wearing off and its' absence was making him feel sick. He still couldn't believe what he had done, that he had just *killed* somebody. In a strange and sinister way that he couldn't explain to himself, something inside him felt accomplished, like he had reached some coming of age moment. He had done something he never knew he could do, become a new person that he never knew he could be. Thinking back to the moment he had descended on Trevor, telling him earnestly "You're in trouble." It had been a completely new Danny, yet somehow he felt like he had known him all along. Stranger still, it felt like the new Danny had greeted him with open arms and a smile that said, *Finally. You made it.*

He crossed the bridge and was able to cut into the cover of the neighborhood streets. The rain had stopped, an eerie stillness had taken over the night and with just four more blocks to Kay's he had only seen a few cars, none of them police. He didn't want to beat Tanner there and have to wait so he started walking... and then it happened.

It was faint but unmistakable. Just as he emerged from the cover of the neighborhood streets and stood on the corner of Bybee and Milwaukie. He stared back down Bybee towards his house. It was coming from the direction of Safeway. He still had the choice, he could go home and throw himself at the feet of the officers, take the wrap like a man, move forward with things honorably...but he was too scared. He stood still until he heard the siren give off two quick '*woop-woops*' before going quiet. In just seconds they would be ringing the doorbell. He remained on the corner. Squeezing his eyes shut in the silence. Then he turned and walked towards the parking lot behind Kay's. Somewhere in the depths of his mind he was aware of something that he didn't want to directly acknowledge. He had been forced to confront the thought twice in one week: life as he knew it, was over.

— — —

SATURDAY, JUNE 18TH 2016
BEAVERTON, OREGON

The Westbrook Building was José's last stop of the night and never took more than 45 minutes. He only needed the small vacuum for this job; it was the smallest of the office buildings that he was contracted for and by far the nicest. He would be in and out within an hour but while he was inside he let his imagination run wild with dreams of grandeur and importance, sitting at one of the conference tables in an expensive suit, finishing a speech and being applauded. The building was an elegant two-story cube of sleek silver metal and crystal-clear glass, standing pretentiously on a manicured lawn just on the edge of the marshland on the wildlife preserve in Beaverton. It glistened with arrogance, starting with the gaudy silver letters on the grass in front:
The Westbrook.

To the east of the building, a boardwalk sliced through the swamps and trees where Sandhill Cranes and blue herons waded about in the mornings. When it was foggy, the boardwalk seemed to vanish into thin air.

The Westbrook was home to two legal practices, two psychiatrist offices, an orthodontist, a real estate agency and two offices that were leased by Nike but had never been used—the Westbrook was less than 2 miles from the Nike headquarters. Reading the names on the directory in the lobby was motivation for 19-year-old José to work hard in his online classes and become something more than a janitor for Pacific Cleaners.

The Westbrook was the last building on a brand new stretch of development along the preserve; everything there was newly built. Even on a weekday afternoon the area was quiet but on a Saturday night it was absolutely deserted. In some of his other office buildings that he cleaned José would encounter employees working late but although he knew all of their names from the directory in the lobby, he had never seen anybody who worked at The Westbrook. As he propped the front door open to bring in his equipment he noticed a black Audi SUV and a silver Volvo parked a few spaces away from one another at the far side of the parking lot.

José had spent the past six hours at four different office buildings in the Beaverton area and now at 11:42 p.m., he was ready to go home and drink some beers with his brother and cousins. He used the key fob to open the front door and carried the vacuum through the lobby to the cream-colored carpet of the staircase. The silver niceties of the lobby gleamed in the ambience created by the small lamps on the reception desk.

He was never nervous being alone in the buildings after dark but tonight there was something uneasy around The Westbrook, he felt as if he were intruding on something, and he was right to have such a feeling. Just as he reached the landing of the stairs he froze mid step. He had heard something.

It was muffled and distant, coming from somewhere on the first floor. He wished he could un-hear it but it had been too clear to ignore. His brow and palms instantly started to sweat. He stood statue-still, listening. Seven long seconds passed until he heard it again, this time it was clear: a scream. Chills shot up his spine. It was a woman. His first instinct was to reload the vacuum into the van and drive away with the cowardly assurance that whatever was happening was none of his business.

You can't ignore this. You have to be brave.

Tiptoeing cautiously back down the stairs and through the lobby, he tried to listen over the throb of his heartbeat in his ears. When he was in the hallway and past the kitchen he heard it again, it sounded like it was coming from the very last office in the hall—*Jenna Aoki MD, 1E.*

His ears were hot, his shirt stuck to his back. The scream had become rhythmic in its' consistency, every few seconds. A few steps down the dark hallway and he could make out whimpers in between the yelps, but no words. A few more steps... he was only a few feet outside her door when suddenly words burst into clarity,

"Oh Fuck! Oh! Ohhh! Oh my God!"

It was sex. He slumped forward and put his hands on his knees, exhaling an enormous sigh of relief, a tiny bit embarrassed at how nervous he had been, but also proud of himself for having the courage to investigate.

He wiped the sweat from his forehead that had formed in record time as he turned and headed back upstairs, chuckling to himself. He couldn't wait to get home and tell the story to his brother and cousins.

- — -

Jenna Aoki's head tipped back off the edge of the couch. She ran her fingers through her black hair as her eyes rolled back and she lost her breath yet again. The only piece of clothing that remained were her black stockings, everything had been stripped off and tossed across the room. She never wore stockings unless she was going to meet Danny. It was part of the fun for her; dressing up, wearing fine lingerie under the curve-hugging office clothes that she knew she would only be wearing for a matter of seconds.

Her legs pointed to 5 and 9 as the warm euphoria of overlapping orgasms flooded through her, each wave stronger than the previous. It was the sex she had always dreamed of but had never had before she met him. Playing the naughty psychiatrist was her way of making up for everything that she had been too timid to experience during college, grad school and the years since. He crashed into her, the domination of his weight pressing her into the chaise longue. She was tangled in the sheets of ecstasy—it was like this every time.

She ordered him to get behind her. The helplessness she felt when he flipped her was exhilarating, a stark contrast to the meticulous control she had over literally every other detail of her life. Even now—after two years of meeting late nights in her office—the surreal, star-struck part of the experience had yet to wear off. Sometimes when her boyfriend Peter was out of the house she would Google Danny and read the articles about him or watch videos of him on YouTube, all the while in disbelief that she was secretly having sex with him in her office after hours.

Before Danny, Jenna was resigned to not only boring sex, but also what had slowly snuck up on her and become a boring *life*. She had obsessed so much over her career goals that she felt as though she had blinked, and blinked, and blinked again until a large chunk of her life had passed her by. It was terrifying, but every time Danny Sheppard would flip her over on the couch or chaise longue in her office, she felt as though she had managed, in a way, to get back something from the time she had lost. For 45 minutes—usually every two weeks or so—she could leave her house, drive to her office, and have amazing sex with a young man who was fast becoming a world-renowned superstar. It was surreal. Unlike anything else she had ever experienced, or ever would experience outside of those 45 minutes.

Jenna was 34. It was right around the time she turned 32—just months before meeting Danny for the first time—that she realized her life was already drifting towards a mundane, vanilla horizon. Her response to the realization was to start working out and in no time it had spiraled into a full-blown obsession. It started slowly; she bought some new work out clothes and a membership to Fuel Fitness, along with a few supplements from GNC. After a couple months she was running 6 miles every morning before work and spending her lunch hour researching green tea detox drinks and reading message boards about supplements and proteins. She was in the gym 6 days a week, headphones in, black hair pulled back into a ponytail, squatting and lunging like a woman on a mission. The difficult thing about being a psychiatrist was having to analyze the issues of her own life and she knew that no matter how much effort she put into exercise, it wouldn't fill the void of the chunk of youth that she bypassed.

Danny started to go faster, Jenna moaned louder. It had to be soon, they had been at it for nearly 40 minutes. As usual, the entire thing had seemed to be one long, pulsating orgasm for her. It wasn't the anvil-hard body or the movie star face or even the length and girth of Danny that made the sex so unbelievable, it was simply who he *was*, and the fact that it was all a secret.

The last two years had been more colorful than the previous 15 years combined for Jenna. She could remember the first phone call, or rather the missed call from an unknown number and the voicemail that would start the whole affair. It was a Sunday. Danny had been home from Brazil for four months when Isabel Silva called.

If Jenna agreed to take Danny on as a patient, it would be his third different psychiatrist since being home. Rich and Isabel had tried everything in their power to get him help. The first two doctors had had both confirmed that he was showing clear signs of PTSD and anxiety but his refusal to talk was making it impossible to move forward with any sort of treatment or progress. He filled his prescriptions but never took a single pill. His eyes were still blank and looked into space as he daydreamed by himself.

Jenna liked Isabel Sheppard immediately, as most people did. Just from hearing her voice—something trusting, almost naïve in her adorably accented English—Jenna was instantly willing to help the woman on the other end of the line.

Isabel would go on to tell her about how her son, Lucas who had died in a car accident. Jenna remembered hearing the news about the Oregon State football player a few years earlier. Then she told her about her other son, Lucas' twin brother who, according to Isabel, had recently moved home from Brazil and was "having some tough times".

At the time when Isabel made the phone call, Danny had only just won his second fight in Northwest Chaos Promotions. He wasn't famous, he had no endorsements or sponsors and none of his coaches had moved to Portland. Things were moving slowly but although he had won both of his early fights quite easily, nobody could have predicted the level of success that was just around the corner. Jenna and Isabel talked for almost thirty minutes before scheduling an appointment for Danny.

He sauntered into her office on a dull and forgettable Wednesday afternoon. Everything about him was confident and languid in a kind of opiate-seduced way. His huge frame seemed to move in slow motion. As he entered the waiting room and saw Jenna for the first time, his brow twitched in surprise, and it was mirrored in her eyes. Neither was what the other had expected. They sat across from each another and talked about Danny's life—his family, his friends, his childhood. His expression never changed, his voice was deep and monotone, he was just going through the motions. He didn't volunteer any information on his own, she had to pull every detail out of him and she could tell that he had no desire to talk about any of it.

She was able to get a good picture of his life—wrestling prodigy, dead brother, loving family, younger sister, adopted younger brother, best friend, dear-to-his-heart elderly neighbor, spending summers in Brazil, ex-girlfriend of his brother—everything that was important to him. But there was a huge void, a few very important chapters to his story that were missing completely. He was so efficient at steering conversation away from Lucas that after four sessions, Jenna was forced.

"You're good at avoiding the things that you're supposed to talk about here."

Danny had no intention of talking to a psychiatrist, he only agreed to it—for a third time—because Isabel had begged him. "If I'm honest, I'm really just doing this to make my mom happy. I don't have much to talk about."

"Your mom isn't happy?" Jenna probed.

"No that's not what I—it's just, she thinks I need this and I really don't."

Jenna didn't need her doctorate in psychology from the University of Washington to see that Danny was in severe need of help, but he was very smart and very determined to avoid all of her questions. In their conversations he was well spoken and engaging but it was easy for Jenna to see that it was forced, and he didn't want to be having a conversation in the first place. He would have called an end to the appointments himself if he hadn't hatched an idea, a project, an endeavor. He didn't know for sure if it would work but over the first month he had slowly started to build a sexual tension, and he didn't sense much opposition. She was maybe a little uncertain, but he could see that something in her was curious, at times even eager.

She had let their conversation become far too friendly; there was very little patient/doctor formality anymore. Jenna began to feel alarmingly flushed when he would venture playfully flirtatious comments. She found herself looking forward to encountering more of his charm and if she was lucky, one of his rare half-mouthed grins. His voice did something to her. It was all so incredibly inappropriate and over the line and she knew it... but carried on.

It was a Tuesday afternoon, meeting number eight. A torrential downpour beat against the window when it happened for the first time. Jenna had decided that she needed to end the meetings. A moment of clarity had smacked her into shameful reality a few nights earlier and she knew that whatever was going on needed to stop.

"Danny. Unless you think you'll be able to open up a little more, this is going to be our last session. Nothing is being accomplished. There's no point in us continuing to meet."

His expression didn't change at all. He seemed indifferent to the news, sitting on the suede couch in her office. He held her brown eyes with un-wavering eye contact as he went all in, "I can think of one reason we should continue to meet." He said in his slow, deep voice.

Jenna's heart absolutely throbbed inside her rib cage, her cheeks were hot and she could feel her chest turning red. She shook her head. "There's no reason to meet, Danny."

Then he let the silence do the talking for a few long seconds. He was impressed by how hard she was trying to stay professional, but it was over.

"I guess I'm no longer a patient of yours then, Ms. Aoki."

Jenna was either going to let him tear her tear open her button-up, or kick him out and for Danny, either outcome was a success. She was both furious and exhilarated that she had let the flirting culminate into this. Voices of reason and desire yelled over one another inside her head. The rational side of her brain was incensed, pulling its' hair out and screaming of the implications, even if he wasn't her patient, she knew it was beyond unethical. Her greedy side sneered condescendingly.

Why do you spend so much time at the gym? Why do you spend so much money at Victoria's Secret? So you can take pictures in the mirror in sexy lingerie when Peter isn't home?

That first day, during working hours on the carpet in her office, was the most amazing hour of her life. Two years and dozens of after-hours meetings had passed since that first day. And now, Jenna had finally rounded back to the realization that what she was doing was wrong and it needed to end.

Alright you've had your fun. Enough is enough.

For the past two years, he would text her and they would set a time for that night. She would then fake an urgent situation with the patient that had come to be known by her boyfriend, Peter, as the "high-risk patient". Even if he wanted to (which he never did) Peter couldn't press for details given the confidentiality of the psychiatrist/patient relationship. He never suspected a thing. Danny did feel a little guilty about the fact that she was in a relationship, but he could also sense how much Jenna enjoyed what they were doing and the sex was just too good. But tonight would be their last meeting. Her mind was firm on this, one last hurrah.

— — —

Danny pulled on his track pants and fell shirtless onto the couch, watching as Jenna shimmied her way back into her pencil skirt. Even though she was half Japanese, her high cheekbones and thin nose gave her a sculpted Nordic grace and refinement and her body was artwork.

"Beautiful day today huh?" He said in complete seriousness. It had been a monotonous grey day with light rain. She looked up from buttoning her shirt with a puzzled look. She giggled when she saw that he was being dryly sarcastic. She finished putting herself back together and settled onto the chaise longue that even she had to admit was a cliché.

Danny's stomach muscles created a collage of shadows in the dim lighting of the brown, olive and cream-colored Feng Shui. Jenna had never stopped being star struck by him. She had been in awe even before he had grown into a superstar. When they first met he was still a long way from becoming Danny "The Python" Sheppard, but even then he carried himself as if he knew exactly what he was about to become. She had watched the transformation with her own eyes. She knew him when he was a lost 20-year-old fighting for crowds of 400 and she now watched on YouTube as he packed arenas of 20,000. It had all unfolded right in front of her; from amateur to icon, and most remarkably, Danny hadn't changed one bit.

His bank account had several new commas and he was mobbed for autographs and photos everywhere he went, but any of their 60 to 90 minutes together over the last years could be completely interchangeable with one another—he had always been the same calm, sad-eyed young man. His gaze still wandered into nowhere and he was still as soft-spoken and evasive as he had been in their first meeting.

"I saw your billboard downtown this week," she said. When he didn't respond she added, "You look so intimidating!"

He didn't share in her excitement. He had brought grapes and was eating them off the vine like an Egyptian prince as he lay back on the couch, "Mm. I guess that's what they're going for with this whole thing—I signed my contract this week." He said without enthusiasm. By *they* he meant Nike, and by *this whole thing*, he meant Modern Warrior, the new line of sportswear for mixed martial arts training. He was the face of it, quite literally. His face now looked out over Pioneer Square in downtown Portland.

"Oh congratulations! I didn't know that was happening *this* week, that's so great!" Jenna gushed, smiling sincerely.

He had signed with the Ultimate Fighting Championship after just four fights in Northwest Chaos Promotions. He had won his first professional fight quietly enough but his second put him on the map, heads began to turn. A vicious highlight-reel kick to the head had sent Japanese fighter Takanori Kondo to the mat like a rag doll. Soon after, the phone began to ring more frequently with increasingly bigger and better news. Endorsements started rolling in and requests for interviews were an almost constant. Fast-forward just two short years and Danny was arguably the most recognizable mixed martial arts fighter in the sport and was signing a $6.4 million endorsement deal with the biggest sportswear brand in the world.

His support came from every direction. Had he been a politician, he would have won any election by a landslide. People fell in love with his soft-spoken nature, something that was so out of place in the world of professional fighting. Arguably his best moment was the weigh-in for the fight against Ryan Thurman. Sitting behind the table in front of thousands of hyped fans in Atlanta, he sat through two and a half straight minutes of ear-shattering trash-talk from Thurman. When the time finally came for him to respond, he leaned forward slowly and in his deep, tired voice said, "I think this is going to be an easy fight. This guy is using all his energy yelling into that microphone." The crowd of 9,000 went delirious. That fight was eight months earlier and he had gone on to win just 2:31 into the first round with an arm bar.

He had responded to Jenna's comment about his billboard with the bare minimum and went back to lowering grapes into his mouth. Hanging on the side of a downtown building was his face, the size of a tennis court, and he had absolutely no interest in talking about it. The grapes seemed to be the center of his universe.

He was picking them off the vine; oblivious or just indifferent to the way Jenna fidgeted on the chaise. She looked at his eyes: the same far-away eyes that she had been looking into for the past two years. She imagined him, as she often did, as a child. A quiet, sweaty-faced little boy competitive to the death in whatever he was doing, always flanked by a slightly taller and louder brother and a shorter best friend. She saw him start to chase girls, she saw him start to understand what kind of person he was going to be. She saw him go off to college, walking campus with Lucas and Tanner. She saw him win his national championship as the wrestling phenomenon. But somewhere after that, it all went blank, his eyes lost life.

"You like grapes." She said observationally, trying to work up the courage to do what she had set her mind to. She was resolute: tonight she would tell him that they wouldn't be seeing each other anymore, but she was nervous.

"Yeah. I used to throw grapes for Lucas when we would barbecue in the backyard." Jenna didn't immediately believe what she had just heard. In two years Danny had never once brought up Lucas voluntarily. A voice in her head begged her to push for more. *I've got nothing to lose.*

"Do you miss him?" She asked bluntly.

Danny didn't have any reaction to the question and instead of answering, pulled another grape from the vine. Painful silence ensued, Jenna didn't think he was going to answer but he finally spoke, and when he did Jenna nearly gasped.

"I miss him all the time."

Her heart jolted into her throat. She was going to push it as far as he would go.

"What was he like?"

He didn't seem the least bit uncomfortable.

"He was a nice guy, friendly to everybody. Really good football player too." Jenna was nearly in a state of shock hearing the words come out of his mouth and she tried to mask her excitement. She wanted more.

"Who was older?"

He sighed heavily but she couldn't tell if it was irritation or if he was simply taking a deep breath.

"He was. By a few hours." He answered, still in a flat and unaffected tone.

"Was he friends with Tanner too?"

Danny's eyebrows narrowed and he frowned with confusion, "Of course. You thought Tanner was just my friend? Why—because he's a wrestler?" Jenna shrugged helplessly, "How am I supposed to know?"

Danny seemed a bit confused, but it wasn't enough for him to continue.

"Well, I think I'm gonna call it a night." He said, rising to his feet, twisting his upper body from side to side then touching his toes. Jenna got nervous then, she had to tell him that it was over.

"Danny." She said sternly enough for him to stop putting on his shirt and look at her expectantly. "We can't meet anymore. This has gone on for too long. It's not right. I know I'm not your therapist, but it's still wrong."

He showed no expression, just nodded slowly.

"But this is so perfect." He said.

"It's been fun. But it's run its' course." She said firmly.

"You're not enjoying it anymore?" He asked. Jenna rolled her eyes in preparation to explain herself. "*Obviously* I'm enjoying it. It's not that. It's wrong and I know you don't want to hear this but you need some real help. You need to talk to somebody and if that's not going to happen here then it needs to happen somewhere else."

Danny got angry in the way that he did, becoming calmer and holding stern eye contact. "*Talk. Get it off your chest.*" He said mocking all the people that had urged him to talk to someone. "Is that what I need to do?"

Jenna had found unexpected confidence. "We've been doing this for two years and I don't know anything about your past. You don't see anything wrong with that?" Her voice was strong and certain of itself.

"It was an enormous loss." She said softly. He stayed quiet, presumably growing more agitated. She had made his life much easier for the last two years; their discreet meetings hadn't been the therapy that Isabel had envisioned for him but it had been an outlet from the rest of life, and he didn't want to lose it.

His eyes searched the floor as if he would find words that might change her mind, but there was nothing. It was over. A wind of defeat and frustration blew over him. Although they weren't romantically attached, rejection was rejection and he wasn't going to argue. Solemnly he held out an arm for a hug. Tears welled in her eyes as she rose and hugged him.

"Don't be a stranger." She said quietly. He released her from the hug and walked out of her office for the last time, feeling low.

WEDNESDAY, JUNE 22ND 2016

Monday had been a disaster. Tuesday was even worse, and when Wednesday's workout started the same way, Danny's coach, Marlos walked onto the mat and waved his hands in the air, shaking his head in frustration. In all his years coaching he had never seen such a sudden and drastic drop in performance.

Mark and Remy stood outside the ring and exchanged a troubled look. Remy shook his head slowly, eyebrows raised in confusion, *I don't know what's wrong.*

Danny had been weighed down all week, nearly a full half step slow on everything like he was wearing a backpack full of sand.

Ricky, Danny's sparring partner, had left the ring at the request of Marlos who was now pacing in front of Danny, plotting his words. A heavy-breathing, sweat-drenched Danny leaned against the cage, expressionless but somehow obviously frustrated. It was a Danny Sheppard that nobody had ever seen. There had to be a clear explanation—fighters didn't just fall apart. His next fight was six weeks away. Joe Vega in Nashville.

Danny's knuckles were nearly white as he gripped the steering wheel on the way home. Taison, sitting in the passenger seat, knew better than to say anything. He had been the subject of a stern grilling from Marlos after Monday's workout about what Danny had eaten the past 48 hours. His diet hadn't changed though—Taison was as confused as any of them, he had no idea why Danny was slow. Again after Tuesday's workout Marlos had taken Taison aside, very seriously asking him to think about what Danny had been eating or not eating and what time he was going to bed but again Taison insisted that he had been strictly following his diet.

Danny was angry, retreating deep inside himself. He didn't need to think about what was slowing him down, he knew damn well that it was Jenna calling an end to their arrangement, but he didn't know why it had affected him so dramatically. They pulled into the driveway of Danny's new condo.

"I'll start your food." Taison called after Danny as he bounded up the stairs. He needed to close the door to his bedroom and think. This couldn't continue. He had lost his breath early and when his second wind came, it was weak.

He was alone but the invisible audience was back. They peeked out of his closet and looked in from his window. Joe Vega was 22 days away. He knew what he had to do. He reached for his phone.

He texted Jenna.

"Can we meet tonight? I have to ask you something"

— — —

Over the two years that they had been meeting the topic of Lucas had only become more and more taboo. It was clear that Danny wouldn't be talking about him but ever since their last meeting, Jenna had done nothing but think about how he had brought him up voluntarily.

Maybe I ended things just as he was getting ready to talk.

She had finished with the first patient of her Thursday afternoon when she checked her phone. Her heart jumped into her throat when she saw the words on her screen. She read it several times before responding.

"10?"

His response came immediately.

"See you tonight"

— — —

9:41 P.M.

A minor ankle injury a few months earlier had left him with a full prescription of oxycodone that he hadn't touched but that was still under the sink in his bathroom. The timeframe in which he was allowed to take them was still open so a drug test wouldn't be of any concern. In the months after returning from Brazil he had turned to the combination of Jack Daniels and painkillers too frequently, it had been a dark time. He had willed himself away from it before anybody could sense a problem, but now he was going to give in. The anxiety was as bad as it was in those first months home from Brazil.

He opened a fresh box of Nike gear that he had arrived earlier in the day. His contract had allotted him $8,000 of catalog money each year and he had spent about $600 of it on this order. Ripping the tags off, he dressed in a forest green Jordan warm up suit and sat on the edge of his bed, two oxycodones on his bedside table next to a pint of Jack.

– — –

He sat on the couch. She sat on the chaise. His muscles were light and pleasantly tingly from the two pills and two shots. Jenna sat there patiently.

"Um. I've been training like shit all week." He confessed.

Jenna nodded slowly. *Go on...*

"I really like coming here. I look forward to it—not just for the sex. I don't want to stop coming here." He realized just how true it was as he said it.

For two years he had used her office to escape to a place where there was a total lack of complication, nothing but cozy dim lighting and great sex. Even when he was at his own house he was surrounded by reminders of the mission at hand. But during the late night hours that he spent at Jenna's office every couple weeks, he could put away his drive and focus and take a brief vacation in the secret little sanctuary.

Jenna's legs were folded, her fingers linked on top of her knee.

"I can't continue to sleep with you Danny. It's gone on long enough."

Danny was expressionless, but he was listening.

"I know you don't want to hear it from me or anybody else but you do need some help. You need to talk to somebody." She said.

"Hm. Well if that's the case, we can continue to meet until I'm ready, yeah?"

Jenna shook her head.

"Not unless you're ready soon. It's not for me to say when you should be ready but I can't keep sleeping with you until you are. It's been fun, but it's not right."

Danny's eyes wandered the room as he tried to come up with a compelling bit of convincing but he could tell that her mind was made up. He relented.

"Well what do you want to know?" He asked, nerves showing.

"I want to know about Lucas." She said softly.

She half expected him to put his jacket back on and stand to leave and in truth, he was considering it. Talking about Lucas was just too difficult. But he tried.

"He was loud. I was quiet—I—I still am I guess." He stuttered.

"I'm not sure—what exactly do you want to know about him?" He interrupted himself. Without hesitation Jenna went all in.

"Tell me about the night he passed away." It was her intention to go straight for the most painful part, the heart of the beast. She knew that if they talked too much about other things first he might lose his nerve. Danny was quiet for a long time. She got a different read on him: still distant, but calm, almost in a trance. Her heart began to race as the silence stretched on. He took another deep breath and sighed heavily. It started slowly, but the words were coming.

─   ──   ─

"We went to a movie with some friends from high school, down here at Cinetopia." He said throwing a thumb lazily over his shoulder, referring to the Beaverton Cinetopia that was no more than ten minutes from her office. Jenna nodded. She knew where it was. He counted on his fingers the friends that had been there, "It was me, Lucas, Tanner, Ryan, Caitlyn, Dion and Michelle. It was January but it wasn't very cold out—I remember random things like that—and we were standing around in the parking lot afterwards, just talking or whatever. Tanner and Dion and I were about to go hang out with some girls that we had met at school and Lucas was going home to hangout with Andrea." He cleared his throat into his fist.

He was fighting for each sentence. Jenna hung onto every word. She couldn't look away from his face. He only made eye contact occasionally, mostly staring towards the floor near her feet. His brow would wrinkle over his glazed green eyes. He tucked his bottom lip in and ran his fingers down his jaw line as he contemplated something to himself. Each word was a small accomplishment. Jenna waited patiently.

"Then it got so loud. This huge red truck pulls into the parking lot and it was like, *deafening* it was so loud with the exhaust pipes that like go up in the air from behind the cab you know?" Jenna nodded, "And it was so strange. We didn't even know who it was but even as the truck drove through the parking lot, I could just sense something bad about it. Like you could tell it was trouble somehow, from the very start."

Jenna's heart started to beat faster.

"It pulls up to the curb in front of the frozen yogurt place that's in that shopping center and just idles there. Three guys get out—like three loud redneck type guys. I wouldn't have paid them any attention but my friend Caitlyn like," Danny rolled his eyes in disgust and sucked his teeth in an attempt to mimic her, "she made some sort of face when she saw who it was. I had to ask who they were but when she said his name I remembered hearing of him and maybe being in the same place a few times, but that's it. We didn't know each other or anything. Trevor Ramey was his name."

The name didn't mean anything to her but as he said it goose bumps bristled on her arms. "What I knew about him was that he was an asshole. Literally, that was the *only* thing I remember being able to associate him with: being an asshole. He looked like it too." Danny's eyes blinked slowly.

"He was like an ultra pretty boy but a redneck at the same time—I don't really know how to describe him. He had blonde hair and huge, blocky, un-athletic stupid looking muscles—I don't know." Jenna nodded.

"Anyway I don't know what they were doing—dropping somebody off maybe, I wasn't paying attention at all but I do remember that they left the truck running when they got out—like I said, I remember all these random things. Anyway people started leaving and stuff and Lucas started walking towards our truck that was parked over near where this red truck was parked by the yogurt place. Ramey came out just as Lucas was getting into the truck and Ramey said something to Lucas. I have no idea what—his fucking truck was so loud even when it was just idling there. It was like thirty yards away and their exchange went on for like twenty seconds maybe. We were just standing there watching it all. They were going back and forth and the body language just wasn't right, it was weird, definitely confrontational. Tanner was hoping something would escalate—I've told you how Tanner was in high school. Always beating somebody up, usually somebody who was fucking with my sister."

Danny swallowed hard, it seemed that he was almost choked up but he continued smoothly. "Anyway. It ends. Lucas leaves. Pulls out of the parking lot in the little Tacoma that we shared and then this guy pulls out of the parking lot in his big red truck." For some reason at that moment it became evident to Jenna that very few people knew the story he was telling her.

"We were driving into North West when I got the call from Lucas. I remember his exact words, couldn't forget them if I wanted. Danny put his pinky and thumb to his ear like a phone.

"'This redneck douchebag is trying to run me off the road or some-thing.' I knew right away he was talking about Trevor Ramey and that it had something to do with whatever was said in the parking lot." Telling the story was taking a physical toll, he felt fatigued and almost short of breath… but it felt good.

"Anyway. He wasn't calling to tell me that Ramey was trying to run him off the road. He was calling to say that Celia—you know, my neighbor, I've told you about her—" Jenna nodded, "he was calling to say that she wanted to take us to breakfast at this place in Sellwood the next day. This place that she always took us to when we were growing up. He didn't say anything more about Ramey trying to run him off the road and to be honest it almost sounded like he was amused by it, I didn't think anything of it. So that was at about nine forty-five. The next call I got was from Andrea maybe an hour later. Tanner and I were at this girl's condo in The Pearl. She wanted to know where he was. I told her that he had left an hour earlier and that maybe he had stopped somewhere. She wasn't worried but it was weird that he wasn't home and hadn't answered his phone. So I hung up with Andrea and then maybe forty-five minutes after that was when we got the call from my dad." Danny inflated his upper lip and slowly shook his head, looking Jenna in her face. Her heart pounded against her rib cage.

"All he had to say was 'Danny.' And I just knew something wasn't right. He told us to get to Kaiser Permanente as soon as we could. I immediately thought back to what he said—about Trevor Ramey." Danny's voice had become even slower and more gravelly, almost hoarse.

"I knew he had done something... I just knew—and Tanner did too. The phone call was on speaker. Dion would have heard it too but he drove separately. I talked with an officer that night at the hospital and a detective the next day, with my dad. The accident was coming down Hillsdale Highway just before the curve where you get onto Barbur? You know where I'm talking about?" Jenna knew exactly where he was talking about, she usually drove that way to get downtown instead of Highway 26. She nodded solemnly, fighting to keep her eyes free of tears.

"So. I don't have any idea how it came to be like this flaming, rolling car type of accident—that part is a mystery. I've had all these questions—*Why couldn't he just pull over, why didn't he have his seatbelt on, why was there no evidence of road rage*—all the questions that you'll probably want to ask, I have those questions too. Shit's all a mystery still." He said the last part with the conclusiveness that meant the story was over.

Jenna was still in a state of disbelief and why she asked him the next question she had no idea, it came from nowhere but it turned out to be the right question to ask, steering them towards something more light-hearted.

"What movie did you see?"

Danny scoffed with amusement as if he'd just been reminded of something. It couldn't have been more out of sync with the mood that the story had put them in.

"We saw *American Hustle*."

"Oh I never saw that. It won awards didn't it? Who was in it, again?"

"Bradley Cooper, Christian Bale, Jennifer Lawrence and—what's her name...Pam from The Office...shit what's her name...Amy Adams."

"No, Amy Adams isn't Pam in The Office."

"Are you sure? Isn't she? Who plays Pam in The Office?" He asked concerned.

"Ugh, what's her name? She's in that ice-skating comedy with Will Ferrell and the guy from Napolean Dynamite...damn it I have to Google it." She said taking her phone from her purse that was on the floor.

"Jenna Fischer!" She said a moment later.

"Oh that's *right*. She's great. I love The Office. Anyway, American Hustle is good, you should see it—what kind of movies do you like?"

"Oh God, I haven't watched many movies in the last few years but I like comedy, drama—anything that's not violent really, I have a weak stomach."

Danny frowned. "Violent? It's not too violent to watch me though?"

"I *don't* watch you. I've told you that. I've seen everything on You-Tube but I can't watch it live, it's too much for me. The only time I tried was when I ordered your fight against the—what was his name, the Russian guy—Krymanski?"

"Kerzhakov. And he's Ukrainian. But yeah close enough."

Several times over the past two years they had met only a week or so after one of Danny's fights but they never talked about it any further than Jenna saying "Congratulations" before being ripped out of her lingerie. He had always assumed that she watched his fights but he realized that he didn't have any reason to make such an assumption.

"Oh oops. Well yeah I ordered that fight but I had to look away for most of it." Jenna remembered sitting on the couch with Peter watching the spectacle of a UFC event. The cameras swooping through the air above the octagon and the cheering of the fans while the announcer yelled into the microphone. Fighters, surrounded by their entourages, streamed toward the octagon while their entrance songs played. Danny didn't have a song that he came out to and he didn't wear some stupid costume when he made his entrances like many of the fighters. He just walked through the crowd surrounded by his team and the security guards. His long arms outstretched like Jesus so his hands could brush through the hands of the fans.

Did you know he's from Portland? Peter had asked her as they watched.

Yeah I think I heard that. Jenna had said.

"Well it's probably better that you didn't watch that fight. Lot of blood," Danny said running two fingers over the thin diagonal scar on the outside of his right eyebrow, "he had some sharp Ukrainian elbows, that guy." He said, reminiscing.

Jenna flicked a finger towards his eyebrow, "Is that how you got that?"

Danny was silent for a moment as his eyes angled off to the right. "No this is from a long time ago." Jenna thought she could hear the faintest quiver in his voice but it could have been nothing. So many questions ran through her head but she wanted to see if he would press forward. "And then you went to Brazil?" She asked.

Danny nodded, still not meeting her eyes. "Well that week after the crash the detective got back to my dad. He said that the accident had nothing to do with road rage and I was mad—for no reason. It's not like it would have helped if Ramey had been arrested. Then the next weekend—the night after Lucas' funeral—I randomly saw Trevor Ramey in a Safeway parking lot. I snapped. Beat him into a coma. *Then* I went to Brazil. *Ran away* to Brazil, more accurately. Got on a flight the next morning. A fugitive on the run basically."

A look of utter horror took over Jenna's face. He had laid it out and breezed through it as if it were just a minor detail. She tried to grasp for a question that would make him elaborate but Danny was done for the night; he had said all he was going to say for now. He closed his eyes and bowed his head, putting his hands on his knees and pushing himself onto his feet.

"Wait—*what?*" She asked in shock.

"That's enough for tonight." Danny said with a yawn.

She couldn't believe the last part but he had already stood up. Happy, hopeful warmth swelled through her—almost maternal. He had done it. She never thought it would happen. What was especially encouraging was the fact that he had said "Enough for *tonight*." She tried not to get too carried away but she thought he seemed relieved and slightly buoyant as gave her a quick hug and left her office.

– — -

The next day coach Remy's French-accented voice powerfully echoed through the gym, "Tsa! Two, three, four, Tsa! Two, three, four, Tsa!" Danny whipped a meaty right kick into the big blue pad that Remy supported with all his weight. From the start of Danny's career his kicking had been highlighted as his biggest weakness and his coaches pushed him hard to improve it. "...three, four, TSA!"

The last kick was so strong that it forced Remy to take a step backwards. Laughter and light cheering came from the coaches standing outside the ropes. Everyone was baffled. Neither Remy nor Marlos had ever seen something like this. Monday, Tuesday and Wednesday had been atrocious, embarrassing training days for Danny. Thursday was starting off very different. It was impossible to imagine that he could be any more agile, athletic or powerful than he already was but somehow, someway, he seemed to have jumped up a level overnight. On the side of the ring Marlos leaned over and whispered something into Mark's ear. Mark nodded.

The stretching routine that was always the last part of the workout had been less painful than normal. Usually it felt like Remy was trying to fold Danny in half or pull one of his limbs clean from his body but today he felt looser, his breathing was easier to control, his muscles felt rubbery and strong. After his five-minute silent reflection, where he lay on his back and closed his eyes, thinking about his movements and imagining himself working in the octagon, he sprang to his feet and headed for the shower to the applause of his team. He threw a thumbs-up over his shoulder. He felt good. He showered and emerged from the locker room to see Tanner standing near the door while Mark, Remy and Marlos huddled around Taison in an interrogating manner. Danny was able to catch a few words of what Mark was saying, "... think back through the week... you're sure you're measuring things correctly?"

Danny's team had come together organically with Marlos

assembling it in the months after Danny had returned to Portland. The big addition was Remy. He was the real deal. In Marlos' opinion, there was no better kickboxing coach in the world. The two had met at a PRIDE Fight in the 90's in Paris; Marlos was coaching Brazilian fighters and Remy Cissé was fighting. A mountain of a man: a meaty six foot six inches of thick Senegalese-French muscle. His bald head always glistened with sweat after five minutes of any workout and his big white smile looked almost neon in contrast to his coffee bean skin. He was very handsome.

He was a kickboxing practitioner and had utilized it to great success in his own career. Before Marlos recruited him to come to the American city of Portland Remy had been operating his own gym in Toulouse where he had developed the skills of top French, Belgian, Polish and African fighters. He was content in France and well respected in the farthest corners of the MMA world, but his excitement peaked when he got the call from his old friend Marlos Vieira.

Marlos wasn't a man who dished out praise easily and when he said that he had found what he promised was "a young fighter with the potential to be a world champion", he couldn't let the chance pas him by. When he arrived in Portland, he wasn't disappointed. He had never seen a fighter like Danny. The athleticism, the power, the controlled aggression—his wrestling was the best he'd ever seen and his Jiu-Jitsu was only getting better under Marlos' watchful eye.

"Don't forget you have the *Men's Health* interview on Saturday at noon. I'll text you a reminder tomorrow." Mark called after Danny as he followed Tanner, who was back from Corvallis for the weekend, out the door.

Mark had been Danny and Tanner's wrestling coach in high school. It was an easy decision to install him as his manager and agent. The Sheppard family trusted him and his gym in Beaverton had turned into training headquarters with the addition of some specialty equipment at the request of Marlos.

– — –

Outside of the gym Danny encountered the same group of 15 year-olds waiting for their wrestling practice. As usual, most of them scrambled to unlock their phones and take a Snapchat of him as he walked through the parking lot. They were there three times a week and Danny always gave them the same acknowledging head nod but today, he startled them, calling out, "What's up boys?"

Their eyes got wide as their heads jerked into sharp attention, "What's up." They echoed back in surprised, uneven unison. Danny could hear the fervent murmuring behind him when they got close to the car—one of the kids gloating that he had captured the moment on his Snapchat. He had felt better than he had in his entire career, so limber and energetic, and he knew why.

Tanner noticed something different about Danny too. They climbed into the Audi, Danny had given Tanner the keys—he usually made him drive when he was around and Tanner loved driving the SUV.

"What are we doing tonight—are we waiting for Taison?" Tanner asked looking out the back window to see if he was coming. "No, he's..." Danny was distracted typing something on his phone, "...he's doing something with Mark."

"What are we doing tonight?" Tanner asked again. "Let's just chill at home for a while. Play some FIFA with Rodney."

Danny wanted to be at home before he went to Jenna's later but he

— — -

Jenna's heart raced when she saw the text. The reality that he had finally opened up had left her fidgety and distracted all morning, and now he wanted to meet again, the very next day. A few times she had caught herself daydreaming about it, thinking back to the moment when he had let out the heavy sigh as he succumbed and started the story—it gave her goose bumps.

— — -

Danny slumped into the cognac colored couch, sedated once again by two Oxycodone and two shots of Jack. He was just as nervous as the night before but he wanted to feel more of what he had felt that day. The sexual energy wasn't there; it was obvious that this meeting was only about the story. He pulled a Snickers Ice Cream bar out of the bag he had brought with him and held a finger up to his lips, "Shhhh. I'd be in trouble if they knew I ate this but I just couldn't resist."

"Your diet is *that* strict?" Jenna gawked. "Yeah." Danny said giving her a look that said *Duh.* "I don't control it myself. I just eat whatever Taison cooks—he cooks all my meals and sticks to the plan." Jenna loved hearing the bits and pieces of his day-to-day life; it was so interesting—a behind-the-scenes look at the life of a world-class athlete. "He's your cousin right? The one who lives with you?"

"Right—my uncle Renato's son. Little party animal right now. Goes out every weekend. Lovin' life." There was affection in Danny's slow, drawling words. "Is that annoying?" She asked. Danny frowned and shook his head. "I couldn't care less. It's annoying when he comes home hammered and wakes me up at three in the morning because the girl he brought home wants to meet me."

"No way…" Jenna said laughing, eyes wide with amusement. "Yeah he did that once." Danny said shaking his head.

"Did you meet her?" She asked. "I shook her hand and politely told them to fuck off and I went back to sleep. He was really sorry the next morning. I wasn't mad."

Jenna smiled. After a long silence she asked, "You really put Trevor Ramey in a coma?"

Danny finished his ice cream and linked his fingers on top of his head, raising his eyebrows as if to say, *That's how you're going to play this?*

"No foreplay? Just straight into it?" He asked without expression. Jenna shrugged. "Yeah."

Danny raised his eyebrows, *Well alright then.*

"It was late at night and he just so happened to pull into the parking lot of Safeway by my house. One in a billion. I snapped. I was sure I'd killed him."

"And you were scared of getting arrested? Is that why you went to Brazil?" She asked.

He took his hands from the top of his head and folded his arms. "Mostly. I also just wanted to get out of Portland. I didn't give a shit about leaving my wrestling but I felt awful about leaving my family. Can you imagine? A week after Lucas died I nearly kill a guy and left without a word, in the middle of the night." He squeezed his eyes shut. It was obviously hard for him to think about.

"I'm sure your family has forgiven you but...why aren't you in jail?" She asked with a wrinkled eyebrow.

Danny almost grinned. "It's a long story. I guess I got kind of lucky but Trevor Ramey fucked up, and he knew it."

Jenna was dying to know what that meant but she would be patient.

"I'm so sorry you had to go through that. That's a lot for a twenty-year-old to have to deal with."

Danny scoffed mildly. "That was just the start."

"What there's more?" Jenna asked.

He closed his eyes gently and nodded slowly. "Lot more."

"Tell. I promise not to analyze anything, I just want to hear what you've been through."

"You're a persistent little Asian."

Jenna laughed. "*Half* Asian." She corrected. He lay back on the couch and pinched the bridge of his nose. "Alright." He sighed heavily.

"I called Tanner to pick me up that night."

– — -

SUNDAY JANUARY 19TH, 2014

Just as Danny rounded the corner into the parking lot behind Kay's, Tanner's white Maxima leapt up the entrance at the far side. *Thank fuck.* Normally he would have welcomed the silence and solitude of the empty parking lot but at the moment it was the last thing he wanted; too much time to think would be the worst thing for him. The tires squealed as they swerved and lurched to a stop with the passenger door an arms length away from Danny. Tanner's driving already matched the urgency of the situation; somehow he was always on the same wavelength. Danny jumped in and instantly buried his head between his knees,

"FUUUUUUUCK!" He brought his head back to the headrest and pressed the heels of his palms into his eyes. In one anxious, rambling sentence he confessed.

"I fucked up man I fucked up big time I went to Safeway and fucking Trevor Ramey pulled in to the parking lot and I freaked out and beat the shit out of him—and his friend—and I'm not sure but he might be dead he's probably dead. Ramey—not his friend. He's dead. He's gotta be dead. He's fucking dead."

Tanner rolled his head towards his window and whispered to himself, "Shit." In all the years Tanner had known Danny Sheppard he had *never* seen him like this; reckless, frantic, hyperventilating, pupils so big his whole eye seemed to be black. They had started heading North towards the city without any real plan in mind. Danny's phone started to vibrate.

"The cops are at the house. Dad's calling." Tanner shook his head quickly, "Don't answer."

He imagined the exchange that had surely happened just moments earlier…

-Mr. and Mrs. Sheppard? Is your son home?

-What's this about Officer?

-We have reason to believe your son has assaulted two men earlier this evening.

-Danny? No officer that's not right. There must be some mistake.

Danny tried to put the thought out of his mind.

"What the fuck am I going to do?" Danny said softly, his voice quivering with panic. Tanner didn't have an answer. He was as street-smart as they came and he knew that the best thing to do was try to convince Danny to go home and face the consequences, however scary they might be. Even if Ramey was dead, it was the best thing to do. Tanner's phone was ringing. Andrea. He put it on silent. Then Danny's phone again: Allie. He put it on silent.

"I'm texting Dre back." Tanner said. Danny didn't fight him on it.

She texted back saying that the police left and had told Rich to call them as soon as he knew something. Danny felt a little encouraged by the fact that they left, surely if he was a murderer they would have at least stayed a bit longer.

"We're gonna lay low tonight. I know where to go." Tanner said.

They pulled off the curb and continued north, they were headed to the Irvington neighborhood in North East Portland. Tanner put his phone to his ear. He was calling Alexis Petersen.

She was a 28-year-old artist from Seattle. Tanner had met her at a First Thursday event the year before and would occasionally spend a sweaty night at her cozy duplex in the Irvington neighborhood under the prayer flags that hung from the ceiling. Danny had been to her house twice before.

Irvington was an eight-minute drive north on 99. They parked next to the playground of an elementary school two blocks from her house. Inside the chain-link fence stretched a sea of asphalt with painted squares and chalk drawings, a wall-ball board, basketball hoops and a tetherball. Danny gazed out at the theater of worry-free innocence and joy. Tanner nudged him with his shoulder, "I kicked your ass on a playground like this."

– — -

The one time Lucas had been to Alexis' place he had described it as "groovy". In truth, it was the only word that did it justice. It was a two-story duplex and she had the upstairs, accessed through a narrow stairway from the right side of the shared front porch. The door was unlocked for them. They made their way up the stairs and could hear the music from her studio. The door at the top of the stairs opened directly into the dimly lit living room. Antique trunks and suitcases were stacked on top of one another for decoration and complimented the maroon walls and wooden beams that crisscrossed overhead.

The house was over 80 years old with original wood floors that creaked with history in certain places. The kitchen had been renovated with rustic copper tabletops and matching handles on the dark wood cabinets. The thick wooden beams that ran across the ceiling had prompted Lucas to joke that the place looked like Vikings built it. They had all met there before going to a concert at Holocene the year before.

Danny planted himself on the couch as Tanner sought out Alexis. The indie rock music got turned off and he could hear the low voices, sounding like Tanner explaining that they just needed some space and time to talk and would she mind just staying out of the living room for the night. "Of course, of course." She said loud enough for Danny to tell that she was crying.

There was more mumbling talk, he heard a sentence end in a question and Tanner said, "Yeah go ahead." Danny saw her shadow on the wall before she rounded the corner, she was *really* crying. Her lilywhite cheeks were red beneath teary, bloodshot eyes. Her rust colored hair was up and wrapped in a purple tribal-patterned bandana. She wore an art-apron over black leggings and a white t-shirt. Alexis had only met Lucas the one time but—as was always the case—he had left his mark on her. His booming laugh and broad smile made her feel like they had been friends for years.

Upon seeing Danny sitting on her couch her face puckered into a sob as she approached and feebly waved him in for a hug. He obliged. "I'm so sorry." She managed between sniffles and sobs. Appreciative of the fact that the boys were looking to be alone, she didn't bother with questions or more condolences.

"There's food in the fridge." She called over her shoulder as she retreated back to her studio. Danny heard Tanner mumbling gratitude then the door closed and the music went back on, Florence and the Machine, if Danny wasn't mistaken. Tanner collapsed into the armchair next to the couch, massaging the bridge of his nose with both index fingers before sitting forward.

"You're on the run now. If it's going to stay that way we need to explain things to your parents. That needs to be priority number one."

Danny was never known to be violent or even confrontational; they must have been so confused. There was a long silence. Tanner couldn't take it.

"Alright. Story time." Tanner said firmly in an *enough is enough* kind of way. He didn't want to pressure Danny, but it was time. 2:07

a.m. Danny took a deep breath and started into the events of the evening, beginning with him leaving the house to go for a drive. In the middle of the story, Tanner's phone rang. It was aunt Judy.

"Hello... yeah... no I don't know... right now?... do they want to talk to me?... sure... yeah hello... yeah I talked to him an hour ago maybe but I'm not sure, he's turned his phone off so... I'm at a friends house... can it wait until tomorrow?... first thing in the morning... yep will do... can you text it to me, my aunt will give you my number... ok... yeah goodnight." He hung up.

"Cops are at my aunt and uncles, if I talk to you I'm supposed to urge you to turn yourself in. Continue." Danny felt a brief wave of nausea but he kept telling the story. When he finished, Tanner shook his head in utter disbelief.

"What are the fucking odds of *that*?" He mumbled.

"So what now?"

Danny linked his fingers on the top of his head, pondering the different paths he may or may not head down in the coming hours. His priorities had become selfish. For Tanner, the seconds were passing as slowly as they did in the waiting room of Kaiser Permanente a week before. He was feigning for words: instructions, a confession—anything. He would have to wait nearly 20 agonizing minutes until Danny sat forward, eyes staring intently into nowhere.

"Alright." He said as if curtains were parting on a stage. Tanner sat forward too. It didn't matter what came out of Danny's mouth next, Tanner would be right there with him.

– — -

Jenna didn't want to interrupt with questions at any point but she couldn't help it when they reached the point where it became clear that Danny was going to run away to Brazil.

"So you threw away your college career? Your *wrestling* career?" The first portion of the story had lasted about fifteen minutes.

Danny nodded but shrugged, "It was so unimportant at the time.

That first week after Lucas died… nothing was important. Nothing mattered. And then after I beat up Ramey…" He shrugged again.

– — -

7:00 a.m. came suddenly. Danny felt as though he had fallen asleep just minutes earlier. Tanner looked outside, it was raining. Both the boys were alert and ready to start the day by 7:12. The first part of Danny's plan was underway as Tanner put his phone to his ear while Danny paced the living room, stretching his arms above his head. It was go-time.

"Good morning this is Tanner Spurling, we spoke briefly last night… yeah… um, Danny called me just a minute ago, he's somewhere on the coast. He wouldn't say where exactly but he's out there somewhere, I would guess that he would be in Newport, he liked it there… yeah I know… no he wouldn't do that… listen I know these are crazy circumstances but I know Danny better than anybody and I know for a fact that he wouldn't hurt himself… yeah I understand, I want that too… I'll be in touch… yep… alright yeah, bye." They were looking at each other as Tanner hung up.

"Alright. You need anything from the store before we head out?" Tanner asked. Danny shook his head.

Danny didn't have the stomach to say goodbye to Alexis and deal with the inevitable emotional embrace that would occur. He wasn't sure if she was even home, she had taken it seriously when Tanner had asked her to give them some space, and Danny was appreciative of that. He monitored Tanner's behavior from his peripheral: anxious, fussing about, not quite sure what to do with his hands.

"I gotta get outta here man. I can't stay." Danny said as if Tanner had asked him the question. Tanner knew it was now or never, "Dude do you realize what you're giving up here? You're national champ, you're supposed to go to the Olympics, man I just—" his words were upset and rushed, very un-Tanner. His hands found their way to the back of his neck.

"I know man. I never thought for a second that I wouldn't finish college." His words sympathized with Tanner's concern. "I'm just not sure of anything here. Even when I'm at home it all feels so strange without him. If there's even a chance that things will be different... I gotta go to Rio. I just gotta go." Tanner didn't need to hear anything more, and a few minutes later they were on the road, headed for Seattle.

— — —

At 8:45 a.m. at the Sheppard house Allie, like everybody else, didn't know what to think. For some reason she couldn't help but suspect that whatever was going on was related to the "road rage" thing that Danny and Tanner had been murmuring about all week. The information she had was that her brother had beat somebody up at Safeway and then gone missing, although she knew he was with Tanner somewhere.

She almost couldn't believe it, a part of her felt that it had all been some epic misunderstanding and that Danny had been completely uninvolved. It weren't as though he was a saint—after all he was a master of dominating other men in physical competition—but his nature was competitive, never violent. Allie had seen both her brothers mad before, but nobody had ever been crazy enough to cross either of them and surely Danny hadn't been the instigator.

The scene in the kitchen was a silent movie of confusion and angst. Almost no words had been spoken and nobody had managed to sleep since being woken by the police. Rich had been at the island in the kitchen for most of the morning, arms folded and brow wrinkled. He seemed more pissed off than concerned. Isabel was a wreck, crying and talking to herself in Portuguese.

"Onde ele está? O que aconteceu com meu filho? Isso não pode ser real—me chame de Danilo! Agora mesmo!"

Celia dabbed the corners of her eyes with her silver handkerchief every few minutes like clockwork. Andrea's parents were there. Wendy and Phil. Phil constantly looked like he was on his way to play 9 holes: polo shirts, khaki pants or shorts and grey hair creeping up from his ears. His look was so *retired businessman* that it prompted Tanner to joke with him, "Phil, when are you moving to Florida man?" Wendy was elegantly blonde and almost never spotted without a face full of makeup. Her eyes squinted at the outsides like Andrea's.

It was reminiscent of a movie scene where the kidnapped victim's family huddled around a phone, desperate for it to ring—minus the detectives and their tracing equipment.

– — -

At 8:52 a.m. the boys were passing through Olympia, well ahead of schedule. Danny had bought his ticket at Alexis' house that night using his credit card. Last minute flights weren't cheap; he had spent $1,317.00 for a one-way ticket. He knew the police didn't have time to get a warrant to freeze his passport. It was a 12:05 p.m. departure, SEA → MIA and then 9:35 p.m. MIA → GIG (Rio De Janeiro).

"Thanks man." Danny said as they cruised on I-5. It was the first thing either of them had said in a while. "I know it's a bitch, but thanks." Throughout the night he had walked Tanner through his plan, which in essence, was him running away and leaving Tanner and his family to do all the cleaning up. Not until later would he realize how awful it was. For once in his life he was thinking selfishly. He didn't want to get arrested. He wanted to be in Brazil. He was frightened, in the purest most primitive sense of the word.

Everything that had happened that week after the accident was flooded in truth. Not a word had been spoken that wasn't completely necessary and true. Death stripped away anything superficial. Danny shredding through Trevor Ramey was truth in action. The pile of bodies on the white tile floor of the hospital waiting room was the truth. Tanner screaming in his parked car outside the Sheppard house, Danny's vacant eyes, Celia's ever-present silver handkerchief: all truths.

Despair illuminated how flimsy everyday life could be, so full of extra nonsense, minced words, murky in common friendliness, but not now. Death had wiped away the thick makeup of everyday life, and the ugly face underneath was impossible to alter. Danny was running away from his problems… and it was the truth.

"No problem. I'll take care of it." Tanner said with military certainty. He had his instructions from the night before. Then, as it had all gone far too easily with the police thus far, Tanner got a call from a number he didn't recognize but the caller ID made it clear: Multnomah County. Stabbing the power button on the radio with his index finger, he flashed the screen at Danny before answering.

"Hello?" The voice that came blasting over the speakerphone was husky and highly agitated. "Yeah hello Mr. Spurling, Detective O'Connell here." Without pausing for Tanner to respond he continued, "Listen, I've done some poking around and I think your claim that Danny is somewhere on the coast is bullshit and after learning just how close the two of you are, I have to say I think you're lying and that you know exactly where he is."

The accusatory tone of Detective O'Connell was acidic and even surprised Danny. Tanner was more offended than surprised, he never tolerated a tone like that, "Well Detective. My *claim*—as you put it— that he is on the coast, is what Danny *himself* told me this morning so I haven't *claimed* shit. I don't appreciate your tone and you're not moving forward by making random accusations and treating me as an adversary." Tanner's words were hard and graceful, his eloquence never ceased to impress. Detective O'Connell was clearly taken aback and a bit lost as he fumbled for a response. He was the type that would never admit when he was wrong… even if he wasn't.

"Well you know… if you speak with Danny you need to tell him to contact me. It's very important. According to Kevin Minnick, Trevor is lucky to be alive—said Danny was completely out of control and that if he hadn't been there Danny likely would have killed Trevor. He needs to come in, he's only delaying the inevitable."

"Okay well this has been nice. Like I said this morning, if he calls I'll try to convince him to contact you."

"You know it's not just the victim that suffers from something—" Tanner hung up. "Prick." He said angrily. Danny felt relieved. He really believed Ramey was dead. O'Connell had said *likely would have killed Trevor.* Tanner turned the music back on and they continued up I-5.

– — -

"Your parents must have been so worried." Jenna said. Danny stared at the ceiling from his back. "That's putting it mildly."

He squeezed his eyes shut. "Tanner gave me an oxy at the airport. I took it when I got to Miami and it wore off like halfway through the flight to Rio. I've never experienced anything like it. I was so mad at myself. I couldn't believe what I had done to Trevor Ramey and I couldn't believe how I had left my family. It was so childish. Cowardly. Whatever you want to call it. I hated myself for it."

— — –

It was 8:52 a.m. local time on Tuesday morning when Danny stepped off the plane in Galeão International. The sliding doors opened and he was embraced by the hot, heavy air of Rio De Janeiro. Everything about being in Brazil was familiar except for the feeling of arriving without Lucas.

Every summer when he stepped off the plane he transitioned from Danny to Danilo: an even more carefree and light-hearted being than Danny from Portland. He slept in board shorts and hardly ever wore socks. His skin turned darker in the sun and stayed sticky with sweat. He would go to one of the cheap street-side barbers and get a buzz-cut just so he didn't have to worry about his hair being greasy. He was one with the rhythm of the beach and the bustling streets; he wasn't a foreigner. Copacabana and Christ the Redeemer were as much his own as they were every other Brazilian in the city. The hot air and familiar smell of the city greeted him.

Welcome back. You made the right decision.

When the oxy that Tanner gave him at the terminal had wore off half way through his flight from Miami the magnitude of his decision began to eat him alive.

What kind of son and brother am I? Lucas would have kicked my ass for this.

He slung his duffel over his shoulder and hailed a taxi, anxious to be at his grandparent's house—they would be expecting him by now. Isabel would have called as soon as Tanner told them what was happening.

Tanner figured that he would text Rich when he reached the Rose Garden exit on his way back from Seattle, letting him know that he was on his way over to the house. He couldn't fathom the confusion and stress that must be ravaging the Sheppard house at that moment or how he would be received when he stepped through the door.

At the sound of the front door opening he immediately heard the frantic movement in the kitchen, stools sliding back, socked feet scurrying along the wood floor to look down the hall. Isabel was first to see him, and without hesitation she hurried up the hall to the entryway and flung her arms around him speaking hushed Portuguese into his neck.

Celia and Rich were close on Isabel's heels with the girls and Rodney behind them. Tanner used his shoulder to wipe away his tears in between the hugs he got from everyone. The welcoming embrace lasted a few minutes before Rich cut gently through the crying that had started and in an open-to-all kind of tone, said, "Ok everybody, Tanner and I need to have a little talk."

In the office Rich authoritatively swiveled a chair around to face his desk. He never lost his power to intimidate, and he pointed to the chair with an effortless dominance that would have made Vladimir Putin sit promptly. Rich sat at his desk, massaging his brow for a long few seconds before sitting back, folding his arms, and directing his full attention at Tanner.

"Alright Tanner. Just what the fuck is going on?"

His eyes were bloodshot, his stare frightening in its' serious simplicity and flatness, his hair disheveled and greasy like a career alcoholic. Tanner swallowed hard, "It was *him*. The guy who Lucas said was trying to run him off the road. Danny went for a drive last night and coincidentally," he paused and shook his head as he himself thought of the incredible chances of the confrontation, "ran into him at Safeway." Tanner hoped Rich would fill in the blanks but he stayed silent, forcing him to continue, "...and he beat him up. Beat him up pretty bad. Apparently."

Tanner expected a swift and unrelenting barrage of inquiry but for the time being it seemed Rich just wanted silence to think. He leaned back and folded his arms; his expression was a sort of weary acceptance as if his theory had been confirmed.

– — -

THURSDAY, JANUARY 23ᴿᴰ 2014
RIO DE JANEIRO, BRAZIL

Three days had passed since Danny had arrived. Three days spent in the perfect symmetry of the bedroom at the bottom of the stairs across from the laundry room. At six or seven years-old Danny had spotted the symmetry of the room that he and Lucas shared every summer.

"If you fold it in half here," he declared dragging a dirty finger down the grout between the square white tiles of the floor, "it's the same on both sides."

He wasn't wrong. The room was perfectly halved at the grout of the tiles with the two single beds against either wall. On the far wall was a central window with Mickey Mouse curtains hanging on either side. In spite of—or perhaps *because of* the bareness—the room radiated character and importance like a bedroom of historical significance behind velvet rope in a museum. Without Lucas in the bed on the right however, the symmetry was destroyed. Still, this was the room Danny and Lucas had shared for years. Being in the room was enough of a reprieve to make him realize that he wasn't going home any time soon.

The dust had settled somewhat. He had made the phone call home just minutes after arriving. His grandma, Rosa had promised Isabel that she would have him call the moment he walked in the front door. His heart had pounded so hard as he dialed the number. It seemed like more sobs had come over the phone than spoken words. Each second seared him with more guilt and shame. There was no other way of looking at it, no way to spin it: he had abandoned his family in the midst of the most terrible time of their lives. It was the act of a weak man.

Everyone pleaded with him to come home. Begged and cried for him to get on a flight and face the music, with them, together as a family. But they didn't understand what it was like for him. It was only a tiny sliver of solace and calm that he found in the symmetry of the basement bedroom, but he couldn't leave it. The quiet. The way the Mickey Mouse blinds swayed gently in the evening breeze, he felt Lucas around him. He wasn't going anywhere.

He had hung up the phone and immediately been sick to his stomach. He hurried down the stairs and out the back door where he squat in the yard as his mouth turned wet before the vomit came.

For the next three days and three nights Danny felt physical pain similar to what he imagined a heroin withdrawal might feel like. He sweat, he ached, he hardly could eat and became weak. He worried obsessively about what would happen to him when he returned home but then he would sink into a dark indifference as he realized how little he cared about life now that Lucas was gone. Rosa would leave food outside the bedroom that he would take into his room and put in a plastic bag until night would fall, then he would take it out back and toss it over the fence into the brush. Somehow the room itself gave him the only company he cared for. Even if Lucas' bed was empty it still had some sort of anchoring assurance about it.

Thursday morning came. Later in the day his grandparents, uncles, aunts and cousins would be flying to Portland… without him. There had been many phone calls since the initial call home and the back and forth had been extensive and draining for both sides; Danny was flat out unwilling to come home and in a stable, patient voice he told this to everybody in no less than 20 separate calls. Rich, Tanner and Celia had seemed to come to terms with it early on but Rodney and the girls were more persistent and they had strong points, none more compelling than,

"You're going to throw away your wrestling career." Which was as true as it was terrifying. He had never pondered life as *Danny-who-used-to-be-good-at-wrestling*, but the fear of years in prison outweighed his fear of normalcy, and his mind had been made up, he was staying in Rio.

Rich's firm would act as legal representation even though, strangely enough, as of Wednesday afternoon there still hadn't been charges filed by the Ramey's family attorney. Nevertheless, Detective O'Connell had been hovering like a determined mosquito that couldn't be slapped away. Blunt, arrogant and insensitive in his self-importance. Tanner was finally able to put a face to the voice when O'Connell abruptly rang the doorbell on Tuesday morning at the Sheppard house. He was as heavy as he sounded. Bald, sweaty, and seemingly enamored with himself and his title of Detective judging by his proudly displayed badge on his belt.

He harped the severity of the damage Danny had done so repetitively that it almost seemed as though Trevor Ramey were his own son. Rich put him in his place on Wednesday morning when he showed up unannounced for a second time. He asked the disgruntled meatball of a man for some respect and privacy, reminding him that they were grieving a loss of their own. When that wasn't enough for him, Rich asked him if he thought Police Chief Warren—whom Rich had known for years—would think his actions were appropriate and necessary. That shut him up quickly and he left the house in a way that made it clear that he wouldn't be back without at least calling beforehand. There was nothing he could do but wait for Danny to come home.

Tanner had called three times and although he hadn't been to Brazil yet (plans of a visit had been in the making for years) Rosa always knew exactly who it was when she answered the phone. She liked hearing from Tanner and had listened to his voice change over the summer months of the years past. Occasionally, when the boys weren't around to take his call, Rosa would patch together some English and Tanner would do his best with his Portuguese and they would talk to each other for a few minutes about simple things. Even over the phone and in a foreign language that he barley spoke he had the same likability. Rosa felt as though she knew Tanner quite well.

He and Danny had a lot to talk about but their calls that week never lasted more than ten minutes and they were straight to the important stuff; what was being discussed at home, who was taking everything the hardest, what the police and detectives were saying, whether or not their friends had heard about the fight (they hadn't), what Coach Avery from OSU and Tanner had talked about.

Three to four calls for Danny came from Portland everyday.

Whoever was calling would talk to Edson or Rosa for a few minutes before the inevitable request,

"Can you go down and get Danny?" They already knew he was in the symmetry of the bedroom. When a call came for him it had become custom for Edson and Rosa to move to the balcony at the front of the house, leaving him in privacy as he sat on the low stool next to the computer and phone desk. In new words, he would assure them that he was okay—that everything would be okay, but that he wasn't going to come home.

— — -

After another restless night tossing and turning in the sweaty throws of half-sleep he lay on his back staring at the ceiling while his Beats by Dre played crystal clear J. Cole lyrics into his ears. He had been alternating between silence and music. Of the 72 hours that he had spent in the room he had either lay in bed or sat on the floor with his back against the wall. He only emerged to take a call, fill his water bottle, or go to the bathroom.

It was 6:30 a.m. He was wide-awake but had his headphones on and didn't hear the door open above his head. He flinched when Paulo's upside down face appeared over him. He pulled off his headphones just in time to hear,

"Sair de cama. Vamos dançar." It wasn't a question—it was happening; Paulo was already heading upstairs before Danny could even find words to put up a fight.

"Get up. We're going dancing." Paulo had said, which meant that they would be going to do capoeira. Even though his conscious had been unaware and numb to the restlessness, he discovered that his body was eager to do something active.

Paulo chose the beach over the studio and they threw their shirts in the sand, and stretched in silence. Uncle Paulo could fold himself in half at the waist, stick one of his feet behind his head while balancing on the other and a number of other stretches that made his limbs appear rubber. Danny couldn't possibly pick a favorite uncle but the opportunity to spend time with Paulo was never something he wanted to pass up.

Paulo was carved by Brazilian culture and tradition. It was easy to see that his wiry muscular body came from somewhere other than the gym. Black hair thinly covered his tan and sun-spotted core, his gangly arms were lean and powerful with intense veins. He was at once intellectual and cultured but with an air of a competitive badass. His thin black hair was cut short and greying above the ears, his face wise and handsome like a youthful Edson. When he wore the traditional white capoeira and jiu-jitsu gi Danny couldn't help but be reminded of Gandhi.

It was 82 degrees at Copacabana. The sun was rising above the green mountaintops at the north end of the beach. A group of teenage boys in shorts and backwards caps juggled a soccer ball nearby, talking about the events of the night before. Danny's forehead was glistening before they had even started. They walked into the golden light of the sunrise and started with slow ginga movements, finding their balance, hopping from foot to foot, forward and backward in triangular patterns. Eventually Danny spun a kick through the air. Paulo responded with an *aú aberto*, an *open cartwheel*. He dug his heels into the sand again, inhaling on the combination of salt and city. Very gradually the movements became more extreme, flips and kicks were more frequent and exaggerated, it was a practice in patience and awareness: growing faster and stronger but with the right tempo. They attracted the attention of several beach-goers.

After ten minutes Danny was dripping with sweat. He stopped and plopped himself in the sand, breathing heavily. Paulo continued on his own for a few minutes longer before joining Danny.

"É bom para trás?" Paulo asked, looking over at his nephew.

Good to be back?

"It's going to be strange without him here."

They stared at the ocean in silence. "We are all still in shock. Life can be so random, so inconsiderate." Paulo's voice was raspy and hinted at tears. He was devastated for his little sister. Nothing more was said before Paulo hopped to his feet, brushed off his pants, and held out a hand to hoist Danny up. They began again, this time more independently of one another; Danny's movements were profound and more energetic, almost angry: waves crashing on the shore. Paulo was more languid, one movement leading poetically into the next, his cart-wheel moves slow and controlled: a lazy stream flowing over smooth mountain stones.

They went longer this time and when it was over they high-fived and fell into a back slapping hug. As they gathered their shirts and shoes and headed to the car Paulo stopped Danny with a firm grip on his shoulder.

"I won't let you stay in that room all day. I know it seems impossible, but you need to stay active, and I have arranged something. We are going there now."

Danny felt suddenly irritation but then the same subconscious relief took over, he knew Paulo was right and whatever it was, it was for the best. They drove for twenty minutes, ending up in the Comte Valho favela at the foot of the mountain on which Christ the Redeemer stood, a rough neighborhood. Paulo pulled to the curb in front of a cin-derblock warehouse with a rounded metal pavilion roof. There were no windows, just two side-by-side garage doors like eyes facing the street. The buildings that continued along the street were stucco and brick; some finished, some unfinished, as well as a few abandoned foundations with rebar sticking from the tops of the hip height cinder blocks. Stray dogs wandered the crumbling curbs and cobblestone beneath the maze of zigzagging power lines. Music blasted from a parked car down the street in front of a shop. A few big guys in tattered tank tops and sandals leaned against it, eyeing the two of them suspiciously. Danny stared back with a confrontational pull of the eyebrow until they looked away.

Paulo opened the chain link gate as if he owned the place and led the way through the narrow walkway between the warehouse and the building next to it. Danny could hear the noise from inside; he knew what this place was.

Behind the building seven-foot brick walls slick with moss boxed in a crude platform of concrete that caved to a drain in the center. Copper shower pipes, three across from three, stuck up on either side.

Paulo walked in the back door confidently, someone was obviously expecting them. Just inside a long narrow corridor with cubbies and lockers ran the whole width of the building. Shoes, shirts stuck out and gym bags littered the floor beneath the scattered benches. It was musty and sweaty like a wrestling locker room but with a distinctly favela tinge of something sour.

Paulo opened the next door and the previously muffled noises burst into clarity. It was loud; the thumps of bodies on mats, coaches shouting instructions and the metal clattering of weights. Danny's suspicion was confirmed; it was a mixed martial arts gym. Somewhere in a hazy, distant part of his memory from a not entirely sober late night dinner conversation he recalled Paulo speak about a friend with a gym and doing capoeira with young fighters there.

The scene mesmerized Danny. All of a sudden he was six years old again at his first wrestling lesson, Rich leading him by the hand and pointing him to the mat where other boys gathered around an instructor. His heart fluttered with the same nerves and childish giddiness. Every inch of the gym was alive. On the far wall six fighters lined up in their underwear, waiting their turn to step on a scale while a coach examined a clipboard and tapped the meter until he had the right weight. In the far corner was what looked to be an official sized octagon where heavily padded fighters sparred at what looked to be 80 percent intensity while a coach in a baseball cap holding a stopwatch pushed them, "Ataque, ataque Gio. Cubra agora! Recuar. Bom, bom."

On the left side of the gym, six punching bags hung from the ceiling beams, three of them being pummeled by the biggest guys in the gym—the heavyweights, Danny assumed. Blue mats covered nearly a quarter of the whole gym on the side of the bags and several pairs of fighters were grappling at 50 percent intensity. The entire right side of the gym was free weights and platforms with bars and plates scattered about. It was a beautiful scene.

An impatient Paulo jerked Danny from his trance, "Danilo!" he shouted as if he had already called his name three times. He stood in the doorway of the office directly to the right. Danny had been so mesmerized by the gym that he hadn't even noticed it.

"Sorry," he stammered, stepping through the doorway. There was too much in the office not to stare. A dusty film coated the photos on the shelf above the desk. Trophies were crowded on a higher shelf—for storage more than display. It had been somebody's office for a long time. Several empty coffee cups sat on the sill of the window that looked out at the gym and the desktops were crowded with stacks of folders and notebooks.

In the weeks and months after Lucas' death there would be a handful of moments—Rodney's silhouette in the coliseum tunnel, Trevor Ramey's red truck in the rear-view mirror, Dre scrolling down her Twitter feed on the couch—that would be branded into Danny's memory for life. That morning, he walked into the office of Marlos Vieira and saw yet another unforgettable snapshot in time.

The man leaned back in a low office chair. At once he reminded Danny of an older version of his dad. It wasn't their appearance; they didn't look alike aside from the goatee and mustache they both wore. It was their demeanor. They both had the same daunting air of serious-ness that spoke a clear message: this man is not to be crossed.

His tanned skin was leathered and freckled from time in the sun. His faded blue button down was lazily opened three buttons from the top. With his grey and white hair slicked back he had the air of a weary fish-erman at the end of a bar in Key West, but with a silent magnitude that belonged in a monastery. He was maybe in his early sixties, a little over-weight but still limber and formerly strong, presumably a fighter himself.

He first reminded Danny of Rich, then of Andrea by the way the outsides of his eyes drooped. He may have had some distant Japanese heritage, which would make sense as he radiated a sobering no-non-sense Mr. Miagi demand for respect. He said nothing and didn't make a move for an introduction but his eyes shifted slowly from Paulo to Danny and back to Paulo while Danny felt a silent communication pass between the two of them; *I see what you mean.*

Paulo was the first to speak, "Marlos, this is my nephew, Danilo."

After an uncomfortable pause Danny took a few awkward steps across the office to shake Marlos' hand even though he hadn't offered it. His grip was firm. Danny then stepped back and Marlos folded his arms across his chest, "How is your Portuguese?" he asked, so far seeming disinterested.

"It's good. I grew up here." Marlos looked at Paulo for confirmation. "A few months a year." Paulo clarified.

Marlos continued, "Your uncle tells me that you are good on the ground, a wrestler." His Portuguese had a subtle accent that Danny hadn't heard before and didn't know what it meant in terms of where he was from.

Danny nodded confidently.

"Are you any good?" Danny nodded again. Judging by Marlos' lack of expression Danny guessed that Paulo had already told him about his wrestling.

Without making any attempt to hide it, Marlos studied Danny up and down.

"How much do you weigh?"

"One hundred and eighty pounds—eighty four kilograms." He corrected himself.

Marlos nodded and seemed to be mulling something over in his head. Then unexpectedly he said, "You can train with the light heavyweights. We have three—all training for fights in the next two months. From what your uncle told me you're not interested in fighting but you're welcome to train here until you prove yourself useless. The only rule we have here is that you show respect to everybody."

Without being told, Danny already understood that this was a privilege—an honor even. Maybe Marlos owed Paulo a favor—it had sounded more like a compromise than an invitation but Danny felt very grateful.

"Thank you." He said waiting for something more to be said but there was nothing so he turned and left the office, eager to look out at the activity on the gym floor. Paulo stayed behind to exchange some light banter—Danny heard Marlos joke that Paulo was a master in fighting without ever actually hitting somebody. Danny took one last glance at the gym floor and was startled to see that a third of the roughly 20 fighters had paused whatever they were doing and were staring at him.

A new guy.

Edson and Rosa, Leandro, Renato, Paulo, Antônio, three wives and seven kids in total boarded a flight for Portland that afternoon. Saying goodbye to them as they headed for the airport wasn't as difficult as Danny had anticipated, there was no final convincing or pleading for him to come home; his decision to stay had been respected. He would be alone at the house for a week.

All afternoon, evening and into the night he felt excited. Paulo had been right; he couldn't carry on siting in the symmetry forever. The gym had looked like a playground, the type of place that he would put in heaven if he were the architect. He was giddy and had to get up from bed a few times and bounce on his toes and stretch.

His wrestling career was finished; he had avoided thinking about it in depth but he knew it was the truth. The thing that had identified him for so long was gone in one uncontrollable moment of rage that lasted no more than a few minutes. He had no plans of fighting, he couldn't imagine himself as a fighter. Regardless, he had been prodded into considering it every summer, mainly by Paulo and his little cousin Jadson. Jiu-jitsu and mixed martial arts were huge staples of Brazilian culture and the country was arguably the most prolific producer of talented fighters. It was a soccer country—that would never change—but MMA was extremely popular and fight posters were plastered on every corner and shop window when a big bout loomed. Even without being a fan of the sport, Danny knew the names of at least a dozen Brazilian fighters. He would never do it, though. It wasn't for him. Still, being held accountable to show up somewhere, a place to be and a time to be there, it gave him a much-needed sense of purpose.

— — —

His instructions were to be at the gym at 7 a.m. the next morning. He took an early bus to the only stop within walking distance and was there by 6:30 a.m. The back door was unlocked. There were a couple fighters stretching on the mat already but the narrow changing room area was empty. Minutes later fighters began to show up. They greeted one another warmly but when they came to Danny, they shook his hand out of common courtesy, only a few even bothered to say their name. He didn't care.

— — –

"Harder with the left, more square, more direct!" Coach Alexandre shouted.

Each weight class rotated trainers daily to get specialized training from each of the five coaches but the main trainer of the light heavyweights was Alexandre. He was less than welcoming to Danny but of course he wouldn't raise a disagreement with Marlos. He found it disrespectful to his fighters—they had worked hard to be a part of this gym. This wasn't a hobby for them. They were here to chase a dream, feed their families and make a name for themselves. It was an insult to allow some unproven kid with no paid dues to just waltz in and start training. He *did* have the body for it though; there was no denying that. Most fighters would kill for Danny's frame: long arms and legs stemming from a thick core.

The garage doors to the gym had been opened. Stray dogs roamed the street and occasionally one would wander inside but would be ushered out by a coach or fighter. Aromas of the street food being sold outside the bodega down the street wafted through the gym. Danny struck the bag with the six-punch combo that they had been training on. He could sense—and decided to ignore completely—the annoyance of the other fighters. He had the fancy Nike stuff, his Portuguese had a slight accent and he didn't have any scars or tattoos. Their best guess was that he was a rich kid with a pipe dream of fighting so he had somehow bought his way into the gym.

"No!" Alexandre shouted. He was quickly losing patience. "Rafael, show him how to do it." Rafael, a light heavyweight at 205 pounds and standing at just 5'11" stepped up to the bag and bounced on his toes before unleashing a thunderous left followed by two rights, a left and a right. Danny wasn't discouraged, and that seemed to frustrate Fred, another of the heavyweights who, with enthusiasm, had taken it upon himself to test Danny by calling him Calvin Klein and mumbling snide comments intentionally within earshot.

Even though he trained with a completely separate group, Danny had been aware of the persistent glances of a smaller fighter. He caught his name when he heard Coach Breno call for him.

Mateus.

A lightweight at 155 lbs., he wasn't taking part in the collective bullying, and while the shit talking continued among the other fighters he stayed silent, waiting patiently to be vindicated. He knew who Danny was.

Every morning, in the pre-dawn darkness of his bedroom before he took the bus to the gym, he would get on espn.com and browse the American football news. He still didn't fully understand the rules but the game fascinated him. The colors of the helmets, the names of the teams—*Dolphins, Jets, Vikings*—it had intrigued him since he was a child.

A few weeks earlier the internet had been buzzing with the news of the talented college wide receiver that died in a car accident and after Googling his name he discovered that he had a twin brother at the same University who was one of the best wrestlers in the country, then he Googled him, and found out that they had a Brazilian mother. When he saw Danny talking to Marlos on Friday morning he was in awe—he had been looking at pictures of him on his computer just days before. While all the other fighters turned spiteful and hostile of an unknown outsider coming into the gym, Mateus was eager to see what he could do.

– — -

A week went by. Danny learned that Marlos was more of a behind-the-scenes coach than he was hands-on. He hardly left his office during workouts but would periodically come out and meander through the workouts giving the occasional advice or direction. He was regarded in the most respectful and serious manner making it obvious that he was the boss of everything and had influence that stretched far outside of the gym.

The workouts were planned meticulously and carried out with intense structure. Most days Danny was the first one into the gym and he would glimpse the gathering of all the coaches in the office writing things on their clipboards while Marlos read from a notebook. Despite the other fighters trying to make Danny feel like an outcast, he thrived in the environment. He quietly went about his work, focusing on whatever it was that the coaches told him to do. He hadn't won their respect—he realized he might never do so—but his humility, work ethic and complete lack of ego had lessened the criticism a bit.

Many of them expected him to explode and show an immature temper or throw a tantrum and storm out, but it never came. In addition to his discipline, he had improved immensely in such a short amount of time. A rumor started to circulate that Marlos himself had said that Danny was good on the ground although they hadn't grappled at full intensity yet so there was no way of knowing for sure.

— — -

Every evening when Danny would call home Isabel made him promise to pray before he went to bed. It felt like a huge set of hands were strangling him every time he heard her cry on the phone. Rich was easier to talk to, but on Thursday there was bad news; charges had been pressed by Trevor Ramey's family. Rich had given the case to two of his partners at the firm. Trevor Ramey had a serious concussion, he needed surgery on his nose and eye socket, he had a total of fourteen stitches and six staples in multiple places, his jaw and one eye socket were broken but he would make a full recovery.

The girls had started to cry less and less on the phone and the day before they had lasted almost ten minutes; unimaginable a week earlier. It was always a relief to hear Tanner's voice. He made it sound like things were under control back home, always relaxed and levelheaded. Rich had put a quick end to his plan to take a semester off and stay in Portland. Andrea needed to though; she wasn't ready to go back.

She had attended University of Oregon in Eugene, another hour south of Corvallis and simply couldn't bring herself to continue. Not yet. She wanted to stay home, close to the Sheppard house. Allie had gone back to school but rarely stayed in her dorm room, making the twenty-minute drive to Eastmoreland almost every night.

Celia herself had called three times that week; it was equally calming to hear her voice. She had told Danny all about the burial and talked about how lovely it was to meet all of the Brazilian family. Her voice never quivered or got weak and her optimism was a blessing that always made Danny hang up the phone in a better mood. Three days earlier she had almost read a thought from his mind, like only Celia could do, when she said, "You need to bring a Brazilian girl home. Do that for your mother."

— — -

On Friday January 31st the handsome bald-headed figure strolled through the open garage door at the front of the gym. The moment the fighters were alerted to his presence there was an eruption of cheering and excitement from everyone, including the coaches. It was a real hero's welcome and the admiration was genuine.

"Who is that?" Danny asked Coach Breno.

With glowing approval of his own he said, "That's Gabriel Souza. He left for France in December to train with a kickboxing coach but he won the Rio Games in October. He's a light heavyweight—ninety-two kilos. Damn good fighter. Best in Rio in his weight."

All workouts stopped, the guys mobbed him, and the coaches didn't seem to mind the interruption in the least. He was a big guy, handsome and extremely athletic looking in his late twenties. A gold chain hung on his bare chest, visible under his hallway unzipped black hoodie. Through the commotion of the crowd he and Danny's eyes locked for a split second. Danny didn't mean to look as unfriendly as he did, and he saw Gabriel's smile fade a bit. They held awkwardly long eye contact before Gabriel's head was pulled into a hug from somebody.

He hung around the training that day and everybody's level

seemed to increase in an attempt to get a compliment from him. He was a benchmark for the younger fighters and appearedto be a genuinely nice guy as he made the rounds and didn't discriminate against the less-popular guys who lit up when he joked with them.

These guys love him. He must be good.

Gabriel didn't seem to have much of an ego and he wasn't loud or boisterous in the least. Danny knew that the calm, modest ones were the ones who needed to be taken most seriously. He knew because he was cut from the same cloth.

– — –

FRIDAY, FEBRUARY 7ᵀᴴ 2014

Another week passed. Still nobody had warmed to Danny and he remained an outsider in the gym. No scars. No tattoos. A pretty boy. Emerson, one of the more thick-necked heavyweights had almost pushed it too far on Wednesday and called Danny a "cadela" the Portuguese equivalent of a "bitch". Danny wouldn't step out of line, after all he was still a guest in the gym, paying his dues, but it pissed him off and he stared at Emerson with his empty eyes until he looked away. He stripped off his shorts and headed for the showers in the yard behind the gym. Emerson followed, "Daddy can't buy you technique, Calvin Klein. You couldn't connect an elbow with a blind man."

Emerson came from a tough place. His tattoos were all religious. He had earned his place in the gym and had taken exception to Danny from the very beginning, making it his own personal initiative to test him with taunts and insults.

"Don't worry Emerson, I wouldn't try to fight a blind man." Danny responded neutrally.

"That's good because he would probably knock you out." Emerson said. He knew as well as Danny that internal fighting was grounds for immediate dismissal from the gym and there was no squaring up or raised voices but he was tired of the rich kid and even more annoyed that Danny didn't seem fazed by his insults.

As soon as Danny woke on Friday morning he was wide awake and decided to get an early start, coming into the gym at 6:10 a.m., Edson and Rosa were still asleep as he tip-toed through the kitchen making his protein shake and taking his lunch out of the refrigerator.

Dust particles drifted through the rays of light that sprayed into the gym through the holes where the cinder blocks met the metal roof. Nothing was more worthy of a deep breath as an empty gym in the morning. He soaked up the silence. In the two weeks since Paulo had introduced him to Marlos, Danny had come to love the gym. It spoke directly to his Brazilian half. It wasn't fancy and clean like the gym at Oregon State. The old and new clashed all over; some of the equipment was fresh out of the box while some of it looked like it was from the seventies. The quarter of the gym floor that was covered with padding was another example brand new and some was old with long veins of duct tape piecing it all together like shifting continents. The six punching bags that hung to the left were new, new, new, old, new, old. It seemed that they were replaced on a need-to-be-replaced basis when they were blown open by a strong punch or kick.

Danny started stretching. Marlos peered out of his office window. This young man was intriguing, and not only because he was related to Paulo Silva. Marlos knew fighters. Training was his life's work. After five minutes of talking to Danny he knew he had the attitude of a champion. His physical attributes were one thing but it was his humility and his willingness to receive and analyze criticism. These things were what set him apart. Marlos had lost track of all the fighters that had destroyed themselves with ego and attitude. The body was only as strong as the mind was willing. Too many fighters didn't understand this.

Marlos saw everything that went on in his gym. He saw the fighters that turned it up a notch when he was around, he saw when someone stayed late to train on a specific defense that had been high-lighted by a coach, he saw their interactions with one another in the changing room, and since Danny had arrived, he saw that they didn't like him. He couldn't fault them for it. They had battled and worked hard to be recruited by his gym while Danny seemed to just waltz in off the street. The Nike clothes that he wore everyday didn't help. If there was one thing that working class kids didn't like it was rich kids with shortcuts.

Marlos was hopeful that after some time Danny would have a change of mind and consider fighting but it couldn't be a decision that was made reluctantly—no fighter ever found success if he wasn't absolutely devoted with his mind, body and most importantly, his heart. Even if he didn't want to fight, he was Paulo Silva's nephew, and he could stay in the gym for as long as he wanted.

— — –

Training got underway that day with Coach Marcelo reading off the three groups for the fitness test: a timed run through a series of hillside trails about two and a half miles long in Parque Lage. They would go in groups of seven; Danny was in the second group. The groups that weren't doing the run would be doing strength work at the gym.

Gabriel was having a private session in the cage with both Marlos and Breno. Marcelo and Alexandre were the coaches conducting the fitness test at the trail and Dante was doing the weight session with the remaining fighters. The weight session turned out to be more balance and core stability. The real focus of the day was the fitness test. Gabriel's workout on the other hand, was quite intense and everybody was sneaking glances.

For the first time in a while, when Danny woke up that morning he had the urge to wrestle, he wanted to go all-out and compete, he hadn't moved around on a mat in far too long. He was focusing on his balance with a ten-pound kettle bell doing an RDL when Marlos' voice ripped through the gym, "Dante! Send us Fred."

Dante scanned the fighters in front of him for a moment then glanced at his clipboard, "Fred is in the first group." Dante called back, his voice echoing off the cinder walls. "Send me a heavyweight. I need a heavyweight." Marlos called back.

Dante scanned the group once more, "Both Fred and Gio are in the first group and Ruben has a bad wrist." Ruben was right in front of Dante with his wrist taped thickly. There were mumbling deliberations that went on for a second in the octagon. Gabriel was shirtless, glistening as he leaned up against the cage. "Ok we will wait until the first group gets done, we need a grappler."

Dante threw a thumbs-up and it seemed that it was settled, until Danny spoke. The words came quick like unexpected vomit, out of his control. He had learned that it was taboo to speak directly to Marlos but something inside him had taken over and had decided to take a chance.

"I can grapple." He called over to the cage.

The cage was far enough away to force Danny to shout. The gym had already been quiet but somehow it got even quieter. Marlos turned and walked to the edge of the cage, grasping the rubber-coated chain-link and pressing an eye closer to one of the holes. While he mulled it over in the silence, the curiosity and intrigue from the fighters and coaches alike was almost thick enough to touch: *Who the fuck does this guy think he is? Why does he think he can get in the cage with Gabriel and why does he think he can talk to Marlos directly?*

"Danilo." Marlos said, as though he had finally realized who had said it. A tense pause followed before he said, "Yes. Come." Waving him over. Danny jumped to his feet eagerly and started toward the octagon. Marlos yelled back to Dante, "Bring them over here, they might learn something from this."

The kettle balls of all 13 fighters dropped to the floor and they hurried over to the cage. Danny was still hovering near 184 lbs. and he was aware that Gabriel was closer to 205 lbs., a difference that should almost certainly give Gabriel an insurmountable advantage, but he didn't care, he just felt like wrestling.

It was the first time he had stepped into the gym's octagon; it didn't feel like stepping onto the mat of a wrestling meet. He felt captured. Gabriel squeezed a water bottle and sprayed a stream of water into his mouth as he looked across at Danny. They had yet to speak to one another in the week that Gabriel had been back. He seemed relaxed, aware of the weight difference, under the assumption that this would be nothing but a beneficial exercise. Danny stripped off his shirt and tossed it over the side of the cage.

"Full intensity but no locks. No striking. Nobody gets hurt today.

Danilo I want you trying to take down Gabriel—this is training for his defense. We will work in periods of forty seconds."

The fighters shared a collective snicker at something one of them had said outside of the cage. Danny paid it no attention. He was getting close to his competitive mode, the mode that had won him a national championship. He focused on one body and nothing else. There *was* nothing else.

Mateus stood apart from the rest of he fighters with his arms folded. He had been waiting for this moment.

"Gabi?" Breno asked loudly. Gabriel nodded.

"Danilo?" Danny nodded.

"Início!"

They circled a few times like wolves positioning themselves for a bite of an elk. Danny reached a hand to the back of Gabriel's neck a few times and pulled it away as if he were touching a hot frying pan, gauging how he would react. He watched Gabriel's footwork, the subtleties of each step; it was like cracking a safe—there was always a way in, and Danny always found it. There was a reason that not a single college wrestler had been able to defeat him in two years. Gabriel wasn't going to try and take him down, he was waiting to defend and hopefully turn defense into attack. Danny had no doubts that Gabriel was a good wrestler; if nothing else he was athletic and probably close to twenty pounds heavier.

Well, fuck it.

Danny faked like he was going high, and Gabriel bit hard, standing up straighter, Danny went low and executed a perfect duck-under, lunging for his back leg. Gabriel tried hurriedly to move it back and make his center of gravity as low as possible but Danny caught it and was able to pull it forward just enough for Gabriel to have to stick his butt back just a bit. It was a pleasant surprise just how easy the next move was being made available; he wasn't defending it well at all, relying on his weight. Danny pulled his leg sideways underneath his body forcing him to bring his other leg closer and he snatched it, he now had both of Gabriel's legs wrapped in a hug, he squeezed them around the knees. Gabriel tried to make himself low but it was over, still Danny paused. He was in total control, a textbook double leg takedown. He looked at Marlos and raised his eyebrows, *Should I do it?*

Marlos gave him a gentle close of the eyes, bowing his head.

Full intensity.

Danny jerked hard and the big body collapsed onto his backside, but he wasn't done. He released his hug around Gabriel's legs and thrusting himself onto his torso while wrapping his legs around Gabriel's. It was what Allie had always referred to as the "Koala Bear move". Only 15 seconds had passed from the moment Danny went in for the back leg to the time that Gabriel was in complete submission. Marlos called them to their feet and ordered them to get a drink and stay loose. Danny scanned the crowd. There was embarrassment, confusion, some shock and even anger. They avoided eye contact, some of them tried to catch the eyes of one another for some clarity, an answer.

That was a fluke right? Did Gabriel slip?

Mateus stood out to Danny, a grin smeared across his face as he stood separately from the group. Danny found himself wilted with appreciation for the kid that he had never talked to but was the only one who had greeted him with any measure of welcoming in the mornings. Breno was speaking hushed words to Gabriel inside the cage. Marlos was far less concerned, standing outside the cage with his arms folded, his expression indifferent.

"Again. Gabriel, whenever you are ready." He said after a minute. Gabriel nodded hastily to whatever Breno was telling him then bounced on his toes a few times. There was some cheering from the side. They began again. Danny very confident now, he was home. He could see that Gabriel was shaken, overcompensating with aggression judging by the way he swatted Danny's hands away from his neck, but it wouldn't help him… Danny was too smart and too composed.

Cheers were uninhibited now from the others and even though Danny had only been in the gym for ten days, he knew this wasn't a normal occurrence. Gabriel, eager not to let his peers down, tried to go low and grab a leg. Danny pushed him down by the shoulders and jumped back. Gabriel got back to his feet and they started circling again. Danny almost felt sorry for him, he didn't stand a chance as he lunged in for a leg but could only catch Danny behind the knee of his front leg. This was supposed to be training for Gabriel to defend takedowns but it seemed Marlos just wanted to see some grappling now.

Danny wrapped his arms through Gabriel's armpits clasping his hands together over his chest, then he pushed his legs back forcing Gabriel to let go of the back of his knee. Just as he had the first time, he looked over at Marlos, but this time he didn't seem to understand; the first time it was clear what Danny would do, but this time Marlos didn't see the potential for a takedown. To Marlos' credit, this was not a normal takedown and he looked back with what Danny took to be permission.

Proceed.

He allowed Gabriel to get one arm loose so that he now had him locked in his grasp around the head and armpit. Danny started walking backward for momentum, fooling Gabriel into standing up straighter…

Nobody knew what was coming, it was a rarely seen takedown and Danny wasn't even sure if he was strong enough to pull it off but he was going to try anyway. It was a highlight-reel move, seen mostly on YouTube, never really in person and would be humiliating for Gabriel. Danny questioned whether or not to go through with it but he wanted to see if he could do it.

As he walked backward taking Gabriel with him his cheeks inflated and then let out a sharp exhale as he exploded backwards, flipping Gabriel clean over his head. The roughly 200 pound body flew through the air, crashing thunderously onto the floor. The room was stunned; there were stunned cries of shock and amazement from the fighters. They couldn't believe what they had just seen. Nobody could. Gabriel was the light heavyweight champion of Rio De Janeiro, and he had been manhandled not once but twice by the quiet pretty boy that nobody talked to. Danny scampered on top of Gabriel and pinned him flat on his back. The silent, invisible audience was back. They watched with excitement from all corners of the gym.

"OK! Back to training now. That's enough." Marlos shouted uncharacteristically irritated. The 13 fighters talked in hurried whispers, confused and defiant, as if what they had just seen had been a practical joke. They drifted back towards the weights, some of them casting astonished glances over their shoulders. Marlos had started towards his office with a head of steam. In a low growl directed at Danny he said,

"In my office."

Danny jumped out of the cage, regretting that he had just done what he had. Maybe he had gone too far. There was such a thing as professional courtesy and he didn't want to embarrass Gabriel but he was doing what he had been instructed to.

Maybe I crossed the line.

Marlos pointed to a chair as he pulled up his own desk chair and sat down with authority, he seemed pissed. Danny fumbled awkwardly with his hands in the short pause that ensued.

"Listen to me, Danilo." Marlos took a deep breath, "Rio is one of the most historic Jiu-Jitsu and mixed martial arts cities in the world. Gabriel is the light heavyweight champion of this city. He weighs maybe ten kilograms more than you, and you have just treated him like a toy."

Danny didn't know how to respond. He glanced away from Marlos' stare. He could hear Dante yell at the fighters, something along the lines of "Back to work…it's over. Focus." This was also something rare: a fighter meeting privately with Marlos. Danny was relieved that he wasn't in trouble. He shrugged uncomfortably. Marlos' dark eyes were narrowed, penetrating yet understanding at the same time. "I don't know what my uncle told you about me but… I—I'm just not a fighter."

"If you're not a fighter, what are you?" He asked, his voice controlled and leathery. Danny was lost for words. He didn't know how to tell him that he would never fight. It felt rude and ungrateful since he was coming to the gym, but he just wouldn't do it. "I'm a wrestler. I mean I *was* a wrestler."

It was difficult to say the words, but it was true. His wrestling days were over. Wrestling had defined him for so long but he knew it was over. He didn't know what he would do with his life now. He had been studying marine biology at OSU—he loved the ocean—but his focus would have remained on wrestling for a time after he graduated. It was, of course, his dream to compete at the Olympics and become a world champion like he and Lucas had talked about since childhood. The gym had given him a temporary sense of purpose but it hadn't been anything more than a productive distraction from reality and his troubles in Portland. No new inspiration or thoughts of fighting had sprouted in his mind.

Danny wasn't surprised by Marlos' wisdom, "You seem lost Danilo. Paulo told me that things were difficult for you right now. What is difficult?"

Danny inflated his upper lip and nodded. "Um, my brother passed away recently..." he shrugged, trying to play it off as a slight bummer and not the complete shattering of his world. Marlos' eyes didn't show empathy, but there was understanding. "How old was he?"

"He was my age—we were twins." Danny said trying as hard as possible to sound casual.

Marlos folded his arms and his brow wrinkled, "Why do you enjoy this? Why would Paulo ask me to take you in?"

Danny was relieved that the questioning had veered away from Lucas. "I like to train and be in this kind of environment. I was a wrestler before."

"Yes you said that. It would appear that you are *still* a wrestler." Marlos said, allowing a sly grin to dance across his face as he tilted his head back towards the cage. Danny glanced out through the window and noticed a few sets of eyes dart in any direction but his.

"You see Danilo, fighting is a controlled man's sport. These days it's lost under the trash-talk and the arrogance." He said waving a hand through the air as if shooing away an imaginary mosquito. "But real fighters are men of great discipline, balance and respect." Danny nodded his understanding.

"Fighters who are unbalanced always get exposed. Your wrestling and ground tactics seem quite good, but in truth, if you were sparring with Gabriel I would place a bet on Gabriel winning—it's about balance."

Danny nodded again, agreeing that he wasn't a purebred when it came to striking. "Greco-Roman wrestling is a good platform—it's better to learn that first—but if you added the locks and submission techniques of jiu-jitsu that aren't allowed in traditional wrestling it would make you into a fighter... who would be difficult to beat."

Danny felt like he was trying to be sold a car that he didn't have the money for, smiling and acting interested but inside knowing that it wasn't even an option; he wouldn't be buying the car, he wasn't going to fight. It wasn't easy to say *No*. He left the office with an unconvincing, "I'll give it some thought."

— — —

Danny dug his feet into the sand then raised them and watched it sift through his toes. His thoughts were on the event of the morning, tossing Gabriel through the air. It didn't give him any high or sense of accomplishment—if anything he was still a bit embarrassed but he knew it would buy him respect. He'd started spending his afternoons at the beach. Sitting on a towel in the sand with his sunglasses on and his headphones in. His thoughts roamed but were always tethered to Lucas. He missed him so much.

He thought about how much Lucas would have loved the gym. In barely two weeks it had already become something Danny couldn't imagine being without. Who knows how long it might have taken him to get out of the symmetry of the bedroom if Paulo hadn't dragged him from it. Every day training seemed to be over too soon and the hours afterward were nothing but sluggish chunks of time that he just wanted to pass so he could go to sleep that night, wake up and go back to training: the two and a half hours when everything else was kept at a distance.

Now he tried to pass a couple hours each day at the beach listening to music and staring out at the ocean, sometimes doing a little capoeira on his own. Usually when he returned to his grandparent's house he would sit with Edson and Rosa on the balcony while Edson smoked his evening cigarette as the sun set, but they were still in Portland and wouldn't be back for another three days.

The connection to Lucas that he felt while at the beach was similar to being in the bedroom. They had spent countless nights there over the years with their aunts, uncles, cousins and grandparents. It was a special place, and as Danny was soon to find out, special things happen in special places.

"Blame Game" by Kanye West with John Legend was playing in his headphones. He would remember that and even listening to the song years later would give him nostalgic goose bumps. It was a chance encounter that just as easily could have been missed altogether. When he saw her for the first time, his heart sped up but time slowed down.

He sat 20 yards from the boardwalk—which itself was the first piece of chance since he usually sat much closer to the water. Then he heard a laugh. It sounded just like Tanner's laugh and as he spun around he saw a group of four guys close to his age laughing at something as they walked along the boardwalk. It was uncanny just how similar a laugh it was to Tanner's, who was almost 7,000 miles away. Just as he started to turn his head back towards the water he did the most dramatic double-take. Everything about her was crystal clear. She was high definition and everything around her was static and blurry. Time was slow.

He was transfixed. She strolled down the boardwalk in dark sunglasses. He was wearing sunglasses too but for a moment he could feel their eyes locked on one another. She walked behind him and he shamelessly turned his head to look over his other shoulder. He continued to watch her until she was out of sight. He found himself in need of a deep breath.

What the fuck?

— — —

Mateus hadn't stopped thinking about what he had seen that morning. Danny Sheppard, the American wrestler, had just tossed Gabriel— *Gabriel Souza*—through the air like he was a child. The other fighters were shocked, but not Mateus. He liked Gabriel as much as the next guy but for some reason he was put in a good mood by the spectacle and decided to stop at the corner bar before going home. It was Friday and there was no training the next day, he had one of the best times on the trail run, and his weight was well under control, he deserved a beer.

At Bar Patricio everybody was a local; the old-timers, the street-hard guys, the middle-age gossiping women, Mateus knew everybody and they all knew him. He sat by himself in the middle of the bar and was greeted by Alda's warm smile as soon as she came around the corner from the back.

"Mateus! Monthly beer time?" she joked as she stretched across the bar for a kiss on the cheek. He had the support and encouragement of the whole neighborhood, an honest kid who had worked hard since his youth and been offered a spot in Marlos Vieira's gym.

"Monthly? Feels like longer." He said with a grin. Alda poured him a cold Heineken before he had asked for it. He was mid-sip when the Soares brothers walked through the door: unbuttoned shirts and shaggy hair, cheesy grins, sun-kissed skin and stoned eyelids from a long day at the beach. As soon as they saw him the jokes began, "Whoa whoa whoa! The superstar in the flesh!" Said Alan Soares.

"Yeah it's the superstar and he can't be seen with low-lives like you guys!" Mateus joked as he stood to hug them; he hadn't seen the brothers in a few months but he had known them since childhood. Life for them was only as important as the last CR Flamengo soccer game or the upcoming UFC bout.

"How's life my friend?" Marco Soares asked as he and Alan settled onto stools on either side of Mateus. "Everything is good. Life has been kind to me lately, all thanks to God. What about you guys?"

They talked and laughed, mostly updates about friends that Mateus hadn't seen in a while. The brothers had finished three beers by the time Mateus decided to order a second. Alda was in and out of their conversation, adding bits and pieces of her own neighborhood knowledge as she bustled around taking care of other patrons and restocking glasses.

"How's training?" Alan asked with excitement, clasping a hand on Mateus' shoulder, he had been itching to ask. The brothers showing up had interrupted Mateus' reminiscing of what he had seen that afternoon. With the mention of training, he was immediately thrust back into the scene from the morning's training, and the Soares boys, who knew all about Gabriel Souza, would be just as blown away.

"You guys are never going to believe this…"

As Mateus played the details over in dramatic fashion, their eyes grew as big as their heavy eyelids would allow and their voices seemed to fail them—it was impossible to imagine *Gabriel Souza* being tossed through the air as Mateus described. "I swear to you. The gym went silent. I knew he was good at wrestling though because I had seen him on the internet—on ESPN. His brother was…"

Mateus continued while the Soares brothers listened with wide eyes. They were all so wrapped up in the story that none of them noticed that they had gained another audience member. At the far end of the bar, a street guy with an unkempt afro and a slanted scar over his left eye had begun to listen just as intently.

— — —

Danny had gotten comfortable. He was lying on his back, looking at the ceiling, at times talking with his hands. He could feel Jenna's interest as he spoke. By the time he finished telling her about the day he wrestled Gabriel it was 12:30 a.m. It had been a while since she spoke but she asked, "Did that change things? When you beat Gabriel?"

"Like the flip of a switch." He said, snapping his fingers.

— — —

Monday came again. As the fighters started to filter into the changing room Danny was greeted in an entirely new way; respectful nods and head flicks, actual handshakes, at the very least eye contact and acknowledgment from everybody. All of a sudden he was respected. From rich pretty boy who couldn't punch for shit to the real deal, a wrestler who may have even been *recruited* by Marlos. They were still nervous to talk to him or perhaps too proud and unwilling to own their mistake, but Danny didn't fault them for that. He had, after all, made them all look like fools.

Gabriel was still there and although they still hadn't exchanged any words it didn't seem that he was either embarrassed or had any ill feelings towards Danny; he was a consummate professional. As fighters started to mill out onto the gym floor, the kid who had been casting glances at him all week walked up confidently, "Hey. I'm Mateus." Extending his callous-rough hand.

"Danilo." He said surprised, a little bit taken aback by the sudden introduction. "It was really impressive what you did on Friday. Gabriel is a very good fighter."

"Yeah that's what I've heard. I guess I got lucky." Danny said. Mateus laughed. His expression stiffened up when he realized Danny hadn't meant it as a joke.

"There's no need to be modest, my friend. I know who you are." Mateus said as if he had foiled the plan, cracked the code, *the jig is up.*

"Yeah?" Danny said uninterested, looking down as he tied the drawstring of his shorts. "Yeah. So I know you didn't get lucky. Also... I'm sorry about your brother."

"5 minutes!" Breno shouted from the doorway to the gym. Danny nodded without looking up. He finished tying his shorts and gave Mateus a hearty pat on the chest as he walked past him and headed to the gym with the crowd, "Nice to meet you man."

– — –

Danny couldn't put his finger on what it was that made her so special but now when he went to the beach after training he was high on the mere hope of seeing her again. He now looked forward to the beach almost as much as training itself. In hindsight, he felt foolish for letting her walk by but something inside him was certain that he would see her again.

Mateus had been going out of his way to make bits of conversation with Danny since introducing himself. He had the buzzing admiration of a little brother and on Wednesday he tagged along to the beach, casually walking with Danny to the bus stop after training. He reminded Danny of a superhero's sidekick; eager to respond to whatever Danny said and sometimes he began nodding in agreement or understanding before Danny even finished a thought.

EDDY PRUGH

He was from Vidigal, a hillside favela with stunning, scenic views of Rio. A few months earlier he had moved into his own apartment near the neighborhood where he grew up. He was 19. He explained that he made a little bit of money from fighting but hadn't yet had a pro fight.

"I'm the youngest fighter in the gym." He said, chin high with earnest pride. "I'm very proud of that. Marlos thought I was ready earlier than anybody else. You know, he won't get you a fight until he knows that you are ready for it—I know *I* won't get a fight for another year at least. It's hard to wait around but I trust Marlos."

Fighters in the gym were always hungry for a chance to prove themselves but Marlos would make their desire fester and evolve, he would make them watch other fighters get a fight, and win. He watched their eyes; he needed to see the hunger and the love. It was a privilege, Mateus explained, and Marlos wouldn't get any of his fighters a fight, old or young, until they had earned it.

"Was he a fighter?" Danny asked.

"He was but he had a bad injury early in his career. He loves the sport though. He's one of the best in the world but he doesn't promote himself, that's why there's never been a world champion from the gym." Mateus explained.

In the almost three weeks that Danny had spent in the gym, he had done what was in his nature to do: observe. Something that he saw in just the first couple days was that Mateus was a talented fighter and got more compliments from the coaches than anybody else. They sat on a concrete picnic table near the boardwalk and slung their shirts over their shoulders. Girls smiled as they passed, Mateus noticed them and usually gave them a polite turn of the mouth but Danny was oblivious. The topic of conversation turned to Danny not wanting to fight. It was impossible for Mateus to wrap his mind around it.

"You could make a lot of money you know? There are fighters who have never even left Rio and have made enough money to retire. You're definitely good enough to make it in one of the big promotions—at least *I* think you are."

"You've seen me—I can't punch or kick." Danny said solely for the sake of Mateus' interest. Shrugging his shoulders and holding his palms up Mateus argued, "You can win however you want—it's not boxing. Of course you have weaknesses but you have actually improved a lot since being here—you still can't defend the body punch but it will come."

Danny was hardly invested in the conversation and vaguely said, "Fighting just isn't my thing I guess." His thoughts were on the girl.

Mateus sucked his teeth in disgust, shaking his head. The next topic to come up was American football. It was difficult to discuss without bringing up Lucas, but they managed—Mateus was respectful and didn't dare mention him.

He listened intently to whatever Danny had to say about the game. As far as he was concerned any American was an expert on the sport. The rules and intricacies of offense and defense were fascinating to him. Danny was impressed by Mateus' obvious desire to soak up whatever he said and his hunger for knowledge shed more light on why he was one of the best in the gym: he was eager to learn.

"You don't have a girlfriend?" Mateus said with ironic timing as Danny had just slipped into a daydream—watching her walk down the boardwalk.

"No, I don't. You?"

"Yeah man of course. Isabel."

Danny scoffed, "That's my mom's name."

"That's good! Deep footprints make strong futures." And with that, he hopped up abruptly and shook Danny's hand. "See you in the morning man." He hadn't stayed more than half an hour.

For the next five minutes, Danny mulled over the last thing he had said,

"Pegadas profundas fazem futuros fortes."

Deep footprints make strong futures.

He had never heard it before but it had to have been a saying. The way Mateus said it was too fluid and familiar to be something he had made up on the spot—unless he was a poet in his free time.

A joyful homeless man with sun-leathered skin and more gums than teeth collected a red bull can from under the picnic table. As he stuffed the can into his garbage bag he looked up and smiled big. Danny smiled back as the man shuffled away.

Next he thought about the way Mateus had sucked his teeth at him. He knew that from a Catholic perspective it was a tragedy: wasting the amazing talents that God had gifted him. Lately, Danny didn't feel like he owed much to God but he still tried to count his blessings before bed. It was hard to feel appreciation for anything in the current state of his life, but he tried.

"My life is fucked up." He said to himself in English. "Minha vida está fodida." He repeated in Portuguese. He wasn't even allowed to stay in one vein of misery; he had to alternate between grief from Lucas and worry for his legal situation back home. Anytime he indulged in a moment of self-pity, it was quickly overridden by self-chastising. After the way he had run away from his family, he knew he didn't deserve even a moment of commiseration.

The thought pestered him constantly and no matter how things unfolded in the future, he knew that he would likely never forgive himself for leaving his family like he had. Just as he felt the familiar downward spiral of sadness, there was a presence. To his right there was a familiar glow. He looked up. There she was.

She moved slowly with her iPod headphones in her ears, the same as his. He felt as though he was back on center stage and for the invisible audience, a narrator spoke slowly:

And so entered the mysterious girl right when he was at an impassable wall of hopelessness. Why she was so alluring, he did not know...but he wanted to find out.

Time slowed down again. Her shiny black shoulder-length black hair swayed gently around her neck. She wore a long navy blue skirt and a white tank top, a casual outfit for a walk down the beach while listening to music.

She walked with a balanced, docile confidence. Even though she moved slowly, she was still closing in too fast, Danny couldn't think. He had obsessed over seeing her again but he hadn't put enough thought into what he might actually say if he did. The lump in his throat was hard to swallow as he scrambled to put his shirt on. Her hips swayed slowly under the dress, she was relaxed but Danny's nerves vibrated—he didn't know what he would say. He took a deep breath, and started to walk towards her as coolly as he could but his legs felt wobbly and unsteady. The narration continued,

He nervously approached the girl he had been thinking about, she was even more beautiful than he remembered. He couldn't believe his luck to see her again.

He still didn't know what he would say but he was certain of one thing; he couldn't let her walk by again without saying something. When he came to within a few yards of her he caught her attention with a little wave and waited for her to take her headphones off.

"Sorry to stop you but I saw you here on Friday." He said, hopeful that she would say the same, but she didn't say anything. She expected him to continue. He shrugged awkwardly. She smiled politely, if not a bit confused. "What are you listening to?" He asked.

Her voice was easy going and sure of itself. "It's classic American rap music. Talib Kweli is his name." She said almost apologetically, as if to say *Sorry, you wouldn't know him.*

Oh thank Jesus. Danny thought, suddenly growing in optimism, "Oh. *Just to get by?*" He asked, switching to English with a sheepish grin, praying that she would understand the reference. She had politely taken off her sunglasses and her big brown eyes looked at him confused for a moment before melting into a smile.

"Ah you know him?" She said with surprise.

Danny couldn't quite describe what he felt at that moment but if he had to try he would say that it felt like his heart had smiled.

"So you like hip hop?" He asked.

She shrugged, "I like words—poetry."

"Even if it's in English?"

"Sometimes *especially* if it's in English. I understand most of it but it's not just about the words." She shrugged again with a beautiful smirk; *I don't expect you to understand.* But Danny felt like he understood perfectly.

"Well I didn't mean to interrupt you. I enjoy walking and listening to music myself so I will let you continue. I just wanted to say hello."

"I'm Danilo." He said.

"Nina." She said coolly. He reached forward, smiling sheepishly, and enveloped her soft, small hand in his. As he stood alone in the middle of the boardwalk, watching her white Chuck Taylors stroll away from him, he could sense that she enjoyed the randomness of the brief exchange. Something had clicked between them in a few magical seconds, and everybody had seen it, the whole invisible crowd. The way her eyes had changed when she suddenly understood his *Just to get by*, reference.

Asking for her phone number would have ruined the moment. There would be another chance. He didn't know why he was so confident of it, but he just knew he would be seeing her again.

Nina.

He said her name softly as he stared out the window on the evening bus home.

— — —

In the small office at the back of the bar in the hillside favela, a man with a slanted scar over his eye stood respectfully before a brittle old man sitting at a desk. Smoke rose from the cigar in the tray on the desk. A gaudy military portrait of a younger version of the old man loomed large on the wall directly behind the desk. Large men stationed on either side of it watched the man with the scar even though he had already been frisked upon entering the bar. The old man took the cigar from the tray and stuck it in the side of his mouth. He nodded his head, granting the man his attention.

"He's light skinned—half American I heard. Somehow he got a spot in Marlos Vieira's gym and the rumor that's going around is that he was grappling with Gabriel Souza and threw him through the air with some incredible technical takedown."

The scar over his eye danced and twitched as he spoke. He had never actually seen the boss with his own eyes but now, in the dim bar through clouds of cigar smoke he saw exactly the man he had imagined. Skinny to the point of being described as frail but being flanked by such massive bodyguards made it trivial. He had a thin moustache and sharp cheekbones. His skin was tanned and hung loosely below his eyes, his grey hair slicked back with oil. He was maybe in his late sixties.

Upon hearing that some kid had "tossed" Gabriel Souza through the air, the old man's brow wrinkled with suspicion, he had difficulty believing it. The man with the scar saw this and elaborated, "I heard Mateus Peres talking about it at the bar and it's been confirmed by two other fighters. They said it was amazing. I know it does not seem possible but it is true. He pinned Gabriel two times. They say he is a Greco-Roman specialist."

The boss sat motionless, eyes angled toward the pool table as smoke rose from the amber of his cigar. "I suppose…I would like to see for myself." He said sticking the cigar back in the corner of his mouth. The man with the scar knew what that meant. He wasn't going to ask about the money, he trusted that it would be a handsome bounty. As he turned to leave the boss called after him, "Tell us your name."

The man turned to face him once again, "My name is Donadel."

— — —

The next few days were the closest Danny had been to normalcy since Lucas died. His grandparents and uncles had returned from Portland. He helped Rosa cook dinner in the evenings and played soccer with his little cousin Jadson in the afternoons after coming home from the beach. At training he joked with Mateus during water breaks—who it turned out was a great friend to have; well respected in the gym and the community—he had started to remind Danny more and more of Tanner. He had his first social outing since Lucas died, going with Mateus and a few of the younger fighters to watch a welterweight bout with one of the fighters from Marlos' gym, Ismael, in his professional debut. He had won.

It still weighed on him like a wet blanket that he was on borrowed time and sooner or later he would have to go home and face the consequences and inevitably, some time in jail.

Rio was kicking into high gear for Carnival celebrations. People came from all over the world to celebrate and the festivities were starting to kick into high gear now that it was just days away. On Friday there was a music festival at Praia Ipanema, perhaps Rio's second most historically significant beach after Copacabana. Danny and Mateus met at a bar near Rocinha a couple hours beforehand. The night was beautiful as the sun set on the white sand and green water. The boys wore sandals as they strolled the boardwalk. The distant beating of drums and cheering gave Danny a nostalgic feeling of approaching a football game in Corvallis.

The boys made their way through the crowds, occasionally stopping to talk to acquaintances of Mateus. Everybody seemed to light up when they saw him. Danny was introduced to fighting enthusiast friends who became formal and overly respectful, it seemed as though his reputation had preceded him. He did his best to act cordial and friendly but his thoughts were elsewhere. He knew the chances were slim at such a large event but he still scanned the crowd for Nina.

Aromas of street food, popcorn, and firework smoke combined for a distinctly carnival aroma. In the distance, a man yelled into a bullhorn provoking loud applause and cheering. Anywhere Danny looked he saw smiles and laughs; children playing with soccer balls in the sand, adolescent groups of skinny guys in tank tops and flat billed Yankees, Phillies, and Dodgers hats acting cool as could be and their counterparts wearing short skirts and brightly painted fingernails, trying equally hard.

He had never been in Rio for Carnival, he was always in school during the time of year but Isabel had come down a few times to celebrate with her family. Still, he had been to many beach festivals with Lucas and Taison and the rest of his family over the years.

At 12:15 a.m. when the festival was in full swing Mateus met three middle-aged women who were friends of his mom. Danny introduced himself politely and was mid sentence, explaining that his grandparents lived in Rio and he was visiting from the United States when something caught his attention. It was strange because there was so much colorful commotion going on all around them but a small glint of shiny, clean silver almost called to him. He turned his head and almost gasped, it was Nina. Once again, she seemed to be in high definition while everything around her was dull. He excused himself as politely as he could and hurried after her.

She was in a group of four girls moving up the beach. He loved the two syllables of her name and he spoke her name in his mind as he gave chase.

Nina.

He hadn't seen her face but he knew it was her. He saw her slender neck and smooth skin, her shoulders exposed above a turquoise halter-top. Her black hair was twisted into a casual but elegant bun and her long silver and turquoise earrings that had caught his attention swayed with her steps. Amidst the chaos she moved like water, effortlessly. Danny sprang into action so suddenly that at first Mateus thought there was trouble. He twisted and turned through the crowd, racing not to lose her, following the turquoise and silver of her earrings that appeared and disappeared like fish scales in water.

He was getting closer but she was slicing through the crowd better than he was able to and by the haste that she and her friends were moving it seemed they had somewhere to be. It was like trying to chase a snake through the underbrush. Mateus didn't have a clue what could be so important as he raced to keep up.

Finally a small clearing in the crowd gave Danny a clear sighting, she was maybe 15 yards ahead of him and he took the opportunity of open space to make up ground. Speed walking and even breaking into a little jog for a few strides he pressed through the huddles, bits and pieces of conversations flying past him; *Yeah but he was only on the field for the second goal—She just started but it shouldn't be much longer—Just call me before it's gone I want to see it.*

He made his way around a group of teenage girls squishing together and throwing up piece signs for a picture when the flash went off. He threw his hand up but it was too late, he was blinded. He blinked rapidly while still pressing forward through the crowd, but he didn't see the turquoise anywhere. He turned in circles, frantically searching for the shine of the earrings, the smooth skin, but she was gone.

Frustration and pessimism took over. Even though he had seen her three times in the space of ten days he now felt like that was all the luck he would have. It was reminiscent of the time he had lost his sunglasses in the ocean; they were so close but in a second they could have been anywhere.

Mateus caught up to him, he let his confused expression ask the question. "I lost her." Danny said as if Mateus would know what he was talking about. He linked his fingers on top of his head, still searching the crowd hopefully. "Who?" Mateus asked, turning and looking through the crowd himself. "A girl I met on the beach the other day— the day you were with me, like right after you left. An angel, I swear."

Mateus smiled, "She'll be around man." He was only trying to be optimistic as he could see Danny was seriously discouraged, but Danny felt as though she had been swept away forever.

"Maybe you'll see her again at the beach or something you know it's…" Mateus was saying but Danny was in a different world, staring at the silver and turquoise earrings. She and her friends were talking impatiently it seemed to a muscly guy in a tank top. They were still trying to go somewhere. Danny rushed away from Mateus in the middle of his encouraging words.

The group of girls had politely shirked the attention of the body-builder guy when Danny was ten yards away and they started off again. "Nina!" He called out. She turned. She smiled. Danny's heart smiled. He hoped it wasn't just wishful thinking but she seemed genuinely excited to see him.

"Danilo!" She said in her smooth voice with a calculated level of enthusiasm.

She remembers my name!

He was thrilled.

The heads of her three friends poked out from behind her, seemingly intrigued. He had been so focused on catching her that he hadn't given any thought to what he would say to her if he did, so he stood there dumbly silent. Finally Nina giggled.

"How are you?" she asked. Danny shook himself back to the present. "Good! I'm good. Where are you going? I was chasing after you." He said bashfully.

"We are going to a friends' gallery. We have been here for a long time." Danny had been playing her voice in his head for the last eight days like a favorite song and to hear it directly from her mouth was a bit surreal. "An art gallery?" He asked. She nodded still smiling and cocked her head coquettishly. Behind her the eyes of one of her friends sprang into recognition of Mateus who had appeared behind Danny. It was the act of a classy wingman as he walked past Danny to talk to her friend, exactly something that Tanner would have done.

Art and poetry and Talib Kweli—who is this girl?

She seemed to be from two worlds: classic and contemporary, old and new, fleeting and forever. Whatever she was, Danny was hypnotized. "Well I don't mean to keep you. I just saw you and I wanted to say hi."

"Oh you have *such* good manners." She said sarcastically. He smirked and she stared back at him as the silence between them grew into an understanding, an awareness...something was happening. "Is it normal to run into the same person more than once in Rio?" He asked.

She shrugged, "It just depends on the undertow of the streets I guess." It was perhaps the most mesmerizing sentence he had ever heard.

He asked for her number. She gave it to him. The giddy glances that her friends passed between one another suggested that she didn't do this often.

They said their goodbyes after Danny had quickly met Maria, Monica and Catia. The rest of the night was like a post-concussion daze, he really had her number now. He had so many questions.

Does she always speak like that? What is her family like? What kind of movies does she like?

He wanted to know everything about her.

— — –

When training started again on Monday Danny felt light in the chest and light on his feet. Trevor Ramey and his troubles at home seemed far away and not of imminent concern. His energy was infectious, resonating throughout the gym—everyone seemed to be training well. He should have anticipated this happening sooner or later. He was the leader. He set the tone. It was a familiar feeling, but he didn't think it would ever happen here in Marlos Vieira's gym. Not only was he accepted... he belonged.

— — —

On Tuesday night he lay in bed, the worst part of every day was about to begin: the hour or so before he fell asleep when his thoughts were free to chew at his brain. He had no defense. The Mickey Mouse curtains swayed gently near his feet from the heaven-sent breeze that drifted in through the screen window.

The heavy sadness of Lucas was the foundation but on top of that his worries compounded and swelled, scenarios painted themselves into pictures—a courtroom packed with family and friends sobbing and hugging one another as the judge indifferently delivered a sentence of 15 years imprisonment with eligibility for parole after seven. He would start to sweat, his hands would clench into fists.

He only had music to distract himself with but it never did much but interfere like static on a radio, never completely drowning out what was going on in his head. Like every night his thoughts eventually revisited the parking lot of Safeway. He could hear the screams of Ramey like an animal falling victim to the food chain, terrified and desperate. He could feel Kevin Minnick's arms around his neck and stomach trying so hard to rip him away from his prey. He thought about when he stood up and looked down at Ramey, his head cocked awkwardly, face already swollen, the pool of blood expanding from under his head like an aerial time-lapse of a flood.

Then suddenly, he remembered something. Something became clear that for whatever reason hadn't been clear before. He had heard something in his reminiscing, words that had always been there but had never been audible and clear until then, flashing across the bottom of his conscience like subtitles written in a tiny text. They had been lost in the manic screams but all of a sudden they were there, and he knew he wasn't imagining things. The voice, the tone, the fear—it all came back to him now like pieces of a drunk night.

Dude, I'm sorry. It was an accident—I didn't mean to hurt him.

He lurched up from bed like someone had hit the brakes at 60 mph, nearly tripping as he scrambled out the door and up the stairs to the kitchen. It was 10:33 p.m. and 6:33 p.m. in Portland; his dad would most likely be home. The ring that came over the receiver was crackly. It rang once, twice, three times. Rich answered. "Hey buddy! How's it going?"

He had talked to him earlier that evening but the sound of his dad's weary yet happy-to-hear-from-you voice still gave him a lump in his throat.

"Dad. I remembered something just now, I don't know why now and not before but in the parking lot... Ramey. He *admitted* to it. He said, *'I'm sorry. I didn't mean to hurt him.'* Or something like that. I—I just remember him referring to it—"

"Slow down, Danny." Rich interrupted sternly.

He swallowed once and gathered himself. "Okay, listen. *Please*, dad. Just listen."

There was a long pause. "Okay buddy. I'm listening."

"See up until he saw me in the parking lot he must have assumed that nobody knew what happened—he couldn't have known that Lucas had called me just before the crash but then when he saw me he must have realized that I knew what he had done and he *apologized* for it. He wouldn't have said anything if he didn't do anything, Dad. Do you understand? He did it. He fucking *apologized* for it."

His breathing was heavy and he could feel the sweat gathering on his lower back. Rich didn't say anything immediately and Danny imagined him at that moment squeezing his eyes shut and massaging his brow, under-enthused and overly-stressed.

"It's useless Danny. Ramey's attorneys will say it was just a spontaneous declaration in the face of fear— " Danny interrupted angrily, "But what could he be apologizing for? *What* didn't he mean to do? *What* was an accident?" He was trying not to yell, Edson and Rosa were sleeping just around the corner, but he was enraged. As far as he was concerned it was undeniable proof.

He tried for another ten minutes to convince him that it was worth something and Rich fianlly relented and said that he would pass the information along to his associates who were defending Danny. They touched base on a few other things before the phone was passed to Isabel. He went through the same sequence of assurances with her—that he was okay, that he loved and missed them and that he would be home soon.

After ending the call he went back to bed where the events of that rainy night began to play once more: the carnage, the rage, hearing the screams, Kevin Minnick throwing his hands above his head—*I got no beef with you man*, Steve standing just outside the sliding doors, waving as cordially and nonchalantly as if he had seen none of it.

There was no mistaking what he had heard and there was absolutely no reason in the world for Ramey to apologize unless he had done something wrong.

Dude, I'm sorry. It was an accident—I didn't mean to hurt him.

The words echoed in his head as he tried to slow his heartbeat by taking deep breaths. In through the nose... and out through the mouth...in through the nose...and out through the mouth...until he dosed off.

— — —

Training on Wednesday started like any other day but something strange happened that left Danny in an uneasy state of mind. The garage doors facing the street were open as they had been for the last several days during the especially hot days. Favela kids often gathered on the sidewalk and peered into the gym with amazement but just after 9:30 there was a visitor who wasn't welcome.

Danny was all the way across the gym near Marlos' office with Fred and Glayson talking arm-bar tactics when a commotion across the gym in the opening of the left garage door turned their attention.

"Get out of here! You are not welcome in here!"

Danny saw a dark-skinned thuggish-looking guy standing a few yards inside the garage door. His afro was knotted on the side of his head, a shiny dark scar slanted over his left eye. His grey T-shirt was far too big for him but Danny could still make out strong shoulders underneath it.

"You can't be here I said!" Breno yelled walking quickly toward him, pointing for the man to leave. He obviously wasn't someone who had just wandered in off the street, Breno's tone was angry but familiar; he knew the guy. There was a swagger of confidence in the way he had walked into the gym that suggested he had been there before.

Danny was too far away to make out the words of the deep scratchy voice but suddenly the eyes of all the fighters in the gym were searching for him. Breno pushed the man back forcefully. The guy was big but no match for 230-pound Breno. He continued to talk as Breno shoved him out of the gym, Danny caught a few words, "...the American with the rugby brother—heard he beat your ass Gabi." He said pointing at Gabriel who was near the cage and had stopped jumping rope. The way he addressed Gabriel was familiar also.

"Where is he anyway?" He asked with a villainous grin as Breno finally herded him past the threshold of the doors and as he said it, he followed the eyes of the other fighters, giving him his answer. His gaze found Danny from 30 yards away and he grinned with a menacing twist of the mouth, pointing a finger straight across the gym as the garage door slammed down in front of him.

– — -

"His name was Donadel." He said to Jenna.

"Mateus didn't know him but the other fighters told me he had a typical Rio fighting story—lots of talent and potential but a bad attitude and a short temper. He got kicked out of a few good gyms in his early twenties and eventually just stayed in the streets, or so I was told. I heard so many stories like that—good fighters with potential but they just couldn't keep their shit together." He shrugged, *what are you gonna do?*

"So what did he want? Did you see him again?" Jenna asked.

He ignored the question.

Thursday was the day. Danny had calculated it in his mind as the best day to send Nina a text. He didn't want to do it on Friday because the weekend would be upon them and it would look like he was messaging her at the last minute and if he messaged her on Wednesday, it was too early in the week and was too far from the weekend. He was over-thinking. For the first time in his life he got a taste of the insecurity that he had seen all of his friends go through over the years, even Tanner.

Oh so this is what it's like.

He sat on the edge of his bed, the text line blinking in the blank space. He wrote words, deleted words, chewed his thumbnail, gave up once and lay down. Through a combination of exhaustion, impatience and saying *Ah fuck it*, he sent her a text that read,

"Ei Nina isso é Danny" or "Hey Nina this is Danny"

The second he hit SEND he realized that she new him as Danilo but assumed that she would connect the dots. With that, he put his phone on his bed and went upstairs to rummage in the refrigerator in an act of discipline, giving his phone space and privacy with the hopes that when he came back to check it there would be a message waiting for him. He made a sandwich and took it out on to the balcony where Edson was smoking his evening cigarette.

They spoke for a few minutes about training and the beach—Edson saying that he should tag along with him one day, as he hadn't been to the beach in a month or more. The pain he felt for his daughter had begun to show in his face, his cheekbones a little sharper under his skin. They said their goodnights and Danny headed downstairs, his heart thudding in his chest. He picked his phone up from his bed and reassured himself that it had only been fifteen minutes and if she hadn't text him back then there was no need to worry. He clicked the top button to wake his phone…

There it was, staring him in the face like the presents under the tree on Christmas morning: the little green envelope. No girl had ever made him feel excitement like this. He lay down and opened the text, a huge smile spread across his face in the symmetry of his bedroom.

— — —

Their text conversation continued late into the night and had come to a beautifully scripted head when Danny asked her if she liked football (soccer) and she declared in capital letters that she loved it and that she was a huge Fluminense FC fan. Danny saw his chance and went for it, sending two texts in a row:

"My uncle is a coach in the youth system!"

Followed immediately by:

"He got tickets for the national team friendly this weekend. Do you want to go with me?"

He was made to wait a little longer for her response and he knew somewhere in the back of his mind that her answer, one way or the other, would dictate whether or not anything would transpire between them. He left his phone on his chest, waiting for the vibrations that would bring either joy or a huge bummer. He wanted her to say yes so bad that he almost said a little prayer. What he didn't want was for her to turn out to be what Rich always called a "Slow-no-er" which was somebody who couldn't say *No* definitively, so they said *Maybe—I'm not sure yet—I'll have to check—Let me get back to you.* It was an attribute of the weak Danny thought. Nina seemed anything but weak. She would say *Yes* or *No*.

His phone vibrated. He took a deep breath.

"Yes! We should get some drinks with my friends first."

For the first time in weeks he felt genuine optimism. It flooded through him. *Perhaps life can go on.*

— — —

It had been almost 7 weeks since the bars of Leo Goia had shut behind him and the biggest hardship in Joris' life was the fact that he would sometimes run out of liquor and would have to wait for Michel's wife to bring him more. He still smoked spliffs daily and did cocaine every few days or whenever it was offered but he never bought it for himself.

He enjoyed uppers from time to time but he was a downer man: heroin, opiates, marijuana and most importantly, alcohol. He admitted it to himself openly; he was an alcoholic, and would be until the day he died. There was no better feeling in the world than having a bottle of whiskey on the green felt of a card game. Holding a hand of cards was also an addiction but through all the thousands and thousands of hands he'd been dealt playing cards over the years, he had never lost the will power to walk away from a table.

He now had a new obsession. In truth it seemed to be everybody's in Leo Goia: Friday night fights. Michel had taken his money the first week, Joris' fighter lost but he didn't care. While betting seemed to be the point of the fights for everyone else Joris just loved the spectacle of it all. Every Friday was a production. The buzz was in the air starting in the morning. The fighters came from everywhere but they were all talented; some were retired but still limber, some were currently fighting professionally and just came in for the cash payment. Leo Goia was the center of the underground fighting world in Rio, which Joris learned was a very populated world. There was big money involved. He had seen large wads of cash on hand at the fights but he knew there were serious behind-the-scenes wagers being made, big money transactions. He knew what a nervous gambler looked like and he could see them in the crowds on fight night.

– — –

At 3:15 p.m. on Saturday Danny leaned against the wall of Botto Bar on the sweltering sidewalk. The corner bar was a 20-minute walk from the historic Maracanã Stadium. Rosa had come downstairs as Danny was rummaging through the drawers in the hallway outside his room. She was beside herself with joy, cupping her hands over her mouth and nose when he said he was going to meet a girl. She refrained from asking too many questions when she noticed that he was frustrated with not having anything nice to wear.

She gave him far more money than he needed to buy something on the way and he had stopped at an H&M and bought a simple polo—cream colored with navy and red horizontal stripes and a navy collar. He was worried about being underdressed but he didn't anticipate Nina or any of her friends being very dolled up on such a hot day. Never before in his life had he been so concerned with his appearance.

He picked nervously at the sun-faded yellow paint that was chipping away from the brick wall. The sidewalks were alive; buzzing with anticipation of the game and other Carnival festivities. A drum beat steadily in the distance at some party nearer to the stadium. He scratched his calf nervously with the toe of his dirty white Vans. Girls would walk by and give him a coy smile. He paid them no attention. After maybe ten minutes Catia and Monica, whom he had met quickly the week before when he got Nina's number, showed up looking like the search results of Googling 'Brazilian women'.

Both of them were extremely attractive with curvy bodies that they apparently didn't like to go unnoticed. They approached Danny without hesitation and he gave them a nervous grin and greeted them with the customary touching of cheeks on both sides. Their smiles were excited as if they had just finished talking about him or knew something he didn't.

"You two look nice. What are you doing tonight?"

They smiled together. Catia was the shorter of the two with long hazel hair and a fair complexion. As she answered him, Danny could sense Monica—taller with long auburn hair, dark Spanish skin and green eyes—studying him from head to toe.

"I think we are going to a friend's apartment for drinks later and then I guess we'll see where the night takes us!" She shrugged, smiling big. Danny cracked a smile in response.

"How long have you guys been friends with Nina?" He asked trying to sound casual but secretly feigning to get as much information as possible about her from the people who knew her. She had left him in such a state of curiosity that he just couldn't hold back when he had Catia and Monica alone and every answer the girls gave made him think of a new question to ask. He could tell by their answers that they adored Nina.

He found out that she worked at an art gallery and lived near the north end of Copacabana in one of the high-rise apartment buildings. She was originally from Rio, she had two brothers, her parents were currently on vacation in Spain and she loved soccer, a little too much for Monica's liking judging by her eye-roll. They wanted to know more about him too but his questioning was so persistent that they could hardly get a word in. Eventually he could sense that he was being too overbearing and he changed the subject.

"So you know my friend Mateus?"

The girls shared the same bashful giggle, again as if there was an inside joke. "Everyone knows Mateus." Monica said to explain why they were laughing and then she added, "Catia knows him better than most though." Catia cried out in shock, as her cheeks turned scarlet. "How dare you!"

Catia playfully resisted the apologetic hug of Monica. Danny smiled with affection, they reminded him of Allie and her friends. That was the last interaction they would have before Nina appeared from around the corner. Danny lost his breath. Yet again she moved in slow motion, which was almost predictable at that point. She wore faded jeans with rips in the thighs revealing patches of buttery smooth skin. A green and yellow Brazil jersey hugged her slim stomach and was just short enough to expose a tantalizing bit of skin above her jeans. The slightest darkening of eye shadow made her eyes an even deeper brown and the tiny mole on the side of her eye stood out in the sea of creamy skin.

The girls greeted each other first, exchanging some quick news about a gallery and a friend named Sergio before Nina turned to Danny. Like when he saw her at the music festival he was a bit lost for words but he managed a fairly normal greeting before they headed inside.

He liked Botto Bar. It reminded him of a bar that might be in Portland; a cozy place where the bartender was a wiry guy with a thick black beard and a man bun and poured beers from any of 20 taps. Ceiling fans spun frantically. The brick walls were covered with memorabilia of the Brazil National Team.

Danny meandered past several pictures of players from the early 1900's that he didn't recognize, then past a framed and signed picture of Cafu lifting the World Cup in 2002, then a picture of Pelé doing the same but in black and white from 1958.

When Pelé won that World Cup in Sweden in 1958, he was the youngest player to ever play in the tournament at 17 years old. As Danny sipped his first beer of the evening, he stood looking at the still of the young man. He was crying, raising a triumphant fist above his head and hugging a teammate with his other arm. Danny wondered if Pelé knew that he would soon be a worldwide icon, and eventually considered by many to be the greatest soccer player ever.

Why did you get to live and not my brother?

Danny's mind wandered away in imagination for a moment. He couldn't say how much time had past before he felt Nina's soft hand touch his shoulder, bringing him back to reality.

"What are you thinking about?" she asked with a giggle that must have implied that he had been staring at Pelé for a long time. Danny glanced back at the photo.

"Nothing." He said sheepishly.

After an hour the bar was packed with people in the yellow and green jerseys. The Maracanã Stadium held close to 79,000 people but Fluminense games only filled about half the seats. Today's game would be different; there would be at least 70,000 fans. The Brazil National Team was playing a friendly against Colombia. The World Cup would be hosted in Brazil later in the year, and The Maracanã had been designated as the stadium where the final would be played.

The last time Danny had been to a game had been two years before; Fluminense played Santos. That day the crowd had been almost 65,000. The attraction of the game was a young player who had been dubbed 'the new Pelé'. His name was Neymar and at the time he was a skinny 22-year-old kid. He was so gifted with the ball that it almost appeared to be tied to his foot. Perhaps one day he would have a picture on the wall in Botto Bar next to Pelé, Cafu, Ronaldo and Ronaldinho. He was already destined to carry the torch of Brazilian soccer for years to come, an enormous responsibility for a 24-year-old. A year after Danny had seen him play he had made the jump overseas and now played for FC Barcelona but tonight he would be back in The Maracanã to play for his country.

Danny spent 15 minutes listening to Nina explain why he was so good and why Barcelona had been willing to pay almost €60 million to sign him from Santos. She said he would be the face of Brazilian soccer for the next ten-plus years. It wouldn't have mattered what the topic was, he was mesmerized when she talked passionately about something. He couldn't be paid €60 million to look away.

The next two hours were the best two hours since Lucas died. Catia and Monica had quickly made friends with several people of similar age at the bar. Danny and Nina were able to drift away and have their own conversation for a while before deciding to join the group.

She seemed almost as curious about Danny as he was of her. The first question she asked led to several more:

"So people call you *Danny*?"

"Well my name is Danilo but I've been called Danny my whole life—I'm from The United States, actually."

Everything was going great until one point when Danny faced a difficult line of questions from a guy named Marcos. Everyone grew quiet as if they had collectively agreed to be interested in Danny. He answered many of the same questions that Nina had just asked and they too learned that he was half American and half Brazilian and was visiting his grandparents in Rio on a "break from school".

When it came up that he was training at an MMA gym, both Catia and Monica shot Nina a look as if they had just won a bet. It was then that Arthur, another of the guys, sprang into animation, his eyes grew wide, "Wait. Was it *you* who threw Gabriel Souza over your head? Are you *that* American?" Everybody's eyes turned to him with intense expectation. He hesitated and almost considered lying. Bashfully he confessed, "Yeah but—we were really just messing around."

They all seemed to know who Gabriel was and their eyes said it all. *Holy shit. This guy must be the real deal.*

Friends and acquaintances of the girls seemed to show up at random, they were obviously very popular. Danny had learned that Nina was best defined by poetry, art and soccer. The only girl he had ever met who was even close to Nina in terms of being so confident and intelligent yet so laid back and beautiful, was Andrea.

Whenever they were separated and started talking to other people at the bar, they would always manage to lock eyes. Sometimes they held each other's stare for a few seconds, neither seemingly capable nor willing to look away. It took Danny back to the first time he had seen her at the beach when they were both wearing sunglasses but they saw each other, he was sure of it.

The game started at 6 and by 5:30 Danny was 6 beers and 2 shots deep. He was talking to a short thick guy wearing round Ghandi-style glasses who it turned out knew his uncle Renato when Danny felt the same soft hand on his shoulder.

"We should go soon."

— — —

The atmosphere inside the Maracanã was electric. The crowd cheered in perfect unison for each good passage of play, yelled shocking obscenities at the referee for every call he made and applauded simply when a nice piece of team passing unfolded. It was a living organism.

Their seats were about twenty rows up at half-field; perfect for analyzing the formations of the team and Nina rushed from observation to observation so quickly that Danny could barely keep up.

"See it's all about balance. You can't have too much attack with too little defense and vice-versa. For me, the midfield is where the game is won or lost—I mean for the *most* part. Of course if your defense is shit then you will give up goals and lose and if you can't score goals you will never win, but the midfield is the most important because it will contribute everything to both the attack and the defense if it's well organized." All the while she was pointing sporadically at the "shape" of the teams as they shifted by the second.

"You see—number ten? The little guy for Colombia? He has a free role. He will be here or there or wherever, he has freedom to do what he wants when they have the ball—he just wants the ball. The coach will want him to be the player with the ball more than anybody else in the attacking third so he gives him the power to decide what he wants to do. Nobody else has the same freedom—in attack at least. In defense everybody has responsibility."

Her gaze was fixed on the game but she spoke as if her attention was solely on Danny. At one point she interrupted herself and turned her eyes to him, "...unless the winger drops back to help—are you listening to me?"

He laughed. She smiled. "I can be quiet if you want." She said apologetically but light-heartedly. "No!" He said laughing, "I like learning. I mean I know a little just from being around my uncle but there's a lot I don't know." He tried to flex the small amount of knowledge that he had, "Colombia are playing a four-two-three-one, no?"

Nina's head spun to look at him, surprise plastered across her face, eyebrows raised. "See! You're not a *complete* disaster." She said, her brown eyes sparkling in the lights of the stadium.

– — –

Danny finished telling Jenna the story of what he would later refer to as his and Nina's "first date". His eyes were back in the Maracanã Stadium and Jenna could see a weary acceptance in his face. Even if she had something to say it would have been inappropriate. Just by being in the room she felt as though she was intruding. Wherever his mind was, whatever memory he was re-living, he was firmly implanted there. Only his body was in the present.

After a moment he blinked and shook his head softly, raising his eyebrows; back to reality. He looked at his phone, 1:44 a.m. Through his yawn he said "Oh man. I should go." He had been talking nearly non-stop for three hours. Danny had told Celia and Tanner about Nina when he returned from Brazil but that was more than two years ago and he hadn't discussed her since then. She had existed exclusively in his memory for so long. It was so strange to speak about her. To say her name and describe her out loud, recite conversations that they had shared, it made her seem more human, more incapable of doing what she had done to him.

The red and blue lights on the interface of Danny's Audi glowed in the black night as he drove home on the empty streets of Beaverton. He always knew that something he would invest in when he had money would be a nice sound system for the car he would be driving, and he had done just that. Lana Del Rey's voice floated crystal clear through the speakers as his mind wandered back to Nina as it always did when he was alone in his car.

He went back to the beach, to the festivals, to Primatas Waterfall, her high-rise apartment in Sao Conrado. He saw her face look back at him over her shoulder as she led the way up the trail through the trees. He saw her look up at him as she rested her head on his thigh on Copacabana. He couldn't shake the curve of her jawline, the shape of her face or the tiny mole on the outside of her eye. He could almost feel the warmth of the rising sun across the Atlantic Ocean that they had watched together.

His feelings for her hadn't tapered off in the weeks, months, and eventually years afterward and he had accepted it: in all likelihood, he would be in love with her for the rest of his life. He wanted her desperately, almost in the same way that he wanted Lucas back. But also like Lucas, he knew it would never happen. He would never see her again.

The reminiscing continued as he pulled onto the smooth black asphalt of his driveway. He opened the front door to find a new row of boxes lining the wall. Free stuff from his sponsors wasn't exciting anymore— he had too much and not enough storage space. Taison poked his head around the corner from the kitchen, shaking him back to the present.

"Come eat. You have to eat this before you go to bed."

Taison was Danny's favorite cousin, an organic substitution for Tanner in the summer months over the years. He was Renato's son, which meant he was smart and never shied away from an adventure— absolutely thrilled at the chance to move to America and be Danny's live-in cook and general assistant for an array of tasks, amongst which were managing his social media accounts. Danny had no interest in keeping up to date with pictures on Instagram or words on Twitter.

Taison reported to Marlos about anything and everything that might affect Danny's performance and he would be in big trouble if he failed to report that Danny returned from his therapist in the middle of the night. Taison was committed to his duty and winning was as important to him as it was to any member of the team. He didn't approve of Danny being out until almost 2 a.m. but at the end of the day, Taison was the same cousin that had created the distraction at the bodega for Danny and Lucas to steal Hustler magazines in 2005. He would never dream of going behind Danny's back.

Danny walked into the kitchen and slid onto a barstool as Taison set a bowl of beef broth and a spoon in front of him.

"Long one tonight huh?"

"Yeah. Long one." Taison knew the distance in Danny's voice meant there was nothing else to be said. Danny never talked about the time he spent at Jenna's.

"Good. I'm going to bed. Make sure you eat everything. Good-night." He said motioning towards steamed vegetables, fruit and a tall glass of a yellowish milky substance.

"Goodnight." Danny said a whole twenty seconds later—Taison was already halfway up the stairs. Then it was silent in the kitchen of his townhouse; he could let his thoughts drift back to Brazil, to the beach, to Nina.

— — -

A week had passed since he had told Jenna more than three hours of story and things were going well. His coaches were all very happy; Remy in particular who said Danny's kicking had advanced "four months in four days". On Tuesday there was an afternoon walk with Rodney and Celia through the Rhododendron Garden near the golf course. Thursday, he went to the University of Portland with Andrea to watch Allie's singles match against a girl from the University of Washington, which she won in straight sets. Normally any media activities and especially sit-down interviews were met with gross displeasure, but on Saturday Danny had sat across from Ryan from *Men's Health,* and found the interview to be relatively painless.

It was a good week—one of the best of the last four years. He and Jenna had planned on meeting on Saturday. He wanted to finish.

— — –

She was wearing athletic clothes and glasses, her hair in a tight ponytail. Danny had never seen her in anything but business attire.

"You come from a workout?"

"No I just didn't feel like dressing up, Peter's not home, so."

Danny lay down on the chaise. "Where did I leave off?"

"You and Nina had just gone to the soccer game."

— — –

The night couldn't have gone any better. Everything about the two of them fit together so well. Their conversations flowed and their jokes and banter made one another smile effortlessly. They were two matching rhythms that had finally been played over one another creating a beautiful new sound. They both felt it.

After the game they walked to another bar, this one a little more *Rio* than Botto Bar had been. They talked for hours, sitting at a picnic table on the sidewalk. Drinks arrived at the perfect times. He fell in love with the little mole on the outside of her eye that reminded him of one of the dots on Tanner's constellation tattoo. Patrons kept the bar alive late into the night talking about the game and Brazil's chances at the World Cup later in the year. Nina told Danny she liked his accent.

The topics of their conversation ranged from one end of he spectrum all the way to the other; capoeira, tattoos, Basquiat, aliens, Bolivia, her family, board games, Obama, The Red Hot Chili Peppers, Canada, Tupac and everything else... except Lucas. Somehow with every drink she seemed to get more sober and articulate. She listened to him talk about his four uncles and all his cousins, his little

152   **EDDY PRUGH**

sister the tennis player, and his younger adopted brother, Rodney who was athletic enough to play any sport but Danny hoped would choose American football. He did feel a bit guilty leaving Lucas out entirely but he just wasn't ready to simply discuss Lucas in the past tense.

At about 3:15 a.m. they stood on the corner waiting for her taxi. There was nothing said about future plans, it was obvious that they would see each other again but it seemed equally hard for both of them to say goodbye for the night. When the taxi arrived she stood on her toes, kissing him on the cheek. They indulged in one final moment of extended eye contact.

In his own taxi ride, Danny wondered if what he was feeling was normal, if it was the same excitement that all of his friends who had girlfriends felt when they first went out together. Surely it wasn't this good—not for everybody. It was a shame he thought, that some people settled for anything less than what he had found because even in the midst of the pain he felt, it was a feeling that made life make sense.

– — –

The next day they met at the beach, Danny texted her at noon when he woke up. In her apartment near the North end of Copacabana she lay in bed thinking about the American who had approached her on the beach who she had just gone to a soccer game with. There was something about him, something mysterious. Monica and Catia had been right about him; he was a fighter, but he wasn't like any fighter she had ever known. His soft demeanor made it almost impossible to reconcile that he had a violent side.

Her phone vibrated and to her surprise it wasn't Catia asking for a ride home from a guy's house. A smile melted across her face when she saw his name on her phone: *Danny*. She liked the name. It was a child's name, a little boy's name, which, despite his broad shoulders, deep voice and square jaw was what he appeared to be: a little boy. It had to be something in his eyes; big, sad Labrador eyes that didn't quite fit the rest of him. There was damage within him; she could see it like she could see the right brush strokes in an original piece of art.

It was there every time they locked eyes from across the bar. There was something he wasn't telling her and it wasn't just his eyes that gave him away. When discussing his life he was incredibly vague on what he was doing or how long he was staying. She wouldn't press him though. It was his business to tell or not tell.

At 2:30 p.m. they sat at a concrete picnic table with an umbrella on the boardwalk. Conversation picked up as seamlessly as it had ended the night before. At one point in their conversation Danny couldn't come up with the Portuguese word for 'spatula' and had to mime it. Nina giggle before saying "esáptula." It was painfully obvious as soon as it came out of her mouth and he flicked himself in the temple in mock self-punishment. It led them into the discussion of language and communication:

"In South America there are different dialects and localized indigenous languages in some places—and in like French Guyana they speak French and in Suriname they speak Dutch—but obviously it's Spanish for the most part—except for here, of course. But in Europe it's amazing how so many different languages have developed—and the proximity of the countries. They are so close to one another you know? It's amazing."

They stayed for almost three hours. All the problems that had compounded for Danny in the recent weeks just weren't as important when she was talking. He could have stayed at the picnic table all day and all night.

— — -

Rosa was frantic when Danny finally came home, she didn't even wait for him to make it through the gate before calling to him from the balcony. Rich had called and he needed Danny to call him back *immediately*. A rock sank in his stomach. He hurried up to the computer. Rosa hovered in the living room inside the door to the balcony. Danny could feel her fussing about behind him, "It's okay grandma." He called over his shoulder as he typed in the number to Rich's cell.

The ring crackled like an old walkie-talkie over the line. Rich answered after the third ring. He sounded exhausted, his voice characteristically gravelly. "Hey bud. You've been cleared of everything. There are no charges."

Danny had heard him but the words didn't mean anything initially. Sort of like when the doctor had shaken his head in the emergency room, it didn't register and seemed more like a lie or a joke. It wasn't real yet and he needed more information. The complete absence of enthusiasm in Rich's voice wasn't making it any easier to believe.

"Hm. What happened?" He asked flatly.

"Well..." Rich sighed once, "...it's been a strange week. You know—I actually knew Trevor Ramey's attorney from Law School, but anyway on Thursday, you called me with that information about what he said in the parking lot about being sorry and all that. We played it close, you know, we didn't let them know exactly what we were accusing him of saying, but I'm guessing Trevor isn't the brightest kid in the world—his attorney either, for that matter. We sent them a request for discovery on what he said before you beat him up and they came back to us pretty quickly with the proposal of dropping charges in exchange for us not pressing any charges of our own. Short version—Trevor Ramey knows he did something wrong."

It was becoming more real to Danny. "We couldn't have built a case with just you and Tanner testifying about the phone call and then your testimony that he said whatever he said in the parking lot. Basically, he got scared and rushed into an agreement that he didn't really need to make but for sure, Trevor Ramey knows that he did something wrong, and he got scared. That's what it all comes down to."

Danny's mind was trying to grasp for more questions, which he had many of, but they weren't materializing into words and the reality that he wasn't in trouble was slowly becoming overpowering. Through the scatter of thoughts racing through his mind, he was only able to ask,

"So if I come home I won't get arrested?"

"Nope. You're a free man." Rich said as he sighed again. "Detective O'Connell has been notified of the agreement. If he's a good detective he'll give me a call but I'm not expecting one—that guy..." Danny could see his dad shaking his head, "asshole. Really poor law enforcement. Anyway. That's that. Heard you went to a game yesterday? With a girl?"

They spoke for only a few minutes more before Rich put on his mom and Andrea. When it was over he stood up from the stool but didn't move. After a few seconds he punched the sky. It felt like literal weight had been lifted from his shoulders and back. He turned to see Rosa clasping her hands in front of her chest, her eyes brimming with concern. Danny smiled big and hugged her, kissing her on the cheek and her concern melted into relief.

"Eu estou livre!"

I'm free.

— — —

"What a relief." Jenna said.

"*Huge* relief." Danny recalled. "Between that news and meeting Nina, things almost felt okay. Almost hopeful. But I should have known...it wasn't going to last."

— — —

It was as if the news had set into motion the next chapter. Every minute of every day he missed Lucas immensely, but life was crawling forward and he was doing his best to move with it. Everything was okay when he was with Nina. He couldn't get enough time with her and she seemed to enjoy it almost as much as he did.

They sat and talked about anything and everything. When questions about his life in America came up he answered as truthfully as possible but at times he was misleading to avoid Lucas. He mentioned Andrea once and when Nina interrupted him to ask who she was, he said it was a family friend—not a lie but not entirely forthright.

Sometimes Danny would ask her a question about art or soccer just so she would keep talking and he could sit and listen. He was in no hurry for anything physical—he savored the hug he got every time they left the beach but the real high came from knowing that she had chosen to give him her *time*. He felt so lucky, even honored, that he got to spend the same two hours with her every day that week.

MONDAY

"When the Basquiat came into town a few weeks ago it was the most amazing thing I've ever seen in person. I got to stand right in front of it. I could hear it when I closed my eyes. I had looked at it online and in books for so many years that when I saw it for real I nearly lost my breath. I don't even remember a lot of things very clearly from my childhood but I remember the first time I saw the painting in an art book."

"He's dead though right?"

"Yeah he's dead. Heroin. But he was so vibrant—so consistent but so erratic. It would have spoiled his work if he had lived into old age. It sounds terrible but I think it's true."

TUESDAY

"LeBron James is the best player in the world—that's not the question. The argument is whether or not he's the best of all time, which means being better than Michael Jordan. Michael Jordan was my hero when I was a kid even though I was too young to really remember him in his prime, but he was the best. And still is—I don't think LeBron is as good. It's a close debate and I understand both sides but there was just something about Michael. If you saw him play you would understand. He just refused to lose. Unbelievable to watch."

Nina was listening attentively. "But are they different kinds of players?"

"Well that's the thing. They were similar in height—Jordan was six foot six inches—or, I mean almost two meters tall—LeBron is like this much taller," Danny showed two inches between his thumb and forefinger, "and they technically played different positions, but I guess in basketball you have to just look at the overall contribution of their play. It's a tight race but I would never say that anybody is better than Michael Jordan. He's an icon. I love him. Kobe can be in the conversation too. We can't leave him out. He is amazing also. Rodney is obsessed with him."

Nina was excited by the conversation even though she knew very little about basketball.

"It must be similar to the Messi versus Ronaldo debate that happens now. It's so hard to say which player is better—and whether or not they are the greatest players in history. Personally, I think they are the two best players in history. I know I'm Brazilian and I'm supposed to say Pelé but the game is so much more fast-paced and technical now. For Pelé to accomplish what he did in his time was amazing but these players now are so fast and precise I don't think there should be any comparison. I need to see Messi play someday. He's the greatest player the world has seen and he exists in *our* lifetime. I need to see him play with my own eyes before he retires."

WEDNESDAY

"We adopted him when he was five. It all happened in like two weeks, really fast. My dad is an attorney and—it was crazy how it happened— he was representing Rodney's dad on drug charges and his mom just sort of left him in my dad's office one day. She had gone to run some errands or something and had gotten arrested herself. He was from a really bad place. He hardly talked in the beginning but he always wanted to play sports with me and…Allie. All the girls love him." Danny said with a devilish yet affectionate grin.

THURSDAY

Nina claimed that her English was decent and on Thursday they tried it out. Danny found that she was being modest and was shocked by how good it was. She laughed when he said that he felt deceived and that now he didn't even know who he was talking to. In English she told him how her brother had been to Yellowstone National Park the year before and had seen a "bear and her small bear—bear baby—bear puppy?"

He didn't mean to laugh but it came reflexively, she lit up.

"Oh so that's what your laugh sounds like. I like it." Danny was warmed to the bone by the remark, since it was what people had always said about Lucas' laugh.

FRIDAY

Nina had the day off and they made plans to go for the short hike to Primatas Waterfall, a popular place to spend a hot summer day in Tijuca National Park. After wading into the mountain water they sat on a pair of boulders in the shade of the trees.

"It's not just about the music and if it sounds good, it's all about the writing. I would like country music if it had the most creative writing—it wouldn't matter the genre—but hip-hop has the best poetry. Some of the writing of some artists is amazing and it's unfortunate that it's overlooked sometimes."

"You would like Tanner. He's really good with words. I don't know if I would call him a *poet*, but he's definitely got some sort of gift with words."

"Tanner sounds so fun." She said, having heard more stories about him than arguably any other member of Danny's group back home. Whatever it was that was going on between them had become serious enough for her to feel obligated to tell him her news.

"Danilo. I need to tell you something."

Danny looked at her with a concerned wrinkle in his brow.

"I accepted a position to study and work in Spain. I'm leaving in two weeks." The words sounded like an apology and even though Danny knew she didn't owe him anything, he was still hurt. He tried to sound excited for her but he couldn't hide the disappointment completely.

"That's amazing! For how long?"

"Six weeks."

"That's not so long is it? I'll see you when you get back?"

She nodded but it was as if she wasn't quite sure about something. "Of course."

— — -

Jenna's heart ached for Danny now that it was clear how much he had cared for Nina. She wondered what had happened between them.

He lay on his back, eyes fixed on the ceiling, back in his own world of memories, allowing himself to stay in the past for a whole minute, paying no attention to Jenna until he asked,

"When you first met Peter, were you like... excited? You know? Were you like thinking about him when you would go home and stuff?"

Jenna bit her bottom lip uncomfortably, "A little bit. But not really. No." She drew her own conclusions on what Danny was wondering by asking such a question.

"We didn't have what you and Nina had—I don't think many people do." He chuckled, "Well thank *God* for that."

There was a faint but wicked trace of spite in his words. Then Jenna knew that it was Nina that had done something to end it, and all of a sudden she hated her.

How could someone hurt such a sweet person?

"It was the best week of my whole life." Danny said with blunt certainty. "Including the time before Lucas died: my whole life."

This confession was a new level of exposure. Jenna was choked up. She managed to ask, "Why did it only last two weeks?"

He didn't say anything.

– — -

Saturday March 1ˢᵗ marked six weeks since Danny had arrived in Brazil. It had been a turbulent ride. He had felt the extremes of several emotions. The constant depression that Lucas was gone, the suffocating stress of waiting for something to happen with the Ramey situation, the euphoric sense of relief after being cleared of punishment, and the pure joy he felt when spending time with Nina.

All he wanted to do was continue healing from the loss of Lucas and spend time with Nina. Training at Marlos' gym would augment the process. At the moment nothing was as important as Nina, and he couldn't wait for the night. It wasn't an overstatement to say that the Saturday night Carnival party at Copacabana was one of the biggest parties in the world.

A week earlier he had chased her through the same crowds while the neon lights danced around them but tonight they walked in the sand through the crowds with no real initiative or purpose, almost as if they had silently agreed that all they wanted was to be in each others company. Although Danny hadn't been there yet, it was known that her apartment was on the North end of the beach in one of the high-rise buildings, so if they were on Copacabana they were never far from her home.

She latched onto his arm as they strolled along the board-walk amidst the noise of the festivities. Strong déjà vu visited him throughout the first part of the evening; it was usually a smell that took him back to younger years running through the streets with his family, skin tanned from long days at the beach.

Nina had never said that she liked to dance but Danny could have guessed that she did, the way her hips moved when she walked suggested that she had typical samba rhythm. The volleyball arena on the beach was central to the entire festival and it had been turned into an open-air stage with some 30,000 spectators standing in the sand. The only time Danny had seen more people there was when the Pope visited in 2007. Samba music from speakers on either side of the stage floated into the warm night. They laughed and flirted and took sips from the water bottle of gin and lime juice that she had brought in her purse.

They wandered around the outskirts of the crowd and eventually took their shoes off and walked in the water underneath the purple and pink sky. Danny was smiling, Nina was laughing. Their touching became more frequent while flirting became more uninhibited, the gin warmly encouraging it all. Finally Danny pulled her into him. She linked her fingers behind his neck and he did the same around her lower back. She looked up at him with a smile was so bright that he felt sorry for the people behind them watching the music because the real show was staring straight into his eyes. It didn't bother her that he was quiet—she liked it. She liked how it was so contrary to his appearance; one would guess that someone so handsome would be loud and maybe even arrogant. Danny was neither.

Seconds ticked by, they continued to look at each other with familiarity and some sort of mutual knowing. For a few seconds it was their 20th wedding anniversary and they were thinking about all they had been through together. Finally the silence became too much, Nina laughed. Danny's sadness was far, far away. Waves washed over their feet in the warm night air on Copacabana. Danny kissed her.

– — -

At around 9:15 p.m. they ran out of gin. "Let's walk to my apartment and fill this," she said shaking the water bottle. They walked the boardwalk, weaving in and around the crowds.

They were near Rua Paula Freitas when Danny began to feel it. At first it was quick footsteps, a sneaking stare, he could sense something behind him. He stopped and turned to look and as he did several people looked at him, but they weren't what he had felt.

"What is it?" Nina asked with some concern, turning her head to see what he was looking for. "Nothing." Danny said still scanning the crowd. They continued, and the bizarre feeling persisted, something not normal behind him, uncomfortable like a spider web trailing off the top of his head, he spun around again, but nobody was looking at him.

– — -

Her apartment was on the fourth floor of the very last tall building on Avenida Atlantica, very desirable urban beachfront property. The view from her living room window was south, a straight shot down the two and a half mile stretch of Copacabana sand. There was something distinctly "drug lord" about the white tile floor and tall windows of the living room. The apartment itself was very nice but there were only a few pieces of furniture in it and it was all flimsy and cheap as if it was a temporary living situation, empty boxes were stacked on one wall. From the kitchen she apologized for the mess but Danny was transfixed by the view of the beach and the neon lights of the festival.

She was explaining that the apartment belonged to her family and that they usually rented it out. She had been living there for a while but was only staying for a few months and would probably get her own place when she came back from Spain. Her parents lived in a suburb in Coehxlo. Then Danny realized that Nina was like him: from a well-off family but without any of the characteristics of a rich kid.

"You ready?" She asked, poking her head around the corner from the kitchen. "Yeah." He said without turning away from the view. It was amazing.

They weaved their way back down the boardwalk; the crowds becoming thicker and thicker the closer they got to the volleyball stadium. It was when they reached the food stands when Danny had the feeling again. Somebody was watching him. He didn't know what made him so sure, but he could feel eyes on the back of his head. This time he turned quickly, positive that somebody would duck away or shift their stare…but there was nothing, just groups of happy people. "Fuck it." He said to himself in English, convincing himself that he was imagining things.

— — –

They drank more and laughed harder, Nina couldn't help but stare when Danny would smile, it was magic. When he wanted her attention he would put his hand gently on her lower back and tap her with his index finger. He had done it four or five times throughout the night and she had come to crave the gentle touch.

It was a night from a fairy tale—the smells, the cool air flowing in off the ocean, the perfect level of intoxication that they had reached, the fluid way they swayed among the crowds of people; heaven on earth. In the thick of the crowd, Nina slung her arms around his neck and pulled him into her as he wrapped his arms around her midsection. He inhaled her creamy vanilla scent when something in the crowd caught his eye over her shoulder—something that didn't fit; a dark and unpleasant figure in a sea of smiles and joy. He focused and saw the dark eyes staring directly at him between the heads of dancing people. As soon as their eyes met he ducked away but not before Danny saw the shiny scar above his eye.

A chill ran up his spine, he had been following them. The image of the garage door slamming shut in front of his pointed finger flashed through his mind and there was no mistaking him: it was Donadel.

"What is it?" Nina asked as he searched the crowd for the afro. "Nothing." He said, still scanning. He returned his attention to her, "Everything is great." And he wasn't lying. Everything was so great.

‑ — ‑

Danny wouldn't describe the next part of the night to Jenna. He hadn't told anybody about it, not even Tanner or Celia. They had gone back to her apartment at around 3:45 a.m. They sat on her couch in front of the floor-to-ceiling windows and had one last drink before going to bed. They didn't have sex. They lay tangled in each-others arms and talked in hushed voices, Danny making her speak English for his own amusement.

They had the conversation that always took place when two people reached a certain point of familiarity to confess their first impressions of one another.

"When you first walked up to me on the beach I was so confused." She said with a giggle. "I was impressed though when you knew Talib Kweli."

Danny grinned, "I would have been screwed if you'd been listening to country music, but I had to say something. When I said *I saw you here yesterday*, I felt so stupid afterward. You were just like, *Okay?*"

"I have a confession to make." She said softly. "I saw you too."

Danny slapped his hand over his eyes. "Oh my God! I knew it! I can't believe you just let me die of embarrassment like that. I can't trust you."

She was giggling with her head on his chest. "I'm sorry but I didn't know what to say. It was so random. I'm glad you said something though."

"I had to. I'd been thinking about you. I saw you on a Friday and talked to you on a Wednesday."

They continued to talk in hushed voices, laughing at normal volume while lying in each other's arms. Danny thought about all the nights that Lucas and Andrea had spent like this over the years.

At around 5 a.m. a stretch of silence almost led them into sleep. Danny stared at the ceiling, the fan at the foot of the bed hummed quietly. He wasn't sure if she was still awake.

"I had a brother. A twin brother." He whispered.

Her head was on his chest. Her breathing was steady. Neither of them had spoken for several minutes and he was pretty sure she was asleep. When she didn't say anything he continued. "He was older than me." More silence.

"He died in a car accident." Nina didn't respond. Two minutes later, just as Danny himself was nodding off, she spoke.

"Is that why you're so quiet?"

"I've always been quiet."

"Is that why you came here?"

"Yeah."

He would save the Trevor Ramey saga for later.

"What was his name?"

"Lucas."

"Lucas… was he as wonderful as you?"

Danny was quiet. Her question had made his heart leap with something other than surprise. He had never felt anything quite like it.

"You think I'm wonderful?"

She lifted her head to look up at him.

"I do. And I've only known you for a week."

Danny wanted so badly to tell her that he felt the same. He didn't know how she became so important to him so quickly but he suddenly couldn't imagine not knowing her. She was guiding him back to life, reviving him from the hollow-eyed empty grey existence that he felt himself drifting towards. He searched for words but he couldn't speak. His voice failed him and before he could say anything she continued.

"I knew there was something you weren't telling me."

She didn't press for details. Instead she rose from bed, "Let's go for a walk. We can sleep for a year afterwards, but I want to see the sunrise."

They brought two beach towels. Just across the street from her apartment they spread one on the sand and lay the other over their legs. The light grew slowly stronger as 6:00 a.m. approached, creeping over the hills at the North end of the beach and casting the few figures along the beach into silhouettes. One of the figures, maybe 30 meters away, was juggling a soccer ball in the wet sand just beyond the break of the waves. Nina lay back against Danny's chest as he propped himself up. It was beautiful to watch: he would stop sometimes and just dance around the ball as if it were his partner. Then he would flick it up and catch it on the back of his neck. Danny and Nina would *Oooh* in perfect unison at an especially fancy trick.

For twenty minutes they watched the shirtless stranger dance and juggle the ball against the pink horizon. Finally he gave the ball a high punt into the ocean, signaling that he was ready for a swim. Nina looked up at Danny in the golden morning light and tugged at his collar, "Let's go to sleep."

None of that night, which he had come to categorize as the best night of his life, was for Jenna's ears. It was his memory and his alone. After playing it back in his mind, all he wanted to do was go home and be alone, so that's what he did.

— — —

Danny didn't feel as good as he had the week before. He had relived the night with Nina thousands of times in the last two and a half years but it was even more vivid now. It had put him in an anxious, hasty way that week. She had been even more present in his mind, menacing and beautiful as always. Unbelievable, he thought, how simply telling Jenna the story had affected his weeks so powerfully and so differently.

His training was harder than normal and Marlos and Remy both let him know that he was heavier on his feet than he was the week before. He was convinced that the only way to fix it was to go back to Jenna and finish the rest of the story.

When he puled into the parking lot of The Westbrook that night it was raining hard, which was appropriate given that this section of the story would be the hardest to talk about.

— — —

Jenna was on the same page as Danny when he scooped her up and planted a playful but firm bite where her neck met her shoulder. She gasped, unable to control her volume. They both wanted it but they also knew that it wasn't the point of the night. After they dressed and settled onto the couch and the chaise he picked up the story when he woke the next day. Cutting out the events of the night completely, "So I stayed the night at her apartment and woke up late the next day."

– — –

At around 1:15 p.m. Danny woke up. He snuck out of bed and got dressed. Nina stirred but didn't wake up. He knelt next to the bed and rested a gentle hand on her neck, stroking her cheek with his thumb. The thought of being away from her was unpleasant and somehow, even while he knelt right in front of her, he already missed her. It had been three weeks since the first day he saw her walk in slow motion down the boardwalk of Copacabana and only a week since they had actually started spending time together but it felt like he had known her for so much longer. She opened her eyes.

"I should go home. Can I see you again soon?" He said softly.

Nina smiled sleepily and gracefully shut her eyes for no longer than a lengthy blink. "You have my number." He took one final look at her before getting to his feet and walking for the door. There was no way he could have known that it was the last time he would ever see her.

– — –

For six hours Danny was on top of life. Six short hours was all that he was allowed before it all came crashing down yet again.

It started with a text from Nina at 7:42 p.m.

"I want to show you something. Can you meet me near Rocinha?"

He would have met her in Venezuela if she had asked him to. Forty-five minutes later he arrived to where she had directed him; a discreet basement bar in an old building. It took a bit of searching before he found the sign he was looking for, sticking out from the narrow walkway in between the white stucco building and it's newer neighbor. It was barely visible from the street and he wondered how it even managed to make money being so well hidden in addition to being in a rough neighborhood.

A narrow stairway took him below street level. The door was heavy but as he pushed it open he heard the distinct colliding of pool balls. It was a dimly lit hidden gem of a bar. Booths padded with purple velvet sat above a sunken floor where three pool tables stood. A red neon sign for Tecate behind the bar and green-shaded lamps hanging above the pool tables were the only light source, it was dim; his eyes needed a moment to adjust.

A chrome jukebox at the far end of the bar played "Country Roads" by John Denver. The bartender was an old man with a ponytail of thin grey hair who looked like he had smoked a pack a day for 40 years. There were four people in the bar and they all turned to see who had entered: two older men smoking cigars in a far booth, appearing to discuss business and two younger guys playing pool and drinking beer at the nearest table.

"What can I get you friend?" The bartender called to Danny as he stood just a few feet inside the door.

"I'll take a beer." He said, settling onto a barstool and pulling out his phone.

"I'm here"

She texted back immediately. More directions. It was a scavenger hunt. She instructed him to go into the back, through the curtain-covered doorway next to the jukebox. Not for a second did he feel suspicious or apprehensive; he was still high on the promise of seeing her face. The bartender slid him a beer as Danny stood, still looking at his phone. "Be right back." He said but the bartender had already turned and was fussing with liquor bottles.

Danny pushed aside the black curtain and stepped into a dark room lit by red lights like a photo-developing room. The ceiling was lower than it was in the bar. A few boxes were stacked next to a metal locker in the corner. His phone vibrated again.

"look in the black box on the far wall ;)"

He saw it. It was locked. Just as he reached for his phone to ask how to get in it vibrated again.

"The key is on the ground behind it"

Still nothing told him that something was wrong. Excitement and curiosity were the only things he felt. He slid his hand along the concrete floor and found a single key. The lock popped open and he lifted the lid. Then he was flooded with confusion. He hadn't known what to expect but what he saw didn't make any sense at all. In the dim red light he could roughly make out the packages but he needed to use his phone to illuminate the contents to make sure. As soon as he did, there was no mistaking what it was. It looked just like it did in the movies. Cocaine. A lot.

Numerous emotions rushed him. Foremost, he felt as though there had been a mistake. Then he felt nervous—he wanted to get away from whatever this was as quickly as possible.

Does Nina do coke? Did she think I would like this?

All of a sudden he felt as though he didn't know her at all. His mind raced to several other places as it tried to make sense of what he was looking at—surely he must have missed some piece of communication that would explain this.

Fuck it I'm out of here.

He slammed the lid of the box and started towards the curtain when he heard the front door of the bar burst open. Things started to move in slow motion. The unseen audience was back in a strong way, watching him from everywhere...with sympathy.

Whoever had entered the bar was singing along to John Denver in terrible English, "...tekk me hooome...Wess Bairginia...mountain momma...contry roooooad..."

Danny stepped through the curtain and froze in his tracks.

"Polícia." A hefty voice said with no real conviction. Danny didn't have words for what he saw. Four police officers stood inside the door.

"What are you doing back there?" The front officer demanded. He was wearing light blue jeans, tennis shoes and a polo shirt, a badge dangling around his neck. A holster was fixed to his hip, the butt of a gun protruding. Two of the officers were dressed in jungle green cargo

pants tucked into combat boots and decorated belts of police accesso-
ries wrapped tightly around their waists. They cautiously edged around
the side of Danny, keeping their distance as if they had been warned
that he was dangerous.

"I'm here to visit a friend." Danny said. His instincts told him
to raise his hands above his head but he reminded himself that he
hadn't done anything wrong and that this was all just some sort of
misunderstanding.

"There's been a mistake though. She's not here." He said, beginning to realize that whatever he said wouldn't help. He was scared.

"Identification." The main cop demanded as the two military cops
flanked Danny.

"I don't have any." Danny looked at the officer in charge who
avoided his eyes; instead he looked past him to one of the officers as he
came out of the back room. Danny turned just in time to see the man
nod at the leading officer.

"Hands behind your back, Danilo." He said mildly as if Danny
should be expecting it.

"What?" He said startled, shuffling backwards away from the
officer before the hands of the officers behind him clamped on his
shoulders. They were nervous too, he could tell by their grip.

"How do you know my name?"

*What is happening? Where did these cops come from? Where the fuck is
Nina?*

His initial instinct was to punch his way to the door but he knew
better. Instead, he put his hands in front of him as the lead officer took
a pair of stainless steel handcuffs from his waist. Danny was becoming
panicky. "Why am I under arrest?" He asked as calmly as he could.

"Drugs." The lead officer said flatly, slapping him amicably on the
shoulder after he finished putting on the handcuffs. His thoughts were
not cohesive or rational. He had to re-visit the chain of the events
throughout the evening that had led him here; he had to be missing
something.

The confusion continued as the officers led him to a nearby booth
and sat him down, then went to the bar and ordered drinks. The

bartender greeted the younger officers with familiarity. None of it made any sense.

"Is this your beer?" The main officer asked from the bar, pointing to the full beer that was sitting by itself. Danny nodded and they brought it to the table as soon as they had their drinks. He didn't want to drink it but for some reason he felt it could somehow help if he did. He brought it to his mouth with both handcuffed hands. The mood of the officers was light, they laughed and drank for half an hour. Eventually one of the military police turned to Danny, "You must be a fighter." His tone was buddy-buddy which allowed for some optimism.

Okay this may be some sort of fucked up joke that she's playing on me.

"I train jiu-jitsu. I'm not a fighter." He said.

One of the military cops said, "I heard about what you did to Gabriel Souza." Danny looked at him with contempt but didn't respond.

One of the officers got up and disappeared through the curtain, returning carrying a small, folded piece of newspaper. He emptied its' contents over the table; a small pile of light yellow powder and tiny pebbles spilled out. The lead officer began sweeping it back and forth with an ID card then he cut it into six large lines. They all took turns, coming to Danny the head officer offered him the rolled up R$50 note. He declined. They did all of it, dragging their fingers through the left-over residue and wiping it across their gums when they'd finished.

"Let's go." The boss said after draining the last of his beer. They began moving to the edge of the booth. "I'm not going anywhere." Danny said defiantly. "I haven't done anything."

"What are you doing with all that cocaine? It's a dangerous drug. It ruins lives." The chief said as the others chuckled, along with the bartender. The biggest officer grabbed Danny by the arm and pulled him to his feet. There was nothing he could do. They hadn't made any mistake; there was no confusion or hesitation, this was all part of some plan.

It would take a few hours before he could find the calmness of mind to realize what would break his heart right down the middle: she had set him up.

– — -

Jenna was lost for words. Even if she had wanted to say something she wouldn't have been able to find her voice.

It wasn't just the death Lucas; it was Nina too.

Whatever amicable feelings Jenna had towards Nina were gone in an instant.

How could someone do such a thing?

Even more alarming was that Danny still seemed to be affectionate towards Nina—a glimmer of adoration in his eyes when he spoke of her, a sick sort of Stockholm-syndrome acceptance of her actions as if somehow they were surely justified. Danny was slumped into the couch, fingers linked on top of his head, eyes towards the ceiling, already thinking about something else.

"So you were arrested." Jenna said. Her voice quivered hard at the last syllable.

Danny looked at her. A tear formed at the corner of her eye. She wiped it away carefully with her index finger. He stood and walked to her desk where he pulled two tissues from the box.

"Here, it's okay." His voice tipped her over the edge and she started crying uninhibited. He sat next to her on the chaise. "It's okay." He repeated putting an arm around her. Jenna sniffled and stammered out an embarrassed, "Oh my *God*," as she continued to wipe the corners of her eyes. "So unprofessional." She said. Danny chuckled. "*Professionalism* went out the window a while ago, Jenna."

It was Danny's selfless nature, he forgot the trauma he himself was currently re-living and instead focused on consoling Jenna. "Should we take a break?" He asked.

"No, no, it's alright." She insisted. "I'm fine. I just don't know how someone could do something like that." Danny squeezed her tighter and rubbed her arm. She had said she was fine and ready to continue but she obviously wasn't.

For a few minutes she cried gently while he thought about the relationship they had forged in the last two years of meeting late at night in her office. He cared about her and she obviously cared about him, but it had never evolved into anything more than just sex. He was incredibly thankful for her though, especially now. Had she not given

172   EDDY PRUGH

him the ultimatum, he would have never told her a thing about what had happened. And even though he wouldn't admit it, he knew it was what he needed.

When she was finally gathered and ready to continue he moved back to the couch. "I'm going to fast-forward a tiny bit." He said as he cleared his throat.

"I was driven directly to a prison called Leo Goia which, ironically, wasn't even that far from my grandparents' house. There was never any real proper, like, intake or procedure for me going into prison, no paperwork or mug shots or talking to an embassy or anything like that. I was just sort of taken through the front door and through some offices—they took my phone and wallet, but they did let me keep a picture I had of Allie and Lucas and I when we were little—but then they just sort of… opened a gate and tossed me into prison." He said with a shrug.

"It didn't take long before I realized I wasn't a normal inmate. I was there for a reason—it all made sense after the first couple days." Jenna waited for him to elaborate. "I was so confused and… and nervous. I had no idea how long I was going to be in there or *anything*. I still didn't want to believe that Nina had set me up."

He thought back to that first night, slumped against the wall of the cold concrete cell. He was cold, the only clothes he had were what he was wearing when he got there and he needed to get ahold of his grandparents. He had been equally worried about letting Marlos know that he wouldn't be at training on Monday.

– — –

It was still too unbelievable to seem real. At any moment he expected there to be an eruption of laughter and Nina to pop out from behind a door revealing that it had all been some ill-humored prank. Danny sat in the back of the dark green military Jeep between two officers who kept sniffling from the cocaine. After a twenty minute drive they pulled up to the front of a massive concrete structure that occupied a whole city block of its' own; towering grey concrete walls and a non-descript front entrance under thick yellow, stenciled letters: PRESÍDIO LEO GOIA.

The officers led him through offices in the front of the prison, fans spinning overhead and more military guards lounging in desk chairs smoking cigarettes and drinking beers. Then they bypassed the different sections of caged intake rooms, barred doors clanking loudly as they slid open and closed behind them. Finally down a long hallway they pushed through metal double doors and into a narrow enclosure behind bars once again. But now through the wide gate of aqua painted bars, Danny could see where he was headed.

"Don't worry. You'll have fun here." The shorter of the two guards said as he squeezed Danny's shoulder in a friendly way, sniffing again. The gate cranked with an ominous, mechanical rumble as it retracted to one side. Danny would never forget the sound. Beyond the bars everything was concrete and he looked out over an open space big enough to fit two basketball courts. His handcuffs were taken off and he was nudged forward. The gate began to crank shut behind him.

Okay, now I'm in prison.

He tentatively took in his new surroundings in the eerie silence that was only broken by a distant strumming of guitar strings. There were seven levels of cells boxing him in a courtyard. Above him was nothing but open night sky. Sheets of different colors hung over the doorways on all the levels and lights within the cells turned the walls into grids of different colored rectangles; a strangely beautiful scene. Huddles of men were scattered on the catwalks outside of the cells leaning over the railings, smoking cigarettes. Danny was taking it all in when there was a voice to his immediate left. He nearly jumped out of his skin.

"Danilo?"

A hefty man wearing a ratty green and orange University of Miami sweatshirt stepped into the light of the single light bulb in the narrow space behind the bars. He stood a safe distance away but his body language wasn't tense.

Danny didn't say anything. The man took a long look at him, starting at his feet and moving up. He bobbed his head in apparent

EDDY PRUGH

agreement with something that he had heard then turned his back and gave Danny a flick of the head to follow.

He led him to one of the first cells on the ground level. It was lit by thick wax candles but would have been pitch black otherwise. The cell was a room the size of a normal bedroom, a perfect square maybe fifteen by fifteen feet. Burn piles in the far corners of the room had provided charcoal that people had used to scrawl things all over the walls.

There was a single mattress pushed against one of the walls. Danny sat on it. Aside from the debris of the burn pile it was the only thing in the cell. Above his right shoulder someone had taken the time to fill in a bold '**THUG LIFE**' with the black charcoal. It looked like the walls of an abandoned mental asylum where people had gone mad and tried to express themselves as best they could through drawings and writing; erratic petroglyphs in a cave.

"You can stay in here tonight. Tomorrow we will move you into your cell." Danny had so many questions but he couldn't muster the energy to ask any of them.

"I need my family to know where I am."

"I'm sure the police that arrested you have taken care of that." The man said as if that would clear it up without concern. Danny was furious and beyond confused but he didn't have anything in his body that seemed capable of putting up a fight.

Everybody knew something that he didn't. The man set down a two-liter Sprite bottle filled with water inside the doorway and left. Danny was so close to climbing to his feet and screaming after him but he just couldn't find the power of will. The walls were closing in on him again. All of a sudden he was right back where he had started. The pitch-black despair closing in on him only this time it was even worse.

— — -

Everything that had happened since January 10th, the night Lucas died, ran through his mind in slow sequence: the phone call, the waiting room at the hospital, the services in Corvallis and at Church, the wet pavement with Trevor Ramey's blood pooling under his head, the plane to Brazil, the first day at Marlos' gym and his grappling session with Gabriel that had made waves throughout Rio's fighting world, the beach and Nina, the neon lights of carnival, the silhouetted man juggling a soccer ball on the beach at six in the morning, the black metal toolbox, the backseat of the Police Jeep. It had all taken less than three months; three short months to go from the top of the world to being slumped against a concrete wall in a cell in a Brazilian prison with a dead brother and a shattered heart.

In the candlelight, he stared at the picture of Lucas, Allie and himself from childhood. Studying the happiness and simplicity of life from a time that was so far gone that it was hard to believe it ever even happened. How shocking had the fates of the children in the photo been: one of the boys was dead and one was in prison in Brazil—the girl was doing okay at least.

He was scared for his family, how they would react to the news of him being in a Brazilian prison. But for himself, stepping into Leo Goia, he wasn't scared at all. He was weak with despair and anger but not scared. He welcomed any confrontation that would allow him to scream and swing his fists as hard as he could.

He didn't know if he ever actually fell asleep but he had zoned out in the misery of the silence for five hours and the next thing he knew the same guy in the Miami sweatshirt was calling to him from the doorway.

"Danilo. Danilo!"

Danny came into the moment.

"Come train!" he said enthusiastically with a flick of his head.

The guy was too friendly, talking to him in too familiar a way. It was becoming increasingly obvious that something larger was at work. Initially Danny thought that the guy meant they would be going to Marlos' gym, and his momentary relief cruel.

He followed the guy out the door into the open courtyard, getting his first look at the place in the light. There was a lot to take in. The design was simple: seven levels of cells boxing in a square courtyard, reminiscent of The Quad at Oregon State; the dormitories building that he and Tanner had lived in during their freshman year. The aqua gate that he had entered through the night before stood central on the bottom level of one of the sides.

Metal walkways with steel railings ran around the whole complex on each level and there were two sets of stairs on opposite sides. Ribbons of razor wire ran around the mouth of the opening, apparently to discourage any grappling hook style escape ideas. High in the pink morning sky a plane was leaving a perfectly straight contrail.

He counted 14 cell doorways on the slightly longer sides and 12 on the other two. The sheets that covered them gave the prison a tongue-in-s sense of urban beauty but were even more beautiful the night before when they were lit up by the lights within. Several picnic tables were scattered about in the courtyard and there was a small futsal court with chain link goals, white lines painted on the ground. Everything was concrete. It had the feeling of a post World War II Soviet building—something that might be seen in the grainy resolution of a documentary on A&E.

Maybe it was just because he was new to Leo Goia—although he had a growing suspicion it was much more than that—but he was the center of attention. Inmates leaned over the railings on all the levels and with Danny's emergence from the charcoal room several of them called into cells and more inmates emerged to catch a glimpse of him. He could hear their murmuring. He looked up at the faces of maybe 60 inmates. He was the star of the show.

The advice of convicted murderers and rapists from shows on History and MSNBC dictated themselves in his mind, *Do your time, don't let your time do you... Figure out how to be productive... They can keep my body in prison but they can't keep my mind locked up.*

They were all caged animals and he expected there to be confrontation. When he would make eye contact with one of them he would stare back until they looked away, he didn't give a shit. He wasn't scared. He was sad. He was angry.

A few pieces of exercise equipment lay scattered by one of the picnic tables. He picked up a standard 45 lb. bar with no plates on it and started pressing it over his head in a sarcastic manner as if it was incredibly difficult. The inmates were amused, laughing and whooping at his joke. The other inmates who were around the weights had stopped what they were doing and collectively stepped back, giving him more space.

After his fourth repetition he tossed the bar to the ground. The other lifters didn't know whether to smile with him or step back even further. There was excited chatter from all sides of the courtyard and Danny knew it for sure now: they all knew who he was.

"Not here Danilo." The guy said flicking his head towards an open doorway across from the cell he had spent the night in. He followed him inside and to his shock he saw a nearly state of the art gym. The floor was covered in black rubber mats like a hockey locker room. There were two punching bags attached to the ceiling, free weights, medicine balls and a bucket overflowing with different rubber bands and weight clamps on the right wall. A CD player was on the floor in one corner playing light reggaeton for the lone occupant, a small, quick looking fighter in his late twenties.

Soaked in sweat, he saw the two of them standing there and immediately became interested, "Is this him?" he asked in an, *Oh it's so good to finally meet you,* way.

Danny was peeved by the easy-going nature of the question and when the guy stretched out his hand for a respectful introduction, Danny wrinkled an eyebrow and kept his own hand at his side. The smile quickly faded from the smaller guys' face.

"What the fuck do you mean, *Is this him?*"

The fighter shook his head and turned around, heading back to his workout but Danny wasn't having any of it and snatched him by the forearm, spinning him around, "I asked you a question little man."

He was maybe 150 lbs. and Danny could have tossed him through the wall if he wanted, both parties seemed well aware of that. "I heard what you did to Gabriel. I—I heard about it. That's all."

Danny released him. He turned to the guy who had brought him, "How the fuck does he know that? What am I doing here?"

The Miami sweatshirt guy was looking at the smaller one angrily, and Danny wasn't supposed to see it because he quickly changed his expression just as Danny turned back to him. He shrugged, "News travels fast. People know people. That's Rio. It's a fighting city."

Danny wasn't satisfied. "Do you know Nina?" He demanded, looking back and forth between the two of them but he could see by their faces that they didn't know anything about her.

Danny decided that for the time being he shouldn't be making enemies.

"Sorry. I'm Danilo." He said to the smaller fighter who became relieved.

"I'm Rafa. I'm one of Leo Goia's fighters."

Danny was piecing things together.

"Somebody will bring you some food soon." The big guy called, stepping out of the cell. Danny threw a thumbs-up over his shoulder. He rummaged in the box of rubber bands for a moment before giving in to the frustration and slumping against the wall.

All he could see was Nina's face. The little mole on the side of her eye had once seemed so graceful and full of beauty but now seemed more like the mark of the devil. He saw her round face, smooth skin and dark eyes looking up at him from its resting place on his lap as they watched the sunrise. Every smile she had beamed at him, every laugh and gentle touch was a lie. Rage overcame him, but instead of punching the concrete wall he rushed outside and threw up, of course drawing the attention of the whole courtyard.

Miami sweatshirt guy was true to his word and around noon a little guy in a bootleg pink Ralph Lauren polo stuck his head in the door, "Danilo?" and then proceeded to hand him a grease stained brown bag with a double cheeseburger and fries from Bob's, a popular fast-food chain in Rio. The fact that it had come from the outside was his first clue that Leo Goia was nothing like the prisons he had heard stories about.

His stomach didn't want to accept anything solid but he ate the burger because he didn't know when he would get food again. He started to stress more and more about talking to his grandparents—and Marlos. For the time being, he stayed in the gym, slumped against the wall, occasionally getting up and hitting the punching bag, focusing on the techniques that had been drilled into him by the coaches at the gym.

The gym cell appeared to be off-limits to normal prisoners—the only people to come in throughout the day were athletic and obviously had fighting minds as they all did some sort of fighting-specific exercise. There had only been four throughout the day and they all showed Danny respect as if he were their childhood hero.

– — -

Jenna had been wearing the same wrinkled brow for ten minutes. At an appropriate pause she asked, "How could they just put you in jail like that? I mean wasn't there some sort of protocol. And what about your grandparents?" She asked, concern rising in her voice.

"It was strange, but…the people who organized this stuff have everything covered. They knew everything about me—from Nina, of course. Officers had been to my grandparent's house but there was never any involvement with the embassy—they're so well connected and powerful it's no use going to the police—Marlos knew that. My grandpa knew that."

"So was it dangerous? Sounds like you were…a *celebrity*."

Danny nodded in agreement. "Yeah I really was. The prisons that you're probably imagining exist for sure. Every summer I'd hear a news story about over-crowded, roach-infested prisons with riots that lasted for a week and killed like fifty people but it wasn't like that at all. I never felt threatened, especially since I was there to entertain. I was like royalty. Nobody would have ever done anything to me."

Danny was amazed at the ease with which he was able to recall the experience; the last time he had done this with Celia and Tanner in the Rhododendron garden his heart had pounded so hard that he thought his chest would bruise.

He could see the dots connect in Jenna's mind as she stared without blinking, "Entertain. You were there to fight."

– — -

The guy in the Miami sweatshirt was, it seemed, his assigned prison liaison. At about 4 p.m. that afternoon he stuck his head into the gym cell. Danny hadn't left all day except for a few minutes here and there to wander through the courtyard.

"Danilo. When you're ready I can take you to your room."

Danny was slumped against the wall as he had been for much of the day.

"I need to call my grandparents. They don't know where I am." He growled.

The guy frowned, "I told you it was taken care of." Danny shot him a look that made him quickly surrender his position of assumed authority. "Okay, okay. One moment." He disappeared for a couple minutes before returning with a silver flip phone that reminded Danny of his first cell phone that he got in eighth grade. He tossed it over.

"My name is Jefferson." The man said.

"Cool." Danny said uninterested as he dialed his grandparents home phone number. Rosa answered quickly. Danny took a deep breath. "It's me grandma...I know...I know but...grandma...I know... it's going to be okay...it's not true grandma, I can explain."

— — —

17 hours after he had passed through the aqua bars of the entrance into the courtyard, in a rambling fifteen-minute conversation with Edson, Danny explained what had happened the day before. Edson didn't get flustered. He only asked the questions he needed to ask to get the information he needed. Danny hurt for his grandparents; he couldn't even fathom how worried they must have been but he assured them that he was safe and that Leo Goia was nothing like what they were likely imagining. He didn't want to picture his own parents when the call came from Edson.

It was so cruel to pile worry on top of the grief and he knew his mom—maybe all of them—would be on a flight as soon as they heard where he was.

Rosa was given the phone again. He couldn't tell if she had heard his assurances that he would be okay, she was crying so hard on the other end of the line and soon Danny could hear his uncle Leandro in the background consoling her. Edson had taken the phone back then. Danny made him promise to pass his love to everyone and as difficult as it was, they ended the call.

— — -

There was an intense game of futsal taking place on the court below as they climbed the grated stairs to the second level. "They have arranged a room for you." Jefferson said over his shoulder. Danny didn't know who *they* were and he didn't care anymore. The phone call with his grandparents had left him feeling sick and wanting to lie down.

The guitar that Danny had heard the night before was playing again and the sound grew louder as they made their way along the metal walkway, passing sheet-doors of all colors until finally, two doors away from the corner of the level, Jefferson pushed aside a dark green sheet that hung over one of the doorways. It was a similar color to his house in Portland.

My new home is the same color as my old home.

Déjà vu from pushing through the curtain in the bar made him clench his teeth. Inside the cell was a desk lamp on the floor in the corner giving the room a warm light. Dozens of books were stacked neatly next to a mini-fridge on the back wall with clean dishes stacked on top of it. A cone of incense burned from a holder in the center of the chipped concrete floor.

The books and the refrigerator threw it off but Danny instantly noticed that the room had the same symmetry of his bedroom at his grandparents' house, there were two mattresses pushed against the walls opposite of one another. The left one was obviously for him, two blankets folded on top of it.

Sitting on the mattress on the right side of the cell was a thin white man with red hair holding a guitar, a bottle of Jack Daniels on the floor in front of him. He wore a loose wife-beater and green cargo shorts. His forearms were tattooed and he wore glasses.

"This is Joris. He's from Germany. Whatever you need, just ask him. He is your friend."

— — —

"I don't think I'll ever meet another person quite like Joris." Danny said with a fond grin of nostalgic adoration. "I miss that guy."

"What was he in for?" Jenna asked.

"Drugs. Cocaine. His sentence was only like eighteen months. If I didn't have him in there…I don't know what I would have done." He said with a sigh, shaking his head, not wanting to ponder the thought.

— — —

Danny was left standing in the concrete cube with his new cellmate, who put his guitar on the mattress and looked at Danny, expectant of an introduction or some sort of exchange. Their eyes locked un-ag-gressively. He was skinny. His glasses made him look smart but his sunburnt skin and cheap tattoos gave him a look reminiscent of a rural Eastern Oregon meth user. Danny could see that his jaw was a tiny bit misshaped when looked at from just the right angle. His black ink that had faded to a dull green hinted at young, misguided mistakes. For a moment, Danny could sense the presence of the invisible audience once again. Watching the exchange between Danny and Joris.

"Is your jaw crooked?" Danny asked bluntly.

"Yes. It is." Joris said earnestly, shrugging his eyebrows, not the least bit offended by the question. He ran a nostalgic thumb down the left side of it. His English took Danny by surprise. His left forearm was covered with a greenish-blue lion head with a grand mane. His teeth were smoker-yellow—a shame, since they were straight and un-chipped. His face had a boyish youthfulness to it, accentuated by the light red hair and freckles. For a split-second Danny saw him as something other than an inmate in Leo Goia. He was handsome in a tough, derelict kind of way.

Danny had started to sweat through his shirt and he stripped it off and sat on the edge of his mattress, arms folded on top of his knees. "So. Joris. I'm here to fight." He said definitively. He assumed that Joris' English was good enough to understand that it was also a question, an open invitation for him to confirm or deny or elaborate upon. Joris nodded slowly, moving a book from his mattress to the refrigerator and sitting up, folding his gangly arms over his knees the same as Danny in what seemed to be a show of courtesy. They sat just feet across from one another and the symmetry of Danny's new bedroom was complete.

"Yes. That is correct. Every Friday there are fights here. People come from all over to see. And bet, obviously."

Obviously, Danny thought to himself sarcastically since it wasn't obvious at all. You are a big attraction—probably the biggest that has ever been in these fights, as far as I am aware of." He cleared his throat. "They have been talking about you. About what you did to this guy... um..."

"Gabriel?" Danny helped.

"Gabriel. Yes that's the name." His voice was tough and certain of itself. Nothing about his demeanor was tense or nervous. His eyes were calm and familiar as if he was talking to somebody he had known for years.

"You will make good money on Friday." He added as a potential cause for optimism.

For a moment Danny contemplated the implications of Joris and everybody else in Leo Goia knowing about Gabriel. "So you've heard about me. You know I was set up." Another statement that was left as an invitation and Joris nodded with what appeared to be genuine sympathy in his eyes. "I don't know how that works. It is not common but somebody probably made a lot of money by getting you in here." He said pressing an index finger to the side of his nose, the international sign for doing cocaine.

Danny went into solitary reminiscence of Nina, staring into space while his heart sank. Joris lit a cigarette. "Don't worry, man. You are not a *real* criminal and they can't keep you here forever—you are American, yes? It will become too serious for them if you are in here for long time and then they have to deal with the embassy and that. Just have a few fights, make some money and you will be out very soon." Danny appreciated the optimism but the cigarette was going to be a problem. "Take that shit outside. Please."

Even in the first few minutes of knowing him Danny could already feel a familiarity with Joris; it was very odd timing to find such a feeling, right in the midst of the emotions he was feeling but it were as if they had known each other and were being re-acquainted after years apart. He had a very easy-going approachableness. It was impossible to imagine him sitting in a classroom but Danny could sense a unique intelligence, like it wouldn't be surprising to learn that he had a photographic memory or some other obscure talent.

"Sorry." Joris said, standing and pushing through the curtain and onto the walkway. Danny followed a moment later, he wasn't done with his questioning but as he leaned over the railing, resting his elbows on the steel, he realized that he was more curious about his new cellmate than he was with his own predicament.

"So you're German?"

Joris shook his head mid-drag, rolling his eyes. "I am Dutch. This guy. *Jeff*erson. He is a little dumb head. He probably does not know the difference: Dutch and German."

"Dutch." Danny said, half to himself, half to Joris.

"Yesssss. Red, white and blue." Joris said glancing at Danny to see if he understood the joke. He did, and he almost smiled at the bit of dry humor. Joris smoked two cigarettes in quick succession as Danny asked questions.

Joris had long since stopped being surprised by people. He had seen men become capable of things that he never dreamed they would be capable of, but when Jefferson told him that he would be rooming with the new fighter that everyone had started talking about a few days earlier, Danilo *or Danny*, was not at all what he had expected. They talked for an hour leaning against the railing over the courtyard in Presídio Leo Goia.

In the conversations that resulted from Danny's inquisitiveness Joris learned that he was reserved and rational yet robustly confident. He was going to enjoy learning more about this American fighter.

After a long string of questioning they eventually moved back into the cell where Danny fell asleep. Exhaustion from the whole ordeal seemed to finally catch up to him and the strange sense of ease he felt around Joris eased his reluctance to fall asleep in prison for the first time. He woke two hours later. Conversation ensued as naturally as it had before, this time over a few dirty glasses of straight Jack Daniels. Joris had an uncanny way of answering questions that Danny had in his mind but hadn't yet asked.

"This is like, how should I say...a *luxury* prison." He said as he mimed an elegant sip of tea with his pinky finger pointed out. "It's for people who can afford to stay out of the shitty prisons and for foreigners too, also people who have friends in the government or something. If a foreign person dies in prison in Brazil it will be a big headache for the government so most of we are in nice place like this."

It all made more sense to Danny then, this place was nothing like the overcrowded and rat infested places that would catch fire and kill 100 inmates the he had heard of.

"I need to be in contact with my family, Joris. I must speak with my grandparents. They are worried."

Joris got up and moved towards the door without a word and Danny thought he might be ignoring him but before he broke through the curtain he said, "That's not a problem."

Two minutes later he returned with a different flip phone than the one Danny had used to dial his grandparents that afternoon. "You can use this phone whenever you want. It needs to be get power in a cell down the—over there." Joris said jerking a thumb over his shoulder. "It is a Rio number, yes?"

Danny nodded.

"Yes no problem then. Use this phone whenever you need." Danny took it and started dialing his grandparents again. He knew Rosa was distraught and he needed to assure her that Leo Goia was more like a cheap hotel than a prison.

Joris moved toward the green sheet covering the doorway but stopped just short. Unlit cigarette in his mouth, he turned and asked, "What was your last name?"

Without looking up from the phone Danny responded, "Sheppard."

"Sheppard." Joris repeated. Then moving out of the curtain he continued talking to himself, "Danilo Sheppard: the shepherd of victory. And I am Joris, your prison shepherd. Follow me...to the riches."

It had only been a few hours since he had been introduced to his new roommate; the Dutch drug smuggler named Joris, but he was already thankful for him.

— — —

The Sheppard house had been plunged back into frantic anxiety since the news came over the phone that Danny was, unfathomably, in prison. Once again, they felt the same surprise as when the police knocked on the door in January with the news that Danny had nearly beaten a man to death. Isabel had bought a ticket for Rio within moments of hanging up the phone with Edson.

— — —

After his afternoon nap, sleep seemed unlikely that night. His thoughts had been so preoccupying that it didn't seem possible to slow them down to a pace that would allow for sleep. Nina was forefront, she pulled the strings of Danny's mania but she was interrupted frequently by the image of Allie or Andrea walking through the front door to hear the news that had just come over the phone, *Danny is in jail*.

But against the odds, he did sleep. It was the calming sound of Joris lightly strumming his guitar that put him to sleep. It was the power of his prison shepherd.

— — —

When he woke the next morning Joris wasn't in the cell but there was a plate of food waiting for him next to his mattress—scrambled eggs and several rolls of bread, a cup of coffee, and a bottle of ketchup. It wasn't a breakfast that somebody would normally come across in Brazil and he felt strangely grateful to whomever it was that was feeding him and had acted upon the stereotype that Americans loved ketchup. He ate everything and was finishing his coffee as Joris appeared, light flooding into the room as he pushed the curtain aside.

"Oh good. You ate the food. How do you like your coffee so I know for the future? What else do you want?" He asked as if Danny could order anything.

"A little milk—in the coffee, I mean." He rubbed his eyes as Joris handed him a brown paper bag with a toothbrush, toothpaste and a mini stick of deodorant. "Do you want to see everything?" Joris asked, at the same time snapping his fingers and pointing at a folded towel that had appeared on top of the refrigerator.

Danny nodded and the morning was spent on a tour of the prison. He saw the cells on the ground level where food was cooked. He saw the cell where there were outlets; tangled jumbles of power strips coming from every outlet for cell phones, iPods, computers and whatever needed charging. He saw the cell on the fourth level where Joris played cards which was much nicer than the other cells and seemingly reserved for only social gatherings, no beds, just chairs and a couch and a large round table but most noteworthy was the rug.

So strange, somebody took the time to furnish a prison cell with a fucking rug. Some inmates couldn't care less about Danny's presence but most sprang from their seats in respect, eager to shake his hand and demonstrate their admiration.

Danny trailed Joris from cell to cell and level to level. They were all furnished differently according to how much money and resources the inhabitants had. After spending the first night in the charcoal-graffiti cell he could never have imagined that the rest of the prison would look as it did, some cells were nicer than places in the favelas. Lastly, he was shown the shower room on the ground level. A solemn concrete room with drains in the middle and sixteen showerheads, eight on either side protruding from the concrete on either side. Several prisoners were showering.

"People jerk off in that far corner, stay away from over there—unless you are jerking off." Joris said, not joking.

Danny wanted to shower and while Joris went to get him the towel from the cell he stripped off his clothes and hung them on a free hook near the entrance. The other men took notice of him as he walked to the farthest showerhead. He didn't know if it was yet another show of respect but almost immediately the other guys had dried off, dressed and left.

The cold water was heavenly when paired with the silence. The room had the first windows Danny had seen inside Leo Goia. Nothing was visible—they were inches thick and greyed out on either side but they let in a hazy light that did enough to make things just barely visible.

He leaned his forehead against the concrete as cold water ran from the end of his nose like a spigot. He was aware of Joris hanging up the towel on the wall near entrance then quickly ducking out, trying to go unnoticed.

When he closed his eyes all he could see was her smiling face. Her laugh echoed faintly as if it were floating from the top of his brain to the bottom, or perhaps it was rising from the bottom to the top. He still couldn't believe it but if he had learned anything from Lucas dying it was that he might as well believe it, it had happened. Still, for Nina to coerce him as she had, it now seemed that anybody was capable of anything. Nobody could be trusted.

He heard her voice explain the nuances and subtle differences of a 4-3-3 formation against a 3-5-2 in soccer, *It's very similar when they are attacking but in defense is where you can see the difference between the two.* She had done most of the talking in the week that they spent together, maybe an 80/20 ratio. He remembered almost every word she ever said but things like, *It depends on the undertow of the streets,* or *It's all about balance. You can't have too much attack and too little defense and vice-versa,* repeated themselves over and over again in his mind. Her slow sultry voice wouldn't leave his ears.

She owned him.

— — -

When Danny came back to the cell after his shower he was alarmed to see his duffle bag from his grandparents house stuffed with his clothes.

"The guards just dropped this off." Joris said, not looking up from his book. "They can bring stuff in here from the outside?" Danny asked.

"Of course." Joris said.

Danny wondered if his uncles were in the offices beyond the aqua gate at that very moment. He could imagine Leandro—the biggest and most intimidating of them—slamming his fists on a table and demanding to speak to the highest-ranking official.

Danny went with Joris to the card game that evening. In the cell with the rug, nine men sat around the table and a few more loitered around the outside, drinking and talking. One of the younger inmates was quickly sent to fetch a chair from another cell for Danny to sit. Joris whispered to him that this kind of respect was unlike anything he'd seen in his three months in Leo Goia. Danny sat by himself but was soon brought a drink by a thirty-something man with a nondescript face and normal build. He introduced himself as Michel then returned to the card game but lost chips on virtually every hand.

The cell was hazy from cigarettes, spliffs and pure joints. A bullet of cocaine was passed around from time to time as casually as if it were a bottle of whiskey.

After what must have been at least his eighth Bacardi and Cola, Michel abandoned the game, taking his remaining chips and moving his chair next to Danny's, apart from the rest of the table.

"I'm terrible at cards. I just play for the jokes and the fun." He said cheerfully. From watching the game Danny gathered that Michel was well respected or at least well liked by the rest of the card players. He was talkative. Danny wasn't sure if it was just his nature or the drink and cocaine but he was a wealth of information. A bookie for the fights; locked up for—like almost everyone; drugs. Without much prodding or questioning, he answered questions that Danny wasn't sure he would have answered had he been sober.

"The boss organizes everything. He has the contacts to bring in the fighters. He takes a big cut—more than he should, if you ask me. It's big business in Rio. Most people think of Rio as a football city—of course it is, Brazil is a football *country*—but fighting is in our bones. Very popular. And this is the where the biggest underground fights of them all happen. Right here in Leo Goia. The most money passes through here. A lot of the betters are foreign—they fly in just for the fights. I promise, everyone is very excited to see you."

"Does he come to the fights? The boss?" Danny asked.

"Always." Michel said, rising from his chair to make another drink. Danny also found out that he would make at least R\$6,000, about \$2,000, maybe more depending on the fashion in which he would win, knockout paid out the most. It was a little annoying that everyone so readily assumed that he would be willing to fight after being set up for a false arrest but in truth, he was *more* than ready, in truth he was grateful for it. His sadness had evolved into something much worse. It had morphed into a toxic blend of anger and spite for the whole world it seemed. Nothing was worthwhile in a place where a person like Nina existed. Michel returned, settling roughly into his chair and strangely, almost recited word for word what Joris had told him that morning.

"Just appease the boss. Have a few fights, make a bit of money and you will be out in no time. You didn't do anything wrong, they can't keep you here forever."

Danny took the glass that Michel was pressing towards him, at least a double shot of straight Bacardi. "Cheers." He said, "To your coming success. You are going to make me a lot of money!" He laughed loud as he clinked his glass against Danny's and threw it back. Danny did the same.

They continued to drink and talk until Joris stood from the card game, gathering his chips and a large pile of cash. Danny was impressed by his Portuguese and chuckled when he heard him say to the rest of the players that he and Danny were, "Going home."

Danny did the smart thing and introduced himself to the players at the table who he hadn't previously met. He wasn't sure who he would need to be on good terms with while he was inside. As he bounced between fits of jaw-clenching anger and slumps of depression, he found that he could count on Joris for a calming bit of conversation.

He was perfect company for Danny, never getting noticeably happy or excited which was nice since Danny wouldn't have been able to join him in either emotion. Joris' damaged serotonin production kept him from smiling or laughing often and even when he would do cocaine—which was fairly often, like many of the prisoners—he never exhibited any of the heightened enthusiasm or rapid speech of an amateur cocaine user. He was a veteran of addiction and it showed in his flat brown eyes and wilted brow. After returning from the card game Danny lay down on his mattress as Joris picked up his guitar. "Any requests?" He asked jokingly.

Danny rolled over and grinned. "Thank you for being my prison shepherd."

- — -

The next few days passed diligently with phone calls to his grandparents, morning workouts and an afternoons listening to Joris tell stories from his time in South East Asia or Europe. Just as Danny had anticipated, Isabel was flying down on Wednesday, distraught no doubt. There wouldn't be anything she could do but she wasn't about to sit in Portland and wait for phone calls.

Before Danny knew it, it was Friday morning. Fight day. The buzz was palpable around the courtyard. Danny called his grandparents again. Now it was always Isabel who answered. She always started crying and it made Danny feel even more hopeless. Of course he omitted the small detail that he was there to fight, although he suspected that Edson knew that part since he had been in contact with Marlos.

As he sat on his mattress and ate his second serving of breakfast he stared into space and tried to feel something for the upcoming fight. It didn't feel any different than an impending wrestling dual. He imagined that he would have more nerves but he didn't feel anything, his confidence was sure of itself; he knew he would win. He took the two-liter bottle of Sprite that he used for water and headed for the gym cell.

There were two other fighters working out, the one he had met the first day, Rafa, and a taller one who introduced himself respectfully, Ismael. At about noon, things really started to get energetic outside. The mechanical cranking of the aqua bars made Danny step into the courtyard with curiosity. Three men in matching green t-shirts and worker gloves wheeled in flatbed trolleys of metal folding chairs. A few cheers rang out from the metal walkways above.

– — -

6:11 P.M.
Danny woke from a nap. Joris was reading a book, glasses on.

"When do I fight?" He asked. Joris didn't look up. "Much later. The first fight is at ten. You fight last so maybe…eleven thirty?" He guessed.

"How many fights are there?"

"Five tonight." Joris said, adding, "I have money on three of them."

"Do you have money on me?" Danny asked. Joris still didn't look away from his book. "Yes of course I do. Pretty much everybody does—your odds do not pay out very well but everyone seems to think it is the only, like, *guarantee*."

Danny strolled outside and down to where the folding chairs had been assembled on three sides of an open square of concrete, dead center in the courtyard. A red wrestling mat was rolled up on the open side of the chairs, not yet unraveled. The green-shirted workers were setting up the poles on the corners of the square where Danny assumed ropes would be strung up. The whole production seemed very organized and professional. There were more guards standing around than usual, he recognized four of them but there were nine now. He strolled past them and studied the scene that was taking shape as one unfamiliar guard mumbled something to another and Danny was able to hear the names *Gabriel* and *Marlos*.

– — -

8:19 P.M.
Danny was jumping rope languidly in the gym cell when out in the courtyard he heard the clanking and grinding of the aqua bars sliding open again. In came the floodlights. Camouflaged guards carried them in teams. Twenty minutes later the whooshing noise of the lights being

turned on brought more cheering. The energy was growing with each passing minute.

— — -

9:14 P.M.

Danny was eager to see the type of people who would be entering Leo Goia to watch and bet. At 9:14 he got his first glimpse.

The gym cell had become more populated with what seemed to be organizers and other people involved with the fights, Michel and Jefferson were both there and Joris had been in and out. He heard the commotion of the spectators before the gate even started opening. He peaked out the doorway and saw people filtering into the narrow space behind the aqua bars.

The gate retracted again, freeing them to spill into the courtyard, more guards were mixed in with them. Now Danny was interested.

It was a diverse crowd but one thing was clear, they all had money. For some of them it seemed as though the fights were just a night out, a weekly routine that they simply stepped out their door and took a taxi to. For others it looked like far more of a production. He watched as a group of three tall, smooth skinned black men, all dressed in black Adidas warm up suits strolled towards the chairs. They spoke pure Spanish; Danny guessed they were Colombian and most likely; professional soccer players judging by their athletic builds.

There were several American or Canadian businessmen. Danny imagined that they had just finished a business trip and decided to bet some money on underground fighting in a luxury prison after company drinks at a fancy hotel somewhere; blue jeans and un-tucked shirts, buttons open at the top, cowboy boots and gold bracelets. There were groups of Rio drug people: flat-bill baseball caps and fresh white Air Force Ones, Cuban links, sagged Levis.

Danny was excited now. He wanted them to spend their money and be happy with him when they won it back. He wanted to be victorious and be the star of the show. He wanted to hear his name and for people to understand that what they had heard about him was true. He wanted to win.

From the doorway of the gym cell he watched as a couple in their forties, the man dressed lavishly in steely greys and his wife in a strapless black dress approached a guard and asked him something. The guard then pointed straight across the courtyard at Danny. Their eyes followed the guard's finger and locked on him. The man gave him a smile and a respectful nod. They were there to see him. Danny unfolded his arms and waved.

All this from tossing Gabriel…

He sat and stared at the photo of Allie and Lucas and himself as bodies ghosted around him, he caught bits and pieces of the conversations between the four fighters and their advice-givers, *But watch for the elbow when you're in that position… Don't get too confident if he starts to retreat, trust me I know this guy…Just keep moving, bouncing, he'll lose focus.*

The photo was incredibly worn out now but the smiles of his brother and sister took him somewhere calm. He stayed slouched against the wall staring into their eyes for the next hour.

– — –

10:18 P.M.

One fighter in the cell was bouncing on his toes vigorously, nerves clearly getting the best of him. Danny didn't know anything about him but he had little confidence in him. He wasn't an inmate but had been in the gym cell since earlier in the evening with his trainer. He couldn't have been much older than 20 and didn't appear to be very athletic; his upper body was larger in proportion to his lower body.

Suddenly outside in the courtyard a bullhorn pierced over the chatter of the crowd and echoed off the walls. The man's voice seemed well practiced, a Portuguese Bruce Buffer imitation, deep and drawn out as he hyped the crowd for the opening fight.

The nervous kid in the cell was named Rodrigo Pereira according to Bruce Buffer. He was kneeling and saying one final prayer as the bullhorn yelled his name in introduction and he bounded out of the cell and towards the ring, followed by his trainer. The aqua bars had stayed retracted and from the doors behind them came his opponent. They were similarly matched, both maybe 5'7" and around 140 lbs. Danny watched as they were brought together at the center of the mat and instructed of the rules—the same as a sanctioned fight but in Leo Goia there were only 3 rounds of 4 minutes so things went fast and knockouts were more likely as defensive tactics fell by the wayside.

Everybody in the gym cell had stepped just outside the door to watch but Danny went back to looking at the picture, still slumped against the wall.

– — –

12:13 A.M.

The fourth fight ended in a submission. It was a god fight but there was an undeniable angst in the crowd.

Alright already let's see what we came here to see.

The second fight had produced a pretty good knockout that had been the most exciting moment so far if judged by the volume of the crowd alone, the cheers rising into the night sky beyond the razor wire. The intermission stretched on for longer than the pauses in between the previous fights; the organizers wanted the anticipation to grow.

Danny hadn't lent even the slightest curiosity to who his opponent would be and in truth, he didn't care. Michel, Jefferson and Joris had returned to the cell. Danny started loosening up casually. "How are you feeling?" Jefferson asked. Of the three of them, Jefferson was his least favorite.

"Fine. How are *you* feeling?" Danny asked sarcastically.

In the place where he should have more butterflies than anywhere, in an event that should have given him more butterflies than any competition, he was completely collected and levelheaded. He just wanted to fight, to be angry, to clench his teeth and swing.

Then the bullhorn crackled. "Ladies and gentlemen...please prepare yourself for tonight's main event!" The crowd cheered and the commotion from the catwalks above was louder than it had been at any point. Danny felt a sense of duty then, he was fighting for Marlos *and* Leo Goia.

"From the famous gym of Sergio Guedes...standing at one meter, ninety two centimeters...the *Bone Snatcher*," the announcer said his nickname in rough English, "Jean Noguera!"

Danny saw his appointment push through the doors at the opposite wall behind the retracted aqua bars. He was bigger and much older than Danny. He looked like he had been a fighter at some point in his life but was now in his early thirties and hadn't worried too much about his gut. Two trainers wearing the same navy collared shirt followed him. He bounced on his toes in the center of the mat, boxing the air mildly.

Then it was the moment everyone had waited for. "Ladies and gentlemen...please make some noise for the last fighter of the evening... Danilo...O Tuburão...Cheppard!"

It was news to him but apparently his nickname was Danilo "The Shark" Sheppard. The cheering was louder as he strolled nonchalantly out of the gym cell, walking barefoot across the concrete yard by himself. He was already loved. The cheering came from all sides. To the inmates of Leo Goia, he was their own; they would have worn his merchandise and sang the words of his entry song if he had either. He had no frame of reference since it was his first experience of the Friday night fights but something told him that this was a bigger occasion than usual.

Danny stood motionless in the center of the mat; he had become a showman, cocky and self-indulged unlike he had ever been in his life. He cupped his hands behind his ears; *I can't hear you*, as he turned in a circle, appealing to every side of the courtyard. The cheering grew at his beckon. They ate it up and for a moment a chant of *Tubarão...Tubarão* had threatened to begin from the walkways above before the bullhorn called the two of them to the center of the mat. Danny stared at his opponent. Jean Noguera stared back, his eyes unwavering and determined.

Danny felt sorry for him; he didn't know what was coming. The referee, a heavily built man around 50 with a bald head and a thick moustache recited the rules, it was nothing but static mumbles in the background as Danny fantasized about the liberation he was about to feel.

The referee finished with his instructions and they touched fists. Danny walked backward slowly as Jean Noguera bounced backwards energetically and beat his chest with both hands.

Jean Noguera was maybe 6'3½", and he probably weighed 15 pounds more than the 185 lbs. that Danny last weighed in at. He wore black shorts cut up the sides and his ankles were taped in classic kick-boxing style.

Danny turned around and stripped off his shirt and sweats, handing them to a teenager sitting in the front row next to his street-cool older brother or cousin. He wore the uniform of a spoiled Rio teenager: white Adidas All-Stars, acid wash jeans with the knees out, a flat bill LA Dodgers cap and dark aviators.

The distant words of the referee reverbed through his mind *a clean fight...if a fighter taps...knockout...the fight is finished*. Jean Noguera glared at Danny with a rehearsed tough-guy stare as Danny looked back with lazy eyes.

"Ready?" The referee pointed at Jean who nodded quickly, nostrils flaring. "Ready?" He pointed to Danny who flipped his hand through the air. The crowd was thoroughly enjoying his showmanship.

"Fight!" Shouted the referee clapping his hands together and back-pedaling. Jean Noguera moved across the mat towards Danny, fists raised, head bobbing from side-to-side, leaning far too heavily on his front leg. Danny had his fists up and as Jean drew close enough to strike, Danny whipped out a viscous kick to his front leg that gave way dramatically sending him to the mat in a heap. The crowd reacted loudly. Danny could have ended it then if he had taken it to the floor but he decided to back off and let Noguera up, mainly because he wanted to take him down again. He liked the noise the crowd made.

Noguera tried his best to keep his confidence in tact as he got to his feet but he was shaken, Danny could see it in his face. There must have been a contingent of his family and friends in the crowd judging by the localized cheering and encouragement that reigned at him from somewhere in the back of one of the rows of chairs.

He came at Danny again with re-energized determination and blind pride. It was time that Danny actually defended some real strikes, and Marlos would have been proud of the way he moved in avoidance of the heavy swings. Then Danny went for the legs, wrapping him to the ground and easily securing him against the mat with pitiful ease. It must have looked good because mixed in with the cheering the crowd chattered vigorously. His technique was flawless.

This is too easy.

"Tap out man. I don't want to hurt you." Danny said into Jean's ear. It would have been the smart thing to do, he had no chance but he was proud and responded by trying desperately to wriggle free. Danny clasped Jean beneath him in a seated position and began to punch. From his back, Jean was able to connect a few punches upward but they weren't powerful and Danny was able to connect with six, seven, eight solid strikes before he began with elbows that were illegal—the same type of elbows he had used to break Trevor Ramey's just weeks earlier.

He dropped the point of his elbow straight onto the head of Noguera as he shielded his face with his forearms. The referee jumped in after just a few seconds.

"That's illegal!" The ref shouted, bringing them to their feet and separating them to their corners of the mat. Talking into Danny's ear in an informal, friendly tone the referee said, "You can't do that. Not even in here." Danny nodded.

After Jean had taken a minute being tended to in his corner by his two trainers and listening to their futile advice the referee resumed the fight, slapping his hands together in the center of the mat once again.

Cautiously, Jean Noguera edged across the mat. For years Danny had relied on his athletic instincts and muscle memory for wrestling and in the time in Marlos' gym he must have developed more because he suddenly felt an instinct that he had never had before: *kick him in the fucking head.*

Years of capoeira with uncle Paulo and what he had learned at Marlos' took control of his body as they approached one another. Like a flash of lightning and with liquid fluidity, he spun his right foot from behind his body, his head nearly grazing the mat as he felt his heel strike the face of Noguera. It was a piece of art, something he wished he could have seen back on film. As Danny rotated through the kick and was able to see the outcome he was himself surprised. For a moment it was as if he had bad tinnitus, all was quiet, a ringing in his ears as if someone had fired a gun right next to his head.

Was it really that simple? Did I just knock out this big 6'3" body with a spinning kick?

The noise brought him quickly back to reality. The crowd was manic, they had seen what they wanted to see and the ones who had doubted the story of him tossing Gabriel Souza through the air now knew that it was no myth. This guy, *Danilo Sheppard*, was the real thing. Jean Noguera lay flat on his back, bleeding from the nose. Out cold.

The crowd was delirious: yelling and clapping and stomping their feet on the metal walkways above. Danny turned his back to his opponent who was being rolled onto his side by his trainers while one wedged the mouth guard from his teeth. He extended his arms like Jesus and spun in a circle, nodding his head slowly. The referee latched onto his arm and thrust it into the air. The crowd grew even louder. Everything echoed in the rectangle enclosure of the courtyard.

This is all for me. This celebration. This noise. I am responsible for this.

Danny thought about how Lucas used to describe the rush he would get from the crowd in Reser Stadium—*I hear the stadium around me... When it gets loud, when I hear my name—I swear I can run faster... the roar, that's what it's all about...*—it all made perfect sense then. The noise from the crowd fed something deep inside him that he didn't even know was there. He wanted to live in it. He wanted more.

The referee released his arm but Danny stayed in the center of the mat, turning in a circle, looking at the crowded walkways above him. He was loved. It felt like a dream. The invisible audience was there too. Somewhere high above him, peering over the spindles of razor wire, they watched this new person: a confident showman full of anger and pain. They disapproved.

After gathering his clothes from the teenager and ignoring the extended hands that stuck out from the seated spectators he walked to the gym cell. The rumors had been confirmed—*I told you!...Yeah I guess they weren't lying...Okay I see what you mean.*

It was the first time he could remember when he craved loud and not quiet. What was more, she had disappeared from his mind for the three minutes of madness. It was pure escape: he felt nothing but exhilaration. What a rush, what a release, what beauty.

— — -

The bookies, of which there were five including Michel, lined up in front of the exit where spectators settled up before being allowed to leave. Guards manned the exit but many spectators lingered and stayed for drinks with prisoners that they knew. Joris burst into the gym cell and joined Danny with a bottle of Jack Daniels that he had already done a number on.

"What a show!" he cried, slapping a folded, rubber-banded stack of R$ notes into his hand. Danny counted it while Joris disappeared out of the cell to get a couple of glasses. It was R$9,500, roughly $3,000. Danny was pleased by the sum; he still had to pay off the costs of running out of the country that he had put on his credit card. Joris stormed back into the cell with two glasses. Shots were poured—and continued to pour—for the next hour. A few people showed up to the doorway asking for a picture with Danny or just to tell him that he had a good fight. Eventually a lull in the commotion led to Joris asking Danny an important question.

"Did you enjoy it?"

It was a follow up question to the conversation they had a few days earlier when Danny said that although he loved to wrestle he didn't think he would like fighting.

"I like the noise."

Joris agreed, nodding vigorously, "I have never *seen* a crowd like that in here! And I have never seen knockout like that! It was unbelievable! It was all so easy for you, no? I think you can fight two of Jean Noguera and win. Amazing!"

It was impossible for Danny not to concede a tiny smile in the presence of Joris' excitement. He was revved up, having clearly done some cocaine during the night.

The two of them continued to drink until the wee hours of the morning. The party of an after-fight-Friday in Leo Goia Prison was something that had to be experienced to be believed. If not for the aqua bars that kept them locked inside it would have felt like a favela party. He lingered in the courtyard for a little while and was offered everything—cocaine, spliffs, alcohol and even women. He declined it all and continued to go shot for shot with Joris as they made their way from level to level and cell to cell, always greeted like royalty. At around 4:30 a.m. they headed back to their cell but continued to drink. Joris was in rare form, and from the topic of sports betting came the story of when Joris had fixed a soccer game in the sixth tier of English soccer years earlier.

Joris' type of intelligence couldn't be taught in any coursework in the world and his language skills were superb; his English vocabulary was nearly as expansive as Danny's own. His grammar was almost perfect and his accent was tweaked elegantly by a combination of Dutch and British. The stories he told were incredible. Most of them were drug-related and involved characters that Joris would describe in vivid detail, becoming so real in Danny's mind that he thought he had seen them in a movie.

"I stayed there in London for like four years—I was seventeen. It was good fun for the time. I was a kid. I made a lot of money with the ecstasy, the club scene was too easy and I had all the connections—but anyway, that's a different story." They had, more or less, been moving chronologically through his life during the week.

"It was between Poole Town and Dartford, I remember that."

Joris seemed to need Danny's understanding before he would continue. Danny nodded.

"Yes, well—I guess it's not right to say that I *fixed* the game. That means that I control the outcome of the game. I did not do that. That is extremely difficult—almost impossible without it being obvious. All I did was guarantee that there would be a sending off—you know, somebody gets a red card—and it had to be in the final ten minutes. And there you go, Reiss Leadbitter. He got his first yellow in the beginning of the second half and then, very smart of him, there was a foul and the ball was placed for the kick and he acted like he was having a tantrum and kicks the ball into the stands. Second yellow. Money in my pockets!"

It seemed like Joris had an endless supply of these stories and they were all entertaining. They started with his upbringing in Amsterdam and the drastic turn his life had taken after meeting Kerem, his mentor in criminal trades.

"And now, thanks to you and your lovely fighting skills, we have even more money in our pockets!" He said pouring the last of the vodka into their glasses.

"Cheers my friend. It is a pleasure to know you." He said. Danny nodded as they clinked glasses. He couldn't agree more.

— — — —

Danny woke the next morning around 11 a.m. with a thumping head-ache. Joris on the other hand was sitting casually with his back against the wall, reading a book as if he hadn't had a single drink the night before.

"Fuuuuuck." Danny groaned as he curled into the fetal position.

Joris cracked a smile. "Are you going to throw up? You need to smoke a joint." Danny didn't say anything and Joris took this as him agreeing. He got up and moved towards the curtain to fetch a joint from another cell. "Get the phone too!" Danny called after him.

Rosa and Isabel must have been camped out next to the phone desk because it was always answered before the second ring. Isabel sounded better, not as beside herself with worry as she had previous days.

"Edson and Paulo and Leandro are at Leo Goia right now. They won't even let them see you." She said.

"No I can't have visitors. I don't want you to worry though. I'm living very comfortably. I have friends. I read books. I'm very safe. I promise."

He assured her that he was being fed three meals a day and that there was no cause for worry. She said that Edson had been in close contact with Marlos the whole time and that Tanner was calling fre-quently. They talked for about fifteen minutes and Danny was left with optimism afterwards, she had sounded okay.

Joris returned with a plate of food and a thin joint.

— — -

Three hours later at around 2 p.m. Danny woke and pushed himself into a seated position. It seemed that while Danny had been sleeping Joris had sprouted an interest in Danny and that for a change, he would be the listener and Danny would be the storyteller.

"So where is your family?" He asked a bit suddenly as Danny labored to get himself seated with his back against the wall. Joris put down his book.

"My family is in Oregon. You've heard of Portland?"

"Of course. More breweries than any city in the world." He said.

"That's right. That's where I'm from."

Joris stared back expecting more information. "Alright…"

Danny had hoped that the fact about the breweries would take Joris into some other vein of thought and maybe even a story but he seemed resolute.

"I came here a couple months ago. My mom is from Rio and all of her family lives here. She is here now also, actually. She came on Wednesday."

"So this is vacation for you? What do you do for work?" Joris asked.

"I was studying in school. Wrestling for the university."

Joris continued, trying to chip away at the gaping holes of mystery. "So you finished or?"

Danny felt guilty leaving him in the dark about Lucas and everything that had led him to boarding a flight for Rio but he didn't want to talk about it.

"I took a break."

Joris nodded. "Maybe you will go back someday. But here in Brazil you were training in some gym? A famous gym, I heard?"

Danny nodded. "I *guess* it's famous. My uncle is a friend of the trainer. That's how I got in." There was a slight crinkle of confusion in Joris' eyebrow.

"But you are *good*. I heard about you, like, throwing this guy through the air or some story—you know how stories are."

Danny conceded a chuckle. "Of course I'm good. I was national champion in America. And I *did* throw this guy through the air—that's what got me set up to come here and fight."

"You were champion for all of the United States?"

"Yeah."

"But that was just for wrestling athletes that were in universities? The best one are not in university, correct?"

"No the best of them are in university. I'm the best, Joris. I have never lost."

"But then why did you stop?"

Danny shrugged. "I didn't like being in school. I wanted to come here."

Joris was too smart. "So why then are you so angry? Yes, you are in prison but you will be out soon and you are safe and making good money." Joris' voice had turned soft and low, Danny hadn't heard it before and he realized that he couldn't leave him in the dark entirely.

"I met a girl. I thought we were friends but it was her who set me up to be arrested and come here and fight."

To say it out loud was agony and Joris, who was as good as Danny at reading people, could sense this. "These girls will tear your heart out without even thinking about it. For them, it is nothing."

He lit another joint and passed it across the bare patch of concrete floor between mattresses.

"What was her name?"

"Nina."

"You say you came here a few months ago?"

"Yes."

"You fell in love with her in those months? Quickly like that?"

He hadn't said that he fell in love with Nina but it must have been obvious. Danny fell silent, not wanting to tell Joris that he had actually only known Nina for one week of the three months, he would sound insane.

"Yes, quickly like that." Joris didn't press him to continue but as he took the joint back from Danny he asked, "I still don't understand why you would leave your studying and wrestling behind. Just because it *was not right at the time.*"

Danny chuckled, feeling his eyelids beginning to droop. "We can save that part of the story for another time." He said as he reached for the bottle of Tanqueray from next to the refrigerator.

— — -

The same sequence of events as the previous Friday unfolded all over again; a trolley of folding chairs was wheeled in, the big red roll of mat was unraveled in the middle of them. Ropes were strung up on metal poles that were inserted in the holes in the concrete. The floodlights were assembled. The buzz was even *more* fervent. This time around, Danny had chosen to find out what he could about his opponent, which wasn't a whole lot. His name was Thiago Barbosa. A powerful hitter, short and sturdy, difficult to take down and like Jean Noguera, he was heavier than Danny by at least 15 lbs.

There were three other fighters waiting in the gym cell this time. They all greeted Danny with admiration that bordered on awe but by now, he expected as much. It was no longer surprising that strangers knew things about him like the fact that he trained in Marlos' gym and one of the fighters had question after question for him about the gym and Marlos himself. They went through a series of exercises together, Danny leading them. The other fighters followed his instructions with intense focus.

9:42 P.M.

The aqua bars opened with their unmistakable cranking sound. Spectators came flooding through the double doors. Danny sat against the wall eating a plate of beans, rice and fried bananas.

The kid who had asked him all the questions about Marlos was fighting first. Leading up to his introduction he was twitchy and anxious, bouncing on his toes, nerves forcing him from one side of the cell to the other like a leopard pacing in a cage.

Half an hour later the bullhorn ripped through the courtyard, welcoming everybody to the fights and moments later it was introducing the kid, "...representing Vila Valqueire...Mano Tavares!" Danny chirped a whistle to get his attention and gave him a thumbs-up to which his face turned hard with determination before he bounded out of the cell.

Mano Tavares: proud, athletic, and hardworking...but not naturally gifted. No amount of training could ever produce the natural talents that were God-given to the select few like Danny. It was a fact in every sport: the talented were better than the hardworking but the talented *and* hardworking were the champions.

There must have been a thousand kids in Rio just like him, praying for a chance to be in Marlos Vieira's gym. How Danny ended up there seemed too perfect to be coincidence: Uncle Paulo just happened to be old friends with one of the most respected and sought-after coaches in all of Rio. For a fleeting moment the grand scheme of things seemed much smaller.

11:42 P.M.

Mano won his fight and Danny hadn't even paid attention to the other two. The crowd had been loud the whole time but there was a distinct angst and impatience in their cheers, everybody was there for the final fight. They had been waiting for it all week and word had spread efficiently—there must have been at least 50 more outsiders in attendance than the week before judging by the crowds that were made to stand behind the chairs on all sides, the red mat was barely visible through the bodies.

The chant started from a walkway directly above the gym cell. It bounced off the walls on all sides.

"Tub-ur-ão!...Tub-ur-ão!"

As the minutes passed it didn't wither away, it stayed strong. They were proud of him. Danny was Leo Goia's own. The light from the floodlights didn't do much to illuminate the gym cell, a solitary rectangle of light stretched in through the door. Danny felt good in the dark and the steady rhythm of the chanting was as comforting as silence had always been.

The bullhorn brought him into the moment, reality crashing all around him as the chanting shattered into cheering. "Ladies and Gentlemen! It is time for tonight's main event!"

No more rhythm, just cheering and the rattling of the walkways as inmates stomped their feet. "Introducing our first competitor, fighting for the gym of Willian Capanema...," again in the heavily accented English the Portuguese Bruce Buffer said his nickname, "Thiago...*The Bulldog*...Barbosa!"

Danny was surprised to hear a few jeers and whistles—the Brazilian form of booing. Even in underground fighting, it was still a sport of honor and most of the crowd respected that, as Danny thought they should. Then it was his turn. He put the picture of he and his siblings back in his pocket.

"Ladies and Gentlemen! Please make yourselves heard for the final fighter of the night!" Danny got to his feet and began bouncing on his toes. "From the esteemed gym of Marlos Vieira...Danilo!...O TUBŪRAO!...Cheppard!"

As he broke the threshold of the doorway and came into sight the sound hit him like a bucket of cold water being poured over his head. Once again he spread his arms like Jesus, turning his back towards the mat and the hoards of spectators on the floor, walking backwards, looking up at the crowded walkways that rose above him. Then he turned back towards the mat, people reached out to touch his hands as he strolled down the narrow walkway between folding chairs.

Thiago Barbosa was appropriately nicknamed; surely 200 lbs. but no taller than 5'9". Bald and dark skinned, he looked like a shorter, bloated and not as handsome version of Gabriel. A layer of fat padded his muscles but Danny was wary of the type: thick but agile. His wrists and ankles were taped. He wore royal blue shorts. He seemed confident, more accustom to being on a mat than Jean Noguera the week before. All the same, Danny stared into his eyes as the referee laid out the rules before sending them back to their sides. It seemed that the ease with which he had won the week before had prompted whoever organized these things to find him a much better fighter.

Well this will be interesting, he thought earnestly as he walked backwards to his side and stripped his shirt. He fought wearing his black

Jordan shorts. He set the photo on top of his shirt on the outside of the ropes. "Ready?" The referee called to Danny. He nodded.

"Ready?" He called to Barbosa. He nodded. Then he clapped. In an instant the crowd grew louder but as soon as the clap of the referee came everything was muted in Danny's head. Neither of them came out fast, they bounced around each other, Danny studied Barbosa's footwork as best he could.

His arms aren't long...try some headshots, see how he defends.

He tossed out a few left jabs, finding his range before, out of nowhere, Barbosa launched himself into meaty right haymaker with no bullshit about it—he was going for a knockout. Danny was at a safe distance to step away from it, but he was alerted to the power of Barbosa's right. They danced around one another for another twenty seconds, neither ready to commit to a serious strike and exposing themselves, but they wouldn't have to. It was Barbosa who masterminded his own defeat in an instant.

Perhaps if he knew Danny's wrestling resume he wouldn't have tried to outsmart him as he did. He thought it was clever but he didn't know that Danny was far *more* clever; he knew all the tricks. It was a millisecond of a glance, a direction of the eyes, intended to be a *misdirection* of the eyes. He quickly looked at Danny's neck but instead of going where he looked, he lunged low for Danny's back leg, trying to take him down. Danny himself had used it many times over the years and had sometimes even used it in reverse as soon as an opponent thought they had it figured out; Danny would look where he *was* actually going and then go there while the other wrestler thought he was going to do the opposite.

Barbosa's eyes only looked at Danny's neck for a blink before diving low for the takedown. The timing was perfection, Danny leapt into the air leading triumphantly with his right knee, smashing it into Barbosa's face just as he was thrusting himself towards Danny's back leg. It was slow motion: an epic collision of bone and bone. Danny saw it from outside his body, somewhere above the red mat. Barbosa's head snapped back violently. It had happened 43 seconds into the first round and was the only time during the fight when their bodies made contact.

A single loud slap with an ugly trace of a crack could be heard clearly even on the top level of the cells. Barbosa was unconscious before he hit the mat. Several people ducked hurriedly through the ropes to his aid, rolling him to his side.

The eruption of cheers as nothing short of pandemonium. Danny soaked it up and was shaped like Christ once again, turning slowly like a wind-up toy as utter mania ensued. Once again, they couldn't believe what they had just seen. He scanned the spectators, looking them in their eyes. Many of them had their hands on their heads in disbelief, too amazed to even cheer. Women covered their gaping mouths with their palms, glossy fingernails and gold jewelry shining in the floodlights.

He saw Joris on the third level, clapping and smiling so broadly that Danny nearly didn't even recognize him; it showed joy. Genuine, high-on-life, joy. Danny blew him a two handed kiss like a Broadway star at the end of a show.

This is what I am capable of.

Danny could feel the attention of the invisible audience once again.

– — -

More outsiders were hanging around than the week before and several different parties were in full swing, crowds of people scattered all over the courtyard. Guards were taking part, drinking beers with spectators and inmates alike. Danny watched it from the doorway of his cell.

This time, his money was delivered in a thick envelope. When he was done counting it and organizing it into stacks of like-bills, he converted it to dollars in his head: roughly $4,200.

Not bad for 43 seconds of work.

But that wasn't all; the next morning there was a small collection of gifts and letters from inmates and spectators organized at the foot of his bed. A box of homemade pastries, a white T-shirt with graffiti-style *Tuburão* in purple and yellow with gold glitter highlights. There were several handwritten letters in envelopes too. They prayed for his continued success and said that he was an inspiration. He read each of them several times before storing them in the pages of books in the cell. His favorite gift made his eyes widen when he first took it out of the pillowcase that it was tucked inside of. On a small wooden-framed canvas about the size of a laptop, somebody had painted him in watercolors. His jaw was comically square, his arms outstretched in celebration in front of the cosmic flurry of black and red backdrop.

He was organizing his gifts as Joris came back to the cell with breakfast.

"People love you." He said.

He wasn't wrong.

— — –

It was Wednesday. 17 days after Danny had passed beyond the aqua gate of Leo Goia. His only focus was on Friday, but he wouldn't get to fight again. As he pushed through the dark green curtain and onto the metal walkway he saw Joris making his way towards him, a bottle of jack tucked under his arm as he cupped a lighter around the cigarette in his mouth. He lit it and then looked up to see Danny.

"You are getting released today." He said.

Oddly, Danny's initial response was disappointment. For one, he wouldn't hear the noise from the inmates again, and two, Joris didn't have more sadness in his voice.

"How do you know that?" Danny asked skeptically.

"Michel said it. Later today Danilo Sheppard is a free man."

Danny didn't say anything and after several moments Joris looked at him, wondering why he hadn't responded.

"You going to find Nina?" Joris asked.

Danny shook his head firmly. He had thought about it. What he would say to her. What her face would look like when she saw him. But sometime during his first couple days inside Leo Goia, in the middle of his grieving, an agreement had been reached by his head and heart; he never wanted to see her again. He didn't even want to ask her why she had done it; he didn't want anything to do with her.

"You should come to Portland someday, Joris. You would love it there." He said, resting his arms on the railing.

Joris scoffed, "I have *been* to Portland. Many times." He said, sarcastically adjusting his glasses in a scholarly manner, a cultured man of the world. Danny frowned at him, *Have you really?*

"No that is a lie. I have been there once though. I will come when you are a big star. You can buy me some nice things." He said with a wink, taking another drag.

–　—　-

"I loved that guy. I still hope to find him one day. We never exchanged any contact info—I wouldn't know how to track him down, a guy like that. I still owe him some *nice things*, my prison shepherd." He said fondly, thinking about the skinny Dutch drug trafficker.

"I'm sure you'll run into each other someday."

Danny seemed to ignore her optimism, pulling out his phone and gawking at the time. It was 3:36 a.m. "I'm an idiot. I have to train tomorrow. I gotta go. Finish this on Saturday? There's not much left."

"Of course." Jenna said.

–　—　-

Danny trained well on Friday even though he was running on barely three hours of sleep. Taison was not amused by Danny staying out so late and was upset in the morning when he came downstairs.

"Obviously I'm not going to tell Mark or Marlos anything but you need to take your sleep patterns more seriously. Vega isn't that far away." Danny nodded and told Taison that he appreciated his commitment to winning and that after Saturday night he wouldn't have to worry about it, the meetings would be over.

–　—　-

Danny was so eager to get the story over with that he considered texting Jenna on Friday instead but he decided he decided to wait. He had to get it over with, close the curtains, burn the frayed end of the rope until it stuck together.

His Audi sped through the wet, heavy Portland night at 10:41 p.m. on Saturday, The Westbrook glimmering elegantly in the dark night as he approached.

He entered the building through a side door as usual. Jenna said it was safe to come in through the front but he always preferred the guaranteed discreetness of the side entrance. She always left it propped open for him. Tonight both doors—the door to her reception area and the door from there into her office—were wide open. He entered to find her lounging on the chaise, dressed for a run or a workout in black yoga pants and matching sky blue Nikes and half-zip, her hair pulled into a shiny ponytail. Tupperware containers littered the coffee table in front of her.

"What's this?" Danny said with tentative curiosity. She had never been dressed like this before nor had the doors been open nor had she ever had food in the office. She shrugged without shifting her gaze from the opposite couch.

"I was going to go home before you came but Peter is still out of town."
Danny nodded slowly, still confused.
"I've just been here for a while, thinking about everything."
He thought she might elaborate but she didn't.
"Well do you have questions or…"
Jenna fixed her stare on Danny before speaking.
"I've been thinking about Nina."
Danny got goose bumps and waited anxiously for her to continue but she didn't say anything. Danny shrugged his eyebrows.
"Hm. Alright then, back to prison. I'm almost out."

– — -

Danny knew better than to tell his grandparents or his mom that he would be getting out with any certainty. He would believe it when he was standing outside the walls of Leo Goia, not a second before.

"Don't get too excited but there's a rumor that I might get out today—nothing for sure. *Don't* get excited."

After the phone call Danny turned to Joris.

"Well I was going to train today but if I'm not fighting… do you want to play some backgammon?"

Joris had introduced Danny to the game during the week and they had played quite a bit as Joris poured drinks and told stories. Jack Daniels or Bacardi. Taipei or Brussels. Croatia or Indonesia. He wished he could bring Joris with him. There was something eternal and sacred about their evenings of liquor, spliffs and stories. Sometimes Joris would play the guitar and sing. The cell lit by candles, the books stacked along the back wall. The refrigerator that never kept anything but chocolate bars and bottles of liquor at a temperature just cold enough to keep the chocolate from melting. The dark green sheet that he could see from the doorway of the gym cell; dark green was home.

He wished Tanner could have met Joris. They spent much of the afternoon on the picnic tables in the courtyard, the sun beating down on their shoulders as they drank and laughed with other inmates. The more it became clear that he was in fact going to be released the next day. A lot of them had heard the news.

Even though Danny had only spent two weeks inside, the day had a heavy feeling.

There was something about the inmates—most of whom he had never even spoken to—that he felt a strange sort of loyalty to. He appreciated them for being there with him, for watching him fight and taking part in his evolution. Even though Danny wasn't guilty of any crime, the reality had become obvious during the first week: he was one of them.

All the men in Leo Goia had done wrong and Danny had made his mistakes right along with them. Nevertheless, their hope bound them together, breaching the surface of their eyes in every conversation whether they knew it or not. Each time they stepped out of their cell to be under the day or night sky, they heard a whisper of freedom, a fresh hand of cards being tossed their way by the dealer at the poker table of life. They were hopeful boys and hopeful men. Most of them had tattoos, but all of them had scars.

— — —

Joris had been right.

Danny was eating a plate of food in the afternoon, leaning shirtless on the walkway railing just outside his cell. On the opposite side of the courtyard, making their way up the zigzagging staircases were two guards, Felipe and Roger. He watched them the entire way. Felipe was shorter, thick and angry looking with hefty arms and squat legs that seemed to cram themselves into his black combat boots. Roger was quiet but tough looking and gave off an air that suggested he was not to be crossed.

"You're leaving today." He said as he came close enough to speak without raising his voice. "There's no conviction. You are free to go."

Danny didn't mean to but he laughed suddenly, turning his head away from the two of them. It was hysterical that they were continuing with the storyline that his arrest had been legitimate, and furthermore, there had been imaginary deliberations by people who had come to a decision that there was "no conviction."

Danny slowed his laughter, "Right now?"

Felipe did a weird sort of nod/shrug that appeared to mean, *Obviously*.

It took him just a few minutes to throw his clothes into his duffle, shake the money out of the pages of the books and fold it into the pockets of the one pair of jeans he had in his duffle but had never worn.

He stopped and looked back at the bedroom. The symmetry. Not as perfect as the bedroom at his grandparents, but it was symmetry. Joris was in the fourth-floor cell where they played cards.

"I need to say goodbye to a few people. I will meet you at the gate. Ten minutes."

— — —

Jenna asked her first question of the night. "So they just let you out?"

Danny nodded. "Leo Goia wasn't even that far from my grandparent's house—I think I mentioned that before. I just took a taxi home. It was a circus. My uncles were all there—my mom obviously. I was hugging people for twenty minutes straight."

"Did you go home right away?" Jenna asked.

Danny smirked. "We were there for a few days." Something in his voice made it clear that things weren't quite finished in Rio.

"My mom and I were going to leave on Monday. It was Friday. I was on the porch with my grandpa while he smoked his evening cigarette and the phone rang. My grandma answered and came out to say that it was for me. I had talked to Tanner when I got out the day before and I thought it would be him again but it wasn't. I didn't know who else it could be. But it was Joris."

Danny chuckled again, "It was so funny like—it reminded me of when you're a kid and your friend calls: *Hi can Danny come out and play?*"

"What did he want?" Jenna asked.

– — -

"Danilo! How is the freedom my friend?"

It was quite strange to hear Joris' voice on the phone.

"Joris! It's nice, man—nice to see my family. How are you?"

"Yes, yes things are wonderful! I did not know when you are going back home to USA. I am glad you are still here in Rio. I miss having you here with me brother. That is a very selfish thing to say because you are out—and you should be—enjoying life, but it is true. These retards can't play backgammon for a shit!"

Danny chuckled silently to himself. "Yes I am here but I am going home with my mom on Monday. Are there good fights tonight?"

"Ah! Yes there are. And this is the reason for I am calling. It is not only because I have missed you. I'm glad that you use this phone to call your grandparents—I found the number here and I have some good news."

Danny's heart started to beat steadily faster.

"If you agree, there is a fight for you tonight. The man is big and talented. He is old, a former police officer. But it would be guaranteed ten thousand real and if you win, more like fifteen or sixteen thousand. There is big money here tonight—gambling men from all places. What would be even more fun is that it is a surprise if you are here. Can you imagine the crowd?"

The last part was all Danny needed to hear. He didn't consider the mention of the man being "big and talented." He wanted to hear the crowd.

"What time?"

— — —

"I have to see a friend later." Danny said to his mom and grandma as he hung up the phone. They were worried to even let him out of the house but reluctantly allowed him to go.

He thought about asking Mateus if he wanted to come but he didn't think it would be right to involve him in anything to do with underground fights and he didn't have his phone number anyway—the guards at Leo Goia hadn't returned his iPhone when he got released.

Danny stood outside the massive concrete structure as the taxi drove away. Luxury cars were parked bumper to bumper on the street to the South. Even standing outside Danny could hear Portuguese Bruce Buffer on the bullhorn from the courtyard.

Upon seeing him climbing the stairs to the entrance, a young guard that Danny hadn't seen before hurried to hold the door for him, nodding respectfully as he entered. Guards were lounging all through the empty offices, smoking cigarettes and drinking straight from the bottle. The ones Danny was familiar with lit up when they saw him. He strode meaningfully through the long hallway towards the double doors behind the aqua gate. The last time he had walked down the hallway had been a very different type of entrance.

The light of the offices behind faded as he moved down the dark hallway. He could hear the crowd on the other side of the double doors but at the end of the hallway there were three people. He saw the burning embers of cigars before he even saw their figures. Blinking to adjust his eyes to the dark he could see that they were all wearing matching dark suit jackets with white shirts. Danny stopped five feet short of them.

"I'm Danilo. I'm here to fight."

They knew who he was. The shortest of them took out his phone, hit a button and put it to his ear. A moment later, "He's here."

The other two men stood quietly, studying him without shame. This annoyed Danny.

"Let me have one of those cigars." He said jokingly. His eyes had adjusted but he could scarcely make out their faces. The tallest one had a thin moustache and deep cheeks; he was maybe 70 years old. A skinny neck emerged from his collar and the black hair on the top of his head was combed straight back making him look like an evil version of Edson. The other man was short and was young enough to be the taller man's son. He had a bit of a gut but he was handsome and full-faced with thick curly black hair and two or three days worth of stubble.

They didn't respond. This annoyed Danny further. "No? Cigarette?"

The taller man blew out a cloud of smoke and started past towards the offices. The younger one followed. Danny wanted a last chide but he let it go.

Focus.

The third man returned from near the double doors. For all Danny knew he could have been the son and brother of the other two men, they all had the same air of important arrogance. It wasn't until they were well gone back in the offices that Danny realized, *Oh shit. That must have been the boss and his sons.*

A guard came in through the double doors, the noise elevating for a moment through the opening. "Two minutes." He announced.

Danny turned away and squatted down, going inside his own mind. *You are here to win.*

He hadn't willingly returned to Leo Goia for the money or to see Joris again. He had come back because he wanted to hear the noise, to hear the chanting, to feel the love.

This is my prison. Nobody is going to take my glory from me.

He thought about his family. How he would see them soon. How sorry he was for abandoning them in the worst possible moment of their lives. He thought about Tanner and Andrea and Mateus and Marlos. He thought about Nina.

The bullhorn was loud on the other side of the door. It introduced his opponent; his name was Bruno Martins. Then it was his turn. The man waited next to the double doors ready to push them open for him. Danny's heart pounded with excitement.

"DANILO…O TUBARÃO…CHEPPARD!" Portuguese Bruce Buffer yelled into the bullhorn. There was a distinct element of frenetic surprise in the cheering and the second the doors were pushed open and Danny stepped into the light and raised his arms, the sound hit him like a strong gust of wind.

I'm home.

— — -

"I take it you won?" Jenna asked in reference to Danny's stealthy grin as he recounted the night.

"Sure did."

The fight had ended in the second round. Bruno Martins had landed several heavy strikes; Danny's eyebrow was sliced open and was bleeding which he had real difficulty explaining to his mom and grandparents the next day. Coming into the second round Danny had taken the fight to the ground, intelligently baiting Martins into getting low to defend a rear-leg takedown, then he got ahold of an arm and athletically squirmed it in between his legs creating a situation that only allowed Bruno Martins a few frantic seconds to save himself before Danny would pop his arm out of its' socket. He tried but as the pain grew intolerable he realized that it was over and he tapped out. They shared a respectful embrace in the center of the mat while the noise blasted off the walls around them.

"Is that when you decided to fight?"

"Yeah." He lied.

It wasn't quite so simple but he didn't need to go into it with her, he didn't want to. Through the entire story he had only left out the night he lay awake with Nina at her apartment and now, the conversation he had with Joris over a few farewell drinks that would set his mind on the new trajectory towards super-stardom.

"And you never heard from Nina…"

"Well…" Danny trailed off. He nearly lied again so he wouldn't have to re-live it.

"I went back to the gym the day before I left—to tell Marlos that I wanted to fight and to say goodbye to everybody. When I saw Mateus he came up to me all concerned. He said that Nina had called him."

Jenna's heart began to pound.

"He said, 'She wanted me to tell you that she's sorry. She's really, really sorry. She said that you would know what she was talking about. She wishes you all the best in life.'"

"WHAT?" Jenna cried out. "You're fucking kidding me."

Danny nodded.

"That's all? *Sorry and good luck?*"

"That's it. I pressed him for more info but that's all she had to say. She must have gotten a conscience. Anyway, that's the last I heard from Nina."

Jenna still had a look of shock plastered across her face. "God I hate that bitch."

Danny smirked and raised his eyebrows, *Welcome to the club.*

"Anyway. I came home and trained at Mark's gym—you know Mark? Tricia's husband?—yeah I trained at his gym in the meantime and got a fight with some little promotion company in Seattle and I had good representation—Mark became my agent and things just got rolling. As soon as Marlos moved up here and Remy came over from France things really started to move fast. I signed with The UFC after a few fights in Seattle and here we are."

He finished by folding his arms and shrugging.

It was true; things had moved incredibly fast but it was all as he had expected. It almost seemed effortless the way he broke into the professional ranks and seemingly overnight, people's heads started to turn. The phone started to ring more often. Papers began arriving at the house in cardboard folders. Mark and Rich would sit next to him lifting the pages and pointing to the X's where he needed to sign.

Jenna toyed with her ponytail while appearing to mull things over. At last she said, "Wow. It's a lot more than I had imagined."

He nodded his understanding, "Yeah you probably didn't think there would be a Brazilian prison or a Dutch drug smuggler involved but," he shrugged, "but there ya go."

"Do you still like the noise?" She asked.

Danny smirked in his slow motion way, not answering affirmatively.

"Well that's it." He said with a sort of tired finality; the end of the presentation, the applause was over and the floor was opened for questions. She deserved to ask some questions about it all and pretty soon Danny found himself talking about the first month home in Portland after returning from Brazil. It had been a difficult time, for everyone.

The fights in Leo Goia were somehow capable of giving him a distraction from how hurt he had been by Nina but as soon as he came home, it really took hold of him. Some days were harder than others. Aside from roam the house and sit on Lucas' bed and go for walks with Celia he didn't do much. If it was sunny he wouldn't even step outside.

He preferred solitude and found it easier to chastise himself in peace. He would sit on the couch at home but was always far away, it often took saying his name three times to snag his attention. He wouldn't talk about it with anybody, not even Celia.

Every possible scenario and motive that Nina might have had to set him up had been scrutinized in his mind but in the end the only thing that made any logical sense was money. He pictured her sitting on the couch in her apartment and counting the bills after the deed was done. The thought had never lost its' power to make Danny sad.

When the pain didn't taper off he started to question the strength of the human soul and whether or not it was built for such resilience, dealing with such horrible events in quick succession. He rarely smiled and almost never laughed, shying away from the prospect of stepping into public or anywhere he might be expected to glad-hand and be personable. If he wasn't home, Rich and Isabel assumed he was at Mark's gym where he was able to workout in solitude.

Mark had started texting Rich when Danny would show up. In fact, there was an entire network of communication between everybody, updating one another on his whereabouts and mannerisms like a team of private investigators: *He ate all the fruit that was on the counter but I don't think he left the house yesterday—Rodney said they played basketball in the morning—I heard him downstairs early this morning but he's been in his room all day—I know he talks to Tanner everyday, maybe he should take a trip to Corvallis?*

He had returned from Brazil a different person, not unlike a soldier coming home after a horrific deployment. After two weeks Rich set up an evaluation with a psychiatrist to see if Danny was showing signs of depression, which he was, but he refused medication or further counseling. Rodney had to accept that Danny didn't want to play soccer as much as he used to, Allie and Andrea had to accept that he wasn't going to laugh at a funny movie even though they knew that he liked to sit and watch it with them anyway.

He still ached and missed Lucas indescribably. Intense waves of grief would strike randomly. They didn't happen in trigger-form where a certain song or driving past a special place would set him off, but when they hit there was nothing he could do but bury his head in a pillow until it subsided.

– — –

He had stayed at Jenna's office all night, talking about all sorts of things—how his training and preparations were going for his next fight with the Joe Vega, how well Allie was doing in the tennis season, whether or not Jenna wanted him to order her some Nike stuff with his catalog money. They talked about Rodney and how he had grown so fast, and how Danny didn't know what would have happened to him if they hadn't taken him into their home. They talked about entertainment, how Danny didn't really watch movies like he used to, but that his favorite movie was still *The 25ᵗʰ Hour* with Edward Norton, and how he still got goose bumps at the end when Brian Cox said, "It all came so close to never happening…this life came so close to never happening."

The sense of finality was there for both of them. Even though Danny had agreed to open up and talk about his past so that they could keep their arrangement in place, it now seemed as though they had reached the end of things. It wouldn't be the same coming to her office and scooping her up into his arms now that she knew everything.

Normally they walked to their cars together but Jenna said she was going to stick around the office for a bit and go over some notes. He left at around 5:00 a.m.

— — —

Danny didn't bother going back to his town house and instead drove straight to Eastmoreland where he could sleep for a few hours before spending the day with everyone. He felt good. Not exactly the weight-off-your-shoulders lightness that everyone had assured him would happen if he talked to someone but it was good to know that somebody else—outside of his family—knew what had happened to him.

All four lanes on Sunset Highway were virtually empty as he headed for the river. His thoughts drifted back to the night of his final fight in Leo Goia. The conversation he had with Joris that he had left out of the story with Jenna, the conversation that had changed it all and set him on his new trajectory.

— — —

Back in the cell he and Joris sat and toasted. To life, to health, to victory, to marijuana and laughter, Joris thrusting a thin joint in the air triumphantly.

"So? What will you do with your life now? Back to school? More fighting?"

It was the last time they would be seeing each other, it was a valid question. Anybody who witnessed him fight would want to know if there was something more to come and ever since launching his heal into Jean Noguera's head three weeks earlier there had been a small buzzing of insistence in the back of his mind.

There would be no criminal charges to face when he returned home. He wouldn't be going back to school—at least not right away.

Joris spoke again, "You have a lot of life left. You are only *twenty* years old. I just saw you beat a man—maybe forty or something—a *man*. You could leave a legacy." His eyes were both drunk and intensely sober at the same time. His face illuminated by the flickering candle like a bandito in a cave hideout.

The word *legacy* seemed to hang in the air. Joris threw back his glass of Jack.

"I have to do something with my life." Danny said. It was only a sentence, but it was so much more. It shut the door on the last three months, maybe even the last 20 years. Wrestling was over. School was put on hold. Before he would do anything, he would return home and make things right with his family. This would be the last time he saw Joris and he knew it would be wrong to leave without telling him just how important that sentence was.

"I had a twin brother. He died in January and I ran away. I came here."

Joris poured another drink without looking up. "I knew there was something you were not telling to me." He said. It was the same sentence Nina had said before they went to watch the sunrise.

"I'm sure he would have been proud to see you beat these men here."

Danny knew Lucas would have loved it but he didn't say anything.

"So you go and make him proud. Become a champion. You have it inside of you. You can be great. I can see it. I see you here. I see you after you have won it all. It won't be easy. But you will arrive. I know you will. And when you do, the only regret you will have is that it was not more difficult."

Danny hardly needed to be told that he had greatness within him, but hearing it from Joris was gratifying. Mateus, Marlos, everyone at the gym, they all knew it. Joris pressed on, suddenly invested in convincing Danny that fighting was his purpose.

"People would know your name. And the money...it's not everything in life, of course, but it's nice to have it."

Joris shrugged as he filled their glasses again and clinking his against Danny's before throwing it back. Danny did the same.

"It would be a shame to waste such a talent." He said. This information was beginning to sound repetitive, but he knew they were right.

"When we were young we had a plan—my brother and I: he would be a professional football player and I would become a world champion. I would win Olympic gold."

"Now you can be a different type of champion. The Olympics are gay anyway. Redemption or revenge or whatever," Joris was looking for a word that he didn't know and he flicked his hand in the air to show that he wasn't finding it, "is a worthy thing for a person to pursue."

Danny pondered that for a good minute as Joris filled their glasses again.

"I want it." Danny said softly, the candle on the refrigerator flickering. Joris grinned.

"If it is what you truly want…you will find greatness. We are all just young men with tattoos…trying…we are all just trying. You can be an inspiration for the rest of us."

Joris reached into the crack between his mattress and the wall and tossed over a thick envelope. "Here is this, by the way."

Danny knew that it was going to happen then. It was the only way to carry on meaningfully, to become a champion of something, to raise his hands in triumph for himself and for Lucas. Fulfill their childhood pact, as best as he could.

"I don't have any tattoos though." Danny said, cracking a bashful smile.

"You want one?" Joris asked in complete seriousness.

"What *here*?" Danny asked confused.

Joris exhaled a cloud of smoke, "Yeah there is a machine. They give them here. Get one tonight. Something to remember where you started this journey."

In the cell of the card game a young inmate set up his tattoo machine and the card game became unimportant. Danny 'O Tubarão' Sheppard getting a tattoo was now the main attraction.

The machine buzzed loudly as the kid drew a small black "80" the size of a quarter in the middle of Danny's shoulder blades. Now he would be carrying Lucas with him as he went forward with his new mission. It took twenty minutes, inmates toasting and joking around them the whole time. When it was over they went back to the cell and poured two final drinks.

Danny knew that he had made the right decision to get the tattoo when Joris took his guitar from the corner of the cell. The invisible audience was back to witness what was about to happen. The first few chords were off but the song became clear after a few seconds. The piano keys of the original sounded just as good in acoustic and Danny's eyes nearly started to water when Joris voice started to sing, "When I find myself in times of trouble, Mother Mary comes to me, speaking words of wisdom, Let it Be…"

Danny thought about his future as Joris played an off-key rendition of Lucas' all-time favorite song. When it came to an end he said, "Don't forget about us here. Now *you* are a boy with a tattoo as well. It has been a pleasure knowing you brother. It has been a pleasure to be your prison shepherd." They clinked glasses together one last time.

– — -

Danny reminisced on the night he had become a boy with a tattoo many times but for some reason that morning, driving to Eastmoreland was more vivid, more colorful in his memory. Eastmoreland was still asleep as he drove past the golf course. He closed the front door as quietly as he could then out of pure habit, went to the kitchen and opened the refrigerator. From back down the hallway he heard light footsteps. He poked his head around the corner and saw a curious Rodney at the bottom of the stairs. As soon as he saw it was Danny he broke into a sprint and leapt into his arms.

"Whoa you're getting too big for me to hold you bro!"

It had been a week and a half since Danny had last been at the house and he wasn't lying, he was growing fast.

"What's this I hear about you having a new girlfriend, hm? What happened to the last one?"

Rodney bashfully tucked his chin to his chest to avoid Danny's eyes. Just then Isabel appeared around the corner, her eyes newly awake and her brow wrinkled with confusion at what was happening in her kitchen early on a Sunday morning but when she saw that it was Danny she sighed and extended her arms for a hug, "Casa bem-vinda meu amor." It was what she said every time he came to the house: *Welcome home my love.*

Same as Rich, the grief of the last few years had taken its' toll in the form of a few grey streaks of hair. Their hug lasted a long time. Danny answered a few questions in hushed Portuguese as Rodney headed down to the living room.

Isabel had never been able to sit through one of his fights. She loved watching him wrestle in college but now that there was the potential for an out-cold knockout it was a different story. In his fight with Hjälmar Svantesson she had tried her best, sitting in a VIP box with Rich and the girls but she only lasted about a minute and a half of the first round before hurrying into the foyer, Rich following. Rich didn't have any trouble watching, he was Irish. He couldn't help himself at a heavy blow or takedown and would spring to his feet and bellow, "That's my boy!" as he was known to do at Lucas' football games over the years.

He had never said anything about it but she knew that his decision to start fighting had everything to do with making Lucas proud. It never ceased to hurt, she was so proud of Danny but she could see in his eyes that he himself couldn't feel the appropriate sense of pride or accomplishment. His face was on the side of buildings, he was on TV, people wanted to take pictures with him...but he never smiled.

It had been just over two and a half years since they lost Lucas and she prayed every morning and every night that her son would be able to find joy and inner peace once again. So far her prayers had gone unanswered and Danny's eyes continued to stare into nowhere.

"Is Taison coming over today?" She called after him in Portuguese as he headed for the living room. Anytime the subject had something to do with Brazil she spoke Portuguese. Danny had just gotten comfortable on the couch next to Rodney, "I don't know but I'll call him later and see what he's doing."

Rodney was wired, high from seeing Danny for the first time in over a week and as much as Danny wanted to stay awake and watch cartoons, he couldn't keep his eyes open and he fell asleep. Rodney was happy enough to just have him on the same couch, conscious or not.

He woke at about 10:30 a.m. to the smells and sounds of a Sunday at home: a sweet and spicy pork marinade being prepared and girls gossiping and giggling. He was still tired and could have easily gone straight back to sleep but he wanted to see Allie and Andrea.

He had heard bits and pieces over the last month or so that Allie was seeing somebody but he hadn't talked to her about it yet. It had been in the back of his mind now for a week though, since Rich had referred to the guy as "this kid that Allie has been seeing". Today he would find out more about it.

Obviously there were no rumors about Andrea seeing somebody new; nobody could even entertain the idea of her going out with somebody else. She wasn't as damaged as Danny, but she had her days—like everybody did—and sometimes she still had to come over late at night to sit in the lamp-lit living room talking to Isabel or Rich before spending the night in Lucas' bedroom.

It was a beautiful clear day, chilly and crisp. Danny stood with his hands in his pockets at the barbecue with his dad and although Rich knew full well that Danny would refuse, he couldn't help but try to tempt him, "C'mon have a beer with your old man." Danny smirked and shook his head. The only drinking he had done in months was the Jack Daniels before meeting with Jenna.

At noon, just before lunch Danny went for a walk with Celia and Rodney and then when he got home he FaceTimed with Tanner from the couch.

"Oh good heavens." Celia said with a shake of her head at the island in the kitchen when Allie opened the latest *Cosmopolitan* to the article that ranked Danny the #19 Sexiest Man in Sport of 2016 behind the likes of Tom Brady, Cristiano Ronaldo, and Kelly Slater.

A day like this was as high as he could go; seeing Rodney and the girls smile and laugh, his parents still very much in love, Celia as loving and caring as always.

Saying his goodbyes was always a production whenever he left the house, as if he was returning to school after the holidays. He backed out of the driveway at 8:15 p.m. and headed towards the river, starting to think about the week of training ahead, focusing on Joe "Payday" Vega at UFC 172 in Nashville.

Vega was a kickboxing specialist with a long reach but his grappling wasn't his strong suit and Danny knew that if he took it to the ground he could end it. Surely this would be his last test. If he won, The UFC couldn't deny him any longer, it would be his turn for a shot at the title. There wouldn't be anybody left to beat. Marlos was constantly drilling it into him: never look past a fight at what might or might not happen next. But he couldn't stop himself from daydreaming about the title.

The tangible things that had come with the success didn't matter. He liked his Audi SUV but if it exploded and his new townhouse burned to the ground he wouldn't be devastated, money was never the point of it. While most fighters sat around thinking of ways to promote themselves, Danny couldn't care less about seeking the spotlight. Contrary to his intentions, his laid-back and calm demeanor only peaked people's intrigue and he had accidentally become a promoters dream come true.

Weigh-ins and pre-fight press conferences were as fascinating as his fights were entertaining. He would sit quietly at the conference table next to Marlos, Mark and Remy facing hundreds of journalists and photographers wearing their yellow lanyards in the forefront of thousands of fans pressed shoulder-to-shoulder, phones raised above their heads. His opponent would grip the microphone and talk trash relentlessly while Danny would sit uninterested as if he were about to yawn in the middle of it.

The wrestling twin-brother of tragically killed All-American football star.

The media ate it up. Lucas' death had made such headlines that it made Danny's rise even more interesting.

From a young age he knew that being quiet only built peoples curiosity and the more attentive they would be to the words that they would get out of him. At the press conference for the Montoya fight he had made the crowd roar just by smirking and rolling his eyes at

Montoya's claim that Danny wasn't even that good on the ground. They loved it.

Before he left the house he had asked Allie about the guy that she was seeing. She told him his name was Cameron and that he played soccer for University of Portland. He and Allie had a class together and they had been spending time together around campus when their schedules allowed, she seemed smitten. Danny didn't like the name, Cameron, but she seemed to think he was a good guy. Tanner wouldn't be so laid-back with his own line of inquiry. Just then his phone started to ring. It was Tanner. They had talked just two hours earlier so Danny expected him to have some news.

He pushed his hands-free button on his dashboard and answered the call, interrupting his music, "What's up."

"*What's up* indeed," Tanner said with the energy and vigor as if he had just finished a second Red Bull, fully expecting Danny to join him in his fervor.

"Did you hear that Allie was going out with somebody?" Danny asked. Tanner almost seemed to ignore the question, "How excited— Wait, *what*? Who?—Never mind, we can talk about that later. Are you *stoked*?" he nearly shouted.

Whatever Tanner was referencing was over Danny's head. He was lost, "What are you *talking* about?" As he pulled into his driveway he saw that Marlos' car was parked just down the street. Tanner seemed to ignore him yet again like a drunk friend calling from a party, "Remy called me like ten minutes ago." Danny didn't know what that meant but he could guess, "Why didn't he call *me*?" He demanded, almost angrily.

Tanner had become good friends with Remy in the last two years and they talked often. "Oh you haven't even talked to them yet? So I'm the one who gets to tell you?" Tanner shouted in surprise. Just then Marlos appeared on the front step of Danny's townhouse.

"I'll call you back."

It was as he suspected. He was getting a title shot. Ryan Corwin had fractured a bone in his foot in training and The UFC decided that instead of making Danny fight Vega and wait another four months for a title fight, they would substitute in Gary Mercer for Danny in

Nashville and move the title back two months to give more time to build the hype. It was happening.

Rolando Avelar, another Brazilian, who had defended the middleweight title four times stood in Danny's way. He was good; a Jiu-Jitsu specialist but also outstanding on his feet with great striking capabilities. Danny needed to be wary of all of it. He was thankful and relieved that he was going to get the chance so much sooner than he had anticipated. He had expected to wait at least four or five months until after the Vega fight to get a shot at the title. Now it was just three months away.

Remy and Marlos sat on the couch. Danny sat across from them on the footrest of the chair that Taison sat in. Remy was left in the dark as Marlos spoke Portuguese, it didn't really matter; he knew what was going to be said. His words were slow and thick, leaving no chance that a single syllable could be ignored.

"I have been near greatness a few times in my life Danilo, but that's all…I have only been *near* it. I have seen it at an arms length as if it was in a museum, but I haven't touched it personally. You know the truth. You know that no matter how hard someone may work towards greatness, they need to be born with something inside them. They need to have it in their bones before they ever set foot in the gym or on a field."

With no revelation or drama in his voice he said, "You know you have greatness in you. If you win this fight, you will be remembered for being the youngest ever champion of any weight division." Danny's eyes were steady and cool with wisdom and understanding that didn't fit a 22-year-old.

"In three months you will achieve greatness."

- — -

MONDAY, SEPTEMBER 19ᵀᴴ, 2016

Ever since the night Joris had played his dodgy version of *Let it Be* in their cell, the only thing that had given Danny any optimism at all was the thought of becoming the Middleweight champion of The UFC.

Being the youngest champion in UFC history would be the tribute that Lucas deserved.

Everybody made the trip, arriving a week before the fight and living comfortably in penthouse suites at the MGM Grand. Danny had been training at UNLV where every workout was open to the media and the public. It had been a hectic week and Danny's focus was so extreme that he had become prone to losing his temper. He snapped at Mark and demanded that all interviews and media appearances of any kind were to be over with indefinitely by Wednesday, three days before the fight. This was completely out of the question and as soon as Danny cooled off he apologized and acknowledged that he knew the request was impossible.

There had been three photo shoots, a dozen phone interviews, and an overly confident hipster journalist who was a little too comfortable in his own skin from *Vice News* in a conference room at the MGM in addition to the lengthy UFC checklist of regulation meetings and appointments. Danny didn't want to shake hands, smile and interact let alone even be around people from outside of his circle in the week leading up to the fight. Their casual and friendly disposition was not at all cohesive with what was going on in his head.

The buzz and excitement surrounding the fight gained more steam each day. Even tourists who didn't know a thing about fighting could recognize Danny from the official event poster of him and Rolando Avelar that was plastered everywhere on the strip. It flashed across the advertisement screen of the MGM every minute and a half and it was on the roof of hundreds of taxis: *Avelar vs. Sheppard*. The picture was nothing more than the two of them staring each other down, face-to-face in front of a white backdrop.

Avelar was bald headed and had dark skin like Gabriel. Marlos, Remy and Danny had poured over hours of film on him, but Danny went one step further. At night when he was alone in his penthouse suite, he would type in 'Rolando Avelar' in the search bar of You-Tube and click on any thumbnail that showed him outside of the ring doing trivial things like greeting fans or talking to the media. It was a habit that he had developed early in his wrestling career. He needed to know who the person was, not just who they were as a competitor. He needed to understand them as people, humanize them and imagine their journey. It made them easier to defeat.

After he had watched a video of Avelar giving a tour of his neighborhood in Coritiba to a local news channel, Danny stood and walked to the window of his suite. The crowded sidewalks of the strip brought back the memory of carnival at the beach with Nina. He thought about her often and wondered if she had ever seen him on TV or in a magazine. He wondered what she looked like now; how she wore her hair and whether or not she had actually gone to Spain. It didn't make any sense how he could feel so much anger towards her and at the same time want nothing more than to see her again.

Some mornings in the moments just before he was fully conscious he could feel the warmth of the beach, the soft sand on his feet, the wash of the waves, and most powerfully, the weight of her body in his arms. It was agonizing to wake up and find himself under a comforter in Oregon. Some nights he would wake suddenly after being electrocuted by a vivid image of her smiling face.

He was in the middle of remembering the afternoon they spent sitting at a sidewalk café a few blocks off the beach, sharing a dish of ice cream when there was a deep thudding knock at the door of his suite. The butt of a fist, he knew it was Tanner. He had heard the knock a hundred times in the dorms freshman year. It was 11:27 p.m.

"What's up." Tanner said, pushing past Danny into the suite. The TV was on with no sound.

"You watchin' Keeping Up with the Kardashians in here?" He asked as he hopped onto the bed. Danny slumped into the sofa chair next to the bed.

"Kim and Khloe go to Miami actually," Danny said.

"Umm, I think you mean *Kourtney* and Kim *take* Miami." Tanner corrected him sarcastically taking offense. Danny chuckled.

"The weigh-in is gonna be a shit show man, I was just downstairs, it's nuts. You're everywhere."

Danny nodded. They didn't do any more talking. ESPN had a hold of Tanner and Danny was deep in imagination, visualizing a knockout, the raptures of cheering from the crowd of 17,000—the maximum capacity of the MGM Grand Garden Arena.

— — -

SATURDAY, SEPTEMBER 24TH, 2016

Fight day finally arrived. As usual Danny sympathized with his mom, she had always been a wreck on the day of the fight. Celia was never as distraught and panicky as Isabel but she never had much to say on fight day.

At 8:43 a.m. everybody gathered in a grand event room with floor-to-ceiling windows and elaborate art-deco embellishments that included thick white pillars on either side of the doorway. Danny wasn't allowed to eat the catered breakfast but for everybody else there were neatly organized squares of Red Bull, Gatorade, and bottled waters next to pitchers of juice and the rows of chrome serving containers. A pair of hostesses in white-collars and cream vests stood attentively but out of the way near the door. Danny could eat and drink as much as he wanted after the weigh-in but all his food was still prepared by Taison.

Rodney pressed his forehead and palms against the window and gave a live commentary—to nobody in particular—on what he was seeing on the street below. Celia, Remy and mark's wife, Tricia, traded observations about the weigh-in from the night before. Danny heard Remy say, "...biggest I have *ever* seen, but that is Las Vegas."

It had been incredible. Two hundred members of the media jostled and elbowed to get their cameras in position as the fighters took the stage with their teams. Behind them nearly 10,000 people packed the floor, trying to catch a glimpse of Danny Sheppard: the young phenomenon.

The noise had been deafening as Joe Rogan yelled into the microphone. When it was Danny's turn to be weighed, he stripped into the black Nike boxers with a big white swoosh across the backside. He stepped onto the scale as the official tapped the marker until the bar leveled in mid-air. Other officials jotted things down on their clipboards.

"One hundred eighty four and a half pounds for the challenger... Danny...*The Python*...Sheppard!" Rogan's voice boomed over the speakers on all sides of the crowd as Danny raised his arms and flexed with confidence. The ring girls applauded politely at the back of the stage, smiling coquettishly. Nevada State Police officers stood behind the scale, as was protocol. It was a raucous occasion.

Since starting his career in The United States he had been dubbed "The Python" for the way he used his long limbs to submit his opponents but in his own mind he was still Danny "O Tubarão" Sheppard, champion of Leo Goia.

After Avelar weighed in, they were brought toe-to-toe for the stare-down. Cameras really started clicking and flashing then. Avelar didn't trash-talk or insult Danny in any way and they shook hands firmly at the end of it, looking each other in the eye. He had a similar build to Danny; long, spindly, strong arms and legs, but he was 6'4", two inches taller than Danny.

Mark hadn't sat down to eat yet and was pacing the wall at the far side of the room talking on the phone while looking at a page in the thick packet of papers that he'd been carrying around the whole week. Finally he hung up and turned towards the tables, interrupting the conversations that were taking place.

"Excuse me guys," he called.

"Thanks. So the schedule for the rest of the day is pretty straight forward—six o'clock report at the locker room slash lounge—there's couches and TV and you'll be able to order whatever food you want—you know the drill. Obviously we are the main event so we have to be there for probably close to four hours. It's pretty standard from there with the officials and medical personnel etcetera—checking their stuff, a few tests and all that. So we will head to the arena at around five fifteen, just to be certain. And that...is all I have for the scheduling info. If anything comes up I will let everyone know in the group chat."

Tanner started a slow clap, "Yeah Mark!"

Everybody laughed, including the vested waiters near the door. Mark bowed comically to the tables. "Thank you, Tanner."

— — -

10:06 P.M.

UFC officials and doctors had vacated the room ten minutes earlier and then there would be nothing left to do but wait for the knock on the door.

"What's happening out there?" Danny asked, breaking the silence that had been stretching on since the officials left. They were so deep in the underground of the MGM Grand it felt like they were preparing for a nuclear attack.

Mark glanced at his phone. "Two minutes and...forty seconds into the third round." Fights were comprised of three rounds of five minutes except for title fights that could go five rounds if they needed to. Danny estimated a 30-minute intermission between the last fight and the main event.

He sat shirtless on a stool, his posture rigid. His eyes were blank but steely-focused, staring straight forward as Remy massaged his shoulders.

— — -

When the knock came it was a man in a dark suit with three hefty security guards in yellow polo shirts with "EVENTS" printed across the backs, clear earpieces coiling from their collars to their ears.

It wasn't time to say goodbye just yet but Danny still got corralled into hugs from the girls and his mom. They all followed the security guards, Danny bouncing on his toes as they walked down the narrow hallway. For other fighters it would have been time for cheers of encouragement but everybody knew that he hated any attempts to hype him up; it was nothing but unwanted volume to him. He wanted quiet.

The team looked sharp in their Nike short-sleeve button-ups that were grey but almost glimmered silver. Danny's biggest sponsor was Nike but Monster Energy, BF Goodrich Tire, Toyota and the UFC logo were represented on the front of the shirt. Danny's fighting shorts were short and black with an imposing white swoosh across the backside. In his corner would be Marlos, Remy, Tanner, and Taison.

They followed the men down the narrow hallway that eventually emptied into a vast cavernous tunnel where semi-trucks would bring in equipment for performances and events that were held in the arena. The crowd became barely audible then, echoing faintly through the hollow cave. The chirps and crackles of walkie-talkies bounced off the walls, more yellow-shirted security personnel milled about. Trucks and forklifts were parked along the walls. Across the tunnel the thick-necked security guards pushed through metal double doors and they were back in a narrow hallway. They waited in silence, Danny staying loose, bouncing slightly from side-to-side, head bowed, eyes closed. His thoughts were calm. A woman in a pantsuit made her way up the slightly inclined hallway. Just before she reached the group the man in the dark suit who had been leading the way turned and said, "Okay, anybody who is not going to be in Mr. Sheppard's corner: this is where we need you to say your goodbyes. You're going to follow Ms. Fuller."

Then, like a solider heading for the trenches of war in a far away land, it was time to say farewell. The girls grabbed him first and although it started as a three-way hug, they eventually got a lengthy hug of their own. Then Celia. Then Rodney. Then Rich. Then Isabel.

"Don't worry mom. I'll be fine. Eu vou ganhar. Eu te amo." He said softly. None of them were very willing to release themselves from their embrace—Isabel nearly had to be pulled away. Rodney didn't want to be put down and raced straight into Andrea's arms when he was. All the girls were teary-eyed.

Rich had been in Danny's corner a few times in the past but he had to stay with Isabel for this one. She had promised to sit through the whole fight. He hugged his son and low enough for only him to hear said, "Whatever happens, I'm so proud of you and you know Lucas would be too."

— — -

Given that Danny was the main attraction, Rolando Avelar's entrance was first. They always saved the best for last, even though Danny would be making zero attempt to entertain. There were no flags carried behind him, no entry song, and—although he had received a few requests, or "offers" as their representatives had worded it—no celebrity accompaniments.

Avelar's entrance song began and the crowd grew in volume. 17,100 people. It wasn't the biggest crowd that Danny had fought in front of—that had been in Stockholm at the Tele2 Arena when he knocked out Hjälmar Svantesson in front of just over 24,000—but there was a much more frenetic and crazed vibe from the noise of the Las Vegas crowd. It was, after all, a title fight and a potential record-setting night.

Danny and Tanner both knew the song that was playing for Avelar's entrance: "Ambition" by Wale. It was a good song; Danny had it on his iPhone. Hearing the song that he had chosen to walk out to was another glimpse into what he was like as a person—Danny always felt like he knew someone better after finding out what kind of music they liked.

OK. Here we go.

He began his pre-fight ritual of visualizations, seeing his life in fast-forward: playing with his younger siblings as children in the backyard, his first fight with Tanner all those years ago on the playground, taking Rodney's hand and leading him out to the driveway to play basketball one of the first mornings after they had adopted him, practicing capoeira with Lucas, strolling the streets of Eastmoreland with Celia, walking the beaches of Rio with his family, his time with Joris and his fights in prison, signing his Nike deal and inevitably...Nina. She always made an appearance. She looked back at him over her shoulder as they hiked the trail to Primitas Waterfall.

As he visualized his life a soundtrack began. Beautiful piano keys, a familiar tune. The crowd roared with surprise and excitement. It rang clearly and beautifully from the arena and as the words came, the crowd started to sing along.

"*When I find myself in times of trouble, Mother Mary comes to me, speaking words of wisdom… Let it Be.*" Danny's brow twitched with confusion for a moment. He looked over his shoulder at the sly smirk that looked back at him. Tanner. He threw him an OK sign just as the dark-suited coordinator responded into his walkie-talkie and waved them toward the tunnel opening as four Nevada State police officers surrounded them.

The singing grew louder as they approached the tunnel mouth until they took their first steps out into the spotlight. The crowd went wild. Fans knew Danny never had an entrance song. It had taken them by surprise and boosted the energy level even higher.

The police officers batted away the outstretched hands from behind the gates and past the guards that already lined it. Cameras on wires whipped through the air overhead.

"And in my hour of darkness she is standing right in front of me, speaking words of wisdom… Let it Be."

All eyes were on Danny, including the ones that weren't there at all. He felt them. The invisible jury. They had been waiting for this.

– — -

SATURDAY, OCTOBER 8ᵀᴴ 2016

A hectic two weeks had passed since Danny Sheppard had defeated Rolando Avelar and become the youngest ever Ultimate Fighting Championship title-holder in history. The front page of the sports section of *The New York Times* from Sunday, September 25th was framed and now hung next to the *Sports Illustrated* in the entryway of the Sheppard house. It was a beautiful, triumphant scene from the MGM Garden Arena. Danny's eyes were wide, almost startled-looking. Blood trailed from a cut below his left eye, his hands were raised to the sky. Behind him referee Herb Dean knelt next to a seated Rolando Avelar, a hand on his shoulder, assessing his cognitive awareness after he had tapped out. Men in headsets on the outside of the octagon were standing mid-applause with marveled looks on their faces. The title of the article read:

THE CHAMP… at 22

Isabel could have chosen the sports page of any major publication in the country; everything was Danny Sheppard. She had ordered copies of all major world newspapers from Sunday, September 25ᵗʰ. But The Guardian, The Washington Times, The Los Angeles Times, nor

The Chicago Tribune said anything different or more interesting than one another. They beat the same drum:

After his All-American brother was tragically killed in a car accident, he took a sabbatical to his mother's native Brazil—the transition from being an All-American wrestler to the world of mixed-martial-arts appeared to be seamless—He has transcended all expectations of what a 22 year-old is capable of—courageously battling through the pain of losing his twin brother...

Nobody ever knew of Trevor Ramey. Nobody knew of Leo Goia. Nobody knew about Joris and the boys with tattoos, and nobody knew about Nina.

Danny had been spending his time at the house ever since he returned from Las Vegas and for the first time since the tap-out heard 'round the world he had some time to himself. Rich and Isabel had rented a cottage on the coast for the weekend. Tanner was back at school, Allie was on campus. Rodney was having a sleepover at Charlie's house. Andrea and Celia were both around and Danny went for walks with them daily, but today he was at home by himself.

His cheekbone was broken and it left him with an ugly black eye that had taken the full two weeks to fade to a greenish/purple. An Avelar leg kick in the 2nd round had almost been the end of the fight, sending Danny off balance and wheeling his arms through the air as he stumbled backwards. The adrenaline of the fight had blocked out just how painful it was but when it wore off it hurt terribly. He had been medicating with the oxycodone that he was prescribed, breezing through the days relatively unbothered and tingly-numb.

The first few days after the fight had been especially hectic with appearances, contractual obligations, and being in and out of the hospital. In two weeks he had done eleven phone interviews in which he essentially repeated himself over and over—*It's a dream-come-true...I owe everything to my team and family who have done everything for me...I know he would have been out of his seat the whole fight.*

Things had finally settled down a bit and the world had turned their attention to other sporting events. Marlos and Taison had gone back to Brazil and Remy had gone back to France for three weeks.

Danny wouldn't fight again for another six months and everybody was well deserving of a vacation.

Not much had changed for Danny. He didn't know what kind of release and rebirth he had expected to have happen after winning the title but whatever it was, he was underwhelmed. Winning, and having the title belt thrown around his waist to the screams of 17,100 people, becoming the youngest ever champion, it had all been amazing but there hadn't been any waterfall of liberation and sudden peace. His eyes still looked into the unseen distance.

He sat in the kitchen of his parent's house looking out the window with the aimlessness of a 90 year-old in a nursing home. He watched the drops of rain on the window. He would pick one towards the top and wait for it to slither its' way down until it had gathered enough other droplets to tumble rapidly to the bottom. It wasn't a half bad metaphor, he thought, for how his life had snowballed, or rain-dropped, into an unstoppable plummet immediately after the accident.

He had a phone interview with *Maxim Magazine* scheduled for 3 p.m. and then he didn't know what he would do with his day.

— — —

The interview had bothered him. The frat-boy sounding interviewer had overstepped and asked too many questions about Lucas in too casual a way, they never understood how real the questions were for Danny; it was just a story for them. He started giving him short answers out of annoyance but when he finally hung up he felt sorry, then he became angry with himself.

Directly after the call, at 4:12 p.m. he was in his Audi driving to Trader Joe's and then to the corner liquor store. He knew what he was going to do with the rest of his day.

Out of fond nostalgia for Joris he bought a fifth of Jack Daniels. On the couch in the living room he stirred his first drink with his pinky finger before popping an Oxycodone and washing it down with a lengthy gulp.

He turned the TV on. He texted Tanner. He texted Allie. He

turned the TV off. He walked onto the back porch. The sky was pink, night was coming soon. For the billionth time Danny yearned so badly to talk to Lucas; there was so much to tell him. Strangely, the thing he wanted to tell him most was the story of Nina.

He hoped he would approve of his decision to drop out of school and start fighting. He knew he would be upset to hear how he had run away after beating up Trevor Ramey. Danny thought about Andrea then, and texted her too. He went back inside and poured a double shot, taking it straight without mixing it with the Coke.

"Joris style! But I forgot to toast!" He said in sarcastic despair, pouring himself another shot. "To Joris. My prison brother. I don't know where you are but I hope I see you again someday. Cheers." He said, flicking the glass with his finger.

He went back onto the porch. There was a new bag of coal near the barbecue. He hoisted it into the air like Simba for the backyard to see. "Ay-Ya-Ah-Way-Ahhh!"

He wondered if Nina had seen *The Lion King* before. He wondered where she was. He wondered if she had actually gone to Spain to study. If it had in fact been another lie then it was very imaginative, she had all the details to go along with it.

He wished he had a phone number for Mateus. He texted Marlos and told him to say hi to Mateus if he were to cross paths with him, he hoped Mateus was fighting and finding success.

He went back inside. Mixed a strong drink and took another Oxycodone. He wondered about statistics, death statistics.

How many twins have died in the last year?

He wondered how many years Celia had left. She was 86 years old. He wished she could live forever. He loved her with all his heart and he realized that he should have gone over to her house before he started drinking. He wanted to see her first thing in the morning.

The numb warmth had crept up on him and over the course of the next six drinks and one more Oxycodone, he started to shed more clothing and talk to himself out loud, blissfully unaware of just how intoxicated he was.

"Why isn't there any music on, that's the *real* question." He

242   EDDY PRUGH

drawled. His fingertips were playfully numb as he fumbled with the AUX cord that came from behind the TV. He plugged in his iPhone and hit play on one of Lucas' favorite playlists from 2011.

"Well that's that huh?" He said with childish light-heartedness. "From larva to caterpillar and caterpillar to butterfly." The words came out of his mouth in a drooling belligerent way that.

"Then the butterfly got smashed by a Fiat. Or a dump truck." He laughed and lifted his drink above his head. "To Nina! The love of my life. I hope you are happily deceiving somebody new these days. Saúde!" He said flicking his glass with a finger before drinking.

"But I can't just thank *Nina*. There are so many other people who have helped me accomplish this. Helped me to become the young-est-*ever* UFC title-holder. I have six and a half million dollars. It's a hell of a thing. I'm kind of a big deal. I have many leather-bound books."

He had transitioned to a rehearsed speech voice.

"I must thank my family, whom I abandoned at the worst possible time, I owe them everything." He raised his glass again and flicked it, taking another drink.

"Then of course there's Tanner, Celia, Andrea and a few other loyal people who stuck by me. I'm sorry. I'm so, so sorry. It's not my fault." He said, his voice faltering to a casual tone.

"I just didn't know what to do, I had to run. My mind wasn't right. I didn't mean to leave everyone like I did... I—I... I was so scared." A long pause ensued as a Kendrick Lamar song played softly from the surround sound.

"I was so scared. I still am. I don't know how to move on without you, man."

It felt good, whatever he was doing. It was like the first night when he had started to tell Jenna the story, some sort of untouchable weight was leaving him and he became a little bit lighter in the chest with every toast. A soft, sweet voice from within like a young Celia, almost angelic, prodded him to continue.

Go on, it's okay.

He was now slumped on his side against the couch, staring into the glass.

"I left them alone. I was the most important one because I was the twin, and I just ran away and left them here. Right *here*." He patted the couch behind him.

"I can't forgive myself for that. They needed me to be here and I left. I didn't tell them I was leaving. I thought maybe if I came back and accomplished something great it would all go away." The last words were strange to hear come out of his own mouth. It was like somebody else had said them for him. He repeated it softly.

"I thought it would all go away, but nothing has changed. My family is sad because of me. They want me to be happy, but I don't know how. I miss my brother and I'm always mad."

He rose to his feet and filled his glass for a final time. He was down to his shorts that he had on under his sweats, no shirt. The rain was tapping on the glass of the sliding door, beckoning. He took his drink outside. His skin was hot. The rain was heavenly and seemed to fall harder as soon as he took a few steps out the door. He walked barefoot to the edge of the porch, raising his glass in a final toast.

He could feel Lucas. He felt alone with him, as if they had been at a formal party glad-handing and smiling all night before slipping off into a vacated stairway with a couple drinks…just the two of them. Not even Tanner or Andrea was around; it was a strong singularity that was made of two imperfect halves that fit together seamlessly. It radiated from the backyard; the dark sea of wet grass laughed Lucas' laugh, echoing from far away.

"I miss you. I've never stopped missing you." He said before putting the glass to his lips and turning it upside down one last time.

— — —

It was Lucas' bed that he face-planted into. Not by choice or for any reason—in fact he didn't remember the walk from the living room through the kitchen, down the hallway, up the stairs and into the bedroom. The room didn't spin as he had anticipated but his heart pounded like an anchor making contact with the bottom of the ocean, over and over. He tumbled into the bathtub of warm numbness. It took a lot to put a body the size of Danny's into such a state but the three 90 milligrams of Oxycodone and almost an entire fifth of Jack Daniels had done a good job. His tolerance for both alcohol and painkillers had been weakened after two and a half years of strict sobriety.

– — –

Danny hardly ever dreamed. He couldn't relate to the stories of tormenting nightmares that other people had after traumatic events. He rarely ever remembered the faint dreams he may have had in his usual deep sleep, but he would never forget the dream he was about to have. He was asleep just seconds after planting himself in Lucas' bed, but somewhere deep in the black tumbles of his mind there was a faint glimmer of awareness: a single office light high in a dark skyscraper.

Lucas' bedroom still hadn't been changed in the 2 years and ten months since he died: the Wu-Tang W and the Michael Jordan poster on the wall, the glow in the dark stars on the ceiling. Perhaps being in Lucas' room was what induced the powerful experience that came next.

The noise was the first part, waves breaking gently on a sandy shore. It grew slowly louder as if someone was twisting a volume knob. Time had no influence in this place but soon after the sound of the waves crashing became clear, there was a sense of warmth and humidity and a swaying sensation made it clear that Danny was in a hammock. Then with a brilliant whoosh his eyes opened, he could see. He was too numb and comfortable to move his head but he could see what was ahead of him, and it was beautiful. He had never been there but for some reason it was very familiar.

He was on the beach of a tropical island, a deep inlet bay stretched in front of him. White sand ran the whole length of the shore and palm trees and lush green vegetation covered the hills behind. He had been there for days and he knew that the party that was going on across the water on the far shore was where he had come from some hours earlier before falling asleep in the hammock. There was a bonfire growing brighter at the party as the night began to fall. The faintest sounds of voices and laughter floated across the water. Then came voices from somewhere closer.

At first they were far away and indiscernible in a way that sounded like they were coming from under water but they were coming closer and growing louder. They were cheerful, two of them going back and forth in a chipper, greeting way like two friends running into one another on the street. Before he even knew whom the voices belonged to he knew that they had just come from the party across the bay and would be going back soon. They were standing behind the hammock that Danny was swinging in and he wasn't supposed to turn around to engage them, it was *their* conversation. It soon became clear who they were: Lucas and Celia.

Celia's voice was sprightly and energetic like the Celia Danny remembered from his childhood. Lucas was happy as usual and from his voice Danny could tell that his face was plastered with a smile.

Their auras had colors: Lucas seemed to be an orange-gold while Celia was a crisp sky blue, both colors spilling down on Danny's upper peripheral. Even though their conversation didn't involve him, it was obvious that he was meant to be listening and there was no need to feel guilty for eavesdropping.

"Yeah I've been hiking a lot lately." Lucas responded to Celia's comment that he was looking healthy or happy or something of the sort. The richness and clarity of his voice was tranquilizing and soul quenching.

"Which *speaking* of... my little sister is absolutely killing it this season isn't she?" Lucas was clearly referring to the success that Allie had been having that season on the tennis court; she was currently 23-6 and ranked 11th in the country in singles. The news was current so wherever they were, they were up to date with what was happening in the lives of everyone.

"How do you think Danny is doing?" he asked with excited curiosity, enthusiasm carrying over from the talk of Allie's season.

"You know, I'm not sure. It's been difficult for him. He misses you so much." Celia said with sympathy that appeared to come with a slow shaking of the head.

"I know but can't he just *live* already? I've been gone for like three

246   EDDY PRUGH

years! He just won the title and he's still pissed off and sad—it's crazy. He needs to get over that girl, too. Good *Lord* it's been too long!"

Their voices started to echo and wither as their colored auras shivered and became faint. They were making their way up the beach, returning to the party.

There was nothing ceremonious about hearing Lucas' voice one last time. No music played, his words didn't echo throughout Danny's head or jolt him awake. It was brief but so fulfilling. Danny's mind didn't try to claw or grasp at the space that the lighted ghosts had vacated and he didn't scramble to yell out questions that he always imagined he would ask in a make-believe scenario where he was able to talk to Lucas again. Outbursts or any intense show of emotion were frowned upon in this place, which somehow he already knew. Whatever part of Danny's mind that was present to witness the exchange didn't cry and plead for him to stay, but instead just felt warmth and peace as he swayed gently in the hammock. Soon his eyelids began to shut and the bonfire light grew weak. He fell forward, sinking into the thick darkness.

– — -

CAMDEN TOWN, LONDON, UK

Joris slid into a booth at a hip tavern in North London. He had been relatively clean for almost 10 months. After serving his 18 months in Leo Goia he had gone directly home to Amsterdam. He had money— between the card game and what Danny had won him he had managed to save almost €5,000. A week of intense drinking and cocaine use had ensued and, as he watched the sunrise from the roof of an Old Town apartment building, he decided that Brazil and Leo Goia would be his final hurrah as a drug entrepreneur. And not just that; he wanted out of the crime world completely.

He pieced together a dodgy resume and applied for several jobs at sports betting companies in England, hoping that one would take a chance on his unique math skills. His applications were never taken seriously with as little formal education as he had but he had an enormous stroke of luck when he ended up drinking at a bar in Statford and striking up conversation with the patron next to him who turned out to be a manager at Bet365, one of the biggest betting companies in all of Europe. He managed to arrange a phone call for the next day and then he did what he did best: became likable. Complex algorithms that his colleagues—scholars with degrees in accounting and mathematics—struggled to fully master, he applied easily; his skills were natural.

A steady paycheck was a new phenomenon for Joris. It wasn't just the income part that he enjoyed. It was the normalcy that he had always been so scared of that he now found pleasant. He leased a flat near the river. He was getting his tattoos touched up, he had a dentist, he joined a gym, he found a new hobby in cooking and he enjoyed practicing recipes and perusing the meat market for a specific cut.

The accountability of having a place to be and a set time to show up had given him a sense of importance and responsibility that he took pride in. For a few months straight he had only drank beer and smoked spliffs but eventually the itch would return and he would call his old friend Martin for a single night's worth of fine black tar, usually about a gram. This was the pattern, and it wouldn't be changing any time soon. Complete sobriety wasn't and never would be an attainable benchmark. The fast life had run its' course but the remnants of years of substance abuse weren't going to be mended entirely, it was too late. He had no regrets. He was alive.

The small things in life were enjoyable. Now, he woke in his flat and looked out the kitchen window at the river. He made his morning coffee and read the newspaper. He would walk or bike to work.

Periodically he would be tasked with contributing to the configuration of the odds for mixed martial arts fights and he would end up looking at none other than his old friend, Danny Sheppard. A happy smirk would spread across his face every time he saw Danny on TV or when he appeared in a pop-up advertisement while he was web surfing.

Joris wondered about him—how he was doing, if he was happy, if he had ever fought off the demons that he was blind to but were glaring to Joris. It was on his bucket list to get in touch with him and pass on his congratulations for the success that he had achieved since leaving prison. He would remind him that he owed him some nice things since becoming famous. It would happen one day, but for now Joris was going to continue on this path of normalcy. One day he would see his friend again, and maybe toast him with a dirty glass of Jack Daniels.

— — —

Danny's eyes opened. He wiggled his toes before trying to move his body. Everything was confusing for a few seconds. His eyes took in his surroundings. It came back to him; he was in Lucas' room, he had drunk the bottle of Jack Daniel's and taken several Oxycodone.

A silver streak of light shot through the curtains in an elegant, Victorian way but it wasn't strong enough to make the room any lighter. Danny lay still and watched the dust particles float through it. He took a few deep breaths before pushing himself up from the bed, squeezing his eyes shut and bracing for the headache, but it didn't come.

The room was crystal clear as if he were testing out new contact lenses for the first time—which was shocking, considering that he should be doubled over in the agony of a violent hangover. He didn't feel sick at all, in fact he felt great, he felt light and well rested.

He swung his legs off the side of the bed so he could start to assess just how real or dreamy the hallucination had been. He was positive in its' existence, the image of the shoreline was still quite vivid. He had heard the waves, seen the water, and felt the presence of Celia and Lucas. There was no telling if it had happened just after he fell asleep or just before he had woken up, but it had happened, of that he was certain.

He smelled of stale sweat and alcohol, which he got a strong whiff of as he stood up. The cold, crisp air of the morning—it was 8:17 a.m.—was refreshing beyond belief as he opened the front door and went for the trunk of his Audi where he was pretty sure there was a box of Nike gear that he hadn't opened yet.

He was still so tangled in his own world that he flinched when Mrs. Gibbons hollered from across the street, "Congratulations Danny!" raising a thumbs-up.

"Thank you." He called back with a sheepish smile and wave.

The hot shower water beat onto his shoulders, his mind calm but pensive, wondering why it had been Celia who had acted as the intermediary in his vision. He turned the water off and stepped out of the shower. Wiping a clearing on the fogged mirror he studied his eyes when it hit him, the ice-cold realization. He raced to put on his track pants and top without toweling off before flying down the stairs and across the street, not having checked to see if any cars were coming. He bounded up the stairs of Celia's front porch. It was locked. Her car was in the driveway. He hopped the fence and let himself in the back door.

He didn't want to call out for fear of not being responded to. The kitchen was empty. Danny passed the picture frames on the walls of the hallway, her daughters and their children as well as Danny, Allie, Rodney, Lucas—Lucas and Andrea. He dashed from living room to guest room before taking the stairs three at a time to where he knew her bedroom was—facing the backyard.

He knocked. No answer. He had to take a deep breath before pushing through the door, but it only revealed a tidily made bed, the sheets tucked tightly into the mattress crack. Then it appeared in his memory, some casual Sunday brunch conversation from a few weeks—even a month earlier—*The bed in the basement is so much better for my back*. He hurried but he knew it wouldn't make any difference if his vision had been based on fact.

The door to the basement bedroom was cracked, he was nervous to push it open. A machine humming noise was coming from deeper within the basement, his heart pounded, it was dark but what he saw was unmistakable; the body on the bed, white sheets mounded in the center of the mattress, skinny at the bottom and thicker in the middle. His heartbeat was in his ears, throbbing as he ran his hand nervously along the wall until he touched the light switch. The last thing he remembered thinking was *At least she went in her sleep*, before the room became flooded in light and Danny inhaled sharply; it was a pile of sheets and pillows piled up.

"Danny?" Celia's voice, soft and concerned, ventured from behind him.

He spun around startled, his eyes wild, relief overpowering every muscle in his entire body. He struggled for a breath as he shuffled awkwardly forward towards her. She studied him concerned to the point of being frightened, "You nearly scared me to death, Danny." She scolded.

The irony made him choke out a startled laugh through his fast breathing. The sight of her cloudy white hair, slouched over shoulders and slightly knock-kneed stance was more than he could bear. She could see it coming and with a look of exhausted relief, she dropped the laundry basket to the ground. It was as if she wanted to say, *Finally*, as she opened her arms.

A stream of hot tears erupted and flowed from Danny's eyes as he squeezed her and buried his face in her shoulder. He couldn't hold it back, and he didn't know if it was sheer relief at finding her alive or a combination of emotions from the morning, the two weeks since winning the title or the last three years compounded.

Something inside him had cracked and burst wide open. He sobbed, his nose running, cheeks hot and salty with a rapid stream of tears. He had been wrapped in this same embrace with the same tears when he was 10, hugging grandma Celia around the midsection after he had his finger slammed in the front door.

"It's okay. It's all okay." She assured him softly, patting him on the back as he cried. He had heard variations of the same assurance for a long time, but he finally believed it. He believed Celia. He heard it from Lucas himself in the night. He finally understood and accepted what he had been told time and time again: *He would want you to move on. Forgive yourself.*

He hadn't shed a single tear for almost three years, but they came now as if they had been stored in reserve since Friday, January 10th 2014, the day Lucas died. The anger, despair, spite, relief, anxiety— they were tears of every kind.

The relief that he felt after recounting to Jenna his story was a weak flashlight beam compared to the flood lights that came on with a loud whooshing noise like the lights used for the fights in Leo Goia, illuminating the dark and bleak prospect of carrying on with life. He felt brand new. Reborn. It was as if the tears were the bacteria that had kept him sick with anger and desperation for three years and as they streamed down his cheeks he regained his health. He had Lucas' blessing and he knew—he had always known—that he could forget the mistakes he had made by nearly killing a man and leaving his family as he had. He knew he didn't deserve what Nina had done to him. He saw himself for what he was: a champion, and a kind human being.

For almost three years he felt like half of his own body was missing. Not his parents, Allie, Rodney—not even Andrea could put themselves in the shoes of the brother...the *twin* brother of the one who had died. A portion of his own soul had left with Lucas, but he finally felt whole. He felt like maybe, just maybe, things would be okay.

– — -

Training wasn't set to start again for three weeks. Both Remy and Marlos assured Danny that the free time was strictly for rehabilitation and relaxation—especially for his cheekbone. He decided that in the meantime, he was going to make an effort to step into the public at least once a day and rejoin society.

He went to one of Allie's home matches, which she won against a girl from the University of Utah. He had dinner with Celia, Rodney, Rich, Isabel and Andrea every night. He went for a walk with Celia every day, sometimes twice a day. He played soccer with Rodney who he could start to tell was going to be quite a talent. He would walk to the park near his townhouse and practice capoeira by himself.

At the end of the week he drove to Corvallis and strolled through campus, accompanying Tanner to his classes and indulging students' Snapchat and selfie requests at every turn, even smiling in most of them. They went to a party at a townhouse of some football players on Saturday. After being spotted on campus a buzz had been building and a rumor started to spread that he might be at a party that weekend. It was a popular townhouse complex and they showed up to no fewer than three hundred students milling about. An impromptu block party ensued and police were called in to cordon the street off. It was the first time Danny had seen Lucas' former teammates and friends.

Phones were raised overhead and flashed from every direction.

Danny smiled and laughed as hands cusped the back of his neck as he was immersed in the chaos of love and praise.

Lucas was alive in Corvallis. Rich and Isabel came down on Sunday and together they walked through Reser Stadium. They posed for a picture with the Athletic Director and the football coach in front of the "LS-80" banner that had been unraveled over the student section. The photo would go on to appear in newspapers and social media for weeks to come.

Isabel and Rich didn't comment on the turn in his behavior, at least not to him. But for weeks afterward, as they got ready for bed they rejoiced and hugged, Isabel would cry as they could see that a corner had been turned in their son's life. It had an affect on everybody; brighter eyes, louder laughs, silly jokes—it was infectious and although over the past few years none of them had completely given up hope, they had reluctantly grown accustom to Danny's blank stare.

He still had small lapses of anxious sadness. Late at night while his MacBook rested next to him playing music softly, he would lay and think about the depths of the last three years. From losing Lucas to nearly beating the life out of Trevor Ramey to hating himself for leaving his family and finally, to being betrayed by Nina.

He thought about Joris, and tried to imagine what he was doing at that very moment. He thought a lot about Leo Goia. A tiny part of him even wanted to go back sometimes. He wanted to gaze up at the different colored sheets over the doorways, curl the dumbbells in the gym cell and bounce on his toes in the concrete courtyard where he had his first fight. Every once in a while just before he would fall asleep he would hear the life of it: cheers echoing off the walls from every level of cells, the clanging of pipe on pipe, the aqua gate cranking open.

No matter what path his mind would wander down one way or the other he would always come back to Nina. He could never shake his head or squeeze his eyes hard enough to get the curve of her smile out of his mind; the soft white sand of Copacabana behind her as she looked up at him from his lap while the sun rose. Sometimes he would get up from bed and walk to the window to look out at the neighborhood that was being built around him. If he was too restless to go back to sleep he would put on sweats and headphones and walk the empty sidewalks, even exploring some of the skeletons of the houses-to-be.

He got the email from Marlos on Thursday. Training would begin the following Monday, which came as a relief. Extra weight clung to his mid-section, which in all honesty was probably no more than four pounds, but it annoyed him and he wanted to get rid of it as soon as possible. He was ready to get back to work.

‒ — ‒

Remy, Marlos and Mark were all greeting one another in the parking lot when Danny pulled in. For a month it had sunken in that they had achieved something amazing, something that would be remembered, a special moment in history. As Danny walked across the black pavement they started to applaud, laughing as he bashfully waved away their cheers but eventually gave in and smiled big, raising a fist. With his gym bag tucked under his arm he gave each of them a one-armed hug.

Instantly they could sense something was different about him. His shoulders were relaxed, he didn't restrict himself from grinning, his body movements were languid and natural—not like the seek-and-destroy robot that had shown up to training for the past two years. There was pre-title Danny and post-title Danny. A page had turned and nobody had to say anything, they could all feel it.

Stepping onto the scale of the gym in his underwear revealed that it had been seven and a half pounds that he had gained in the three weeks, not the four that he had estimated. The first session back was cardio and core strength; there wouldn't be any sort of contact for at least another two weeks. His cheek was technically healed but there were still precautions to be taken. The mood of the first session was light-hearted and Marlos let it carry on like that but at the end he reminded everyone, "The most important fight of any career is always the *next* fight."

Hearing Marlos' Portuguese and Remy's English with his thick French accent was reassuring. There was a lot to discuss after training and Mark—reading from his iPhone and counting the tasks with the fingers of his other hand—laid out the schedule for the business side of the next week.

"There was talk—*just* talk, nothing solid—of a cross-training shoe in the Modern Warrior line so that's on the horizon but no need to even discuss—I don't even know why I brought that up in the first place. Forget that. Let's see here…you have more Fit-4-Fight protein and supplements on the way this week so keep an eye out for that and don't forget to have Taison post at least twice about it on your Instagram…" he scrolled down with his counting hand, "GQ interview is next Monday at The Nines…and lastly… Taison. He doesn't come back until Thursday? Is that right?" He said glancing at Marlos for confirmation. He nodded.

"So you're on your own for food until then. Think you can handle it?" He added with a smile.

Danny grinned from his back where Remy was stretching his hamstring, "I won't starve."

— — —

The next Saturday was Rodney's birthday and it had turned into quite an event, he was really popular at school. It seemed like there were almost as many parents as there were kids. Everybody always wanted to be involved if it had anything to do with the Sheppard family. Of all the attendees, most notable was Cameron, Allie's not-yet-official boyfriend. He was tall and well dressed. He introduced himself politely if not a little too confidently for Danny's liking and admitted that he was a big fan before making a hoeful and rehearsed joke about how he had been a little intimidated to meet him. Danny responded, "You don't have to worry about me but good luck with Tanner."

Andrea and Celia laughed close by.

Rich recorded on his iPhone as Rodney blew out all 12 candles at the end of the rapturous 'Happy Birthday'. Danny thought back to when Rodney became a part of their family. How quickly love could transform a person, or maybe just a child. His life had taken on an entirely new trajectory since moving out of the bedroom of a rural Oregon drug house and into the spare bedroom of the Eastmoreland house. He was too young to understand but someday he would know how lucky he was to be swooped up by Rich and Isabel. The thought put Danny in a somber mood and he suddenly wanted to go visit Lucas' headstone.

The party wasn't dying just yet but he didn't want to wait. Isabel was cutting the cake on the back porch and then there would be presents and after that parents would be gathering their kids. Danny retrieved the gift he had gotten Rodney from the closet in the entryway. It was slightly over-the-top, a nearly $900 remote control car.

"Rodney!" Danny hollered as he stepped through the sliding door onto the back porch, instantly commanding the attention of everybody, old and young.

"I gotta go man. Come open your present."

He set the large gift in front of Rodney to a collective *Whooooaaa* of all the kids. He tore into the wrapping paper. Rich was licking frosting off of his thumb in a hurry while fumbling with his phone to catch it on video but Celia was already filming anyway from the opposite side of the table, a better angle to capture Rodney's priceless expression as the car was unveiled.

He rounded the table and wrapped his arms around Danny, "Thank you!" he said learnedly. Danny squeezed him with one arm and bent down to kiss him on the top of the head.

"Happy birthday little bro."

Then while Rich carried the box down the hall and everyone went back into eating their cake Danny hugged Andrea, Allie, Celia and his mom and waved goodbye to the other parents and Cameron. Rich waited for him in the entryway. With a raise of the eyebrows he puffed out his cheeks and chuckled as he exhaled—*kids huh?*

They hugged. Rich's embrace remained the only thing in the world that could make Danny feel like the lesser man.

"I'm gonna go see Lucas for a bit."

Rich swallowed the lump in his throat as his eyes turned glassy. He cupped the back of his son's neck and nodded in a way that showed much more than just approval before he headed back to the party.

- — -

The sun was setting when Danny parked in the loop of Skyline Cemetery, it would be dark in 20 minutes. An older woman was walking a small dog near a minivan further up the loop. Portland stood silently below as the gravestones lined the hillside peacefully. Mount Hood loomed gigantically to the right and Mount Saint Helens to the left. When Danny was a child he imagined the giant mountains as dueling enemies: Mount Saint Helens of Washington versus Mount Hood of Oregon.

As he walked the gravel pathway he thought about a night in high school where Tanner had explained his theory on ghosts and spirits. They had been out all night and in the wee hours of a Sunday morning they sat on the crest of a sand trap on the golf course, droopy-eyed and sobering up. Even though Danny couldn't remember his exact words, he remembered that it had made perfect sense at the time. It was something along the lines of a spirit's connection to physical objects that had been important to them in their lives.

You know time moves in frames so, like, when you spend a lot of time with a certain object, a frame from the past might make another pass or something. My mom was always sitting at her vanity and I swear I've seen her sitting there after she died—she was connected to it.

For some reason, it was a comforting notion. As Danny came closer to the end of the gravestones he could see that somebody was sitting on the bench that was a few yards away from Lucas' headstone. Somebody old judging by the skinny build and hunched shoulders but as he came closer he realized who it was and was delighted by the sight of him. It was Steve from Safeway.

"Steve!" He almost yelled. The look on Steve's face was priceless, first startled then quickly enthused.

"Hello Danny!" He said with his autistic, super-formal politeness. He extended his hand while Danny was still twenty yards away.

Danny smiled and broke into a little jog. They shook hands and with the same etiquette Steve said, "Join me." Motioning to the bench with a sweeping hand as if he were presenting a jazz band to a small audience. Danny played along, "Why thank you, sir."

"The last time I saw you—I believe—" Steve said raising a scientific finger as a prop, "was when you were fighting with somebody in the parking lot of Safeway."

"That's right! Wow. That was almost three years ago now."

"You went a little bit crazy." Steve said, smiling a big yellow-toothed smile that couldn't have been more out of context. Danny had to chuckle just because of how bluntly honest he was without really comprehending the severity of what had happened that night.

"I sure did." He agreed.

"Are you here to talk football with Lucas?" Danny asked. Steve couldn't get rid of his smile, "Yes, yes, I come every once in a while. Of course I need to tell him how bad the Forty-Niners are these days." He said as if Danny had been in on whatever joke he was referring to. This must have been a common topic for them he assumed, and smiled along with it.

"That's really nice, Steve. I know he really enjoyed coming to Safeway and talking to you." Danny could see a twinkle of pride in Steve's eyes and his posture straightened up slightly.

"Yes I enjoyed it very much too. I miss him." His formalness didn't falter but Danny could see how honest the words were.

"Me too." Danny said softly before they sat in silence as the shadows from the gravestones grew longer and longer. Eventually they decided to walk up to the loop where Danny asked if he needed a ride but it turned out that the older woman walking the dog was his mom. Leslie. She was near to tears when Danny introduced himself as the brother of Lucas.

"Steve just *loved* Lucas. What a kind young man." She gushed. Danny smiled.

"He was a great guy—and I know he loved talking football with this guy." He said jerking a thumb toward Steve whose face was proud once again. "I'll come into Safeway sometime soon!" He promised as he gave Steve a hug and then Leslie too.

"But I have to warn you," he called back as he climbed into his Audi, "I don't know football like Lucas did!"

At 22 years old Danny had become—by some distance—the youngest-ever title-holder in UFC history. He had made history, but something wasn't quite finished. Ever since raising his hands in triumph in Las Vegas he felt like there was still something to come...and he was right.

After studying up on his potential next opponent he lay in bed watching a Netflix documentary series called *Making a Murderer*, when he got a phone call. It was Tanner.

"Yo."

"Hey. What are you up to?" Tanner asked, sounding nervy.

"Not much, just at home. Watching that *Making a Murderer* show that everyone's talking about. This poor guy totally got set up—"

"Yeah I saw it. Listen I'm on my way over, don't fall asleep yet."

Danny was instantly sensed concern in Tanner's voice. Something was wrong.

"What's going on?" He asked sternly, his heart starting to beat a little faster.

"Nothing. I just need to come over for a minute."

The following pause was nothing but confusion.

"Yeah, alright man. Come on over."

Danny turned his show back on and waited anxiously. It was unlike Tanner to be secretive and there was no need for him to talk to Danny in person unless something was seriously awry.

Danny couldn't pay attention to the show and he pulled on some sweats and went downstairs. Taison was still in the living room watching ESPN.

"What is it?" Taison asked as soon as Danny appeared with a wrinkled eyebrow of concern.

"Tanner is coming over. Said he needed to talk about something." Taison's eyes narrowed to match Danny's. He knew it was weird.

The two of them sat in silence but they didn't have to wait long. Just minutes later headlights flashed through the blinds as Tanner's Maxima pulled into the driveway. Taison got up and went outside, leaving the front door open. He greeted Tanner. Even without being able to make out the words Danny could tell that Tanner was nervous as he spoke to Taison. The car door shut and another opened. Somebody was with him. Danny stood and moved to the doorway peaking around the corner to the driveway.

She had changed her hair. It was long now but her face was the same: the contour of her cheekbone, the tiny mole on the outside of her eye, the face that had tormented him for three years. He took a tumbling step backwards into the house before everything went black.

— — —

Nina boarded her flight from Orlando. Nerves were evident from the way she flipped through the pages of the Sky Mall Magazine before takeoff. She had been living and studying in Florida for eight months. Since meeting Danilo "Danny" Sheppard on Copacabana almost three years earlier her life had been full of adventure and good fortune, but it was missing something…something significant.

Everyone she knew said she was crazy—her parents, her friends, her brothers—everyone. They didn't think it was possible to fall in love with someone in such a short space of time and especially not at such a young age. They were all wrong. Time passed and his footprint on her heart didn't become less shallow. She missed him ceaselessly. There was still so much more to learn about him and she couldn't bring herself to accept that he didn't feel any of what she had felt.

After several days and several unanswered text messages, she decided to get in touch with Danny's friend Mateus. Catia gave her his number and she called him.

-*Hey Mateus this is Nina—friend of Catia. We met on the beach?*

-*Oh yeah, Danilo made me chase after you! How are you?*

-*That's right. I'm just wondering if you can pass a message to Danilo for me?*

-*I haven't seen him in a few days but when I do I will tell him, of course.*

-*He hasn't been in the gym for a few days? You don't know where he has been?*

-No but Danilo...he has some family stuff happening...I don't know where he is.

-Yes he told me about his brother.

She started to choke up and rushed to get it out: her final peace. If he wasn't able to see her again she would at least let him know that she was sorry he was in such pain.

-If you see him, tell him I'm sorry. Tell him I'm so sorry and I hope he finds happiness and peace. Tell him I enjoyed meeting him.

-I will, Nina. I will tell him.

They ended the call and she started to cry. She was desperate to receive a phone call from Mateus and hear that Danny had a message of his own for her, but it never came. It was over, but the mystery of his disappearance had left an open wound that wouldn't close.

It had been almost three years. Enough was enough. She needed to look him in his eyes and ask why he had disappeared. A message on Facebook or Instagram wouldn't cut it—although she had tried that too. Predictably, they were ignored along with the thousands of other messages he received from girls all over the world.

She had toyed with the idea of tracking him down and confronting him but it took a triggering moment for her to decide to follow through. At the very least she would finally have closure. The day after he won the title she sat in class. Dr. Fontaine walked into class and greeted everyone in a hoarse voice.

"I apologize for my voice, I was yelling at the television all night. Did anybody else watch the Danny Sheppard fight?"

The classroom chorused affirmatively and small conversations broke out. A group of girls sitting behind Nina gossiped, "Did you hear about him and Kendall Jenner?"

Nina spun around, *"What* about him and Kendall Jenner?"

A little stunned from how toxic Nina's tone had been the girl's smile faded.

"Oh, I just heard they went out or something."

Embarrassed at how rude she had just come across, Nina packed up her things and headed for her apartment, searching for flights to

Portland, Oregon before she had even arrived. She almost considered stopping in Los Angeles first to give Kendall Jenner a black eye.

– — -

Danny came to consciousness slowly. His thoughts were muddled and confused.

Oh no, I got cocky. It must have been a kick that I didn't see coming. Why is there carpet in the octagon?

Taison and Tanner were standing over him in the doorway. Tanner was saying something but the words weren't in order and didn't make any sense. He could hear a fire alarm somewhere in the distance and a phone vibrating on a table somewhere closer. He blinked. There were voices speaking frantically over one another. Slowly he realized he hadn't been knocked out at all. He was at home in the entryway of his townhouse. One by one, details started coming back to him. Nina had been there. She had gotten out of Tanner's car. He didn't believe it though.

"Relax man, you fainted. Holy shit." He heard Tanner say as he rolled over and pushed himself to a squatting position, still dizzy and not ready to find his feet, Tanner and Taison held his arms on either side.

"What is going *on?*" He said with a grimace as he stood up.

"Let's go outside, get some air." Tanner suggested, ushering him towards the doorway like an elderly man. In the driveway he linked his fingers on the top of his head and breathed heavily.

"You alright, man?" Tanner asked after a minute. Taison was still too confused and shocked to say anything. He had no idea who this girl was or why Danny had suddenly fainted.

Danny had seemed to steady himself and was breathing normally but his eyes were still a bit wild. Taison looked back and forth between the two of them nervously, not sure where to start questioning or if he even should.

"Listen man, I didn't mean to spring this on you but—" Tanner started to say but Danny cut him off.

"What is *she* doing here?"

"I'm trying to explain." Tanner said patiently. "She messaged me on Facebook and asked if I would help—"

"Stay out here." Danny interrupted again.

— — —

He couldn't believe his eyes. There she was. Sitting on his couch in Beaverton, Oregon. He couldn't believe his eyes. When he spoke the words were in English but he shook his head and started over in Portuguese.

"Did you see me on TV and decide to check in?" He asked. He was in such shock that his voice quivered. She stood up from the couch and seemed confused whereas before she only seemed nervous. This was not the reaction she had anticipated. It didn't make any sense why he would be upset with her.

"What do you want?" He pleaded, his voice nearly failing with the last syllable.

"I needed to ask…" a small tear rolled down from her eye and she paused to wipe it away, "I needed to know why you left me without a word."

Danny's eyes narrowed in confusion. He didn't understand. It would only take a few more words. They would break through and discover the truth.

— — —

The worst part about having her phone stolen was that she lost the conversations that they had shared. At night she would read them while lying in bed and before long, realize that she was smiling. She had saved all her contacts on her computer and when she got a new phone the next day she texted him immediately, but got no response. She waited nearly two hours before sending him another message. No response. She didn't take him for the type to play hard-to-get and surely he would text her the next day. He didn't. Every time her phone vibrated she snatched it up only to be disappointed.

A day passed, then another, then another, then a week. She didn't understand. No explanation ever came; he had disappeared.

She didn't have much time before she would be leaving for Spain. As the date drew closer and closer she found it harder and harder to accept that he was gone without so much as a goodbye. And hadn't he wanted to see her again? Wasn't that clear to both of them? Had the grief from losing his brother sent him into despair and scared him away from whatever was happening between them? It was the only explanation that could have made any sense. She told herself that his heart was still so broken that he was incapable of spending time with her.

In her final days in Rio she spent more time at the beach, embarrassed as she self-consciously looked over her shoulders, scanning the boardwalk with hope that his wide frame would be walking down it, but it never did.

The night before she left for Spain there was a dinner party for her at her parents' house. She decided that at the very least she wanted to wish him well. Pulling Catia aside, she tearfully asked for Mateus' number. Her final act was to ask him to pass on a message for her. She just wanted Danny to know that she hoped he was doing well and that she was sorry for the loss of his brother.

Her friends all assured her of the same thing: *time will go by and you'll forget about him, you'll meet someone new, someone better.*

At first she believed them but as time crept by, she realized that they were wrong. They didn't understand. She thought about him more and more. Days turned to weeks and then months and before she knew it, a year had passed but she couldn't get his face out of her mind.

The nearly three years that crept by were tainted, even haunted by her not knowing what had happened, why he had disappeared. His stardom had blossomed before her eyes. He started appearing on newsstands and television screens consistently. She heard people talk about him; gossiping and sharing rumors that she knew first hand were true. On a random Thursday afternoon she realized that she needed to get to the bottom of it before she could carry on with life. The professor lectured about Flemish painters from the 15th century, Nina stood to leave. She needed to find Danny Sheppard. She couldn't wait even one more minute.

- — -

A week had past since Danny had walked into his house and fainted from the sight of Nina sitting on his couch. A couple days afterwards it occurred to him that he should tell Jenna what had happened. He felt it was important to let her know that Nina wasn't the monster that he had made her out to be. On his way home from training he pulled into the Best Buy parking lot and parked on the far side of the lot where there were no other cars. He called Jenna.

"Danny!" She answered enthusiastically.

"Hey, how are you?" He asked, cracking a smile.

"Fine everything is fine. How are *you* doing?"

"I'm great actually. I've got a story for you. You'll never believe this." He chuckled. "Are you ready for this? Guess who showed up at my house last week…"

"Who?"

"Nina."

There was a few seconds of silence before Jenna shouted into the phone, "*WHAT?*"

He laughed and went on to explain everything. The night Nina arrived it hadn't taken more than a few seconds for them to break through to the truth of what had actually happened, the epic miscommunication and misassumption.

The last night they spent together in her apartment had come to an end. They had watched the sunrise and the man juggling the soccer ball on the beach before going back to her apartment and falling asleep until the afternoon hours. Danny had woken up, said goodbye and headed for home at around 3 p.m. A few hours later, she had left her apartment to go to dinner at a friend's house. As soon as she walked out of the building a well-dressed businessman approached her, smiled and politely asked for a favor. He claimed his phone was dead and that he needed to let his friend know where he was, asking apologetically if he could use hers to make a quick call. Without thinking twice she unlocked it and handed it to him.

He said thank you and then promptly turned and jogged down the street and around the corner. As far as she knew the man would be headed straight to a pawnshop. The reality that her phone had been used to manipulate him into setting himself up for a staged police sting was so far beyond belief. After Danny accused her of setting him up she broke down. It all made sense. It wasn't a random mugging, it was calculated and for a larger purpose. She explained what had happened, the man who had came up to her and asked to use her phone, tears streaking down her face as she too learned that what she had assumed about him was entirely untrue. Then he asked why she had asked Mateus to apologize. It wasn't an apology for setting him up like Danny had assumed for three years. It was an apology for the news he had shared about his brother passing. It was, after all, one of the last things he had said to her before he left her apartment.

His eyes started wandering the floor of his living room as he connected the dots. It all made sense to him, too. He remembered Donadel following them the night before at the festival. He had seen where Nina lived. He had organized the theft of her phone and the scavenger hunt that sent him to the cocaine in the bar. It was his plan.

Danny had so much to say he didn't know where to begin, but for the moment he let the realization take over. He felt the joy of knowing that she had been thinking about him the same way he had been thinking about her for the last three years.

Jenna was blown away.

"I can't believe it, Danny. It's incredible. What have you guys been doing?"

"We've been to the coast, we've been all over the city, we've been to Corvallis, we've chilled at my place, we had dinner at my parent's house a few times—of course she met my family and stuff, Celia and Andrea and everyone. She leaves tomorrow so we're gonna go to dinner tonight. Downtown."

"She came all the way from Rio?"

"No she's in school in Florida actually—studying art and working for a private dealer."

There was a long pause before Jenna asked a final question in a delicate voice.

"So what now?"

What now?

Whether or not Danny had asked himself the question directly, it had been hounding him for the last three years.

When Lucas died: *What now?*

After almost killing Trevor Ramey: *What now?*

When he dropped out of college: *What now?*

Stepping into the courtyard of Leo Goia: *What now?*

Stepping out of Leo Goia: *What now?*

He had won the title. He had made history. He had won over the girl of his dreams and still…*What now?* He found comfort in knowing that he wasn't the only one who didn't have an answer. They were all in it together: Danny and every other person in the world. Time marched on and people asked the question with varying degrees of terror or enthusiasm. There were more struggles to come. Dealing with the reality that Lucas wasn't able to live his own life was a constant battle. Knowing that Andrea would one day find somebody else was crushing. Knowing that Celia would one day take her last breath was devastating.

Uncertainty was the only thing that was certain. And now that he was able to take part in the struggles of life alongside the rest of humanity, he felt as though he were a part of something larger than the struggle that he had been enduring. Whatever was to come, he knew he would face it head-on. He was part of a clan of young men who were just trying to do the best with the cards they'd been dealt. Everybody's struggle was different, but he was a boy with tattoos, and he wouldn't hide from life.

What now?

"I'm not sure. But I think I'm ready for it."

CPSIA information can be obtained
at www.ICGtesting.com
Printed in the USA
LVHW011121190620
658111LV00004B/446